JOYCE CARY
MISTER JOHNSON

A NEW DIRECTIONS BOOK

TO MUSA

'Remembered goodness is a benediction.'

Manufactured in the United States of America
New Directions Books are printed on acid-free paper.
Originally published in Great Britain by Gollancz, 1939; published by
Michael Joseph, 1941; reissued in Carfax edition, 1952
First published clothbound in the United States by Harper Brothers, 1948
First published as a New Directions Paperbook in 1989
Published simultaneously in Canada by Penguin Books Canada Limited

Library of Congress Cataloging-in-Publication Data

Cary, Joyce, 1888–1957.
    Mister Johnson / Joyce Cary.
        p.   cm.
    "Originally published in Great Britain by Gollancz, 1939"—T.p. verso.
    ISBN 0–8112–1030–8 (alk. paper)
    I.   Title.
PR6005.A77M5   1989
823'.912—dc 19   88–35710
                                                                          CIP

New Directions Books are published for James Laughlin
by New Directions Publishing Corporation,
80 Eighth Avenue, New York 10011

SECOND PRINTING

a prefatory essay by the author specially
written for this edition

——————— ★ ★ ★ ———————

Mr. Johnson is a young clerk who turns his life into a romance, he is a poet who creates for himself a glorious destiny. I have been asked if he is from life. None of my characters is from life, but all of them are derived from some intuition of a person, often somebody I do not know, a man seen in a bus, a woman on a railway platform gathering her family for the train. And I remember the letters of some unknown African clerk, which passed through my hands for censorship during the war, and which were full of the most wonderful yarns for his people on the coast. He was always in danger from the Germans (who were at that moment two hundred miles away); he was pursued by wild elephants (who were even further away from our station); he subdued raging mobs of 'this savage people' with a word. In his letters he was a hero on the frontier; actually he was a junior clerk in one of the most peaceful and sleepy stations to be found in the whole country. That was one recollection. Another was of a clerk sent to me in a station in remote Borgu who once spent all night copying a report, which he had done so badly in the first place that it could not go with the mail. I had not asked him to do the work again, for I saw that it was beyond him. I meant to do my own corrections. But at six o'clock in the morning, as I sat down to the letters, he appeared suddenly and uncalled (much to the indignation of the sleepy orderly at the door) and offered me the sheaf of papers, written in his school copperplate (we did not own a typewriter) which looked so reassuringly firm, and was so delusive. I saw at once that this second copy was worse even than the first. A whole line was missing on the first page; whole paragraphs were repeated.

This clerk had been a disappointment; he was stupid, and he could not be trusted with the files. He seemed also, a rare thing in an African, unapproachable. He did not always respond even to good morning. His shyness had a sullen grieved air. What he now suddenly and unexpectedly disclosed was not only a power of devotion but the imaginative enterprise to show it.

Affection, self-sacrifice, are very common things in this world. You find them in any family, school, regiment, service, factory or business. But so is daylight, and yet we do feel a special moment of recognition (perhaps descended from times when every return of the lost sun seemed a miracle of grace) at every sunrise, we remember certain days, not merely summer days, but all kinds of days which have struck us for some reason with special force of enjoyment, so that they stay with us for a long time, for years. Everyone of us has pictures in his brain of some sparkling day among boats; a frozen lake with skaters, and a sky like tarnished silver, full of snow; as we have memory of some special act of generosity.

So the clerk's effort stayed with me. I can still see his very look as he shambled into the office (he was a shambling person in every way, with limbs too big for his flimsy body, and features too big for his face), brought out the new copy and explained that he had been working at it all night. What struck me so forcibly I suppose was that this unhappy boy who was a failure at his job, who felt much more of an exile in Borgu, among the pagans whom he both feared and despised, than I did; who seemed so feeble and lost, was capable of this dramatic gesture. I say gesture because all he could say (unlike Johnson, he was very inarticulate) was that he had not wanted me to 'catch trouble'; that is, to get a reprimand for being late with my quarterly report.

This poor clerk was nothing like Johnson, but I remembered him when I drew Johnson. He reminded me too of something I had noticed as a general thing, the warmheartedness of the African; his readiness for friendship on the smallest encouragement. I remember an occasion when I was riding over a parade ground towards the end of the Kaiser war, when a sergeant drilling his men in the distance suddenly dismissed them, and the whole half company came running to surround me. I could not even recognize the men. We had come together for one night in the midst of a very confused and noisy battle (Banyo) when some lost units had attached themselves to mine.

No officer who has ever commanded a Nigerian company can forget the Hausa Farewell, that tune upon the bugles played as he rides away for the last time. But I don't know why, having met and greeted plenty of veterans, I remember so vividly that scene on the parade ground—perhaps only because I was taken by surprise, I can still see the sergeant's face, the men running; I can't forget their grins (and laughter—an African will laugh loudly with pleasure at any surprise), the hands stretched out, the shouts of greeting from the back where some young and short soldier felt excluded. It is not true that Africans are eager but fickle. They remember friendship quite as long as they strongly feel it.

As for the style of the book, critics complained of the present tense. And when I answered that it was chosen because Johnson lives in the present, from hour to hour, they found this reason naïve and superficial. It is true that any analogy between the style and the cast of a hero's mind appears false. Style, it is said, gives the atmosphere in which a hero acts; it is related to him only as a house, a period, is related to a living person.

But this, I think, is a view answering to a critical attitude which necessarily overlooks the actual situation of the reader. For a critic, no doubt, style is the atmosphere in which the action takes place. For a reader (who may have as much critical acumen as you please, but is not reading in order to criticize), the whole work is a single continuous experience. He does not distinguish style from action or character.

This is not to pretend that reading is a passive act. On the contrary, it is highly creative, or recreative; itself an art. It must be so. For all the reader has before him is a lot of crooked marks on a piece of paper. From those marks he constructs the work of art which conveys idea and feeling. But this creative act is largely in the subconscious. The reader's mind and feelings are intensely active, but though he himself is fully aware of the activity (it is part of his pleasure) he is absorbed, or should be absorbed, in the tale. A subconscious creative act may be a strange notion, but how else can one describe the passage from printer's ink into active complex experience. After all, a great deal of rational and constructive activity goes on in the subconscious. We hear of people who dream solutions of difficult mathematical problems. What is called intuitive flair is nothing but subconscious logic, where the brain works with the speed and short cuts of a calculating machine, upon material that no machine can deal with. In short, though talk about the mental machine, the mechanical brain, etc., is highly misleading, for no brain is in the least like a machine, yet it is useful because that organism does tend to work automatically. Having been taught certain reactions, it will repeat them, on the same stimulus, till further orders; that is, until the intelligence steps in again to ask what exactly that reaction is worth.

But until the moment of criticism (which also arises from the subconscious. It, so to speak, rings a bell for the managing director to warn him that there is trouble in the factory which can't be solved by any routine operation) the reader's conscious self is at liberty to feel

v

with the people of the book; he is at one with them. So if they are in the past tense he is in the past, he takes part in events that have happened, in history, over there. This is a true taking-part, whether the history is actual history or a novel. A reader can tremble still at the crisis of Waterloo; or rage at the fate of Huss. He has in *War and Peace* a concentrated and lasting experience. But it is still a special, an historical experience; it derives much of its quality from the recognition of general causes, it is charged with reflection (such as a man among actual events may use even at a crisis, and in the middle of distress, but first withdrawing himself from among them), with comparison and judgment.

But with a story in the present tense, when he too is in the present, he is carried unreflecting on the stream of events; his mood is not contemplative but agitated.

This makes the present tense unsuitable for large pictures 'over there'; it illuminates only a very narrow scene with a moving ray not much more comprehensive than a handtorch. It can give to a reader that sudden feeling of insecurity (as if the very ground were made only of a deeper kind of darkness) which comes to a traveller who is bushed in unmapped country, when he feels all at once that not only has he utterly lost his way, but also his own identity. He is, as they say, no longer sure of himself, or what he is good for; he is all adrift like sailors from some wreck, who go mad, not because of the privations inside, but outside, because they have nothing firm to rest their minds on, because everything round them is in everlasting motion.

This restless movement irritates many readers with the same feeling, that events are rushing them along before they have time to examine them, to judge them, and to find their own place among them. But as Johnson does not judge, so I did not want the reader to judge. And as Johnson swims gaily on the surface of life, so I wanted the reader to swim, as all of us swim, with more or less courage and skill, for our lives.

J. C.

THE YOUNG WOMEN OF FADA, in Nigeria, are well known for beauty. They have small, neat features and their backs are not too hollow.

One day at the ferry over Fada River, a young clerk called Johnson came to take passage. The ferryman's daughter, Bamu, was a local beauty, with a skin as pale and glistening as milk chocolate, high, firm breasts, round, strong arms. She could throw a twenty-foot pole with that perfect grace which was necessary to the act, if the pole was not to throw her. Johnson sat admiring her with a grin of pleasure and called out compliments, 'What a pretty girl you are.'

Bamu said nothing. She saw that Johnson was a stranger. Strangers are still rare in Fada bush and they are received with doubt. This is not surprising, because in Fada history all strangers have brought trouble; war, disease or bad magic. Johnson is not only a stranger by accent, but by colour. He is as black as a stove, almost a pure negro, with short nose and full, soft lips. He is young, perhaps seventeen, and seems half-grown. His neck, legs and arms are much too long and thin for his small body, as narrow as a skinned rabbit's. He is loose-jointed like a boy, and sits with his knees up to his nose, grinning at Bamu over the stretched white cotton of his trousers. He smiles with the delighted expression of a child looking at a birthday table and says, 'Oh, you are too pretty—a beautiful girl.'

Bamu pays no attention. She throws the pole, places the top between her breasts against her crossed palms and walks down the narrow craft.

'What pretty breasts—God bless you with them.'

Bamu recovers the pole and goes back for another throw. When Johnson lands, he walks backwards up the bank, laughing at her. But she does not even look at him. The next day he comes again. Bamu is not working the ferry. But he lies in wait for her in the yam fields and follows her as she carries home her load from the field store, admiring her and saying, 'You are the most beautiful girl in Fada.'

He comes again to the yam field and asks her to marry him. He tells her that he is a government clerk, rich and powerful. He will make her a great lady. She shall be loaded with bangles; wear white women's dress, sit in a chair at table with him and eat off a plate.

'Oh, Bamu, you are only a savage girl here—you do not know how happy I will make you. I will teach you to be a civilized lady and you shall do no work at all.'

Bamu says nothing. She is slightly annoyed by his following her, but doesn't listen to his words. She marches forward, balancing her load of yam.

Two days later he finds her again in the ferry with her short cloth tucked up between her strong thighs. He gives her a threepenny piece instead of a penny; and she carefully puts it in her mouth before taking up the pole.

'Oh, Bamu, you are a foolish girl. You don't know how a Christian man lives. You don't know how nice it is to be a government lady.'

The dugout touches the bank, and Bamu strikes the pole into the mud to hold firm. Johnson gets up and balances himself awkwardly. Bamu stretches out her small hard hand and catches his fingers to guide him ashore. When he comes opposite her and the dugout ceases to tremble under him, he suddenly stops, laughs and kisses her. 'You are so beautiful you make me laugh.'

Bamu pays no attention whatever. She doesn't understand the kiss and supposes it to be some kind of foreign joke. But when Johnson tries to put his arms round her she steps quickly ashore and leaves him in the dugout, which drifts down the river, rocking violently. Johnson, terrified, sits down and grasps the sides with his hands. He shouts, 'Help! Help! I'm drowning!'

Bamu gives a loud, vibrating cry across the river; two men come dawdling out from a hut, gaze at Johnson, leisurely descend and launch another dugout. They pursue Johnson and bring him to land. Bamu, hidden in the bush, explains the situation in a series of loud, shrill cries. One of the boatmen, a tall, powerful man of about thirty, stands over Johnson and says, 'What did you want with my sister, stranger?'

'I want to marry her, of course. I'm clerk Johnson. I'm an important man, and rich. I'll pay you a large sum. What's your name?'

'My name is Aliu.'

The man scratches his ear and reflects deeply, frowning sideways at Johnson. He can't make out whether the boy is mad or only a stranger with unusual customs.

'It wouldn't do to-day,' he says at last.

'Why?'

Aliu makes no answer.

'When shall I come? How much money shall I bring?'

12

'Money? H'm. She's a good girl, that one.'

'Anything you like—ten pounds, twelve pounds.'

The two men are visibly startled. Their eyebrows go up. They gaze at Johnson with deep suspicion. These are high prices for girls in Fada. 'Fifteen pounds!' Johnson cries. 'She's worth it. I never saw such a girl.' The two men, as if by one impulse, turn to their boat. As they push off, Bamu darts out of the bush and jumps in amidships. Neither look at her. She sits down and gazes at Johnson with a blank stare. Aliu says over his shoulder, 'Another day, clerk.'

Bamu continues to stare. The two men give a powerful, impatient thrust which carries the dugout far out across the water.

Johnson goes on shouting for some time, but no one can make out what he says. The village children come and stare. The general opinion is that he is mad. Finally, he disappears into the bush.

Johnson, with his morocco bag of letters under his arm and his patent-leather shoes in his hand, travels at high speed, at a pace between a trot and a lope. In his loose-jointed action, it resembles a dance. He jumps over roots and holes like a ballet dancer, as if he enjoyed the exercise. But, in fact, his mind is full of marriage and the ferry girl. He imagines her in a blouse and skirt, shoes and silk stockings, with a little felt hat full of feathers, and makes a jump of two yards. All the advertisements of stays, camisoles, nightgowns in the store catalogues pass through his imagination, and he dresses up the brown girl first in one and then in another. Then he sees himself introducing her to his friends: 'Missus Johnson—Mister Ajali.'

The idea makes him laugh and he gives another spring over a root. How he will be envied for that beautiful girl. But he will not only make her a civilized wife; he will love her. He will teach her how to attend parties with him; and how to receive his guests, how to lie down in one bed with a husband, how to kiss, and how to love. Johnson's idea of a civilized marriage, founded on the store catalogues, their fashion notes, the observation of missionaries at his mission school, and a few novels approved by the S.P.C.K., is a compound of romantic sentiment and embroidered underclothes.

Bamu has spoken of the mad stranger once or twice to the other women. Aliu now tells his mother that a clerk has offered a large sum for Bamu. The mother says nothing. She is busy. But the next day she speaks of it to a brother and gradually the whole family find out one detail or another. Then they all talk of it and so it comes to be felt that something important has happened. About four o'clock one afternoon the old mother exclaims, 'So a rich man wants Bamu?'

Everyone ponders this for a while; at last Aliu says, 'Yes, that's about it.'

About an hour later it is agreed that Aliu shall go into Fada and ask if there be really a government clerk called Johnson.

Aliu enquires first in the market, where he learns that there is certainly a new government clerk. But nobody knows any name for him except the 'new clerk.'

'Go to the hamfiss,' an old market woman says. 'Hamfiss,' 'hamfish' or 'haffice' is the Fada translation for office.

Aliu goes to the station. He has lived within six miles of it for thirty years, but he has never seen it before. Fada natives avoid the station as English villagers avoid a haunted manor. It seems to them a supernatural place, full of strange and probably dangerous spirits.

Fada station has been on a temporary site for twenty years, because nobody has had time or interest to move it. It stands in the thin scrub which covers two-thirds of the emirate; that is, all but the river valleys and swamps, where high jungle and tsetse-fly are still more discouraging to progress of any kind.

The station has no bungalows. It consists of six old bush houses, with blackened thatch reaching almost to the ground, a fort and a police barracks, scattered at random, far apart from each other, on bare patches in the scrub.

It is as if some giant had tossed down a few scraps of old rotten hay on a mangy lion skin, tufted with moth-eaten fragments of the hair and scarred with long, white seams. These are the marks of temporary water-courses or drains.

The fort, on a slight hill which represents the flattened head-skin of the lion, is a square of earth rampart which has been levelled by time almost to the ground, so that the guard-room just inside it, a mud hut with a porch of corrugated iron, stands up like a miniature cracker hat, a *kepi*, stuck there, on one side of the lion's battered head, in derision. The tin porch is slightly crooked over the gaping door, like a

14

broken peak pulled down over a black, vacant eye. The gateway of the fort is merely a gap in which dogs like to sleep.

The barracks, across the parade ground from the fort, are four rows of neat huts, like nursery counters arranged for a game. The Union Jack, just outside the guard-room, hangs upon a crooked stick, shaped like one of those old gig whips with a right-angled crank-turn in the middle.

The office, Aliu's mark, the centre of Fada government, lies beyond the parade ground in a bare patch of its own, like a small wart of mange grown out of a huge, dried scar, polished brown. It is a two-roomed mud hut with a mud stoop and half a new roof. On the mud stoop between the two door holes a messenger and an orderly are asleep. The orderly's blue fez has fallen off.

Aliu, a brave and stout fellow nearly six feet high, who has hunted lions with a spear, stares at the office, and the office stares at him under its shelving eaves, as with a dark suspicion.

He looks round at the huge bush houses, each alone and unprotected in the scrub, like sulky and dangerous beasts, at the guard-room with its crooked white eyelash, at the rag of pink and blue hanging over it, at the mysterious pattern of the barracks, and his flesh shivers. He steals away from the incomprehensible, terrifying place, as from devils. This brings him again to the town road and the store.

The Fada Company store, a tin-and-wood shack with the usual labourers' compound behind, stands on the river close to the town gate. Since it is almost part of the town, natives do not fear it like the station in the bush, with its bush devils. Since it belongs to a white man and has an English-speaking clerk in a cotton suit, it is regarded as part of the government.

Aliu, nevertheless, approaches with care and peeps through the door to spy out his ground. Even when he has been reassured by the familiar store smell of half-cured hides, mixed with the bitter, tinny stink of cheap cotton, which blasts out of the dark twilight within like the fumes of a slaughter-house boiler, he takes five minutes to stiffen his nerve. Finally, he goes in sideways, bowing with his neck at every step, like a hen.

Ajali, the store clerk, is alone behind the broad counter. He is a light-coloured southerner with a long jaw, a thin mouth, small, round eyes and a flat, yellow skull. Cut off at the waist by the counter, on which he rests his fingers, he seems to lurk in the hot, stinking twilight of the shed like a scorpion in a crack, ready to spring on some prey. But Ajali does not move at all and his insect face wears a most human expression of boredom.

He is obviously as bored as a reasonable creature can be; not to desperation, but exhaustion. He turns his eyes towards Aliu with weary disgust and, making a great effort, says slowly, 'What do you want, you?'

Aliu pulls in his neck and then shoots it out.

'Master, lord.'

'Hurry up, clodhopper.'

'Pardon, it's about Johnson.'

'Johnson.'

'He's rich, isn't he? He's a great one here?'

'Rich? Great? Who told you so?'

'He did.' Aliu explains that Johnson has offered a large sum for his sister. Ajali roars with laughter. He is full of excitement and delight.

The fact is that Johnson is a temporary clerk, still on probation, called up on emergency from a mission school. He has been in Fada six months and is already much in debt. He gives parties almost every night and he seems to think that a man in his important position, a third-class government clerk, is obliged to entertain on the grandest scale, with drums and smuggled gin.

To Ajali, perishing of boredom, the follies of the new clerk are as exciting as scandal in any country village. They fill his empty mind with ideas and his empty time with a purpose.

'Oh, it's too good!' he cries. 'Rich and great? Dat fool child, Johnson?' He rushes to the door and screams at an old woman passing along the road. 'Has Johnson paid you that debt?'

'No, master.'

'That's funny, because he's rich now. He's marrying a wife for fifteen pounds.'

'But he owes us all money for a long time. What a rascal. And he really has money, has he?' She goes off in indignation. Ajali, roaring with laughter, shouts after her, 'Tell it to the whole market—Johnson is rich now.'

Aliu says, 'What shall I do?'

'Do, pagan lump? Go home. You smell.'

Aliu salutes him and goes with grave dignity and a thoughtful expression. In fact, he is not thinking. He does not know what to think.

16

But he is not surprised at his failure to find out what to think in Fada town. His experience has taught him already how difficult and unusual it is to get any sensible explanation or advice, anywhere.

Authority, as he knows it, is always dangerous, selfish, inexplicable. It looks after its own mysterious affairs in a dark privacy. It never explains. Its servants, even the most approachable, like store clerks, resent nothing so much as a request for explanation. Even when they do give it, it is generally false.

But he feels no grievance, because he fully understands that this is the way things and people are. All things are stubborn and dangerous; all men, except one's own family, find their chief pleasure in tormenting the helpless stranger. After all, what else could anyone do with a stranger, except fleece him?

Ajali spends a happy night and wakes up to a new world full of interest. He puts on his yellow suit and goes to the government clerk's compound.

This is three broken huts among a mass of scrub and weed. One has no roof; the second has lost half a wall and is furnished chiefly with an enormous water pot, four feet high. Behind the pot lies a bundle of what looks like charred sticks, scaly and glistening, covered by a dirty rag. The third and largest has an immense hole in its rotten thatch, but is carefully barricaded at its windows and door.

Ajali, smiling with joyful anticipation as he comes into the clearing, shouts, 'Oh, Mister Johnson!'

He gives to the title mister a peculiar emphasis common on the coast where mister is still a title.

The sticks move, a thin old woman trembling with cold peeps round the wall at the visitor. But as he advances she is seized with panic and again makes herself small behind the pot. Ajali goes up to the closed hut, puts his head through a hole between two mats and stares within. He makes his small, prominent eyes round with dramatic astonishment.

But he has seen the same thing hundreds of times before; the dirty little hut containing one tin box, one three-legged table propped on a packing case, a deck-chair with a torn seat and a native bed of split bamboo hung with dirty butter muslin. Bits of rag and cotton wool are

17

stuck through this muslin to plug the holes. A tin chamber pot and a kerosene tin stand in the middle of the dirt floor. The window hole is blocked with a mat, but the hut is brightly lit from the big hole in the roof. The hut smells foul and cold. The watcher rounds his eyes till they seem to bulge like crab eyes, and screams in a kind of mock horror, 'Mister Johnson! Mister Johnson! Seven o'clock! Oh, by Lawd-gee! you late again for sure.'

The snores have stopped. Mr. Johnson has heard. But he does not get up. He is feeling too tight with life. It is pricking him all over. He has an enormous happiness and excitement swelling inside him urging him to do something extraordinary; leap into the air or utter a yell. The happiness takes form at once as his love of Bamu. He's going to be married to Bamu, that beautiful clever girl. He feels so light with joy that the hard bed seems to have dropped away from him. He could spring through the roof and float into the sunlight. He lies still, enjoying the sensation and preparing to spring.

'Mister Johnson, I hope you catch no trouble to-day. I hear some of dem market people angry with you. Dey say, if you so rich to marry why you no pay dem?'

Johnson resolves, simply on caprice, not to jump out of bed with a yell, but to ride his energy on a tight rein. He puts his net aside, therefore, with a slow movement, slowly brings his feet to the ground, yawns and says in a careless tone, 'Dat you, Mister Ajali?'

The other laughs, turning up his eyes with a kind of leer. 'I tink Mister Blore he make trouble for you debts.'

Johnson, who is fully dressed except for his bare feet, rises with a languid air, strokes down his crumpled suit, spits at the chamber pot and says, 'I don't care for dat ole Blore.' He shouts: 'Sozy.'

This shout throws the old woman into agitation. She crawls out from her corner and runs towards the hut; then, seeing Ajali, turns and dodges behind the wall.

Old Sozy is one of those women, found even in African villages, who have lost their homes. She has lately attached herself to Johnson. But she is still in terror at her own audacity in joining such a magnificent household and she loses her head in all emergencies.

'Sozy, where you?' Johnson shouts. Sozy at once disappears again. She is quite sure that this affair is beyond her. She hopes no one will notice her. Johnson suddenly lifts one leg high in the air and pivots slowly on his heel.

18

'You late, too. I tink you catch big trouble,' Ajali says, laughing. 'You lose you job.'

'I don't care for dat ole government.' Johnson throws up his two arms and pivots on the other leg.

A ringing stroke is heard from the fort. Ajali counts 'One—two—three' to the seven. At the end he cries, delighted in horror, 'Seven o'clock! Oh, you Mister Johnson, you too late now.'

Johnson shouts at him, 'Why you no tell me, you bitch?'

'But I do tell you, Mister Johnson.'

'You tell lie——'

'What, how I tell lie—you heard de beats.'

'You no believe dem youself.'

Johnson pulls his patent leather shoes on bare feet, makes another attempt to wipe out the creases in his suit, and then, cursing himself as well as Ajali, rushes away towards the office.

Ajali, laughing with delighted humour, rounds his eyes and cries, 'Oh dear! What going to happen to dat poor Johnson now?'

He walks towards the store, smiling and shaking his head. Old Sozy creeps out from her refuge, lights the fire and scuttles about collecting sticks. She has failed to give Johnson any breakfast, but she feels that she must do something. She therefore lights the fire and heats a kettle. She does not know what to do with it now Johnson is gone, but she must do something while she lives, and watching the kettle gives her the sense of doing something useful.

Johnson, rushing to the office, is in a panic. But his legs, translating the panic into leaps and springs, exaggerate it on their own account. They are full of energy and enjoy cutting capers, until Johnson, feeling their mood of exuberance, begins to enjoy it himself and improve upon it. He performs several extraordinary new and original leaps and springs over roots and holes, in a style very pleasing to himself. He begins to hum to himself a local song, with his own improvements.

> *'I got a lil girl, she roun' like de worl'.*
> *She smoot like de water, she shine like de sky.*
> *She fat like de corn, she smell like de new grass.*
> *She dance like de tree, she shake like de leaves.*
> *She warm like de groun', she deep like de bush.*

19

How doo, lil girl? I see you dar.
How doo, lil girl? Why you 'fraid for me?
I no got nuttin, no stick, no knife——'

Suddenly he flies out of the cool green cave of the bush into the hot sun-rays, falling on the parade ground. He looks anxiously at the office and sees that the orderly is not among the group of messengers at the District Officer's door. This means that Mr. Blore has not yet arrived. Johnson smiles with relief; takes an old muslin rag from the crown of his helmet and flicks his shoes. Then he puts back the rag, sets the helmet with a tilt over his left eye, and saunters towards the office with an easy and dignified gait. He is still humming to himself, 'I got a lil girl.'

The long morning shadow of the office, bright blue on the white dust, reaches his glittering shoes and he calls out to the messengers, 'Good morning, messengers. God give you health.'

At once half a dozen figures come rushing at him from the far sunny side of the office. They are all shouting at once, 'I'm ruined——'

'I've no more patience——' shouts an old woman.

'I'm going to the judge.'

Johnson, taken by surprise, looks like a child caught robbing the jam. His mouth and eyes open wide; he seems about to burst into tears. He falters, 'But—but—but——'

Old Blore, the District Officer, with his orderly, is seen coming across the station from his house. He is a short, fat man with a snub nose and gold spectacles. He walks with a hasty scuffle, like one pushing his feet through deep slush.

'You pay me now!' shrieks the woman. 'I go to judge now!'

'But—but—but——'

'Robber—liar—I tell judge how you rob me——'

Johnson puts down his head and rushes past her into the clerk's office, where he collapses into a chair. He rolls up his eyes to the roof and mutters, 'Oh, Gawd! Oh, Jesus! I done finish—I finish now—Mister Johnson done finish—— Oh, Gawd, you no fit do nutting—Mister Johnson too big dam' fool—he fool chile—oh, my Gawd.' He hits himself on the forehead with his fist. 'Why you so bloody big dam' fool, you Johnson? You happy for Fada—you catch government job—you catch good pay—you catch dem pretty girl—you catch nice gentlemen frien's—you catch new shoes—you big man—now you play de bloody fool—you spoil everyting—oh, Gawd—what you got to do is to give dis fool good whipping—you no fit stop when he yell—you take off his skin—you cut him up small wid you big whip—you beat him to fritters—you kill dis dam', bloody, good-for-nutting, silly fool bastard, Johnson——'

Blore is heard saying 'Good morning' to the messengers; Johnson stops and holds his breath. The District Officer goes into the office and calls for the first case, about the ownership of a goat.

Johnson, relieved, notices on the table in front of him his half-finished copy of the assessment report. The Fada typewriter is, as usual, out of order. The works are solid with a mixture of fine sand and hard oil. Johnson is obliged to copy everything in longhand. But he much prefers writing to typing, because he is a bad typist and a good writer. He pulls his work towards him. The copy of the report ends in the middle of a word, so: 'This district, scene of the desperate battle between the Emir's rearguard and the British forces in 1906, still has a reputation for fanati——'

Johnson glances at the report and reads 'fanaticism. Schemes for the amalgamation have therefore——' At the sight of the capital S (S is his favourite capital), he smiles, takes up his pen and, having completed the word fanaticism, wipes the nib, dips it carefully in the ink, tries the point on a piece of clean foolscap, squares his elbows, puts out his tongue and begins the fine upstroke. His ambition is always to make a perfect S in one sweeping movement. He frequently practises S's alone for half an hour on end. He looks at the result now and smiles with delight. It is beautiful. The thickening of the stroke as it turns over the small loop makes a sensation. He feels it like a jump of joy inside him. But the grand sweep, the smooth, powerful broadening of the lower stroke is almost too rich to be borne. He gives a hop in his chair, coming down hard on his bottom, laughs, puts his head on one side and licks his lips as if he is tasting a good thing.

Yes, but afterwards, on the up turn, is that a splutter in the first stroke or a flaw in the paper? He stoops down. A splutter. He is full of rage and despair. He curses himself. 'Oh, you fool chile, why you no swing you hand? Don' you never learn nutting all you life?' He throws the whole sheet into the waste-paper basket. 'Oh, you no good bastardly dam' silly bloody——'

A messenger puts in his head and shouts '*Akow!*' in a powerful voice, meaning 'Clerk.'

Johnson leaps up and scurries into the next office. It is full of his creditors; on every side he recognizes faces long forgotten and creditors whose debts he has never tried to remember.

Blore, bald and pensive as a Buddha, sits at the table watching Johnson through his small, gold spectacles. His expression is mild and benign, but the truth is, that he dislikes all negro clerks and especially Johnson. He is a deeply sentimental man, a conservative nature. He likes all old things in their old places and he dreads all change, all innovation. To his mind, a messenger in a white gown, even if he speaks and writes English, is a gentleman; but a clerk in trousers, even if he can barely do either, is an upstart, dangerous to the established order of things.

He looks mild and says nothing, because he respects himself too much to show his disgust. Johnson therefore gets in the first word: 'Oh, sah, I going to ask you if you kindly would advance me a little small portion of next month's pay.' Johnson talks good English to the District Officer, but in the clipped accent of one using a foreign tongue.

'I'm afraid that I can't do that. I never give advances,' Blore says. 'It wouldn't do any good. It would mean simply that you would have to borrow again at the end of the month.'

'Oh, sah, but just a little small——'

'Mr. Johnson, I think I told you before that these continual complaints against you must stop. Three months ago you undertook to settle your debts. But since then they have doubled.'

'Oh, sah. I explain to you, sah.'

'I should be very glad of an explanation, but what's wanted is a settlement. You know what will happen to you if this sort of thing goes on.'

'Oh, yes, sah.'

'I'll give you till to-morrow.'

'Tank you, sah.' Johnson walks out of the office like a sleep-walker. His brain has ceased to work. He goes home, sits down on the bed, gets up and walks round the hut and then sits down again. He is still without ideas. The next day he begs for one more day. He will then explain everything, and pay all his debts.

He is given one more day, and next day, in the office, he suggests again that Blore give him an advance. Blore, losing his temper, says that this is his last chance. He must pay or be sacked. He moves his lips as if saying 'Tank you, sah,' but is not conscious of it.

Blore's hostility, which he feels, has made him perfectly idiotic. He goes out. On the stoop he is confronted by a short, stout, white man with reddish hair, Assistant District Officer Rudbeck, who, fourteen months before, has been Johnson's master during Blore's absence.

Rudbeck, new to the service, has treated Johnson, his first clerk, with the ordinary politeness which would be given to a butler or footman at home. He has wished him 'Good morning,' hoped that he enjoyed his holiday, sent him a bottle of gin for the new year and complimented him once or twice on a neat piece of work. Johnson therefore worships Rudbeck and would willingly die for him. He thinks him the wisest, noblest and most beautiful of beings. The very look of him now on the stoop gives him such a shock of joy and relief that he bursts into tears. Johnson, after all, is only seventeen and completely alone. He falters, 'Oh, Mister Rudbeck, may God bless you—I pray for you all time.'

Rudbeck, not very good at distinguishing one black face from another, or remembering them, stares at the boy from under his shelving forehead and says, 'Hullo-hullo. What's the trouble? Why, it's thingummy-tite, aren't you?'

'Mister Johnson, sah.'

'Yes, dammit, Johnson. Which Johnson, though? Excuse me. Of course, yes, I remember now—why, it's Johnson. Hello, sir'—the last is in answer to Blore calling from the office He walks in and Blore jumps up to welcome him with both hands. Blore is the most hospitable and amiable of men. He is especially kind to all juniors.

'Well, well. This is a pleasure, and I've got to congratulate you, haven't I? When was it—in August? Rather a short honeymoon, I'm afraid.' He is really delighted that Rudbeck has just been married. He, as a married man, would like to see everyone married. 'I hope she'll be able to come out.'

'I've applied,' Rudbeck says, looking very glum. As a young married man, he does not like to be congratulated on his marriage. He is still so much excited by marriage that he feels every reference like an indecency.

'I hope you're successful—excellent plan—the bush is just the place where a man needs a wife. I only wish mine could be with me. What about breakfast?'

He carries Rudbeck off to breakfast and every five minutes he smiles at him and says, 'Well, well. I didn't know you were coming to take

23

over—not till yesterday. That's very nice.' He tells him all the gossip. 'The Emir is playing up again—he ought to be sacked. I'm afraid you'll soon be without a clerk. The sooner you get rid of him, the better—he's the worst type—probably dangerous, too—a complete imbecile, but quite capable of robbing the safe.'

Blore flushes. He really hates Johnson. The shouts and songs from the clerk's compound, during several nights, have filled him with what he takes for indigestion, but which is chiefly fear. All exuberance alarms him, as if he feels in it, from Nature itself, some threat to established things.

'He'll end in jug as the sparks fly upward. I knew what was coming when he asked for an advance in the first month. That's the one thing I never do—give advances. You might as well ask them to ruin themselves.'

Rudbeck listens respectfully. He is a modest young man. He is ready to take knowledge from his seniors. He soaks it in unconsciously and has picked up even mannerisms from his various district officers. He still pokes his head forward and utters loud exclamations like his first D.O., Sturdee; and he sits at his office table, with his chin in the air and his eyelids cast down, like Blore.

Meanwhile Johnson has called on Ajali at the store. 'It's all right, Mister Ajali—my friend Mister Rudbeck done come.'

'How, you no go to prison?'

'Throw away dat ole prison. Mister Rudbeck done come now.'

Johnson is laughing. 'He my frien'—soon as he see me—he smile and say, "Why, is dat you, Mister Johnson? Is you still here?" Den he shake my hand and he say, "God bless you, Mister Johnson—I 'gree for you—I pray for you." '

Ajali is astonished. He raises his eyebrows almost into his hair and cries, 'He say so, Mister Johnson?'

'He say so, Mister Ajali. Oh, Mister Rudbeck is jess the fines' man in de worl'.'

'Yah, but who go pay dem witness? You tink Mister Rudbeck len' you money?'

'Why, of course, he do everything for me—he my frien'. He fines' man in de worl'.'

'Yah, but ole Blore no go 'way yet—he stop week, two week—he call de case to-morrow—he go finish de case quick.'

'No, no, he no finish—Mister Rudbeck my frien'—he save me. Oh, Jesus, he dear, good man—he got a big heart like de Lamb of Gawd—oh, Jesus, it make me laugh—Mister Ajali, what you say, I tink I get dat lil wife now, dat Bamu.'

'Oh, by Jove! Mister Johnson, dat's too fast. How you pay fifteen poun' for native wife when you no fit pay you store bill?'

Johnson laughs. 'My frien' Mister Rudbeck go lend me five poun' for start—den I pay small-small each month.'

The next morning is Sunday. Johnson puts on his best suit and goes to visit his Bamu. In the cool of the early morning, in his clean white suit he goes at high speed. He carries his shoes in one hand, his white helmet in the other, his new sun umbrella under his arm, and skilfully avoids the least touch of a leaf or creeper on his shining trousers. He is as happy, probably, as even he can be, in the sense of his beautiful suit, his new shoes, his friend Rudbeck's support, and of the approach to Bamu. He improvises all the way, humming or chanting.

When he comes in sight of the ferry village, called Jirige, he puts on his shoes and his white helmet, and advances with the dignified steps of a governor-general in full uniform, picking his way among rubbish. Jirige is a new town, planted three years before to serve the ferry, but it has already created for itself a little desert surrounding it on all sides. Every tree has been cut or burnt down. The soil has been cropped and then left to blow about in dust. Close to the mat walls of the three compounds, large rubbish heaps throw a powerful stench of fish refuse down wind. These rubbish heaps are also village latrines. The paths to the village wander through and over them. No one has planted a shade tree, much less a fruit tree, but the sticks supporting the mat walls of the compounds have insisted upon taking root, so that in the village itself, thanks only to Nature, there are patches of green leaf and blue shade.

At eight o'clock in the morning this village is just waking up. Women are beating corn and fetching water; a dirty child with a large sore on its chin is sitting on the largest rubbish heap and holding a goat. Two men are dawdling towards the shore, holding themselves with crooked languor as if just out of hospital. Infinite boredom and disgusted resignation are expressed in their languid, crippled progress.

Johnson, from among the rubbish heaps, hails them. They stop,

25

slowly thrust their crooked necks towards him and stare with bloodshot eyes. One, the taller and older, frowns slightly, as if he has difficulty in getting Johnson into focus.

'Where's Brimah?' Johnson shouts.

'Brimah?' one says and looks at the other, who then repeats 'Brimah?'

'Brimah,' Johnson shouts.

Brimah?'

'Where is he?'

They stare at him and at last the taller asks, 'What do you want?'

'Brimah.'

'Brimah.' They shake their heads.

Suddenly Aliu comes out of the nearest compound, and says, 'Good morning, clerk.'

Johnson is delighted. He shakes him warmly by the hand and says, 'I've come about Bamu. Where is your father?'

Aliu, still staring at Johnson, points with his chin at the tall old man on the shore. Johnson cries out, 'So you are Brimah,' and goes to shake his hand.

The old man presents his hand to be shaken, and then thoughtfully scratches his left armpit with his right hand. He stands on one leg and gazes at the river.

'I want to marry Bamu,' says Johnson. 'Have you decided how much you want?'

'You said fifteen pounds.'

'Very well, and how much down?'

An old woman's voice from behind the mat wall screams, 'Five pounds now at once.'

'Five pounds,' Brimah says.

'And ten shillings a month,' screams the old woman.

'That's all right,' says Johnson. 'Five pounds now and ten shillings a month.'

There is a long silence. Then old Brimah gives one quick glance at Johnson's umbrella and mutters something in the act of turning away; he leaves it in the air, so to speak, as a man drops an empty can in a ditch.

'And the umbrella,' Aliu says.

'No, no. You said five pounds.'

There is another long pause. Then Brimah murmurs something to the river and Aliu says firmly, 'Six pounds with the umbrella.'

26

'But you said five,' Johnson shouts. 'You said five.'

Aliu walks off into the compound; the old man wanders towards the river. Johnson, disgusted, says to himself, 'These savages—they think I'm a fool.'

He walks away from the village towards the bush. Old Brimah pays no attention, but Aliu comes out of the house and calls, 'Hi! Wait!'

He runs after Johnson and shakes his hand, smiling. He exclaims, 'Come into the house, friend—let us discuss this matter—after all, Bamu wants you.'

'Does she want me?'

'Oh, yes, yes.'

Johnson is delighted. 'What, she loves me?'

'Oh, very much—and she's a good girl, too.'

Johnson, laughing, is brought into the compound; the family surround him with attention. One takes his umbrella, another pushes up a chair. He thanks them in all directions. 'Oh, thank you—thank you— you are too kind. So Bamu likes me, does she? What a good, beautiful, intelligent girl she is, isn't she? Yes, I noticed her at once.'

'What did we say?' Aliu says. 'Oh, yes, it was about the umbrella——'

'Oh, never mind about the umbrella—the umbrella; ha, ha—what is an umbrella!'

'Yes, it's nothing. So we agreed—six pounds now, and——'

'No, no, it was five.' Johnson begins to shout. Aliu says something to a dirty little girl, who runs off with the important high step of a hackney. In two minutes, Bamu appears in the compound. She comes in as if by accident. Her brothers look at her watchfully like men selling a horse, and Johnson with shining eyes and parted, greedy lips.

Bamu dawdles slowly across the compound from one side to another, moving each leg only when the other is at rest. Aliu continues to make conversation.

'We hear Judge Blore is going away.'

'Yes, he's going.'

'And Judge Rudbeck is coming.'

'Yes, he's coming.'

'What sort is he?'

But Johnson can't bear any more. He calls out, 'Bamu, Bamu. Don't you know me?'

Bamu is shocked at this breach of etiquette. She squints sideways at the young man and scowls.

27

'Will you marry me, Bamu?'

Bamu stares at him full face, with an expression of surprise and horror. Her brothers look at her sympathetically and one says briefly, 'It's the clerk.'

'What's he want?' Bamu asks in a severe tone.

'He wants to marry you.'

Bamu looks at Johnson for a moment and then she says, 'But what is he?'

'He's a clerk in the government.'

'Oh!' She obviously makes nothing of this.

'A very important man.'

'But what is he?'

'I tell you—a big man.'

'But why is he like that?' She looks Johnson up and down.

'He's a stranger, you understand—from the south.'

'Oh!'

'He loves you very much.'

'Oh!'

Johnson jumps up. 'You are the most beautiful and the nicest girl in Fada.'

Bamu frowns at him and then turns to her brothers: 'From the south?'

'Yes.'

She looks at Johnson with an air of surprise. Johnson takes another step towards her. 'Everyone knows how good and clever you are.'

Bamu turns again to her brothers: 'Why does he go on like that?'

'He's a stranger, you understand—a foreigner.'

'Oh!' She takes another close look at Johnson, who advances towards her: 'Bamu, if you could marry me——'

Bamu suddenly disappears through the mats into the next compound. Aliu from behind says, 'Seven pounds down was the bargain, wasn't it—and eight to follow.'

'No, five.' A shrill scream is heard and a little old woman comes hopping in. She is bent into a ball. Her face is all nose and chin. She is like a shrivelled embryo. She hops across the floor in a frenzy of excitement, pokes her humpy face at Johnson's wrist, gives another scream and hops out again.

'Six and that machine on your wrist,' Aliu says.

'No, no.'

'But that is what mother says and you know she alone can give Bamu leave.'

Johnson springs up. 'What? So you take me for a fool—do you know who I am?—I'm the friend of Mister Rudbeck. Do you think a big man like me, Johnson, is going to be swindled by a lot of savages?' Johnson gets very angry, curses and bawls for ten minutes. At the same time, the old woman is screaming and moaning behind the mats, as if in agony of pain. Everybody else is calm and even appears bored. Old Brimah wanders through whittling a stick; Aliu chews a nut and speaks again to the dirty child.

Bamu dawdles from behind the mat and stares at Johnson in perplexity. Johnson gazes in admiration. He has never seen such beauty. What a nose, straight cut and polished as oil. What a beautiful mouth; the lips are calm and vigorous; they seem to be cut from some soft wood without polish. How serious and responsible she looks, a clever girl.

He smiles in absent-minded delight. In the middle of his trance, he is suddenly aware that his helmet has disappeared. He jumps up just as old Brimah quickly replaces it back-before on his head. Brimah then goes out, and is heard on the other side of the mats to murmur something. The old woman gives another scream. Aliu says, 'Six pounds, the machine and the clothes.'

'The clothes? What clothes?'

'Instead of a robe for the old mother—or ten shillings if you like. What about the shoes?'

Johnson leaps a foot into the air. 'Shoes—how dare you? My shoes are English shoes—the very best shoes—they're not for savage people— bad thievish people like you.'

Aliu begins to leave the compound. Johnson shouts after him. 'But we won't quarrel about a wrist-watch.'

The bargaining goes on all day. Finally, it is decided that Johnson will pay six pounds down, ten pounds at ten shillings a month and give the umbrella, wrist-watch and coat.

As soon as the bargain is struck, it is discovered that Johnson has only three and fivepence. He promises another pound on pay day. The old woman flies into the compound and screams for twenty minutes. Brimah disappears with the wrist-watch. Aliu, unperturbed, begins bargaining again.

In fact, though no one knows how much can be got out of the

foreigner, nobody is surprised to find that he cannot pay six pounds down.

After three hours, therefore, it is arranged that Johnson will borrow, on the strength of his government rank, two pounds from the village chief, out of ferry dues, on a promise to repay three at the end of the month, and after that a pound a month to Bamu's family up to the full sum. Also he will hand over his trousers to the old mother for Bamu's maternal uncle, who lives abroad, and his shirt to herself. The bargain is struck. At the last minute, the old woman begins to scream again and old Brimah comes in with a long stick and the village policeman. He touches Johnson's shoes with the stick, mutters to the policeman, and languidly marches into the forest. The old woman is heard shrieking in short bursts like a ship in a fog. The policeman claims the shoes. Johnson shouts that he will bring down his friend Rudbeck with the government police and arrest the whole village. Aliu accuses him of bad faith, of breaking his bargain; Johnson curses, calls God to witness, weeps and after three hours' bargaining compromises for his hat.

At five o'clock, naked except for a loincloth, he returns joyfully to arrange for his marriage. As he enters the station in triumph, he turns aside to greet Ajali and the post office clerk, Benjamin, who are taking their evening walk.

'Look here, Mister Benjamin, Mister Ajali—I got dat Bamu.'

'Why you go without you clothes, Mister Johnson?'

Johnson waves the shoes at them and laughs. 'Dem pagans tink dey tief ma shoes, but I too much for dem. I say, I know you, you savage people, all a lot of tieves. I no stan' no nonsense—I tell my friend Mister Rudbeck put you all for prison.'

'What, so dey give you Bamu?'

'Oh, dat Bamu, she 'gree for me, she love me too much. We make de fines' wedding ever known for Fada. You come, Mister Benjamin, to my wedding. You come, Mister Ajali.'

Both accept the invitation. Benjamin, however, a tall, grave man of good education, always dressed formally in dark clothes, says in his gentle voice: 'I think sometimes I take a wife, but I think these native bush girls are so ignorant and dirty. It is no good till they have some educated girls.'

'Oh, but, Mister Benjamin, my Bamu is mos' beautiful, clever girl you can tink. First time she sees me, she says, "Mister Johnson, I 'gree for you, I don't like dese savage men—I like civilized man. Mister

Johnson," she says, "You good nice government man, me government lady. I love you with all my heart—we live happy, loving couple all time everyday." '

Ajali bows forward and twists up his eyes at the enthusiastic Johnson.

'What, she says so, Mister Johnson?'

'Yes, Mister Ajali, and she say she love me so much when she see me, she feel like de spirit fly right up out of her bress, and jump into my warm heart, lie down dere like bird in de nes'.'

'She certainly 'gree for you.'

'Oh, she love me more dan de sun make de water shine; she tink of me more dan de corn grow deep in de earth.'

'And how much you pay for dis Bamu, Mister Johnson?'

'Six pounds down and pound a mont' for ten mont'—very cheap. She is a girl fit to marry de King of Kano.'

'But, Mister Johnson, can you pay six pound?'

'I pay'm—Mister Rudbeck my frien'—he give me advance. I get rise of salary next month.'

'You better be quick with dat advance. I hear dat station headman Moma go native court, make complaint there.'

Johnson is suddenly angry. The truth is that his debt to Moma, the station headman, is of a peculiar kind. It is his duty each week to pay the gang of station labourers and gardeners; Blore gives him a lump sum of thirty-six shillings, and he distributes it, six shillings to Moma and five shillings to each man. But for the last weeks he has paid five shillings to Moma and four to each man, promising to make up the rest at the week-end with sixpence interest. He is not troubled much by this debt, which can be wiped off by a single advance, but by a dim fear that he may have infringed some law or regulation of the service by taking forced loans from the labourers. He therefore hates even to think of Moma and now he makes a vigorous gesture as if to knock him out of the air and cries, 'What you talking about? I don' care for dat ole Moma now. Mister Rudbeck my frien'. You come dis evening, Mister Benjamin, we drink to Missus Johnson, and you, Mister Ajali, for a happy evening.'

'I thank you, Mister Johnson, for a kindly invitation.'

'Oh, tank you, Mister Johnson, I like to laugh.'

The Waziri's boy, Saleh, approaches. He is a languid boy of fourteen in a scented blue gown, embroidered in white. He carries his head on his long neck with a lazy, arrogant grace. Black pimples darken his smooth fat chin and his eyes are puffy with too much kola. He wears red morocco stocking boots and slippers over them, like a chief. He throws the stiff gown across his shoulder with an affected gesture and says in a drawling Hausa, 'The Waziri salutes the clerk Johnson, clerk of Fada.'

'I salute Waziri.'

'He sends this message. Will clerk Johnson come to speak with Waziri? It is about this man Moma.'

'No, no. He can't speak about that rascal Moma. Tell Waziri that.' The languid boy says nothing, but stands opposite Johnson.

'What is it?'

'I think you give me a shilling.'

Johnson looks furious, but Benjamin says in English, 'I advise you to give him some small cash—he is very great friend of Waziri.'

'I have no money here—if you would lend me a shilling, Mister Benjamin.'

Benjamin at once gives the shilling. He is generous with money. Saleh takes it without a word and dawdles away.

But at eight o'clock that night he returns with Waziri. Mr. Johnson is enjoying his party. He is giving, to the gramophone, an impromptu dance, while Ajali, Benjamin and half a dozen station servants including Rudbeck's cook, Tom, are clapping the time. Their faces are serious and wistful. Only Johnson is laughing and excited. This is as it should be at any native dance, the artist under possession of the spirit; the spectators critical of the production.

Waziri is a small, wiry, very black man of about fifty. His features are sharply cut and distinguished; the long nose has a high, thin nostril. He wears a thin, grey moustache and a goatee. His small, bloodshot eyes are surrounded by bright crimson lids. They seem to glare like the windows of a burnt-out house whose embers are still hot. These eyes fluctuate in their redness like embers, as he moves them quickly.

He is dressed in a shabby, washed-out blue turban, cracked at the folds, and a dirty gown. It is unwise for any Oriental minister to look rich.

Waziri is received in a very careless manner by the station staff. Ajali says in English, 'Good night, Waziri.' Blore's groom also salutes him. The Waziri is not put out. He has the affable expression of the nobleman travelling in a democratic country; ready to meet every kind of rudeness with good humour. He whisks up his gown, sits down and applauds the dance with cries of, 'Oh, good, oh, excellent, Allah, how well he dances.'

The record is finished, and Johnson stops, panting and sweating. Waziri beckons and a house slave brings a bottle of gin, which he presents to Johnson.

'A present,' Waziri cries.

'But I must pay,' Johnson says in Hausa. 'I must give you a return present.' A great official does not take presents without returning something.

Waziri waves his grey palms in the air and cries, 'Oh no—no—it's not necessary. A penny then—one penny—one cowrie—one kola nut.'

Johnson laughs and says, 'What, one penny—that is a small present.'

'From you it is all I could ask.'

Johnson is amused. He borrows a penny from Ajali and gives it to the Waziri. All laugh. The gin is opened and drunk. Waziri asks Johnson to sit beside him for a private conference. He says, 'You are a clever man, Mr. Johnson, a very important man in Fada. I hear, too, that the new judge, Rudbeck, is your friend.'

'Quite true, Waziri. I am Mister Rudbeck's friend.'

'You know all that happens in the office?'

'Quite true, Waziri. In the government, we know all orders.'

'You read all the letters, all the wires—you read all the old judge's letters, and the young judge's too?'

'Of course I do, it is my job.'

'Mr. Bauli, who used to be the clerk before you, was a good friend of mine.'

'Yes, I know, and he showed you all the government letters.' Mr. Johnson laughs gaily.

The Waziri laughs also. 'Of course he did, he showed me all the letters. Sometimes if a letter came about the Emir's pay, or some debt or other, or the new taxes, he would tell me even before the judge knew.'

'And you gave him ten shillings a month.'

'More than that, clerk Johnson, much more. Many presents beside.'

The whole party has now gathered round and is listening with all its ears. This does not disconcert the Waziri or Johnson. The arrangement with clerk Bauli is well known and, moreover, it is a very common one.

All the clerks, even Ajali at the store, receive presents from various native ministers.

'Mister Bauli had plenty of presents.' Johnson was laughing.

'Yes, for his wife too.'

'A wife is expensive,' Johnson says. 'Especially a pretty wife.'

'Yes, indeed, husbands need money, if they would keep their wives. Suppose, Mr. Johnson, that you should need money, to pay some little debt, you know I am your friend as well as Mr. Rudbeck.'

'You could give me presents like Mr. Bauli?'

'Of course—of course—and if there happened to be any complaint against you, I could take care of that too. When, as you know, there were complaints against Mr. Bauli, something about cattle tax, did I not see the witnesses against him and satisfy them, so that nothing more was heard about the case?'

'Would you do that for me, Waziri?'

'Of course—of course.'

'For nothing.'

Waziri spreads out his hands in the old Eastern gesture. 'For friendship.'

'Not for any letters?'

'Letters?'

'The office letters? Don't you want me to bring you any of the letters?'

'Oh, well.' Waziri rocks gently on his hams and gazes at the roof. 'As Mr. Bauli has always given us information, I was sure you would not object——'

'It is nice to get presents,' Johnson says, smiling and looking round the group. He does not know what he is going to do yet. At the moment he is the centre of interest. He has an audience. It is waiting to follow him and his deeds. The situation has been given into his hands, like wood to be carved or a theme to be sung.

'You want me to show you all the government letters, Waziri?'

Waziri laughs gaily and rocks; Saleh looks still more supercilious.

Johnson, for a greater effect, speaks in English. 'You say to me, Mister Johnson, you government man, you belong for de King, you know de King's thoughts, you tell me dem King's thoughts, I give you plenty money.'

Waziri throws out his hands and cries in Hausa, 'It is the custom. Mr. Bauli——'

Johnson jumps up with an indignant gesture. Benjamin, Ajali and the half-dozen boys from the station gaze upwards with intense interest. The whites of their eyes beneath the iris are like thin crescent moons lying on their backs. They hold their breaths with excitement.

Johnson throws out his arm and raises his chin.

'I not Mister Bauli, Waziri, I Johnson—I belong for government. I belong for de King. I Mister Rudbeck's frien'—I no take money for King's letters. I no fit do such a ting.'

Waziri gets up and bows low. Saleh closes his eyes, as if overcome by the oppressive vulgarity of the scene.

'I surprised at you, Waziri.'

Waziri smiles, bows again, and rises with a perfectly blank, bored face. His eyes are also half closed, and his expression is that of the slum visitor who having finished the day's visits and smiled through a hundred smells, is suddenly projected into a still more revolting smell, which is actually outside her district.

'I think you forget I government man.'

Waziri answers in a flat voice, 'Pardon, I was told you were like the others, like Mr. Bauli, who was a very sensible man. Good night, Mr. Johnson. God prolong you.'

'Bauli was a damn rascal, Waziri, and so are you.'

Waziri gives a cackle of laughter and then, even more bored, sweeps out. Saleh strolls after him, shaking out of his new gown a powerful smell of musk. Saleh, as Waziri's latest favourite, runs a weekly account with Ajali at the store for scent and scented soaps, clothes, tea, jam, sugar and cigarettes; as much as he likes.

The moment he is gone, Johnson turns to his friends. 'Damn old rascal, he tink I tief man.'

His friends congratulate him, and all drink Waziri's gin.

'He tink I show him dem government letters.'

Johnson walks up and down in the compound and every moment his walk becomes grander; it is like the walk of the royal guard, but a guard of poets fresh from a triumph of loyalty. Johnson slaps himself on the chest. 'I belong for de King—I 'gree for de King. I Mister Rudbeck's frien'.'

Beer is going round in large calabashes, all the clerks and servants are talking at the top of their voices and the words, 'King,' 'home,' 'England,' 'royal' are heard. Everybody is excited by the idea of patriotism. Every now and then, as Johnson walks among his guests, he makes a few dance steps, and sings through his nose, 'England is my country, dat King of England is my king.'

Then Ajali chimes in with a bass 'Oh, England is my home, all on de big water.'

At one in the morning all boys and clerks have gone except one small boy. But half a dozen townspeople are still gossiping in the shadows. Johnson is walking restlessly in the compound. He has taken off all his clothes except his bright shoes. A thin moon glitters on the shoes, on an empty gin bottle and the dregs of beer in scattered calabashes. Johnson is singing softly with quick changes of pitch and tone:

> *'England is my country.*
> *Oh, England, my home all on de big water.*
> *Dat King of England is my King,*
> *De bes' man in de worl', his heart is too big.*
> *Oh, England, my home all on de big water.'*

Two of the gossipers dimly seen in the shadow are clapping softly while they talk about their own affairs; an old Yoruba trader in the corner, very drunk, with an English cloth cap on his head, sings the chorus with Johnson, and utters loud sobs. God knows what the word 'England' means to him, but he is an old man who probably learnt his English at some English mission.

> *'Oh, England, my home, away der on de big water.*
> *England is my country, dat King of England is my King.*
> *His heart is big for his children—*
> *Room for everybody.'*

Johnson sings alone, falsetto, dancing with peculiar looseness as if all his joints are turned to macaroni.

> *'I say hallo, I act de fool.*
> *I spit on de carpet of his great big heart.'*

'Oh, England my home,' the old Yoruba sings with a loud sob, 'Away, away, over de big water.'

> *'Hi, you general dar, bring me de cole beer,*
> *I, Mister Johnson, from Fada, I belong for King's service,*
> *Hi, you judge dar, in yo' crinkly wig,*
> *Roll me out dat bed, hang me up dat royal net.'*

36

The clapping grows louder and someone throws in a syncopation. Four or five voices hum and wail the tune with the effect sometimes of clarinets, sometimes of kazoos. Johnson's dance grows even looser, his legs seem to bend in every part, as he sways and sings, clearly but softly:

> 'Hi, you coachy man with you peaky hat,
> Bring me dat gold pot for I make my night water.
> I, Mister Johnson from Fada, I big man for Fada,
> De King, he tired, he work all day, it's mail day.
> He wanna sleep. He feel me dar like hot pain in his bress.
> He say Dass some fool chile in my bress
> Runnin through my bress like he was drunk.
> De Pramminister he come running from his clerk-office.
> He shout out to de King, Up on top; you majesty, I see um,
> I see um like lil black ting no more big than stink bug.
> He drunk, he play de fool, he black trash,
> He no care for nobody. He bad dirty boy,
> He spit all over de carpet of you great big heart.
> All right, you majesty, I go catch him now,
> I go trow him right out right over de top of Pallament right
> In de river Thames, kersplash.
> De King, he say, oh no, Mr. Pramminister, don't do so,
> I know dat Johnson from Fada, he my faithful clerk from Fada,
> He drunk for me, he drunk for love of his royal King,
> He drunk becas he come here, he doanno how to be so happy,
> He got no practice in dem great big happiness,
> Why, what he do now, he laugh. Poot, what's de good to laugh.
> He dance. Poot. What's de good to dance.
> He walk on his han's.'

Johnson makes an attempt to walk on his hands and falls back on his knees.

> 'What's the good of walking on his han's.
> Dat's why he drunk, Mr. Pramminister.
> Dat's why he play around like he low black trash.
> He spit on my carpet because he wanna die for me.
> He——'

At this moment a furious voice bawls across the bush, 'Who's that? What the hell are you playing at, there?'

Johnson stands in a trance of astonishment with eyes like a hare's. He licks his lips and cries in a trembling voice, 'Johnson, sah—I sing small small, sah.'

'Johnson? Who's Johnson? Oh, you mean Johnson. Are you drunk, Johnson?'

'Oh, no, sah, I never——'

'Oh, go to bed, go to bed, Johnson.'

'Yes, Mister Rudbeck. Goo' night, Mister Rudbeck.'

'Oh, the hell, good night, damn it all.'

The guests are already in the bush. Johnson goes to bed still in a trance of surprise. How, he wonders, should Mr. Rudbeck hear him at two o'clock. How should he be awake at such a time?

Johnson's wedding is fixed for Sunday, the office holiday. When the news is known in the town drummers and dancers at once come to offer their services. The beer women go down to the river banks to wet their corn for malting. The scale of Johnson's bachelor parties raises high expectations in Fada. But Johnson sends away the drummers and gives no orders for strong beer. He says to Ajali, 'Dese savage people tink I make savage wedding like bush people. Dey never understand Christian marriage.'

'But Bamu not Christian?'

'No, but I make her proper marriage for government lady.'

Since there is no parson and Bamu cannot be baptized, Johnson asks Benjamin to read the marriage service in the Post Office.

'We must have proper government office for wedding.'

'But do you think a book-wedding good for this bush girl, Mister Johnson.'

'Oh, but she very clever girl, Mister Benjamin—I tell her now she government wife; she fit to be civilized in the beginning. She say, Yes, she do everyting I like. So I say we begin with Christian marriage, which is full of mos' beautiful words and true Christian love.'

Benjamin is seated at his table in the little tin office checking the stamp sheets. He turns over a sheet of red pennies and looks suspiciously at the back, as if fearing that there may be some secret defect there, lying in wait for him. 'It is indeed a very fine service,' he says in his gentle voice. 'It gives the noblest thoughts on which marriage can

38

be conducted, but do you think that book-wedding does any good for such ignorant people. Will they not think it some government juju. I fear, Mister Johnson, that these people don't understand anything at all—it is quite impossible for a long time to come when perhaps we are all dead and gone.'

'No, no, Bamu understand—I tell her. So you will do the wedding for me?'

'I shall feel so foolish.'

'Oh no, Mister Benjamin.'

'But it is certainly my duty for ordinary friendship. It is very little to make myself foolish on your behalf.'

Johnson shakes Benjamin's hand and cries, 'God bless you, my dear friend! Now I see you are truly a friend.'

The wedding is fixed for the morning, but it is postponed because Bamu's wedding dress has not arrived from Dorua store. The store has already wired refusing to deliver it to Johnson's messenger until the money is paid and Johnson has wired the money. But the messenger is late.

At two o'clock Johnson loses patience and flies off with Ajali and Rudbeck's cook, Tom, to fetch the bride. She is waiting with her family, who raise loud shouts and screams when Johnson and Ajali appear and claim her. This is the usual ceremony, meant to show she is being carried off by force. But it is only a ceremony. Bamu, whose box is packed, at once places herself between Johnson and Ajali and walks gravely to Fada. The family, behind, chatter all the way and make all the universal jokes, at which Bamu laughs as heartily as the rest.

Johnson also laughs, but every now and then he remembers that the dress has not yet come and strikes himself on the forehead and kicks himself with his heel.

'You fool, Johnson. Why you no send them money week ago? Now you spoil everything.'

Benjamin is waiting in the Post Office beside the transmitters. Johnson and Bamu stand before him. Ajali and Tom, twenty or thirty of Bamu's relations, with the station servants, fill all the rest of space and extend far beyond the door. They crowd into every corner, even behind Benjamin, enclosing the bridal couple in a small circle. The pagans gaze with amusement and awe, first at the telegraph apparatus and then at Benjamin. Every now and then they are taken with grins and some of the women giggle; the next moment they are frightened; they show the whites of their eyes, mutter and even struggle to get out of the door.

Johnson, holding Bamu's hand, has forgotten his disappointment over the wedding frock. He himself is in a white suit, starched to the consistency of planks; a blue tie, blue silk socks and new patent shoes. His expression is grave at the beginning, but at the words 'which is an honourable state, instituted of God in the time of man's innocence' he smiles and quickly blinks his eyes like a child who is suddenly brought before a lighted Christmas tree. Benjamin reads well with great enjoyment of the words; at phrases which especially please him, he raises his eyebrows as if in surprise and there is even surprise in his voice, as if to say, 'But this is better than I thought.' When he asks Johnson to take Bamu for his wife, Johnson answers in a loud voice and looks round at the audience to see if they have noticed his decisive action.

Bamu makes no answer until first Johnson, then Benjamin, then her brother explain to her that she is expected to consent to the marriage. She says then in a tone of contemptuous surprise, 'But you know I did.'

She refuses to repeat the woman's undertaking, saying only, 'Don't be silly—I know how to get married.'

Johnson argues with her for a moment and is just growing indignant when Benjamin reproves him and says, 'Give her the ring, Mister Johnson.'

Bamu accepts a silver ring and says, 'Thank you.' She continues to look at it for the rest of the service and occasionally murmurs, 'I thank you, husband.'

Johnson, however, holding her hand, is now smiling and gazing at a coil of copper wire, hung on the wall, in a kind of trance.

'Thy wife shall be as a fruitful vine upon the walls of thine house.

'Thy children like the olive branches; round about thy table. Lo, thus shall a man be blessed.'

In imagination he is living already in a kind of paradise; or rather in a series of strange and delightful states which rapidly succeed each other. He is the happy husband adoring and adored in a perpetual and rather solemn dignity like an oleolithograph of the Royal Family; he is the triumphant lover begetting many children; he is the comforter of an unhappy Bamu, suffering from mortal disease; tears come to his eyes when he thinks of her sufferings and his own goodness. Below all he feels a triumphant pride in his own achievement of this splendid and beautiful wedding.

Bamu, comforted by the assurances of her family that all this is a wedding in the foreign style and by the ring, bears the rest of the service with patience. She waits obediently while Johnson, after the ceremony, goes round shaking hands with everybody and saying, 'Good-bye now and thank you. I am now going away privately with Missus Johnson and we wish to be alone. That is the proper thing. But Ajali and Mister Benjamin have beer for you in this place.'

She is following Johnson out of the hut when he puts his hand through her arm, clasps her hand and conducts her through the crowd outside. Bamu does not like this. She wants to walk behind her husband, but she allows herself to be pulled along, saying only, 'What strange things you do.'

Johnson does not hear her protest. He is too happy. He keeps on smiling at her and saying, 'Now you are Missus Johnson—you are a government lady. I think you are a beautiful wife—I love you more than the sky is big. I am going to make you so happy that you will laugh all day and feel quite surprised at your happiness. You don't know how happy it is for women to stop being girls and to be civilized wives with loving Christian husbands who never beat them and are their kind friends—just as good as brothers.'

As soon as they are out of sight, the whole concourse of visitors streams after them. It is impossible for Benjamin to explain that a marriage feast can be held elsewhere than in the presence of the bridal couple. Moreover, Bamu's family are not going to be separated from her on this joyful occasion. They mean to see her properly married in their own method.

Meanwhile Johnson and Bamu reach the compound, which has been swept. New mats have been set up behind the house to enclose Sozy's old hut and the kitchen hut in a woman's compound. In Johnson's hut a table has been laid with a cloth, plates, knives and forks, a cold chicken, fried yam and two candles. Two chairs have been borrowed from the store. A large parcel lies on one of the chairs.

Johnson, with cries of joy, tears open the parcel and takes out a white muslin dress, spotted in pink, with frills at the neck and short sleeves, appropriate underwear, white stockings and white canvas shoes.

'Your dress, Bamu. Now you shall be a government lady at once. Here, this is the first thing to put on.'

He holds up a pair of old-fashioned drawers, mission style.

'But that is for white men.'

'No, no, it is lady's dress—for white ladies. Now you are a government lady, you must wear this too.'

'But they will hurt me.'

'How can they hurt you. You will be proud to wear white lady's dress.'

'But what is the good of such things—I have my own cloth, quite new.'

'But Bamu, you silly girl, don't you understand—this is a great honour. Come, I'll show you. You will feel quite different when you have put it on.' Johnson pushes Bamu down upon the chair, catches her left leg and tries to put it into the leg of the drawers. Bamu suddenly gives a scream and at once two brothers, an uncle and her mother come rushing in, laughing. They are astonished at the scene and stand gazing.

'What is it, Bamu?'

'I don't know. I can't make him understand anything.'

Johnson turns on them and screams furiously, 'But she must—she must dress properly—she's not a bush girl now—tell her not to be silly. I want to give her great happiness.'

Bamu suddenly springs away from the drawers, takes up her cloth and rolls herself into it. She says, 'No, I won't be married to him.'

The mother jumps forward suddenly with loud screams. 'I always said he was bad—take her away from him now. But we won't pay anything back, so it's no good you asking, you brute. It's all your fault.'

Johnson now loses his temper and shouts that they are a lot of rascals and thieves; he will go to Rudbeck, he will call the police. Everyone shouts for half an hour, when it is suddenly noticed that Bamu has disappeared. Johnson rushes out in a panic, shouting, 'Bamu! Bamu! Come back!' The family equally are in consternation. They don't want to pay back the bride-price, of which they have already spent the whole sum handed over. They also hunt for Bamu and she is found making for home and brought back.

'But I won't put on those silly bad clothes—they are indecent for a girl.'

'No, no,' Johnson reassures her. 'Never mind about the clothes now—only stay with me.'

42

'Very well, I will stay.'

'We will eat now.'

'Very well, as you like. You are the husband.'

'You sit there and eat.'

Bamu looks at the chair. 'But I can't sit while you eat.'

'Yes, yes, yes—that is right—it is right for a wife.'

'No, I must attend to you properly, like a wife.'

'No, no, sit down.' He pushes her into the chair. Bamu jumps out of it and gives a scream. In come the family. There is another dispute. Johnson sheds tears and cries to Ajali, 'What can you do with such savage people—I too tired—I die now.' He lies down on his bed. Sozy comes and takes his shoes off. The family, meanwhile, paying no attention to him, decide that Bamu has every right to attend to her husband, and that it would indeed be indecent for her, as a married woman, to sit down to feed with a man.

Bamu brings Johnson, still lying prostrate, a calabash of broth and gives it to him with a low curtsey, turning her head politely to one side so as not to breathe on him.

He weeps loudly and cries, 'I am dying now—the wedding is all spoilt.'

Bamu urges him, 'Master, you must eat—remember, I shall expect you to be strong. Everyone will be looking. You won't make me ashamed.'

'Oh, Bamu, you are a too nice girl—I think perhaps I will teach you to be civilized.'

'This is a very good broth with plenty of pepper—good for making you lusty.'

'Yes, you are so pretty—I think I will teach you afterwards. But now I am sad, all the same.'

He puts down his legs and accepts the broth which he eats with a melancholy expression. 'I am hungry, but I am sad too. You have caused me a great grief. You have spoilt my marriage.'

'But we are not married yet.'

'Is that all you think of, you savage girl—you are too ignorant. But I shall teach you, because you are clever too.'

'I cook very well—you like that.'

'It is good, for savage food.'

'There is more.'

'Very well, my dear, I will have a little more. I am so hungry—but you mustn't think I am not sad.'

Meanwhile, the drums have arrived, brought by Bamu's friends. They are outside sketching a first tune and trying each other's rhythm. Hands are clapping and every now and then a voice shouts out the line of a nuptial song or merely a phrase.

> *'The snake lifts his head,*
> *The tortoise modestly retires.'*

'Yes, it is nice and peppery,' Johnson sighs. 'But I have no appetite.' The drums are settling down to an easy lolloping tune: 'Poom-poom-peroompy-poomety poom.'

The women's voices sing:

> *'Oh snake, why do you look at me with your eye?*
> *What do you want among the maidens?'*

A small drum throws in a comment like chattering teeth or running feet and the bass drum answers with poompy-poom.

Johnson's right foot dances by itself on the floor; his head swings to the tune, so that he has to pause a moment with the spoon. 'I must eat, but my heart is broken.'

The girls outside sing together:

> *'I fear this snake, he is dangerous.*
> *He strikes like the arrow in the darkness.*
> *He bites like fire. Oh—oh—don't let him near.'*

The drums are playing:

> *'Poom-poom-peroompty-poopety-poom.*
> *Tarraty, tattarary, tatty, tattararatty, poom.'*

Johnson is on his feet, jerking his knees and thighs.

> *'Where do you hide, little tortoise,*
> *Under the leaves of darkness.'*

Bamu bursts out laughing and darts out among the girls. She takes her cloth in both hands, throws it quickly open and shut again, singing:

> *'I saw a strange creature in the forest.*
> *A centipede, as big as my arm.'*

Johnson comes slowly from the doorway of the hut, dancing stiffly and jerkily, throwing up his knees like a stallion; the men utter shouts and rush to range beside him in a line. They advance with the same stiff, sudden movements and sing:

> '*Oh, maidens, we sought you in the corn field.*
> *When we looked it was only the shadow of a cloud.*
> *We saw you far off and dived into the white water,*
> *But when we grasped you, it was only the sparkling wave.*
> *We heard your voices in the air and sprang from the branches,*
> *But only the bright bird flew between our hands.*'

The girls with Bamu in the middle, their arms interlaced behind their backs, sway without moving their feet, so that the dance is simply an undulation of the whole row, and sing:

> '*What do I hear, a lion roaring after his prey?*
> *What do I feel, an elephant shaking the ground?*
> *What do I fear, a crocodile lifting his eye from the pool?*'

Then, all together with a quickened note:

> '*I fear the snake, he is dangerous to women.*
> *See, he has struck my poor sister.*
> *She is all swollen with his bite, she cries out, "Aie, aie!"*'

At midnight Johnson, dressed in nothing but the calico drawers, is performing a bridegroom dance among such a thunder of drums, yells, clapping, that his own song can scarcely be heard:

> '*Oh, Bamu, I see you dar in de forest.*
> *Why you 'fraid of me, lil girl?*
> *Why you run away under de leaves?*
> *I do nutting to you, Bamu.*
> *I no got no stick, no knife.*'

Johnson wakes in the morning after the wedding with a headache which makes him stagger. He has black spots in front of his eyes and buzzing ears. But he smiles with self-satisfaction while he hurries, at earliest dawn, to the station in order to avoid his creditors and to get an advance from Rudbeck.

He is just in time to see Rudbeck mounting his pony. He stands with one foot in the stirrup talking to a native official, secretary to the native minister of roads. Johnson has forgotten that Rudbeck has a passion for roads.

Just as Blore is particular about tax assessment and is always collecting statistics, so Rudbeck, even as a junior, as soon as he comes to a station, sends for the chief and complains about the roads. He spends his afternoons riding or driving about the country inspecting bridges; and he loves to make maps and draw on them, in dotted lines of red ink, new trade routes.

In this he has no sympathy from Blore, who considers motor roads to be the ruin of Africa, bringing swindlers, thieves and whores, disease, vice and corruption, and the vulgarities of trade, among decent, unspoilt tribesmen.

It was the same, he says, with the railways, when he was a junior. They spoilt the old Nigeria wherever they went.

In fact, Blore and Rudbeck have already had a slight quarrel about the Dorua road which Rudbeck is now going to inspect. When Rudbeck has suggested, the night before, that a certain curve needs straightening, Blore has smiled and said, 'Still on the road game?'

Rudbeck has looked haughty and wooden, like a small boy being chaffed. Although he is modest and respectful, he has a strong will of his own. He doesn't change his mind easily, after he, or somebody else, has made it up for him. He says now in a cool and defiant voice, 'Don't you think it's about time we had a few motor roads?'

'The voice of old Sturdee—I heard him declare——'

Rudbeck turns red and looks still more obstinate. He says coldly. 'I didn't get the idea from Sturdee—it's obvious.'

Old Sturdee is a resident well known for his enthusiasm in road-building, and Blore is fond of suggesting that Rudbeck caught it from Sturdee, with whom he spent his first six months in the service. This is quite true. Rudbeck, like other juniors, had no idea when he joined of what would be expected of him. If he had come to Blore first, no doubt he would have fallen into a routine of office, drinks and an evening walk; prided himself on his assessment and considered census much the most important duty of a political officer. But from Sturdee he has caught the belief that to build a road, any road anywhere is the noblest work a man can do. He has also found it enjoyable. As Sturdee is fond of saying, 'When you make a road you know you've done something— you can see it.'

But by now, two years after his last contact with Sturdee, Rudbeck honestly believes that he has always advocated roads. He admits to a warm admiration for Sturdee's work, but doesn't acknowledge that his own creations in Fada owe their being to anyone else's inspiration.

'It's a great game,' Blore says, showing a little malice; he can be spiteful with innovators and disturbers.

Rudbeck makes no answer, but gets up next morning early to inspect a broken bridge. He is feeling both virtuous, in getting up early for important public service, and obstinate, in the knowledge that he may be late for the office and that Blore may be put out. He is not, of course, thinking of any disloyalty to Blore; but he is feeling it and acting it. When, therefore, he is suddenly greeted with low bows and loud blessings by a young clerk, very like any other clerk, he doesn't notice him at all, answers with a brief 'G'morning,' and canters away.

Johnson is still admiring his hero from the back, with his broad bemused smile, when Blore's orderly suddenly taps him on the shoulder and says that the District Officer wants him at once in his own house.

Johnson becomes physically and mentally deficient. His aching legs bend under him, his brain turns to water. He creeps into the dark, frowsty inner room of the Residency, where Blore is still in bed.

Blore's bed is a ruin. Its net poles are tied up with string; its net has even more plugs of wool than Johnson's. But the reason is different. Blore loves his net because he has had it for twenty years; he cannot bear to throw it away; Johnson never troubles about a net at all, until he is bitten, and then he buys an old cheap one because he prefers to spend his money on parties and beer.

Blore is lying among frowsty, patched sheets and old threadbare blankets. At the end of the bed, against the wall, a little thin man in dirty rags is standing, cap in hand. Blore in a lively voice says to Johnson, 'Mr. Johnson, I have sent for you to tell you of a serious complaint sent on to me from the native court. This man Moma tells me that you have not paid the station labourers their full wages.'

Johnson, seeing Moma, is already in despair.

'I gave you thirty-one shillings for these men, Mr. Johnson—Moma tells me they only had twenty-five.'

'Oh, sah, oh, sah, I explain to you——'

'I think you'd better, You understand the meaning of embezzlement?'

Blore's voice is cheerful and he shows no anger against Johnson. In fact, he feels none. He is sure that Johnson is done for. He is conscious of power in dealing with him; the force of law is on his side.

'Oh, yes, I explain, sah—to-morrow, sah.'

'Why not now, Mr. Johnson? You realize that this is a serious matter. I have not signed a warrant, but I must try the case—it can't be kept out of court. If I find that there are grounds for a prosecution within the criminal law, I shall be obliged to order your arrest.'

'Oh, sah, oh, sah, but I explain everything.'

'You'd better go away and think it over—I won't need you in the office. I think indeed, after this revelation, that I would prefer not to have you there. I will look into the case to-morrow morning.'

Johnson goes home in tears. Bamu, who has begun her household duties with a great scouring of Johnson's old calabashes and pots, which she has collected in the compound, looks up for a moment, murmurs 'How do,' takes a firmer tuck of her cloth and throws another handful of sand and pebbles into a water pot.

Johnson goes into his own house, sits down on a chop box and sobs. The old woman Sozy creeps in, runs several times round the house in terror; finally she takes off his shoes, rubs his feet and murmurs to herself, *'Ohey-ohey-ohey.'*

She would comfort him aloud if she dared. Ajali and Benjamin appear at the door. Ajali looks in and says to Johnson, 'Good morning. You in at home, Mister Johnson?'

'Yass, I in.'

They come in and Ajali says, 'I hear Mister Blore go try you for bezzlement.'

Johnson is sitting in his bare feet and shirt sleeves. He says in a deep sad voice, 'I finish now.' Ajali turns up his crab eyes and laughs as if in surprise. 'You lose you job now, Mister Johnson.'

'If I lose my job, I go die.'

Benjamin says thoughtfully, 'Why do you think you would die Mister Johnson. Many labourers seem most cheerful in their hard work.'

'I government man—I no fit work like common man.'

'No, it is true. The labourers are too ignorant to know better. It is very hard for people to go backwards when they have had some civilization.'

'What you say to Mister Blore at you trial?' Ajali asks.

48

'Yes, native labourer's food in this country too bad for clerk—I expect it would make him sick, then he die,' Benjamin says thoughtfully. 'The civilization of all people in this country is too unequal. That is why we must depend on government jobs for a long time yet.'

Ajali gazes at Johnson with curious eyes, trying to extract from his despair some definite idea. 'You tink you go to prison, Mister Johnson?' he cries.

'I no go to prison. I die before.' Johnson's voice rises to a scream. 'I no fit be shut up for prison—I no fit.'

'Perhaps a man may learn some good things from prison,' Benjamin murmurs. 'After all, he wouldn't be afraid to lose his job—he'd be more free.'

'I no fit—I no fit.'

'No, I don't think so too,' Benjamin says with sympathy directed apparently towards himself also. 'Fada is a bad place for civilized people, but I think they die in native prison. That prison is too backward except for the bush people.' He sighs deeply.

Outside they can hear Bamu humming to herself like a bee in a box; sometimes loud and determined, when she is attacking a new pot; sometimes subdued, even and mellow, while she pauses in absent-minded repose and calm satisfaction.

The next morning Johnson is very ill. He groans and says that he is dying. 'I can't go to hamfish—I die.'

Bamu stares at him. She goes to old Sozy and says in a tone of surprise, 'The man is ill.' Sozy runs to her beloved and rubs his feet. Johnson weeps and turns up his eyes. He looks haggard and flat as after a long illness. 'I die—I die,' he says. 'They can't put me in prison—I'll die first.'

'Is he really ill?' Bamu asks.

Sozy shakes and wags her head.

Bamu is troubled. Her brow wrinkles. She says, 'But what can we do—he's a stranger.'

Sozy begins to weep. No tears come, but her face works and she is suffering perhaps more than those who have tears. '*Ohey*, he's dying.'

'Perhaps we'd better get the white man,' Bamu suggests. 'If it's a stranger illness.'

49

'Yes, yes, I'll go.' Sozy totters off to the station, but finds no one in the office. The messengers are all at the district officer's house. He is ill.

No one will attend to Sozy. Benjamin is sending urgent wires for a doctor; Blore's servants are packing.

Old Sozy goes home in despair; she staggers into the hut and says, 'Judge ill too—they're going to take him away. I couldn't get any medicine. *Ohey*—he'll die.'

Johnson sits up and exclaims, 'Judge Blore ill?'

'Very ill—they're taking him away.'

Johnson jumps out of bed and calls for his trousers. He can't help laughing. Old Sozy, surprised but relieved, dresses him, Bamu brings him a drink and says, 'You well again, husband?'

'Yes.' Johnson thinks for a moment, runs his hand over his forehead, stomach, ribs; coughs and spits, 'Yes, I feel almost well. Isn't that a good thing?'

'Oh, very nice,' Sozy says, using the Hausa phrase '*da dadi.*' 'Very nice.' It is the only phrase she knows expressing pleasure. She has forgotten the rest.

'Are you well enough to go to the homfice?' Bamu asks.

'Yes, I think so—yes, Mister Rudbeck will be there this morning. Yes.' He feels himself again and laughs. 'I really do feel quite well again—almost—I shall go to the homfice.'

As he goes down the path he is heard singing:

> *'England is my country, de King of England is my King.*
> *De bes' man in de worl'—his heart is so big.'*

But when he comes in sight of the office, his steps falter. He sees there Moma, the headman, and every one of his creditors. He feels again very ill; he has a pain in his stomach. He half turns away. But suddenly the head messenger, Adamu, catches sight of him and bawls, '*Akow.*'

He wavers towards the office, tacking like a drunk man. The creditors and Moma, in a little group by the office door, look at him with the sour and revengeful faces of the betrayed. He shrinks from them. Johnson cannot bear to come near so much bitterness. But suddenly he has an inspiration. He goes up to Moma and says in a low voice, 'My friend Mister Rudbeck is going to give me an advance. Then I will pay. But if you complain, I won't be able——'

'Hurry up, Johnson,' Rudbeck shouts. 'Where've you been?'

Rudbeck is at Blore's table smoking a curly briar and turning over papers with a disgusted air. A small, dirty sack, carefully tied and sealed at the mouth, lies beside him. He is plainly in an impatient mood, seeing before him a whole morning in the office.

'What have you been doing, Johnson? You're bloody late.'

Blore in the same circumstances would have said politely, 'I'm sure, Mr. Johnson, you can explain this unpunctuality,' but Johnson far prefers Rudbeck's speech because it is entirely thoughtless and impersonal. It is not that of a white official speaking to a negro whom he despises, but simply an angry exclamation. 'Damn it all, are you dead or what? Don't you know it's mail day?'

'Oh, yas, sah. My watch go wrong.'

'When you were late yesterday, you said you hadn't got a watch.'

'No, sah, but I done have a watch last week.'

'I see, you're late to-day because your watch went wrong last week. Come on,'—suddenly laying hold of the sack—'let's get this damn mail out of the way.' He lifts the sack by the seal over a file basket, and gives it a shake, whereupon a stream of letters pours out of a large hole in the bottom. The post office bags at Fada are old, but no one wants new ones, because they would have to be tied and sealed for every journey; and untied and unsealed at the other end. This as everyone agrees, would be a waste of time. There has never been a mail robbery in Fada, and there never will be until civilization and private enterprise are much further advanced.

Three private letters for Rudbeck and one parcel without a stamp have tumbled out of the bag. The letters are from his wife, the parcel from the Resident. It contains a new six-inch prismatic compass on loan from provincial stores. Rudbeck whisks the letters into his jacket pocket and opens the parcel. He gazes at the bright brass of the compass with the expression of a carpenter handling a new tool. He waves his hand impatiently at the mail.

'Take it away, for God's sake, Johnson. I've got work to do. Oh, damn, what is it now, Adamu?'

The old messenger curtsies with magnificent grace and says, 'A case, lord.'

Johnson quickly seizes the file basket and shoots round by the stoop into his own office next door.

'What case?'

'Some people who say Mister Johnson owes them money.'

51

'But dash it all, Adamu, don't you see that Mr. Johnson and I are busy. My men are waiting on the road. We've got work to do.'

'But, lord——'

'Oh, yes, yes, I'll hear the blessed case, but not to-day—this is no time for petty cases.'

'Yes, lord, but——'

'To-morrow, Adamu, to-morrow for cases.'

One of the petitioners, at this moment, unluckily puts his head into the office and says, 'Lord.'

Rudbeck jumps, but before he can discover who this intruder is, Adamu sweeps upon him, 'Go, you blackguard—off with you.'

All the messengers and the orderly rise up and throw themselves upon the creditors, whose faces suddenly change from righteous indignation and complacent expectation of triumph to amazement and guilt. They wonder what they have done wrong, but before they can act they have been hurled into the sun. Here they attempt a stand, but Adamu and the orderly at once charge them, shouting, 'Out of it, you scum. What, do you want to be run in, you undereducated dogs?'

They retreat at full speed. Moma, the headman, after some reflection, says to an old woman to whom Johnson owes seven shillings for five months, 'It's the old judge going ill like that.'

'Yes, that's it. God's will be done.'

Since the mud wall dividing the clerk's office from the D.O.'s office does not reach the roof, every word or sound in either cubicle is heard in the next. Johnson has listened with a most alarmed face to the conversation next door. Now at the defeat of his creditors, he bursts into a light perspiration, murmurs thanks to God and Rudbeck and begins to tear open the mail with great speed and noise.

He is loyally determined to complete the filing with extraordinary speed and skill. Besides, he thoroughly enjoys opening a mail—that is, tearing open large, expensive envelopes and throwing them on the floor. This gives him a sense of the wealth and glory of the Empire and he becomes part of it. Reading official letters is a pleasure to him, for it makes him feel like part of His Majesty's Government, and he even enjoys filing so long as he has to deal with established correspondence—that is, letters headed 'In answer to your 174.19.32,' because then he has only to attach them to the cover of file 19. They carry his own file number and he is able to feel at once the pleasure of important and necessary duties and confidence in the results.

What always puzzles him are letters referring to two different subjects; or to new subjects. For instance, here is one in which the first paragraph refers to the new police barracks; and the second to a cow claimed by the company sergeant-major at the provincial capital, Dorua, from a policeman in Fada. Johnson stares at this with blank eyes, while barracks, cows and sergeant-majors perform a sort of witches' dance in his brain. He feels alarmed and depressed and gets more confused every moment. He puts the letter down and grabs another. This is about native tobacco. His eyes grow round. He has never before seen any official reference to native tobacco. What shall he do about it? Why should such a letter come to him just now. He feels a sense of injustice and bewilderment, as if the bottom of the world has dropped out. Nothing can be trusted any more; certainly not intelligence. He takes up the police letter again and finds that it is even more incomprehensible. Finally, he rushes at the heap of files, turns them over, reads odd titles and waits for inspiration. He does not know why at last with deep relief he discovers two upon which he can get rid of the difficult letters. He puts these two at the bottom of the heap, and takes the whole file into the next office.

Rudbeck is not in the office. He is standing in the sun just beyond the stoop, with the plane table set up on its tripod, taking a bearing with the new compass. The whole staff of messengers and several petitioners stand respectfully round him, as they have stood with the same respectful faces, a month before, round Blore while he lays out a putting course. For them the two operations are equally important.

'De mail, sah—I file all letters,' Johnson says.

Adamu answers indignantly, 'Be silent, clerk—the lord is busy.'

Rudbeck murmurs, 'Just a minute.'

In fact, he is only taking a few sights across the station for the pleasure of the thing. He cannot deny himself the delight of handling his new compass.

Johnson goes back to the office and happily writes up the votes ledger. It seems to him now that he has not a single care in the world. Mr. Rudbeck is his friend. The creditors have been put to flight, Moma appeased, he has the prettiest and most enviable wife in Fada, he will

53

get an advance, a rise of pay, he will become the most important man, after Rudbeck, in the government.

He smiles to himself, kicks off his shoes and, revolving his big toes in opposite directions, subtracts sums expended from sums allocated. 'Seven from three is same as seven from ten plus three is five——' a great many of Johnson's additions and subtractions come to five because it is a middle figure, not committing him in either direction, and because he likes writing fives. He is in the middle of the five, with his tongue out, when Rudbeck, in a tone of agony, shouts, 'Johnson!'

Johnson comes into the outer office. He can't imagine what is wrong. Rudbeck, once more suffering from the office, glares like an exasperated bull.

'Look at this, Johnson. What in God's name has the sergeant-major's cow got to do with local exports?'

'I don't know, sah.' Johnson is still more amazed.

'Why did you put it in the export's file?'

Johnson suddenly sees why. 'I tink, sah—perhaps de hide.'

'But the bloody cow isn't dead.'

'Oh, I tink perhaps he going to die soon.'

Rudbeck stares at Johnson with gloomy disgust for a moment and then says, 'Are you pulling my leg, Mr. Johnson? Damn it all, you know, it's like a bad dream—and look at this, my holy hoke, just look at it.'

He jerks the file furiously across the table. 'Look at that—are you mad—drunk to-day, Johnson? What in the name of Nelson has tobacco, native, got to do with elephant poachers in the Fada Kurmi?'

Johnson stares like a lunatic and tries to discover what the connection was, in his own mind. Suddenly he recollects it. Delighted at actually knowing what the truth is, he cries out, 'I tink, sah, you say once dem native tobacco——'

'What did I say about it?'

'I tink you say she look like elephant dropping, sah—he all green like elephant dropping.'

Rudbeck slowly puts down the file and stares at Johnson with wide-opened eyes. For several seconds they remain fixed in this dramatic attitude of wonder. Then Rudbeck slowly and mildly says, 'Mr. Johnson, either you or I have got softening of the brain. Kindly tell me, are my brains porridge, or are you talking any slight degree of nonsense? For God help me if I know.'

'Oh, sah, a tink perhaps I put dem tobacco letters in bush fire file,'

'Yes, oh yes, in the bush-fire file. I'm sure that's an excellent idea, Mr. Johnson—what is the connection between tobacco and bush fires?'

'All dem tobacco field got burnt up, sah, last year——'

Rudbeck suddenly grasps both files, springs to his feet, stretches both arms above his head and throws the files on the floor. He then falls back in his chair with his hand over his eyes and in a feeble voice says, 'Go away, go away, Mr. Johnson—before I murder you. Take them away before I strangle you.'

Johnson gathers up the files and then, in a despairing voice, he murmurs, 'But, sah, I read all dem file list. I no see nutting about any tobacco.'

'Oh, yes, you don't see anything about tobacco—in fact this letter opens up an entirely new subject.'

'Yes, sah, no file about tobacco.'

Rudbeck gets up slowly, leans forward and gazes into Johnson's face. 'Then make one, Johnson; make a new file. Can you write "tobacco"—can you spell "tobacco"—can you copy "tobacco"—have you any ink—have you any intelligence—have you anything inside your skull—are you a filing clerk, Mr. Johnson, or did you come here to polish a bloody chair with your bottom and drive me into the asylum?'

Johnson droops out of the office. Rudbeck, using strong language, mounts his pony and gallops madly across the station to breakfast.

But half an hour later, when Johnson comes beaming into the office with the new file and says proudly, 'I make dem new file, sah,' Rudbeck, full of bacon, eggs and grilled chicken, is in the most easy, absent-minded and friendly temper. He glances carelessly at the file cover and says, 'All damn nonsense, anyhow. Native tobacco for export, my giddy fundament—put it in the other basket and let it mature for a week or two. It will need all it can get.'

He answers the mail in half an hour, leaves Johnson to copy and dispatch it; slings the new prismatic over his shoulder, mounts his pony and goes whistling to the work which he enjoys more than play, and at which he works much harder. Rudbeck cannot whistle any tune, but he enjoys whistling on different notes. The effect is lugubrious to anyone but himself.

Johnson, left in charge of both offices, marches about for a little while, passing from one to another with an important air. He takes up the file baskets and says to the messengers, 'Give way there.' Adamu and his staff not only give way, they take the file baskets from him with polite bows. The procession to the clerk's office is a little triumph.

Johnson makes an important face and sits down to copy the letters. The three messengers sink down on the stoop and doze in the sun as motionless as lizards. Only Adamu's jaw slowly moves as he chews a kola nut. Johnson is heard humming to himself and suddenly utters a laugh. He has forgotten already to look important. He finishes copying the mail in half an hour and bawls for a messenger. He is now important again. He says, 'Take the letters, Adamu, and then you can all go home for the morning. Mister Rudbeck excuses you.'

They thank him with deep curtsies and go away. They know that Rudbeck has not authorized this holiday; they understand perfectly the complicated motives of good nature and glory which cause Johnson to give it; but they will, if challenged, look stupid and pretend innocence. Johnson, left alone, performs a little step dance round the table, hums a tune, and as soon as the messengers are out of sight, goes into the D.O.'s office, tries the safe, which is locked, closely examines Rudbeck's table drawers, sucks at a spare pipe from one of them and goes through the pockets of his uniform left hanging on the corner of the safe.

Like other devotees, he cannot know too much, however trivial, about his idol. He carefully examines an empty cigarette packet, a piece of string, a cartridge and a broken pencil found in the pockets, and reads the last two letters from the young Mrs. Rudbeck at home. He discovers that her name is Celia and that she wants to join Rudbeck in Africa, and this gives him a great deal of pleasure. He is convinced that she will admire Bamu very much and he imagines himself displaying Bamu to her and explaining that he is a civilized husband and how much Bamu appreciates being a government lady, like herself.

Benjamin suddenly appears in the doorway. He wants the mail bag He says in mild surprise, 'What, are you here, Mister Johnson? Are you taking the post of Mister Rudbeck?'

Johnson, caught sitting in Rudbeck's chair, reading Rudbeck's letters, answers with the grave responsible air which he always uses to Benjamin, 'Mister Rudbeck leave me in charge of political office this morning, Mister Benjamin. He got work for road.'

'Excuse me, I think for your sake you take care to put those letters back in the same pocket where you find them. I wish only to avoid trouble for you, Mister Johnson, as my friend.'

'These letters are most interesting, Mister Benjamin. Missus Rudbeck say she come here soon.'

'Oh, dear, how very bad news.'

'How so? I think government ladies make station more civilized,' Johnson says, repeating a judgment which floats everywhere through West African conversation. 'I like to see her for my friend Mister Rudbeck.'

'My experience is that ladies make trouble in all stations.'

'Oh, how so, Mister Benjamin?'

'They have nothing else to do.'

'I think you are too sad, Mister Benjamin. I am enjoying this new event.'

'No. I am not sad. Why, I am four years in this beastly place, without any sensible people at all, and I am not at all heart-broken. I have a strong disposition. Also I wear clean shirts every day, by very good advice. But I am sorry to hear of a government lady. It is a true misfortune, because this place is not fitted for them. Excuse me, I will take the P.O. bag.'

Benjamin takes the bag and walks away with his usual calm and resigned dignity. Johnson goes home to lunch and gives Bamu a long description from imagination of the beautiful Mrs. Rudbeck who is coming to the station. 'She has hair like the sun falling on the river and her eyes are like the sky on the far side from the sun—her cheeks are as white as your teeth and her breasts are as big as pumpkins. She is the most beautiful woman in England and the King himself wanted to marry her. But she preferred my friend, Judge Rudbeck. She will be your friend, my dear Bamu, and you must study her carefully and see how she behaves herself. She is a government lady and you are now a government lady and must learn civilized behaviour.'

To which Bamu replies, 'My brother Aliu has a bad toe.'

'Let him come to my friend Mister Rudbeck and I will ask him for medicine. He has all kinds of medicine.'

'How could they be good for Aliu?'

'Why not?'

Bamu makes no answer. She thinks Johnson a fool to ask such a question. It is obvious to her that white men's medicine cannot cure black men's toes.

After lunch, Johnson is back in the office. He hates to be alone, especially when he might be with Rudbeck. Suddenly he has an inspiration. He puts Rudbeck's letters in his pocket and sets off to find him.

Four miles from the station he comes upon him, in the dry bed of the Fada River. A gang of labourers is setting up the trestle of a new bridge. Rudbeck, in filthy bush kit, covered with mud and sweat, is instructing the gang in Hausa, Yoruba and English, none of which they understand. Rudbeck has therefore done most of the work himself and this is what he enjoys. To work is an occupation for the mind as well as the body, and Rudbeck is not a great reader and takes no pleasure in his own thoughts, which revolve in a good deal of confusion. He would rather plan and build a bush house, a bridge or a market than write a report.

The sight of Johnson on the bank twenty feet above him gives him a shock of indignation. He thinks that the office has no right to pursue him into the bush.

He exclaims, 'Not another bloody wire?'

'Your mail, sah—your private mail.'

'But I had it.' Rudbeck climbs a trestle and scrambles to the bank. He looks with surprise at the letters. Johnson says, 'I find 'em for floor, sah——'

'That's very kind of you.' Rudbeck speaks in a thoughtful absent-minded tone, usual to him in the bush.

'I tink you no want Missus letters to be lost.'

'No, no——'

'I hope she quite well, sah.'

'Yes, oh yes, thank you.' Rudbeck does not even enquire how Johnson knows the letters to be from his wife.

'I tink Missus Rudbeck has mos' beautiful han' writing.'

'Yes, it's a neat hand—Helleman—Tasuki——'

Tasuki, the headman, puts his head over the edge of the bank. He resembles a little old colobus monkey with a Kruger fringe beard all round his clever, wrinkled little face. 'Carry on, Tasuki, and see that they give the trestles a good spread—you know how the current will run when the river is full.' Tasuki springs up and stands with his legs apart. He grins and says, 'Make them stand strong like this.'

'That's the idea, Tasuki—like a man standing against the current.'

He goes into his grass hut, calls for tea and re-reads the letters. After tea he comes strolling out with his pipe alight and is surprised to see Johnson.

'Hullo, Mr. Johnson. What is it—not another wire? No, of course, I remember—have a cup of tea—better take my chair—there isn't another.'

'Oh, tank you, sah.'

Johnson sits down and takes tea. Rudbeck strolls about, looks at the trestles. Johnson goes to thank him. 'Oh, sah, I tank you too much—I just admire you beautiful road.'

'H'm—not much of a road I'm afraid, and a perfectly rotten bridge.'

'No money, sah, for good road and good bridges.'

'No, and every penny spent on them would bring in twenty in trade—but what's the good of telling 'em that?'

'Oh yes, sah, we want a good road in Fada—a motor road way up north to all dese bush people—get plenty shea butter.'

Rudbeck is pleased and surprised by Johnson's interest in roads. He says, 'That's it exactly, Mr. Johnson, but we won't get it—not a hope.'

'Oh, sah, I tink you make it now—right up, forty mile.'

'Forty miles—and where's the money coming from. It costs money to make roads. Have you worked out what even these repairs will cost?'

Johnson has no special interest in roads, but he is as sharp as a sharp child to know what pleases Rudbeck. His enthusiasm therefore throws out new ideas every second.

'Oh, sah, we make it easy. You tell people new road make dem rich—dey do it for nutting.'

'Catch them—I've tried it.'

'Oh, sah, I tink perhaps if you make it like game for dem—get plenty drums, give dem plenty beer. Dis pagan people like game.'

'What's this, Mr. Johnson?' Rudbeck stares at Johnson under his long forelock. 'What's the idea?' He raises his eyebrows and studies Johnson with obvious surprise.

Johnson, seeing the impression he has made, grows lyrical. 'Oh, sah, den you make big north road up—fifty—ninety miles—right up join the P.W.D. road.'

'P.W.D. road?'

'Yes, sah—dem concrete road Governor make for lorries—go right up to Kano.'

59

Rudbeck's eyebrows go up still higher. He says, 'Do you mean the main Kano road—that's a hundred miles away at the nearest point.'

'Oh, yes, sah—you make motor road join Kano road—great big north road for Fada—catch lorries, too.'

But this is too much for Rudbeck. His stare suddenly changes from enquiry and interest to amusement. It is like the pulling down of a blind, so that, instead of a lighted interior, the watcher sees a neat floral pattern with domestic shadows upon it.

'My dear Mr. Johnson—a hundred miles of motor road—and about fourteen rivers in the way.' Suddenly he gives a snort of laughter through his nose. This snort means, 'It's interesting and amusing but I've no time just now.'

'Yass, sah—I tink you make a real big road—important road.'

Rudbeck throws up his lock, nose and pipe in one upwards nod. 'You run away and play, Mr. Johnson. Kano road my foot—go and write a nice copy of something or other—a hundred miles, you make me laugh at the other end. Kindly return to your official duties in the bumf-dirtying department.'

Johnson goes off in the highest spirits. He calls at the store especially to report the conversation to Ajali. Although he knows perfectly well that Ajali is not really his well-wisher, that he is a spiteful and dangerous man, he prefers him greatly as a confidant to the honest and friendly Benjamin. The reason is that Ajali can never hide his wonderment at Johnson's deeds and Johnson needs an admirer far more than a friend. He is one of those people who scarcely notices whether he has friends or not; he gives friendship but he has no time to ask whether he gets it. He is too busy.

He finds Ajali in the last extremity of boredom, buying hides from a little group of Fula cattlemen. Ajali's face, his eyes, mouth, movement of his hands, his flat, disgusted voice all express his complete lack of interest in everything and anything.

Johnson comes prancing in and shouts at him, 'There you are, Ajali—you don' know where I been—I been on the road with Mister Rudbeck.'

'On the road?' Ajali's eyebrows go up; his eyes bulge. He is not really interested yet; but he expects to be, and his face prepares for it.

'Yes, and do you know what he says to me. My Gawd, he say, Missa Johnson—what done happen to you to-day. I tink you god damn bloody fool, Missa Johnson. I good mind trow you in dem river.'

Johnson goes into a shout of laughter and repeats, 'I tink you god damn bloody silly fool to-day, Missa Johnson.'

Ajali, gazing at him, gives a snort through his rocking-horse nostrils and says, 'Why you laugh at dat, Mister Johnson?'

'God damn silly fool to-day, Missa Johnson,' Johnson shouts from the door. He is on his way to tell the story to Benjamin.

Ajali reflects with astonishment upon Johnson's strange behaviour and decides that he is even a bigger fool than he took him for. This idea keeps him happily employed all the afternoon. He waits impatiently for the time when he will be free from the store to go and tell Benjamin, 'Did you hear about Johnson? He really is quite mad.'

He knows that Benjamin will probably know all about it, but he wants to discuss it with somebody, to have an audience for his new idea about Johnson. Even Ajali is a kind of poet when he cries for the tenth time in one evening, in new astonishment and interest, 'Oh dat fool chile Johnson—what he do next?'

The next morning Johnson and Moma go together to the office. Moma waits outside for his money; Johnson goes in to get it. Rudbeck is already at his table, writing the annual report. He looks at Johnson with a distracted expression and murmurs, 'Good morning, Mr. Johnson. What was it I was going to say to you?'

'I don't know, sah.

'Oh, yes, your quarters. Are your quarters all right? I see they were condemned last year.'

'Oh yes, sah—very good quarters. Jess one roof got hole.'

'But you must have a sound roof. Probably the whole place ought to come down. I'll come and see. Don't let me forget.'

'Oh, tank you, sah. You too good to me. Please sah——'

'All right, Johnson. Run along now.'

'Please sah, I was going to ask you if you would be so good to give me a small advance of salary.'

Rudbeck looks at Johnson as if he has committed a crime and says sharply, 'An advance?' Rudbeck has not, however, considered the question at all. He is simply following Blore's advice, though he probably does not know where he got it.

'Yes, sah, please. A small small advance.'

'But I can't give advances, Mr. Johnson. You know what would happen if I did. You'd be short next pay day and simply get into debt.'

'Oh, sah, I tink you give me.'

'I'm sorry, but a rule's a rule. No, Adamu, I can't see anyone to-day. I'm busy.'

Johnson opens his mouth again, catches Rudbeck's eye, and goes hastily away. Rudbeck sucks his pipe and glares angrily at the blank paper in front of him. He growls, 'What on earth shall I say about that old ass Adamu—and Johnson, he's a hopeless liar and probably a bit of a crook, too. Blore caught him at all sorts of dirty work.'

He makes a dash at the paper and writes of Adamu, 'Well meaning and honest, but slow,' of Johnson 'Willing, but careless. Has little idea of filing.'

Three days later Johnson's application for an advance of pay is refused on the grounds of a bad report. This brings his financial difficulties to a head. Moma goes to the native court and charges him with embezzlement. The other creditors join in a claim for seven pounds fourteen shillings. Rudbeck is fortunately on the road, but Johnson is in despair. He does not tell Bamu of his troubles, because he owes her family an instalment on her price. He sits in his hut on an upturned mortar with his hat over his eyes and his arms crossed, while old Sozy rubs his feet.

Johnson's despair is extreme. He feels it even more acutely than he feels his pleasures, because when he is happy, he simply enjoys, forgetting himself; but when he is unhappy, he hates himself and dwells on his own faults. He murmurs to the air, 'Oh, you bloody fool, Johnson—you no good for nutting—you see how bad stupid fool you are. Here's Mister Rudbeck your frien'—de bes' man in de worl'—you only go to do you job proper, and dere you go making trouble for him all de time. I glad you get no advance. I glad you get no rise—now p'raps you catch some sense—go and trow yourself to the crocodiles.' The old woman cries, 'Ohey, Ohey' in a heart-broken voice, and tries to comfort him by rubbing his feet with peculiar tenderness. She longs to pour comfort into the boy; her knotted old fingers work like pistons.

'I'm a fool. I'll take a knife and split myself up—that's all I'm worth. I'm a bad fool—I'll pour kerosene on my English suit and set myself on fire—I'm tired of myself.'

'Ohey, ohey,' cries the old woman. Grief and sympathy, squeezing

62

up her bare gums and wrinkled lips, make her look as if she has a bad taste in her mouth.

'And how am I going to pay for Bamu, and how am I going to pay the store. Why,' he says in a tone of astonishment, 'I'm done for—I'm finished—I'd better hang myself.'

The voice of old Brimah is heard outside; Bamu's father come for an instalment. Johnson gives a cry of despair. 'There he is—somebody's told him already that I've not got my rise. Who told him? It's magic—it's some witch—oh, God curse me, I'm done for—oo—what are you doing to my feet? Do you want to take the skin off?' He gives a violent kick, which causes the old woman to fall over on her back, and rushes barefoot out of the hut.

Brimah is standing on one leg like a stork, his right foot is clamped on his left ankle. His skinny right shoulder is hunched up to his ear. He gazes at the air past Johnson and says, 'How do, master?'

'How do, father.'

A long pause follows. Then Johnson says, 'What do you want?'

'Nothing.'

Johnson goes into the house and shouts at Sozy, 'Where are my shoes, you old fool.'

Sozy puts on his shoes and caresses them with sympathetic love. She feels safer with the shoes than with the feet. Johnson, fortified by shoes, goes out and finds the old man in the same position, but he is looking at the ground.

'What do you want, father?'

'Nothing.'

'You want the ten shillings I promised you.'

The old man slowly raises his left hand and scratches his right armpit; at the same time he raises his chin and looks sideways at the bush.

'Well, I haven't got it—I haven't got any money at all till the end of the month.'

The old man says nothing, but continues to scratch his armpit.

An hour later he is still standing in the compound, but on his left foot. Johnson rushes out and yells at him, 'What do you want?'

The old man starts and his thin face expresses a mild reproach. 'Nothing.'

'Go away, then.'

Johnson goes to the store and drinks a bottle of beer with Ajali. He explains to Ajali that if the government does not raise his pay, he will send them an ultimatum; either ten shillings a month more or resignation. Afterwards he goes to town with Benjamin and drinks native beer. He comes home drunk at two o'clock in the morning and finds old Brimah sitting on a stump in the compound.

'What do you want?' he screams.

'Nothing.'

'I haven't got any money, I tell you. I haven't got anything.'

He goes into Bamu's hut. Bamu is not there. He rushes out again and shakes his fist at the old man. 'Where's Bamu?'

'She went home with her brother.'

'She can't go home. She's my wife.'

The old man scratches himself and looks at the moon.

The next morning Johnson learns that the native court has heard Moma's case, and that the Emir's prime minister, Waziri, will report it to Rudbeck. Johnson feels very ill and cannot get up.

Ajali and Benjamin, finding him in bed, urge him not to avoid the office. Ajali, in the highest spirits, cries, 'Oh, Mister Johnson, what's the good of you no go to office? It only makes things worse for you.'

Ajali gazes at Johnson with the joy of those who rush to see a murderer dragged to prison and death. He gets a definite feeling and almost a definite idea from Johnson's misery. Benjamin is wise and sad. 'I fear you're bust up, Mister Johnson, but if you stay away from office, Mister Rudbeck will be sure that you are guilty in conscience.'

Johnson staggers to the office half an hour late and explains that he is ill. He looks very ill. Rudbeck is much concerned.

'My hat, Johnson, you look absolutely putrid.'

'Oh, yes, sah, I got fever.'

Rudbeck sends for his first-aid box, and asks with sympathy, 'What are your quarters like? Want any repairs? I'd better come along and look at them.'

'Oh, no, sah. Very good house sah—only de roof.'

'Oh, go on, Johnson. Why can't you say a thing straight out? Here, stick that in your armpit.'

He takes Johnson's temperature, feels his pulse, gives him five grains of calomel, ten grains of quinine and a dose of salts, and sends him home to bed. An hour later Johnson feels very ill indeed; his head sings like a kettle, his stomach is swollen and sore, he has violent diarrhœa. He sits perched on the crooked stick which is the seat of his latrine, with his head in his hands and cries, 'I die, I die, and I die—oh Gawd, make me die soon.'

The Waziri and his boy approach along the town road. Old Sozy peeps out of her kennel door, stares with panic-stricken horror and draws in her head again. When Waziri and Saleh reach the compound, she comes out and runs about like a hen with its head off. Finally going up to the mat wall of the latrine, she murmurs through the mats, 'Waziri comes.'

'Oh, oh-oh, tell him to go away—it's no good—I'm too ill—Mister Rudbeck gave me the best medicine, but it's too late—it isn't any good with a bad illness like this—it's a real terrible illness—I'm dying this minute.'

Waziri comes up to the mats and makes them a formal curtsey. The boy Saleh, after one look of contemptuous surprise, sits down at a distance and admires his right hand, which has been newly stained bright pink with henna. His left hand and forearm are hidden in a long cylindrical pot of wood which contains the dye.

'God save you in your indisposition, Mr. Johnson.'

'Oh—oh—Waziri—I'm very ill. Go away.'

'I was hoping perhaps to do you some good.'

'Have you a medicine for this illness?'

'I come because of this complaint of Moma's; and then, too, I hear there was trouble between you and Brimah the ferry-man.'

'That rascal—he's taken four pounds from me and now he wants three more. I'll complain to my friend, Mister Rudbeck.'

'And I hear your wife has gone back to her family.'

'Oh, no, Waziri, that's a lie—she has gone to see a friend—she would never leave me—I had to beg her to go. She is a very good, affectionate, loving wife—she loves me too much.'

'But suppose this Brimah brings a complaint to the native court?'

'Let him try it, the rascal. I'll break his face and Moma's.'

'You owe Moma twelve shillings and Brimah two pounds and old Marimi——'

'I will pay them all.'

'Good-good—for if you pay them now I can stop all these complaints and I can catch Bamu and bring her back. I could even give her a little beating to teach her sense.'

'No, no, in England, Waziri, we do not beat our wives. That is a savage, low custom.'

65

'Then I shall bring her back.'

'Yes, bring her back, Waziri. Don't hurt her, but bring her back. It would be better for you to do it, because it is not proper, you understand, for the King's clerk to go running about the country after little girls. A government official has to consider his dignity.' Mr. Johnson tears up newspapers with a slow dignified gesture. Even the sound is dignified.

'Exactly, Mr. Johnson. That's what I thought. Then if you will give me three pounds——'

'But I haven't got three pounds, Waziri.'

'Oh, yes, yes. How foolish I am. But what a pity. With three pounds, Mr. Rudbeck will never hear of all these complaints. He will hear nothing against you.'

Johnson gives a kind of combined groan and curse and cries, 'But what can I do—I haven't a penny.'

'Suppose, Mr. Johnson, that I lent you three pounds to pay off these low rascals who will spoil you with Mr. Rudbeck?'

'Oh, Waziri, I should thank you ten thousand times. God will bless you too.'

Johnson springs out, pulling his belt tight with one hand and holding out the other. 'You are my true friend.'

'Yes, I have always been your friend, so I will pay these three pounds to your creditors and bring back Bamu.'

'Thank you a thousand times. God bless you, my dear friend.'

'Here is a paper for you.'

'What paper?'

'A paper for the three pounds. The Treasurer made it for me.'

Johnson looks at the scrawled Arabic characters, and says, 'But what's the need of this?'

'You put your name on it. It says that you have had three pounds.'

'But it is not necessary.'

Waziri waves his hands. 'For me, not—but the Treasurer insists. The three pounds, you see, are coming out of the Treasury.'

'But what does it say?'

'It says, Three pounds received by Mr. Johnson, to pay when he likes.'

'When I like.'

'You need not pay at all, Mr. Johnson.'

'No, perhaps I don't pay at all.' Johnson laughs.

Waziri laughs for a long time and cries, 'Perhaps not, and then what will the old Treasurer say?'

'He can't say anything—he's no business to lend money out of the native Treasury.'

'Ah, Mr. Johnson, you're the clever one—full of guile.'

'But if he says nothing, nothing will happen. Three ponus. dYou take a shilling out of some bags, sixpences out of others.'

'Yes—yes—ah!—you know how it's done.'

'Or have a little wax under your finger when the tax is counted.'

'That's it exactly. Ah, you are full of all the tricks. Shall I give you a pen? Saleh, bring a pen.'

The languid boy pretends not to hear and does not move. Waziri is now infatuated with him and he uses all the airs of a spoilt beauty There is nothing else for him to do and he has discovered, besides, that fits of caprice, boredom, indifference greatly increase Waziri's passion.

'Saleh, my sweet one,' Waziri calls.

Saleh with his free finger carefully rubs a little unwanted dye off the edges of his thick nail.

Waziri gets up patiently, goes to him and unhooks the long pen-case from the string round his neck. The boy does not even glance at him.

Waziri brings the pen to Johnson, who signs the paper with a powerful flourish and says laughing, 'That Treasurer is a good Treasurer. He understands book-keeping very well.'

'But he doesn't understand holding on to his money.'

The Waziri goes off, followed by Saleh, who nurses his right arm in its pot of henna with the self-absorbed air of a sufferer. The same evening Aliu and Brimah return with Bamu, who at once, without a word, begins her duties.

Johnson sends for strong beer and a bottle of gin. He celebrates Bamu's return with drums and a dance. At one o'clock everybody is drunk and the noise can be heard five miles away.

The next morning Rudbeck sends for Johnson. He is calm, polite and serious—dangerous symptoms. Even his voice is like Blore's when he asks, 'Mr. Johnson, have you been borrowing money from the native Treasury?'

'Oh, no, sah, I never do such ting.'

'Have you been trying to do it?'

'Oh, no, sah.'

'You know what would happen to you if you did?'

'Oh, yes, sah, but I never would, sah.'

'I hope you're telling me the truth. I'm inspecting the native Treasury this week, you know.'

Johnson is astonished and dismayed. He asks advice from everybody he meets, thus informing the whole town that he has in fact borrowed money from the native Treasury. The matter is discussed in the market, in the store, in the barracks and the native council. It is agreed that Waziri has brought off a neat coup, for he has not only caught Johnson, but the Treasurer. The Treasurer will probably have to pay some of Waziri's debts, run up on Saleh's account, before he is clear.

Johnson will undoubtedly be sacked and perhaps sent to prison, unless he can raise fifteen or twenty pounds to pay his debts, and also satisfy Waziri. Ajali and Benjamin, all the market women, all the police except the sergeant, and all the station servants advise Johnson to go to Waziri. They say, 'Waziri is a clever man. He doesn't do anything for nothing. He doesn't lose his temper or take revenge. You can trust him to do what pays him and the Emir.'

Johnson goes to Waziri, who is surprised to hear of his difficulty and grieved about the Treasury predicament. He thinks that the Treasurer is probably twenty or thirty pounds short. Of course, he will be obliged to show Johnson's paper to cover himself as far as possible. He may try to pretend that Johnson has had the whole sum. Waziri has only one suggestion. The Emir is anxious to see Mr. Blore's staff reports. These, giving the characters of the Emir and the principal chiefs, are confidential. If the Emir could see a copy of them, he would be willing to make the Treasurer hand over Johnson's receipt.

Johnson goes home in such despair that he will not allow Sozy even to enter his hut. The old woman, hearing his groans, can only sit on the ground outside the hut and pat the wall.

At six Ajali and Benjamin arrive. Johnson comes out at once to greet them and to describe his interview with Waziri. He does this with great expression and says now and then, 'What a damn rascal—it makes you laugh.'

'I think I be damn rascal too. I go write him a report for Emir—I take it to him. I say, "Here you report, Waziri. You give me dat paper now?"'

Ajali shakes his head. 'Waziri too clever. He know how Mister Blore write.'

'Perhaps I go take one little report, one little old report from two-three years ago; I give it to Waziri.'

'How you fin' 'em, Mister Johnson. Dos' reports live for safe—safe key on Mister Rudbeck's belt.'

'How I fin' 'em, Mister Ajali—I get 'em in one minute—I get 'em now.'

'How you do so, Mister Johnson?'

Johnson laughs. 'I go take 'em from de safe right from under his eye.'

'You no fit do so, Mister Johnson. He catch you, he put you in prison.'

'What, you think I 'fraid.' Johnson laughs. With his hat on his ear, he swaggers away to the office.

Rudbeck is busy writing a letter to his wife. He writes for every day and he is three days behind. Having just written, 'To-day rather a funny thing happened,' he is tapping his teeth trying to remember something funny that happened on Friday last. Four petitioners gaze anxiously through the door. A gang of road labourers drawn up in line by their headman is standing patiently in the sun waiting for its money.

Rudbeck says to Johnson, 'What did I do on Friday?'

'You went to bush, sah, all day on de road.'

'Yes, oh yes.'

'Road gang waiting for money, sah.'

'Oh, yes, damn them—I told 'em to sit down—you might pay 'em, Johnson. Six days at ninepence works out to two pounds nine and six. Take it out of the petty cash drawer.'

The safe door is standing ajar, as often during morning office hours. Johnson swings it back. He has done the same thing a dozen times since Rudbeck took over, and knows every inch of its interior; the two drawers at the bottom, the flat iron shelf above them, and lying on the shelf half a dozen confidential files. Three bags of broken money, tied up with red tape and bearing enormous labels covered with small subtraction sums, lie on the files. A cigarette tin full of pewter florins and lead shillings, a cardboard box full of Maria Theresa dollars, two bunches of handcuff keys and a broken wrist-watch stand in the back of the shelf.

Johnson pulls out the drawer, peeps at Rudbeck, who is writing hard, and then quietly and calmly takes hold of the top file and slides the money bags off it. He is just opening the file, inside the safe and behind the safe door, when Rudbeck says from the table, 'What are you doing Mr. Johnson?'

He jumps up and comes to the safe. Johnson hastily jerks the two-shilling bag forward on top of the file.

'Money no live, sah.' Johnson, in his excitement, falls back on Cook's English. 'Money no live for drawer.'

'What?' Rudbeck pulls open the drawer and shows about five pounds' worth of mixed silver. He counts out two pounds nine and sixpence, shuts and locks the safe and goes to pay the labourers himself.

He has a thoughtful air, and when he comes back to the office, he says to Johnson, 'Why did you think there wasn't enough in the drawer?'

'I look for wrong drawer.'

Rudbeck opens the safe, pulls open the other drawer and shows a cheque book and bundles of notes. He closes it again with a snap, locks the safe and says, 'All right, you can go.'

Johnson goes, trembling at the knees. He thinks, 'Oh, you fool, Johnson. Why you tell dem bad lies? Why you no say you tink he mean you take money from bag.'

After lunch he comes back early to the office. But the safe is locked. The messengers have orders to see that it is locked before Rudbeck leaves the office. This is Blore's rule, which he has loyally admired and copied.

Johnson is now astonished at his undertaking to steal the confidential files. He sees that it is impossible and that it always was impossible. He goes home in wonder at his own folly. 'You fool chile, Johnson, you bigges' god damn silly fool in de whole worl'—I like to kick you to hell, you idjit, I tink I give you damn good hiding—serve you right if you done for. Dat's what I say, serve you damn right, you silly, god damn bloody fool chile, yam-headed son of a hole.'

He goes by the market road to avoid Ajali and Benjamin, dawdles by the river, and comes home after dark. There they are waiting for him. The report is all over the town that Rudbeck has caught Johnson trying to rob the safe.

This rumour, like many more in the native markets, is founded on an intelligent or intuitive penetration into the white man's mind by his own messengers and orderlies. They know him and his thoughts far better, probably, than his own family relations at home. They give more concentration to the study of them; and they have less distractions.

As soon as Johnson enters the compound, Ajali pops out of the house and shouts joyfully, 'He catch you at de safe?'

Benjamin, stepping out with slower dignity, says, 'I hear, Mister Johnson, he nearly catch you. Are you not afraid of that prison?' He looks at Johnson with a kind of wondering curiosity.

Johnson laughs and tosses his hat to Sozy, hovering round him as usual at three yards' range, afraid to come nearer, but unable to take her eyes off him. 'He no catch me—I do what I want—I see everyting in dem safe.'

'What de good of dat—you no catch nutting?'

'I no try to catch him. You tink I fool?'

'What you do den, Mister Johnson?'

Johnson has no idea. But he opens his mouth to utter something and at once his imagination provides him with a plan, glorious and impressive.

'I go take 'em when Mister Rudbeck not dar.'

'How you do so, safe locked?'

'I open him with de key.'

'De key, Mister Johnson? Mister Rudbeck has key on his chain. Key always on Mister Rudbeck's chain.'

'Yes, Mister Ajali. So I take dem key.' Johnson strikes an easy attitude, throws up his chin and looks down at Ajali.

Ajali, grinning from ear to ear, cries, 'Oh, you take 'em—perhaps you steal 'em.'

'Yes, I steal 'em.'

'You steal the keys?' Benjamin gazes at Johnson with dreamy wonder. 'How you do so?'

'Why, yass, Mister Benjamin—I tink I go to-night—moon come up pretty late.'

'But Mister Rudbeck puts his keys under his pillow.'

'Yes, and his pistol,' Ajali cries. 'His revolver all loaded with bullets in every hole.'

'You tink I 'fraid, Ajali.'

'I tink you better be 'fraid.'

'Perhaps you go to prison for a long time—many years,' Benjamin says.

'I tell you I get dem key to-night. Stay here—I show you.'

71

Ajali begins to be less incredulous, Benjamin ever more astonished in his calm way.

'You no do so,' Ajali cries.

'It is a most dangerous plan,' Benjamin says.

This astonishment makes Johnson more bold and confident. He laughs at all warnings and enlarges his promises. 'You stay here. I bring you dat key—to-morrow I take letters to Waziri. You go tell um if you like—to-morrow Mister Johnson bring dat letter.'

He is so much excited by his own words and by the idea of the glory to be won in this difficult enterprise that he would be greatly disappointed if an earthquake were to crush the safe and a tornado blow the confidential reports into his hand. He describes in detail how he will steal the keys, with appropriate action. 'I creep along by de garden —along by de tomatoes.' He takes a few steps in the compound crouching double, then waves his hand upwards and says, 'Night all full of dark'—climbs up an imaginary step. 'I go into house.' He squats down on his heels and plucks with his hands. 'I see Mister Rudbeck— he lie so on his left cheek.' He bends his own head to the left and closes his eyes. 'He frown—he breathe strong through his nose—he tink he angry with road headman for make dem bad bridge. I slip my hand under de pillow, slow, slow——'

'What you do if cook come in, cry out tief, tief——'

Johnson jumps up as if his legs are springs. 'Cook no dare—I look at him, he no dare.'

'Why he no dare?'

'I show him my big knife.'

Not only Ajali, but even Benjamin grins at this. Benjamin's grin is a little tight grimace as of pain.

'What, Mister Johnson? No, you are joking.'

'If dey tink dey catch me, I kill 'em,' Johnson says, strutting round the compound with the new springs in his legs. 'I kill 'em, I kill 'em.' crouches suddenly and clenches his hand as if on a knife handle; then makes a leap and stabs the air. 'So I kill 'em.' He struts forward, avoiding the imaginary body, then stops, looks at it over his right shoulder, shakes his head. 'I sorry for you, you poor fool chile. Why you do so foolish ting—why you try to catch Johnson?'

Ajali and Benjamin will not leave him. They stay and share his supper, eating most of it. Afterwards they sit drinking watered beer, and now and then Ajali, peering through the small trees, will say, 'He go to bed now.'

Johnson stoops and looks at the lantern still hung on Rudbeck's stoop where he smokes and reads an old newspaper.

'He no go bed yet.'

At half-past ten the light disappears. A few minutes after eleven Ajali says again, 'He go now for tru'.'

Johnson stoops again and sees that the lantern has gone. He feels hollow inside, as if all his stomach has fallen out. He remains stooping for a long time.

'He go now,' Ajali says in a laughing voice.

Johnson sees that he must act. He rises with dignity and answers, 'Yes, time for me.'

He goes into his hut, strips himself except for the loincloth between his legs, carefully oils his body all over with ground-nut oil. Sozy, appearing from nowhere, assists and takes particular care to oil even the back of his ears and the inside of his thighs. Johnson then slips into his loincloth Sozy's cook's knife, a black-handled French knife with a sharp point. He takes a small torch, newly bought from the store. When he comes out again, Ajali and Benjamin leap up in horror. Benjamin steps backward as Johnson advances.

'Wha-a-at?' Ajali falters.

'Johnson, you m-a-a-d,' Benjamin wails in a high childish voice. 'They will catch you—it is quite certain.' And he added surprisingly, 'Do you like to go to prison?'

Johnson suddenly perceives his grandeur. He has, at a stroke, become like one apart, a terror in the world. He feels the wonder and charm of greatness. He takes out the knife and carelessly feels its edge in the firelight. Ajali turns and flies; Benjamin retreats backwards, with a wondering gaze, and then suddenly disappears.

Johnson is astonished. He looks after them for a minute with open mouth and wrinkled forehead. He can hardly believe that it is he, Johnson, who can produce such extraordinary effects on other people.

He becomes gradually accustomed to this surprising power. In half a minute, he is used to it. He hollows his back, gives a short, important laugh and says to old Sozy, 'They're frightened.'

Sozy smiles and shakes her head. Then she approaches and carefully rubs her oily hands over his flanks. That is all she understands of the work, the rubbing, the cherishing of Johnson's flesh. She polishes him like a chair. Johnson, torch in left hand, knife in the right, slips along the bush path and turns into the thick bush behind Rudbeck's house. The moon has not yet risen, but the stars are bright enough to show the difference between the open ground and the bush. They even strike a reflection from Johnson's body, so that a faint radiance, like the shine of coal among coal-dust, marks the smooth muscles of his thighs and flanks. He moves so quickly along the open ground that he seems like the shadow of a cloud in a strong wind. He steps under the eaves of the house, not in shadow, because the stars are all round, but part of the dark mass of the house. It is a still night because of the darkness. Leopards, hyænas, all night-hunting beasts are waiting for the moon to rise. There are no drum parties in town. The police sentry at the fort can be heard clearly, at half a mile distance, bringing the butt of his carbine to the ground. Different kinds of snore come from Rudbeck's kitchen huts; and the grinding of his pony's teeth in a calabash of millet.

Johnson is trembling all over, why he does not know or enquire. He feels as if every muscle is alive by itself with its own nerves tingling, and yet all are perfectly subordinate and waiting like an army for his command. He cannot think by himself, and yet his brain is coolly judging for him. His foot feels for the edge of the stoop and carefully mounts. His hand touches the side of the door and guides him into the sleeping-room.

Rudbeck's lantern, turned low, is standing on the far side of the bed-net, which, hanging down by its corners from the frame of the bed, takes the shape of a clumsy boat with high, steep sides and hollow midships. It is like a ghost or glass boat, for the lantern can be seen through it.

Beside his bed head stands a box and on the box a torch, a box of matches, a pipe and tobacco tin, a water bottle, and a roll of toilet paper. Rudbeck is facing Johnson. He is curled up under the thin woollen sheet, with one foot out and his left arm thrown up and crooked across his face, like a child who has fallen asleep all at once in the middle of some impatient gesture.

Johnson drops down smoothly and quickly and goes round to the bed head. He squats on his hams, and pulls up the net. He does not need the torch. The lantern shows him the end of Rudbeck's key chain with its leather button hole, hanging out below the lowest pillow. He takes the chain and gently pulls it. The keys slip into his hand. In three minutes he is in the office. There is no guard at the office. It stands open day and night without even doors to close or windows to be latched. Birds often spend the night roosting on the files and at least once a hyæna has eaten part of a chicken on the floor. Johnson walks in therefore and takes care only not to show his torch-light on the barrack side, where the sentry might see it. He leaves it on the floor pointing to the wall; opens the safe by reflected light; takes out all the files and squats down on the floor to examine them. The first is marked, Native Administration. The topmost letter contains in Blore's neat, ladylike writing, characters of the Emir, the Chief Justice, the Treasurer, the Waziri, and the five principal feudal chiefs of Fada. Johnson copies it in ink on a sheet of official paper, stamped with the crown.

He hides this copy in last year's files still standing in a corner of his own office, returns the confidential files to the safe, locks it and hastens back towards Rudbeck's house. The moon is now close to the horizon and the sky on that side is turning green. Johnson, when he moves, can see something move beside him, like the ghost of a shadow. He knows that in a few minutes the moon will show its edge and pour light over the whole ground. He darts into the house, approaches the bed with no precaution, and slips the keys under the pillow with a sharp jerk. Rudbeck gives a snort, rolls on his back, opens his eyes and looks straight upwards. Johnson is already squatting. He creeps away towards the wall.

Rudbeck suddenly shouts, 'Boy! Jamesu!' Johnson crouches by the wall, waiting to creep to the door. Rudbeck shouts again and a faint, astonished voice is heard from one of the huts.

Johnson creeps to the door along the wall. The moon has risen and the compound is as light as a knife, grey and glittering. Johnson darts out just as the boy Jamesu, a young Yoruba boy, comes sleepily out of the hut. He sees Johnson and stops, opens his mouth. His eyes with half a moon reflected in each of them, seem to pop from his head. Johnson whisks out his knife and puts his left hand up palm outwards, like a speaker in council protesting against interruption.

'Boy!' Rudbeck yells. Jamesu dashes into the house; Johnson dives into the bush and flies home. In five minutes, still breathless, he is lying in bed, pretending to be asleep. But his chest is panting like a bird's, and his head is singing. He wants to laugh. He is drunk with triumph and excitement. He thinks of Jamesu's terror and says, 'Why you no kill him, you fool chile? Now he go talk.'

Then he thinks, 'Let him talk. I say he mad—I never go from my bed. I *swear* I never go. I swear by Gawd.' Johnson sees himself assuring Rudbeck that he is not a thief; he can even hear, in imagination, the sob of indignation in his own voice and see the innocence in his own eyes. He laughs again in glory. He almost hopes that Jamesu will denounce him.

In the morning at six, Johnson puts on a clean suit and his English patent leather shoes to celebrate his triumph. He takes his copy of the report and goes singing to Waziri's house. Waziri lives in the east ward behind the palace. His compounds are exactly like those of any poor labourer in Fada, a confusion of huts scattered without order, some new, some ruinous. Only there are more of them, greater confusion and more dirt. Waziri is in the new hut belonging to Saleh. He sits there shivering on a bamboo bed among dirty blankets. His shaved head without its turban looks as small and narrow as a dog's. The skin hangs on his face in deep wrinkles like an old boot and his eyes are sunk and bloodshot. His skin is grey and his expression is bewildered and terrified. Saleh is walking about the hut naked. He is still wearing a henna pot on his right arm. His light-brown skin is polished and oiled, so that the morning sky, as light and clear as sea water, shooting rays, mixed with the cold air, through the dirty window holes, makes blue light on his shoulders and smooth thigh muscles. Saleh is admiring himself in imagination. He is moving about the room in order to feel the beauty of his movements and the delight of his life. His face is absorbed and contemptuous. He pays no attention to Johnson or Waziri. Outside the women's voices are screaming like parakeets, sharp and brisk.

'What are you doing with those pots?'

'Where's my pestle?'

'Did you hear about Oba last night? She went out to——' A scream of laughter.

'What are you laughing at? Very well, then, I'll tell them about——'

'Get out of my way. You'll make me spill it.' The strained voice of one with a heavy pot balanced on her skull.

These voices too come into the hut like sharp rays of clean life, working life, mixed with the cold fresh air. Waziri gazes at Johnson

76

with hanging lips and stupid, flat eyes like grapes from which half the juice has been squeezed.

'Here's your letter,' Johnson cries.

'Letter—letter.'

'The chief's letters. I'll tell you what they say.' Johnson carefully pulls up his trousers and perches himself on the corner of Saleh's bed. He translates in a sing-song voice.

'The Emir has always been useless and he is now dangerous. He has large debts and still levies illegal taxes whenever he can. His women and servants freely rob the market. He cannot even be trusted to look after his own interests, as he is subject to violent fits of temper. He has recently had two of his chief ministers, the Waziri and the master of the horse, flogged for some imaginary offence. The former has been flogged many times.'

Waziri sits listening with a look of astonishment and horror. He mutters, 'No—no—I don't understand—it's impossible.'

'It's true. Every word is here,' Johnson cries. 'You give it to your scribe and see. The next is your own character—shall I read it?'

'Oh, God! Oh, God! I can't believe it.'

Saleh, stopping by the window, carefully pulls off the henna pot, which comes away from his arm with a pop like a cork. He holds out his dripping pink right hand and examines it with an anxious and affectionate look, like a shrewd mother summing up the exact condition of a sick child.

Johnson hollows his back and reads out in his voice full of triumph and self-confidence, 'The Waziri is the only intelligent member of the council. He never stops plotting and he is a skilful liar. You cannot trust a word he says. His position is difficult, because he is surrounded by enemies who would try to destroy him if the Emir withdrew his protection. He will certainly be got rid of at any change in the Emirate. He himself is fully aware of his desperate position and he is therefore a most dangerous man.'

'What? What?'

'A most dangerous man.'

'No, before.'

'He is surrounded by enemies.'

'Yes, of course, but before?'

'You cannot trust a word he says.'

77

'Oh, dear, it's terrible, it's terrible. Does he really say that—oh, dear—if the Emir hears that.'

'Shall I read the rest?'

'No, no, give it to me and don't tell anybody. Saleh, you know, don't tell anyone about this.'

Saleh, having finished the inspection of the patient, is carefully fitting it back into the henna pot. He says with contemptuous disgust, 'So you'll get another flogging old man.'

Waziri gives a moan and shakes his head. 'Oh, no; oh, no. It will kill me.'

'Last time you had to lie on your face for a week.'

Waziri says in a flat voice, 'As my lord pleases.'

'Perhaps they'll give you a hundred this time,' Saleh suggests with relish.

'It can't be helped,' Waziri says. He has remembered his manners and recovered his dignity; noticing this himself, he draws himself up and repeats, 'It can't be helped.'

Johnson is carefully smoothing the seat of his trousers. He says gaily,' So I won't hear any more from Moma or Brimah or the rest of them?'

Waziri rises. 'No, of course not. I thank you, Mr. Johnson.' He lifts the door-curtain for the guest and makes his distinguished curtsey. 'God be with you, my friend.'

Johnson, still amazed and delighted by his unexpected brilliance as a thief, greets Rudbeck with explosive joy. 'Oh, good morning, sah. God be with you, sah.'

'Oh, good morning, Mr. Johnson.' Rudbeck is gloomy. He has come nearly to the end of his road money. It has been obvious for three weeks past that the money would not last much longer, but Rudbeck, like Johnson, has the power of refusing to notice unpleasant things until they force themselves upon him. This gives him much happiness and many sudden depressions. He is now very much depressed.

He says to Johnson in a disgusted voice, 'You might bring me the Treasury votes book.' He is answering queries just arrived from the central Treasury department:

'176. Payment shown on 4th October. Repairs to office roof. Labour and materials. Two shillings. Receipt shows two shillings paid labour. Explain materials.'

Rudbeck writes in the opposite column: 'One ball office string, elbow grease, £0 0s. 0d.'

'177. Voucher 33. Road gang on Marima bridge. Three pounds four shillings. This involves overpayment of one pound one shilling and three pence on your capital work's vote. Explain or refund.'

Rudbeck, who has feared such a query, is now enraged. He shouts, 'Hurry up with that Treasury vote book.'

Johnson has been hastily bringing the book up to date. It is his duty to post all payments into it, and to subtract them, on the opposite page, from the totals allocated to Fada division at the beginning of the financial year. He is proud of the book because of the august word 'Treasury' printed outside. He also admires the neat patterns made by the oblique descending rows of subtraction sums. He blots the last entry and comes in proudly. Rudbeck flings the pages back to the heading 'Capital Works,' and the sub-heading 'Roads and Bridges.' The total unexpended shown under Johnson's lowest subtraction sum on the right side of the page is fourpence.

'Fourpence!' Rudbeck shouts. 'Is that all I've got left? Why in God's name didn't you tell me?'

'I tink I tell you when all finish, sah.'

'Good God in heaven, Mr. Johnson. I was sending out a hundred men to-morrow on the new clearing job—that's about five pounds a day. Do you realize that these votes are authorized and not a penny more? Do you realize that if I hadn't seen this book, just now, by pure luck, I'd have had to pay that gang out of my own pocket.'

'Oh, no, sah,' Johnson cries, full of encouragement and helpfulness. 'Oh, no' sah.'

'What—what the hell do you mean? No, sah. It's cost me a quid already.'

'Oh, no, sah, I tink you take 'em from one of de other votes.'

'Take 'em? Take what?'

'De money, sah. You look, sah.' Johnson turns the pages. 'Uniforms, sah—plenty money in uniforms. Extra services, sah—four pound five shilling. I tink you take 'em.'

Rudbeck is amused. It is a common enough practice to spend one vote on another purpose. No honest hardworking official likes to see good money disappearing into the hands of the Treasury at the end of the financial year. He hates the thought of a Treasurer's jubilation when the axe falls upon unexpended votes and swells his surplus. He would rather throw money out of the window or bury it in the ground.

Rudbeck himself only the week before, has shown the native Treasurer how to spend his vote for *dogarai* uniforms—that is, new uniforms for the Emir's police—on a mosque. He has often drawn up the time-honoured voucher, 'To Suli, twenty days special enquiry. Cattle tax. Extra services, one pound ten shillings,' drawn a cross underneath, written, 'Suli, his mark,' and signed, 'Witness, H.G. Rudbeck.'

Or the even more popular form: 'To Suli and gang, twelve days on the Yoga road, five pounds,' with a similar cross and testimony.

'I go write voucher, sah,' Johnson cries, delighted to see Rudbeck's half-grin.

'Why, damn it all, Johnson. I didn't know you were a bloody thief.'

'Yes, sir, I tief.' Johnson roars with laughter.

'But I can't steal this money back, you know.'

'Oh, yes, sah, plenty money in extra services.'

'No, I can't—that would be a real steal.'

'Oh, no, sah—money all dere, sah.'

'Yes, but I've spent it, Johnson.'

'You spend it on de road, sah—government road.'

'Yes, but I didn't mean to—no, the Treasury has caught me out proper. But you can make out a voucher for Extra Services and we'll keep the gang on another couple of days. Not all in one voucher, you know—the Treasury are bloody nuisances, but not god damn imbeciles. Make out two separate vouchers for different dates and leave 'em a surplus of one and sixpence—no—one and fourpence halfpenny. One and sixpence looks too obvious.'

'Yes, sah—one and fourpence halfpenny.'

'No, damn it all, why should I give the Treasury a shilling? Fourpence halfpenny's enough. Make it fourpence halfpenny.'

Johnson draws up a voucher. But he is flattered by Rudbeck's compliments. His imagination is at work. When he comes back, he enters with a broad grin.

'Are you laughing at me, Mr. Johnson, or what?'

'Oh, no, sah, only I tink of something.'

'I suppose I'd better not enquire what you think of.'

'Oh, sah, I tink how you get plenty more money—finish you road.
'What's the new bloody swindle?'

'Oh, sah, you get another hundred and fifty pounds for Fada vote in de next year?'

'I suppose so—it always is a hundred and fifty.'

'Why, sah, how much money you got for Treasury cash tank, tree tousand pounds. You take hundred and fifty now pay dem road men all you want, when money comes in April, you make de vouchers—cross 'em all.'

'I see, embezzlement of public funds. You want to get me kicked out of the service with seven years' imprisonment on top? That's the idea.'

'Oh, no, sir.'

'I may be a thief, Mr. Johnson, but I'm not an embezzler. Where are those vouchers? My God, haven't you any sense? You've made 'em both out to Suli.'

'Oh, sir, I thought we always make 'em for Suli.'

'Not in the same month. Good heavens, and I thought you had some savvy at stealing. Go and make out another.'

'Who I make him to, sir?'

'Good God, anyone you like—the Pope or the Emperor of Turkey. Anyone but Suli.'

Johnson goes away and writes down, 'To Turki and gang, twelve days on special service.' Rudbeck signs it without a glance. He has gone back to his Treasury queries.

'But, look here, Johnson—how does the Treasury make out that I had two pounds two and ninepence last week? I believe they're wrong, Mr. Johnson. By God, we've got 'em. That's worth a quid any day. Let's see now.' Rudbeck is so delighted at the notion of proving the Treasury wrong that he begins to grin. He adds up the column of expenditure in the vote book aloud, and says at the total, 'It shows an expenditure of one pound one shilling and threepence. Why, that's what they said it was. God damn to hell, Mr. Johnson—what is it you've done now? Fourpence? Where d'you get fourpence from? Oh, my God, my dear bloody yamhead, what the father and mother of hell is seven and twopence from fifteen and a tanner? Look at it, look at what you've put? Oh, go away, Mr. Johnson. Go home—go and boil yourself.'

He writes stiffly in the opposite column. 'Regret clerical error. One pound one shilling and threepence is refunded herewith.'

He is now so much enraged that he sulks. He refuses even to gratify himself by smoking. His temper is such that the messengers stand up in a row on the stoop, instead of sleeping there as usual; and visibly jump whenever he grunts, swears, throws his blotter on the floor, or a broken pencil out of the window. He comes out for lunch. scowling, with his shoulders hunched up and his head poked forward. When the messengers salute him, throwing into their voices the most tender notes, like nursemaids crooning at a fractious child, he makes no answer at all. When his horse-boy with an anxious and terrified expression, comes running up with his pony, he walks past him without a word. In fact, he walks all the way home, followed by the horse-boy, in extreme trepidation, half-distracted, because the pony, with his chin tugged into the air by the reins, cannot walk so fast as Rudbeck.

He eats his lunch as if each mouthful were an insult from an enemy, and after lunch, in the heat of the day, he goes out shooting with the orderly. He wants to kill.

Still scowling and sulking, he shoots a wart-hog, but falls, immediately afterwards, into a mud hole. He is so much surprised by the adventure that even while the orderly is fishing him out, he forgets to be sulky and repeats several times, 'I say, that was a bit unexpected.'

Going home, with the pig carried between two policemen, he breaks into a loud whistle which is meant to deceive the world into believing that it is a new work by a new modern composer. He sees Mr. Johnson going home from work with a melancholy, stooping walk, because he fears that Rudbeck is displeased with him, and suddenly he bursts out laughing. 'Stealing from my own Treasury—that's an idea. And yet, why the hell. What's the money for?' Rudbeck looks surprised. 'But it's an idea—yes, it is an idea. Of course, it's impossible—but it's an idea.'

The road gang has already been warned that there is no money for it beyond Thursday. On Thursday Rudbeck spends the whole day working with it and driving it to exhaustion. On Friday it rests; on Saturday it is about to disperse when the headman arrives and says that the judge wants it on Monday. The road is to go on.

'And what about the money?' one asks.

'Judge pays us the same rate.'

In fact, the road goes on at three times the speed. Rudbeck is out every day with the gangs. There is a new road staff of headmen, pioneers, bridgers, quite independent of the native minister for roads. There is even a road treasurer, Mallam Audu, promoted from secretary in the district court. He has his own cash book, showing an initial capital sum of a hundred and fifty pounds, and his own treasury box, an ancient tin box which he keeps inside the native Treasury cash tank.

All this new staff, from Tasuki, chief bridgeman, who six months before was a bush pagan in gaol for elephant poaching, to Audu, is young and boundlessly hopeful. Tasuki, who works as only a negro can work, when he sees the value and purpose of it, who gets up every day before dawn, and can be found at midnight sorting timber by lantern light; Audu, who is responsible not only for supplies but stores, and who spends most nights on the old station bicycle between Fada and road head; and a dozen more who serve them, obviously believe that some kind of millennium is at hand. When Rudbeck tells them that the road will bring wealth to Fada, they cry, 'Yes, lord, of course—much wealth,' but their imagination at once builds up for them out of this word 'wealth' a kind of paradise in which they will enjoy, not only rich food and many wives, but glory.

Of course, Rudbeck has chosen these men precisely for this quality of optimism, ambition and imagination. He does it unconsciously as a school captain picks a team and chooses little Smith instead of big Jones, because, as he says, Smith has got jump to him.

Rudbeck himself has jump though only for the one game; the one idea that has been given to him, the Fada north road. He dreams of it, and when he goes out at night by moonlight to look at the long gulf stretching away through the forest, he feels something so keen and exciting, an emotion so unusual in his experience, that he doesn't know what to do with it and the sleepy boys hear once again the snort of laughter which means for them that it is no good saying anything more to the master; he won't understand.

But Rudbeck wastes a good deal of time standing under bridges with Tasuki in common admiration of the timber work, under the illusion that he is doing necessary and important work. He is on the road every day, simply to enjoy it. He can't keep away from this keen new pleasure. He is like thousands of Englishmen who every year, from some accidental source, get the idea to make a garden or build a summer house, and labour night and day in it, neglect their business and their friends for it, risk double pneumonia for it, and when you say, 'There's going to be a war,' answer, 'Impossible,' because they have just planted tulips or ramblers.

Rudbeck has always despised office work, because someone, probably his father, when he was young, has said something contemptuous about it. Now he neglects it. When he does visit the office, he scowls, swears, shouts at everyone, or talks roads to Johnson.

Johnson is in charge not only of the Fada office, but what is much more important in his and Rudbeck's mind, the construction of the big road inn behind Fada market.

Fada, like most of Africa, has no inns or hotels. Travellers and traders must find some private householder to take them in or sleep in the open. As they cannot sleep out in the bush, where they might be eaten, and must spend each night in a village, their choice is between a private compound where they might be robbed or poisoned, and the hard clay of the local market-place. The poorer ones sleep in the market-place. Every moonlight night thousands can be seen in Fada villages and in the capital itself, lying on the hard earth with their heads on their precious loads.

Rudbeck's plan, long cherished, was to build inns, or, as they are called, *zungos*, at fixed places on the main road and one in Fada town itself, for these travellers.

A *zungo* is like a little fort. It consists of a quadrangle surrounded by a high mud wall. On the inside of this wall there is a leanto roof of thatch covering a long row of cubicles, like loose-boxes. Each of these is a lodging to be taken for the night at a cost of a penny for men and a halfpenny for women. A porter stands at the single entrance to take fees and to keep out robbers.

The biggest *zungo* is in Fada itself, with a hundred cubicles. Its walls are two hundred feet long. Johnson is the head of this work as well as the office. In the morning after breakfast he is in charge of the office. The messengers sit at his door and go upon his errands. The petitioners follow him across the station, crying, 'Mister Johnson, lord, master, hear us.' Benjamin sends him the wires and he decides upon their importance. To a wire marked 'Urgent,' he says, 'I think I leave that, Mister Benjamin. It is not important enough. I am going to the *zungo*. I have real work to-day.'

But when a wire is marked, 'Clear the line,' then he says, 'I think perhaps I attend to this—I go to see Mister Rudbeck.'

In the afternoon he goes to the *zungo* and watches the builders making round bricks of mud, or thatching the first cubicles. He feels a few bricks, complains that they are too small or too large and tells the headmen builders how walls should be constructed. However, if the builder should object and say, 'No, no, you can't do it like that; it will fall down,' he answers cheerfully, 'Yes, of course—I can see that at once.'

Afterwards he may call upon Waziri, tip Saleh a shilling for introduction money, borrow five from Waziri to defray expenses, and tell him all the political news.

'The Resident will not give us any money for the *zungo*.'

'What? Then will you stop it?'

Both the Emir and Waziri hate the *zungo* almost more than the trade road. They say that the road will bring thieves and rascals, but the *zungo* will encourage them to stay in Fada. It will be a refuge for convicts and a fortress against their own authority in the town.

'Good heavens, no, Waziri! Mister Rudbeck and I don't stop for nothing—we have plenty of money in the cash tank. Besides, the *zungo* will soon be making money. It will be finished long before the road.'

'Ah, that road—what a misfortune.'

'A misfortune.' Johnson laughs. 'Why, it is the finest work in Fada—it will bring wealth to the whole country. The motors will run through Fada from end to end.'

Waziri shakes his head. 'That's what will make all the trouble. The Emir is very angry about this road.'

'The Emir is an old savage fool—he has no idea of civilized things. Roads are a most civilized thing. When this road is opened, Waziri, you will be surprised.' Johnson waves his hand. A feeling, more than a vision, of satisfied desires floats through his experience. 'The markets will be full every day of every kind of thing—there will be heaps of money for everybody, all you in Fada will be rich——'

'I won't be surprised,' Waziri says. 'I know what your road will do—I've seen it before—everything turned upside down, and all for nothing.'

Johnson laughs at this pessimism. 'You are not civilized, Waziri. You don't understand that people must have roads for motors.'

'Why, lord Johnson?'

'Because it is civilized. Soon everyone will be civilized.'

'Why so, lord Johnson?'

'Of course, they must be—they like to be,' Johnson says. 'You will see how they like it. All men like to be civilized.'

Johnson then returns to Bamu and tells her of the glories of the day, and the magnificence which is in store for her when the road shall be finished and Fada full of money. 'We shall have parties every day and I shall buy you a motor car, like the gumna's wife.'

Bamu listens in silence and then suddenly utters a scream like a parrot. 'Sozy, the pepper.' Old Sozy rushes out from behind the water-pot and rummages in the kitchen. Bamu goes to find the pepper. Bamu never looks at Sozy, and never converses with her. Since Sozy belongs to another village and is, besides, old and rather stupid, she feels her to be a different species from herself. Probably she would react in the same way to a strange dog. She is kind to her, politely bears with her scatterbrains, and feeds her, but she does not give her a bed or a blanket. Sozy still lies all night trembling with cold, aching with rheumatism, in the narrow space between the water-pot and the wall, but this is only because it has not occurred to anybody that she may be suffering. Sozy herself has not the least self-pity. On the contrary, she is so delighted to be a member of the family, and to think herself useful in the world, that she is full of gratitude all day long. If she had any idea of a god or could imagine such an august being's taking any interest in her, she would thank him heartily for his extraordinary goodness in guiding her to Johnson's household.

Johnson, in prosperity, of course has enemies. Those who, when he was in danger of ruin, merely enjoyed the idea of his folly and certain humiliation, are disgusted by his success. It seems to them unjust that such a fool and rascal should escape punishment. Rudbeck's boy, Jamesu, is so furious that often when he looks at Johnson, he screws up his eyes at him as if they smart at the very sight. The cook, Tom, also glares. Jamesu has told him of the robbery. Johnson laughs at them both and once he calls out to Jamesu, 'Jamesu, take care some tief don' come cut you troat some day.'

Ajali, too, is disgusted with Johnson He can no longer occupy himself with the idea of Johnson's latest folly. He is bored to exaspera-tion, to that condition of fretful spite in which he has existed, like many other store clerks, for years before Johnson's coming. He hates

the sight or the name of Johnson, yet he cannot keep away from him.
Jamesu, Tom and Ajali are found in the clerk's compound every day
because they cannot think of anywhere else to go, or any other occupation for their spare time. Jamesu and Tom sit silent, drink Johnson's
beer and look at him sometimes with rage, sometimes with wonder;
Ajali laughs at him as before and shouts, 'You big man now, Mister
Johnson.'

'Yes, Ajali, I pretty big man, I tink. Mister Rudbeck say to me to-day,
"Mister Johnson, I hope you take care of yourself, because you are
mos' indispensable to me and to His Majesty's service. I pray for you,
Mister Johnson." '

'How much Waziri pay you now?'

Johnson laughs. He perfectly understands Ajali's malice and it has
the same effect upon him as Jamesu's indignant stare. It acknowledges
his distinction and achievement. It excites him to recklessness. It is like
a dare. 'He pay me anyting I ask, Ajali. Waziri and me, we understan'
each other—we both big kind of men in Fada.'

Ajali grins more widely and repeats, 'Yes, very big man,' like one
chewing on a sore tooth.

Rudbeck is now camping at road head thirty miles away and visits
the office only on alternate days. One morning, he comes in unexpectedly, wanders about the office with a perplexed expression and
finally stops before Johnson. 'Johnson, I'll be leaving here to-morrow.
I have to go and meet Mrs. Rudbeck at railhead. That means four days
altogether. Do you think you can go up to road head and keep an eye
on Tasuki and Audu?' He gives long and elaborate instructions about
the road work, to all of which Johnson says, 'Yes, sah—I do 'em, sah.'

'I'm depending on you, Johnson.'

'Oh, sah, you depend on me for my life's worth. I hope Missus
Rudbeck like dis Africa country.'

'She is looking forward to it very much. Why shouldn't she like it?'

Johnson can't refer him to his wife's own letters, from which Johnson
has discovered that she is longing to come to Africa, whereas Rudbeck
is afraid that she may be bored there. He says therefore, 'Oh, I'm sure
she like it very much. P'raps I go build her a new grass house up road.'

'Yes, that might be a good idea.'

'With a nice little lady latrine.'

'What d'you mean, a lady latrine.'

'Dose latrine for white lady so dey go in all by herself—nobody see 'um.'

'That's a good idea.'

'I make um, sah—he ready so soon as Missus Rudbeck come here.'

'Yes, I expect you'll have to look after Mrs. Rudbeck a bit, Johnson—if I have to be moved down the road. I want to get this bad stretch finished before the rains.'

'Oh, yes, sah. I like dat very much. I like to make Missus Rudbeck too happy in Africa.'

'Show her round a bit, you understand.'

'I show her everyting—prison, market, all tings ladies like—I keep her too happy for you, sah.'

'Thanks. By the way, what about that roof of yours—has anything been done to it?'

Nothing has been done to the roof, but Johnson feels a delicacy in mentioning it. He says therefore, 'Very good roof, sah, now, only jes' one little small hole,' as if the hole were growing smaller by itself.

'I must come and see the clerk's quarters. They were condemned three years ago. It's quite time that they were pulled down.'

Johnson goes and tells the whole town that Rudbeck has charged him with the care of his wife. Naturally, this greatly increases his prestige in Fada, where the Emir does not even trust his chief eunuch with his wives. Saleh demands half a crown and the Waziri gives him ten shillings and a bottle of gin. Only Ajali and Benjamin, who understand white manners, are not impressed. Benjamin shakes his head and foresees trouble; Ajali goes to Johnson and cries hopefully, 'I hear Missus Rudbeck come soon.'

'She come in two day now.'

'I tink she give you plenty trouble, Mister Johnson.'

'Oh, no, Ajali. She very nice kind woman—she ma frien'.'

'What, she you frien' now. How she see you?'

'She don't see me, but she tink of me. She say many times to her husband, "Mister Rudbeck, I feel very kind to dat Mister Johnson. I congratulate you with him. I hope to see him very much." '

'What, Mister Johnson, when she say so?' Ajali pokes out his neck and opens his little eyes as bright as half-sucked brandy balls.

'She say plenty more, Ajali.' Johnson's imagination is now at work upon the theme. 'She say she like me better than anyone. She very pleased I make her new house—she mos' glad to hear I make a lady latrine for herself; she say nobody ever thought of that good idea except Mister Johnson. Did you hear, Mister Benjamin, dat Missus Rudbeck de mos' beautiful woman in England; she dance with Prince—I tink she will surprise dese savage people in Fada. Dey never see any government lady so beautiful—she got hair like corn, her eyes are so blue dey burn you right up with blueness like de sky. She six feet high, higher than Rudbeck, and her arm is so white as elephant tusk and more big than ma leg. She big as two men and her teeth so white as de moon. Her mouth so red as henna and she sing and laugh all day, she like dis country too much.'

The next day Rudbeck drives up in his old roaring Bentley to road head, bringing a pale dark little woman with very black eyes. She jumps out of the car in front of Johnson's new grass house and cries, 'How perfectly lovely.'

Rudbeck presents Johnson to her. 'Celia, this is Mr. Johnson.'

She shakes hands warmly, then looks at Rudbeck as if to say, 'I did that right, didn't I?'

'Mr. Johnson is my right-hand man in the office.'

'Oh, but I expect he's the real boss.'

Johnson, overcome, bows, grins, wriggles and exclaims. 'Oh, mam, you make fun for me.'

Celia gives his hand another shake and says, 'I have to thank you for looking after him till I came, Mr. Johnson—he needs a lot of looking after, doesn't he?'

'Oh, mam, but he look after me—he too good.'

She drops the hand and looks round her with the same affectionate curiosity, smiling at the gaping labourers, the drummers bowing sideways with their drums under their arms, Audu curtseying to the ground, at a broken hoe left lying by the roadside and at the trees behind.

'How marvellous,' she murmurs. 'You couldn't believe it, could you? Oh, Harry, you will show me everything, won't you?'

Rudbeck, assuming his most stolid air, takes out his pipe and growls, 'There's not much to see.'

'Oh, mam, I will show you,' Johnson exclaims.

'Thank you—you must take me round.'

'Oh, yes, mam. What you like to see?'

'Everything. It won't be a nuisance for you, will it?'

'Oh, no, mam.'

'Where shall we go first?'

Johnson looks round and sees the house. 'I show you you house mam—de new house.'

Rudbeck takes out his pipe. 'Johnson made it for you.' His tone means, 'So be careful to admire it.'

'Oh, I asked you not to make any difference—but how perfectly palatial——'

They are in the big *rumfa*, a square room of woven mats about twenty feet each way. The new mats are bright gold. The bars of sun, falling through the gaps of leaves, sparkle between the straws like hundreds of small suns.

'What a marvellous house—and what's this door?'

'Dat's you own latrine, mam—you own lady latrine.'

'Oh, I see—a kind of drawing-room.'

'Yes, mam—latrine, mam.' Johnson leads the way into a narrow passage of mats roofed over and points to a hole in the ground, neatly shaped to the broken neck of a large water-pot. In front of this hole two short, forked branches carry for perch another round stick almost straight and carefully peeled of its bark.

Johnson catches up a straw pot cover from the floor and puts it over the hole. 'You see, mam—he catch cover you no fit put you foot der in de dark.' He rubs his hand along the peeled stick. 'I scrape you seat he no fit scratch you legs.'

Celia bursts out laughing and says between peals of laughter, 'Oh, thanks, Mr. Johnson—I see, it's a beautiful arrangement.'

Johnson also laughs. He does not see the joke. He has taken much trouble with the latrine, especially to make the perch firm and give it a smooth stick. He has suffered, like all Nigerians, from rickety perches which collapse at the wrong moment and top bars with bark like sandpaper, splinters like needles, twig ends sharp as chisels. He has set out to compose a masterpiece of sanitary engineering and he is extremely proud of it. But, since Missus Rudbeck laughs, he also laughs. He is delighted by her good humour.

Celia, afraid that she has hurt his feelings, puts her hand on his arm and makes solemn eyes at him. 'Thank you so much, Mr. Johnson—it is a beautiful latrine.'

'I tink you like him—I make stick smoot.' He pats his favourite stick again'.

'I'm sure I shall. Oh, what a lovely tune. What are they singing? It's like a shanty.'

She hurries out to see the road work, tries to learn the tune by ear, asks for instruction in playing the hour-glass drum, tests the weight of a Fada hoe, and tries to swing an axe.

She works at axe-swinging till she has blisters on both her hands. She shows these proudly to Johnson and Rudbeck, who stands always in the background, gripping a cold pipe in his teeth. He does not take the pipe out of his mouth in case he should grin or otherwise betray his delight in Celia's brilliant qualities of heart and head. As soon as he does take out his pipe, as they go in to breakfast, he smiles, rolls in his walk and says, 'Nice of you to be nice to Johnson.'

'Oh, but he's a darling—anyone could see.'

'Yes, but then you're a good sort.'

'Oh, no, darling—not really.'

Celia does not know whether she is a good sort. Sometimes she thinks so; sometimes she thinks that she is a fraud, that she is acting a part; that all her life is acting She is determined, however, not to be a fraud as Rudbeck's wife. She is going to be useful to him, an encouragement and an inspiration. She means to enjoy Africa, to admire his friends and his staff, to understand his work. Above all, she refuses to be a nuisance to him. When, therefore, she wants to see the survey gang at work, she insists that he shall not leave his labourers; Johnson will take her. The next day Johnson takes her to a village to see a village assembly. Every day there is a new excursion, to see women making water-pots without a wheel, to see a house being built, mats being plaited, cotton woven on the native loom.

Everywhere Celia is curious, attentive and charmed by the African people, and tells Rudbeck in the evening how much she has enjoyed herself, how marvellous Africa is.

Rudbeck is extremely busy. While Johnson is away with Celia, he has to do his own office work and type his own letters. Office work in a bush camp is always troublesome, because the files, kept in a tin case, are not easily consulted, mail-runners are erratic, and wires take three days to get an answer. At the same time he is planning the most difficult section of the road, where it runs through high jungle among lakes and swamps. Swamp road is expensive and he has to pick the driest route, in spite of deviations. He thanks goodness very often while he wades through half-dried swamps, from dawn to dark, in clouds of tsetse, that Celia is happy with Johnson, visiting the sights. Rudbeck adores his young wife, but is still, like other young married men, the essential bachelor. He cannot do with a woman except for amusement.

Celia doesn't notice this while she is enjoying Africa with the delightful Johnson, with whom, as she says, she is quite in love. She calls him privately, 'Mr. Wog.' Rudbeck hears her laughing at six in the morning and asks, 'What's the joke, darling?'

'Only Mr. Wog.'

'He's a comic, isn't he?'

'A perfect quaint.'

'Where are you going to-day?'

'I don't really know. Mr. Wog said something about weaving.'

'You've seen that, haven't you?'

'Oh, yes, but we must do weaving again for Wog's sake.'

In fact Johnson now finds Celia difficult to amuse. Instead of ecstatic exclamations, she utters a sigh, gazes blankly and says, 'Oh, yes, they're making pots,' or 'It's a fish trap, isn't it?' She knows Africa.

Johnson can't understand this. He has seen pot-making all his life, but he is always interested to hear the life history of each pot, to criticize its form, to argue with the potter about its quality, or to discuss the general state of the pot trade at that moment. To him Africa is simply perpetual experience, exciting, amusing, alarming or delightful, which he soaks into himself through all his five senses at once, and produces again in the form of reflections, comments, songs, jokes, all in the pure Johnsonian form. Like a horse or a rose tree, he can turn the crudest and simplest form of fodder into beauty and power of his own quality.

But to Celia Africa is simply a number of disconnected events which have no meaning for her at all. She gazes at the pot-maker without seeing that she has one leg shorter than the other, that she is in the first stages of leprosy, that her pot is bulging on one side. She doesn't really

92

see either woman or pot, but only a scene in Africa. Even Mr. Wog is to her a scene in Africa, and one morning when he suggests going to see a fish-hunt in a river pool, she yawns in his face without even knowing her rudeness. Yet she is a most kind and considerate girl. Now she begins to notice that Rudbeck doesn't seek her company at road-head. She cannot decide whether this is a slight or injustice, or whether it is just what a sensible girl would expect and a silly one resent. She says nothing, but she is sometimes a little stiff and uninterested when Rudbeck climbs into her bed at night. She begins to be critical of his broken nails, his too long hair, his bad shaving, his stoop, his monkey jaw, his rolling walk, his affected bluntness of speech. She remembers that he prefers Edgar Wallace to Jane Austen and cannot distinguish 'God Save the King' from the 'Marriage of Figaro.' She thinks calmly that he is rather stupid, obstinate, clumsy and greedy. She sets him apart for the first time as a distinct and real person and examines him with critical judgment. She is astonished above all by his sensitiveness.

One day she ventures to hint that he ought not to grunt and puff smoke in her face when she asks him a civil question. He takes out his pipe, turns crimson and exclaims, 'You think I'm an ape, don't you—a ring-tail baboon? Well, I'm sorry, Celia—it seems we've made a mistake.'

Celia, amazed and furious, answers, 'If that's the way you take a simple remark, it obviously is.'

'It isn't what you say, it's what you think.'

'If you must invent a grievance, why not choose something a little more plausible?'

'You've been thinking me a hog for about six weeks—and a fool for the rest of the time.'

'Do you always read thoughts that aren't there?'

'I'm not blaming you—I know I'm a blockhead, I haven't got an eye and an ear. I wish I had. Everybody wonders why you married me, and you know it knocked me over a bit myself—it was too good to be true. Well, it was, that's all.'

'If you think like that about me, of course——'

'Thank goodness there's no baby—we can split up evens.'

'As soon as you like—I'm not so terribly amused in this god-forsaken hole to stay on sufferance.'

'I must apologize for the hole.'

'I must apologize for being so much in the way.'

For the next twenty-four hours they meet only for meals and converse only in the presence of the servants, with extraordinary politeness. But they are full of such hatred for each other that everybody in the camp feels it, and Mr. Johnson looks and behaves so nearly like an imbecile, when either speaks to him, that Rudbeck damns him for a fool and Celia suspects him of robbing her bag. She has missed money and Johnson cannot look her in the face, because she is angry and full of hatred.

At the same time, each is obsessed by the other. Rudbeck hates Celia with such continuous passion that he cannot even think of his work, writes letters at random, and allows the road to go two miles into a cul-de-sac of bluffs; Celia cannot eat, sleep or read or sit still out of pure spite. She loses weight, her cheeks are chalk blue, her eyes are red and sunken. She looks like a debauchee, a Messalina after some long, frenzied orgy.

On the third night, when both have created for themselves, out of a chance remark, a romantic epic of despair and revenge. Rudbeck is found, at one o'clock in the morning, tugging at Celia's mosquito net.

'Wha-at is it?' she says in a voice trembling with astonishment.

He clambers over her, planting his bony knees on her tenderest spots, and crushes her in his arms.

'Go away!' she screams.

'Bill, darling—forgive me.'

'Oh, Harry, what a perfect beast I am.'

'I was simply mad.'

'We always said that the honeymoon would be difficult—thank goodness it's over.'

'Dearest.'

'What's this damn thing?' Rudbeck mutters in a fearful rage.

'What? Oh, wait—you're on the wrong side of the sheet—yes, darling, tear the beastly thing.'

The next day they both wander about still more absent-minded and hollow-eyed, but in a tranquil and dreamy condition. They are silent at meals, even in the presence of the servants, but tranquil happiness surrounds them. The servants are cheerful and shout at each other; Mr. Johnson, coming up with the mail, greets Rudbeck with a confident, frank smile and says, 'I tink dem Treasury ask you query about dem road voucher.'

Rudbeck puffs his pipe into his face and utters a dreamy grunt. 'I think you're a match for any Treasury, Mr. Johnson. Tell 'em they ought to be glad to get any voucher at all, the bastards.'

Johnson roars with laughter and composes various fantastic letters to the Treasury department. Afterwards he takes Celia to see a fish-hunt and, after gazing for two hours at the men and children splashing and shouting in the pools with an expression of ecstatic delight, she says in the voice of a sleep-walker, 'The people here like Mr. Rudbeck, Johnson?'

'Oh, yes, mam. They 'gree for him too much. He too kind.'

'He's doing wonderful work for you all.'

'Too good work—he too wonderful man for work.'

However, three days later, Celia and Rudbeck for no reason that either can remember, hate each other so violently that Celia begins to pack her trunks, with the intention of taking refuge with the nearest Resident's wife.

The reconciliation is even more violent and prolonged, and it leaves both so enervated that Rudbeck falls asleep over the mail and Celia prolongs her siesta to dinner-time.

Now she is so bored with the road camp that she scarcely leaves the hut. She reads, yawns and writes letters all day. She is delighted when in February the office is taken back to Fada so that reports can be written. She inspects the offices, the old fort, the market and takes tea with the Emir's wives. She is introduced to Mr. Benjamin. Johnson puts on his best suit and takes her to see his household.

'I tink you meet my wife, mam. She like to see you. She mos' clever girl, got very good brains.'

'But I should be delighted—do introduce me.'

'Oh, yes, mam—I like you to know her. She too lonely for all dese bush women in dis place. She too much civilized.'

'But you must bring her to see me.'

'Oh, yes, mam, I bring her. She bless you den. She long to see some civilized lady in Fada.'

'Did she come from the mission with you?'

'She come small small from mission—just a little—she no talk English too good. But she always do like educated girl—she got clever brains. She always dress herself like proper government wife. She no 'gree for bush girl in Fada.'

'No, poor thing. She must be lonely.'

'Oh, yes, mam. She too lonely. She never fit to come to dis savage place, but she love me too much. She got too kind heart. She mos' clever kind girl in Fada. I tink, mam, you wait here small small I go tell her you here.'

Johnson, perspiring with excitement, dives into the compound and leaves Celia in the narrow clearing, in front of the three tumble-down houses, surrounded by walls of rotting straw. She makes interested eyes at the black decaying roofs, of which one has an immense hole in it, and says, 'How picturesque.'

She hastily swallows a yawn and turns her eyes for fresh objects of experience. Her eyes are full of curiosity, carefully fostered, but they are blind to the reality before them. They see only native huts, African bush; not human dwellings, Johnson's home, living trees.

Johnson's voice is heard appealing, protesting and abusing. In fact, Johnson has been preparing for this visit during a week. Bamu, after much violent argument and the intervention of her brother, has agreed at last to put on her muslin frock, stockings and shoes. Johnson finds her in her oldest rag, sweeping out the women's huts.

He screams at her 'But you promised to put on the lady's dress.'

Bamu says, 'It won't go on.'

'What do you mean, it won't go on?'

'It won't go on. I tried.'

Johnson then snatches up the dress and rushes at Bamu. 'Here, I'll put it on.'

Bamu retreats into the hut and cries, 'I won't—I won't—I'll run away—I'll go home.' She is really angry, more agitated than Johnson has ever seen her before.

'But why, you silly girl? The government lady is waiting. You don't want her to think you a savage bush girl.'

'I don't mind what she thinks.'

'What—what—oh, you silly girl. Now you are talking nonsense.'

Bamu comes out of the hut with her newest cloth wrapped closely round her and says, sulkily, 'I'm ready.'

'But you're just like a bush girl.'

'You don't know about women's dress,' Bamu says.

'She'll laugh at you. You're shaming me,' Johnson cries and strikes himself on the forehead. 'Oh, you are the most stupid, ignorant girl.'

'I laugh at her, too,' Bamu replies.

Just then Celia, losing patience, comes stalking through the outer compound and calls out, 'May I come in?'

Before Johnson can speak, she comes in, sees Bamu and cries, 'Oh, you're Mrs. Johnson.'

She shakes hands with Bamu and says to Johnson, 'I think you are very clever to get such a pretty wife.'

Bamu stares at her with a look of penetrating contempt and says nothing.

'She wear a cloth this morning, small small for clean de house,' Johnson explains.

'Oh, but it suits her beautifully—I hope she always wears the native dress. It is so much nicer than those terrible mission frocks.'

Celia is delighted to find a sensible remark and to say something that she means.

'Oh, yes, mam, dem mission frocks very bad for women.'

'They don't suit them at all.'

Johnson gazes at Bamu with a broad smile. He is admiring her in the cloth.

'Oh, no, mam, dey too ugly.'

'Mrs. Johnson is too pretty to wear such awful garments. But you must bring her to tea with me, Johnson. Tell her that she must come to tea with me.' Celia is delighted with Bamu for giving her the excuse for a reasonable thought and a definite opinion.

Johnson, now once more in the highest spirits, tells Bamu of the invitation and adds, 'She says she likes you very much; you are so pretty.'

Bamu glares at Celia and says, 'I don't like tea. Is she going away now?'

Johnson turns smiling to Celia: 'She says to tank you mam, too much, she proud to be you frien'.'

'I'm so glad. I think she's a darling.' Celia shakes hands with Bamu. But she has exhausted the subject. She turns away, saying to Johnson, 'What else had we to do this morning? Oh, yes, the gaol. Have we time for the gaol?'

'Oh, mam, I tink no time now before breakfast and too hot for you after breakfast.'

'But the heat doesn't matter if this is the day.' Celia speaks with the air of one doing a duty. 'No, we'll go after breakfast.'

She goes virtuously to breakfast. Johnson gathers up the muslin frock, the drawers, stockings and shoes and flies to the store.

'Oh, Mister Ajali, I tink you change dese clothes for me.'

'What, you take away Missus Johnson's clothes?'

'Missus Johnson no like dem clothes,' Johnson says with a lofty air. 'I never agree for native girl wear dem foolish dress. I always say to Missus Johnson, you too clever beautiful girl to spoil yourself with dem nasty clothes.'

Ajali stares at Johnson and cries, 'What you say?'

'Come, give me a cloth—a good cloth. Missus Rudbeck ask Missus Johnson to tea—I tink she need new cloth.'

Johnson's lofty air suddenly disappears. He smiles broadly and exclaims, 'Oh, Ajali, she come see Missus Johnson to-day. Missus Johnson say, "How do do, Missus Rudbeck. I welcome you." Missus Rudbeck say, "Oh, Missus Johnson, I only heard of you. I tink you mos' clever beautiful girl I ever see, now I make you my frien' for always.' Den Missus Johnson say, "Oh, Missus Rudbeck, now my heart is so happy I can't help laughing, I love you better than my mother because you are my real true frien'. We are the only two government ladies in dis wild place." Then Missus Rudbeck say, "You must come and have tea with me now at once or I shall be too lonely and sad." Yes, she like Bamu too much.'

Ajali listens to this with a blank stare and says at last, 'Bamu say so?'

'She say plenty more, Ajali.'

'How she talk—in English?'

'How she talk? What does it matter how she talk. I didn't trouble about that. Give me the cloth, Ajali, because Missus Rudbeck waiting for me.' He takes a cloth in exchange for the clothes, at one-tenth of their value, and carries it away in a parcel under his arm to meet Celia.

She, hurrying out into the glaring sun, with white determined face, does not notice the parcel, so Johnson says to her smiling, 'You see dis parcel, mam.'

'Oh, yes, Johnson—something for the prisoners.'

'Oh, no, mam, I get new cloth for Bamu. I tink she look more pretty in native cloth.'

'Oh! how far is the gaol?'

'Not too far, mam.'

Johnson, with his parcel, full of his new idea that Bamu is prettier in a cloth and anxious to see her in the new cloth, does not notice any distance; Celia, perspiring and exhausted, will not allow herself to slacken pace. She feels that she is sacrificing herself to some good purpose and when she gets to the gaol, she peers into each corner, shakes hands with the head gaoler and says, 'What a fine gaol you have here—better than we have in England.'

When Johnson has interpreted this, both he and the gaoler look surprised and gratified. The gaoler looks round at the dungeon of mud and says, 'Better than England.'

Johnson says, 'You say, mam, it is better than England?'

'Oh, much!' Celia cries without any thought at all. She has never seen an English prison.

'Much better,' she says decisively, and she does not ask herself if this is the truth. Questions like these, about institutions, politics, government generally, have for Celia nothing to do with truth, but only with a set of ideas. She turns to Johnson: 'Where are we going next—is it the courts?'

In the next two days they see the courts, the dye-pits, the Treasury the butcher's market, the half-finished *zungo*, and peep into the mosque.

Celia admires all and to all she says, 'How charming, how picturesque how interesting.'

Fada is the ordinary native town of the Western Sudan. It has no beauty, convenience or health. It is a dwelling-place at one stage from the rabbit warren or the badger burrow; and not so cleanly kept as the latter. It is a pioneer settlement five or six hundred years old, built on its own rubbish heaps, without charm even of antiquity. Its squalor and its stinks are all new. Its oldest compounds, except the Emir's mud box, is not twenty years old. The sun and the rain destroy all its antiquity, even of smell. But neither has it the freshness of the new. All its mud walls are eaten as if by smallpox; half of the mats in any compound are always rotten. Poverty and ignorance, the absolute government of jealous savages, conservative as only the savage can be, have kept it at the first frontier of civilization. Its people would not know the change if time jumped back fifty thousand years. They live like mice or rats in a palace floor; all the magnificence and variety of the arts, the ideas, the learning and the battles of civilization go on over their heads and they do not even imagine them.

Fada has not been able to achieve its own native arts or the characteristic beauty of its country. There are no flowering trees or irrigated gardens; no painted or moulded courtyard walls.

99

The young boys, full of curiosity and enterprise, grow quickly into old, anxious men, content with mere existence. Peace has been brought to them, but no glory of living; some elementary court-justice, but no liberty of mind. An English child in Fada, with eyes that still see what is in front of them, would be terrified by the dirt, the stinks, the great sores on naked bodies, the twisted limbs, the babies with their enormous swollen stomachs and their hernias; the whole place, flattened upon the earth like the scab of a wound, would strike it as something between a prison and a hospital. But to Celia it is simply a native town. It has been labelled for her, in a dozen magazines and snapshots, long before she comes to it. Therefore she does not see it at all. She does not see the truth of its real being, but the romance of her ideas, and it seems to her like the house of the unspoilt primitive, the simple dwelling-place of unsophisticated virtue.

But since such an idea is only an idea, without depth or novelty, it is quickly boring. In seven days Celia cannot bear even to look at Fada from the distance. She has photographed it for her album and what else can she do with it? She takes her evening walk into the bush to avoid its smells, and when its drum tunes wake her at night, she swears at them and demands that they shall be stopped.

She points out also that it is eighteen months since Rudbeck came out and that he is due for leave. Rudbeck answers that no one can expect leave immediately it is due and that, as a matter of convenience, he doesn't want leave yet. He wants to finish the first section of the north road before the rains. Doesn't she agree that it would be better to finish the road now and take leave in May or June, for the English summer, or even wait for August, when Uncle Bill may give them a shot at the grouse.

Celia agrees and declares that Rudbeck's work must come first. Then she begins to fret about his health. He is looking thin. Of course the work must come before her pleasure, but it mustn't come before his health. He swears he is fit; she swears that he is worn out. A violent quarrel follows which leaves him worn out, and Celia more nervous, more obstinate; and, as it were, more falsified. That is to say, she feels irritated, not only by Africa and Rudbeck, but by everything that she herself says and does. She cannot, as a thoroughly sensible girl, approve of this Celia who talks nonsense, affects an interest she does not feel, gets into tempers, plays the martyr and makes a nuisance of herself, but she has no other. She has lost the old one, the oldest daughter,

Mamma's standby and Papa's reliable wonder, and she never recognizes Rudbeck's darling. What is she? Where is she?

Like other young women whose marriage has not meant a rapid breathless passage from one social berth to another, both well secured with local ties, but a rocket explosion out of the nursery into the inane, she is in fact lost. She doesn't find anything sincere in herself except her nerves. She therefore indulges the nerves. To her own astonishment and helpless disgust, she begins to have crying fits, she says that Rudbeck does not love her, that he is killing her, and so on. He may ignore his own health, no doubt, if he so obstinate; but how selfish never to think of hers.

To prove how ill she is, she goes to bed and at once has a temperature. She is really ill, eats nothing and wishes that she could die. What makes Celia's breakdown genuine is her own disgust with herself. Rudbeck, frightened and conscience-stricken, drives her to provincial headquarters at Dorua, where she is sent into hospital. The sympathetic Resident insists that the young couple shall not be parted. Rudbeck is put into the provincial office for a fortnight and then boarded for leave. The sympathetic board find him unfit to extend his tour, and the senior doctor slaps him on the back and says, 'So you can take her home yourself by the next boat.'

Young Tring, Resident's A.D.O. in the provincial office, is sent down to Fada, to take over from Rudbeck.

Tring is a popular young man, thin, small, handsome, with very smooth fair cheeks and blue eyes. His shirt is clean every day; his shorts are pressed down the sides so that they stand out like a Greek guard's kilt. He is hardworking, shrewd, even-tempered, obliging, and already people say of him, 'Tring will get on. He's the stuff for a chief secretary.'

He is junior to Rudbeck, who hands over to him therefore with careful explanations. But, as usual in all handings-over, extraordinary and unexpected deficiencies come to light. The police ammunition is short, the medical stores have almost disappeared two bags of shillings sealed by some former D.O. six years back are three pounds short, and Mr. Benjamin's office is in strange confusion. Stamps are missing, the accounts have not been kept for several weeks. What's more, the grave, serious Benjamin offers no explanation. He says in his melancholy voice only, 'I think I have spent the money, sir. Perhaps you will give me the sack, sir.'

'No, no. There's no need for a fuss. But I can't understand it, that's all.'

Rudbeck is surprised and annoyed because he has been praising Benjamin to Tring. 'About the accounts? You've never let them slide before.'

Benjamin himself is obviously a little surprised. He says at last, 'It must have been a lapse, sir. So you will inform the police, sir.'

'Good God, no! What nonsense! It's only a few shillings. I'll make it up myself if you're broke.'

No senior has ever told Rudbeck that it is unwise to make up a deficiency in stamps and no one happens to use the word 'advance,' so he cheerfully gives Benjamin seventeen shillings to balance his accounts. But the incident depresses him. He keeps on saying, 'Funny thing about old Benjamin—he seemed such a sound feller.'

'They need keeping up to the mark,' Tring says in his mild voice; 'especially in the bush.'

'But Benjamin—he's like the Bank of England. Talking about prison like that. Wonder what's going on in his mind.' Rudbeck reflects for some time and then gives a loud snort which makes Tring jump and look pained.

'Just one of their remarks, I suppose. I say, have you seen the store.' Rudbeck grows more cheerful when he opens the store and shows a heap of new picks and shovels just arrived. He feels that they will not let him down before the junior. 'That's the last indent—straight from Birmingham—I checked 'em in last week.'

'How many are there on charge?'

Rudbeck, mildly surprised, calls a messenger to check the tools again. Johnson comes at once to take part in any glory which may radiate to him from their bright labels and gleaming edges.

Rudbeck, reviving again from an anxiety lest, after all, a pick-shaft or a shovel may be missing, cries out, 'Oh, here's Mr. Johnson. Tring—this is my right-hand man.'

Tring shakes hands with Johnson and says, 'I've heard of your work on the road.'

'Oh, no, sah, I do nutting; it's all Mister Rudbeck who makes de road.'

'You must show me this famous road.'

Johnson likes Tring at once, as he likes everybody who gives him the least excuse to do so. As he goes away from the office, he cocks his hat over his ear, hollows his back and picks up his legs in a kind of goose-step, which makes Tring, looking from the office window, smile. Rudbeck, seeing the smile, says, 'Yes, he cuts a dash—but he's a good chap, all the same.'

'What did your wife call him?'

'Mr. Wog—oh, yes.'

'A real piece of intuition.' And Rudbeck, who greatly respects Tring's brain, looks after Johnson with a slight frown, trying to see what deep truth about Johnson his clever wife has discovered and revealed to the clever Tring in the single word 'Wog.'

Johnson, meanwhile, full of pride and good nature, grins at every passer-by and shouts the warmest Hausa greetings, 'Hail—God go with you.' The more he swaggers the more he is charmed by all these nice people in this nice world; the nice trees, the nice sky, the nice sun. The very curl of his hat is a gesture of universal appreciation. He is full of gratitude to the whole world. He puts his head into the Post Office and shouts, 'You come to-night, Mister Benjamin, I make you a party— I get a bottle of real English gin from home—two bottle.'

He hails Rudbeck's cook and Jamesu passing from the town. He shouts, 'Cuku, Jamesu—I give a big party—three bottle gin—plenty beer—we get drums—you come to-night.' Cook and Jamesu stare at him with looks of amazement and disgust. Johnson does not even remember that Jamesu is his enemy and does not notice the blank stares. He catches sight of the store and turns off his road.

Ajali is languidly and haughtily serving an up-country pagan with salt. The road has already brought many new customers to the store, barbarians who cannot make up their minds what to buy or how much to pay for anything. Ajali resents the trouble and tedium of waiting upon them.

'Go on,' he says. 'Hurry up—do you want it or don't you?' To Johnson he says in a different lively tone, 'Excuse me, Mister Johnson, dese bush apes are a perfect nuisance; dey got no sense at all.'

The peasant fingers a corner of a cheap white cloth, filled with clay, and looks out of the corners of his eyes at the two townsmen.

Ajali, not having seen Johnson since yesterday, holds out his hand: 'How do you do, Mister Johnson.'

'How do, Ajali, have you got some nice new cloth for Missus Johnson? I tink I like de very bes' cloth you got.'

'But, Mister Johnson, you buy tree new cloth for Missus Johnson dis month—I tink you bill too big.'

'Never mind about dat ole bill, Ajali—I pay it. Have you got some velvet cloth—some red velvet. I like to see Missus Johnson in native cloth—de very bes' cloth—I like some red velvet cloth—with gold stripes.'

'I got some red velvet cloth with gold spot, but he very dear cloth, Mister Johnson. He cost two poun'.'

'I take him, Ajali. I wan' to give Missus Johnson de bes' cloth in Fada, because she de bes' wife in Fada.'

Ajali gets down a roll of crimson plush and throws it over the counter. The pagan gazes at it sideways with a stupefied air. Johnson carelessly gives it a twist and says, 'I like more gold spot—you no got one with diamindy.'

'I got diamanty by de strip—you sew it on.'

'I want it all over cloth—big diamind. All right. I take some strip.'

Ajali unrolls a strip of diamanté across the cloth. The pagan turns away his head like a dog offended by a flashlight; then slowly twists it round again and gazes. He is quite confused by these wonders. This new life opened by the road is inconceivably enlarged for him and he can't believe it yet.

'I take two yard for top, two yard for bottom,' Johnson says; 'two yards for make stripe down the middle. You tink two stripes better?'

'Oh, yes, Mister Johnson.'

'Or tree stripe—dat ten yards diamindy. I tink Missus Johnson like dat.' Johnson, in spite of his dignity as a government official and a friend of Tring, cannot help smiling broadly in anticipation of Bamu's joy. 'I tink she got bes' clothes in Fada.'

'I tink so—dar four poun' five shillings, Mr. Johnson—you pay now?'

'Put him for my bill, Ajali.'

'But I tell you—— You bill grow too big, Mister Johnson—seven pounds.'

'Too big—I pay you eleven poun' last time.'

'But perhaps Waziri no 'gree.'

'Waziri—what you mean, Ajali? Waziri ma frien'.'

'Waziri no like road—Emir no like road—say bring all kind of rascals to Fada—spoil dis bush people.'

'Dat fool talk, Ajali—dat Emir old savage man.'

'I say he right—dese bush people come here every day—dey drive me mad here with der stupid heads, stay here two hours. Never buy nutting. Bush ape like dis man—look um.'

Ajali waves at the pagan who is in the act of taking another panic-stricken, fascinated glimpse of the velvet cloth and the diamanté. He meets the eye of Johnson and Ajali fixed on him, Ajali contemptuous, Johnson amused and gaily condescending, and at once his brows come down, he scowls and twists his upper lip like a savage dog about to bite.

'Good for nutting savage.' Ajali says. 'Better he stay for bush like de udder apes—I tink Emir, Waziri quite right.'

'I tink you fool child, Ajali. De King he say, I want plenty new road everywhere, so my people fit to go walkum, see de worl—all government officer bound to do what de King want—dey bound to make road. De King he tink what bes' for de people, dats his job—Mister Rudbeck and I we tink so too—we say "God Save de King, we make dis road in Fada." And we do so, Ajali. Mister Tring he tell me jus' now he heard about de road.'

'Mister Tring, who he?'

'Mister Tring, he from Resident office. He de cleveres' man in Nigeria. What, you never hear of Mister Tring—frien' of mine?'

'He frien' of yours?'

'He my frien'—very old frien'—my special frien'. When he see me, he take me by the han', he look in my eyes, he say, "Mister Johnson, I hear all about dis famous work you do for Mister Rudbeck—I admire for you—I tink you bes' government clerk for whole province." And he shake my hand—he say, "God bless you, Mister Johnson." '

'What, Mister Johnson, he no say God bless you?'

'You say I lie, Mister Ajali?'

Johnson is angry because he feels that his description is even more truthful than Tring's bare words; that his speech, repeated in cold blood, could not possibly convey to a third party, certainly not to a stupid and suspicious person like Ajali, the real effect of this remarkable experience which still makes Johnson's heart beat with pride and gratitude.

'What I want to tell you, Mister Ajali, that I only tell you one little bit of truth because I know you can't hold more'n a small piece without it give you a pain. The big whole truth don't agree for dirty little house lizards like you. If I tell you all ting Mister Tring say for me, you just swell up like a dead goat, bust in tree halves.'

Johnson pulls the plush towards him, throws the diamanté into it, rolls it up, cotton side out, and tucks it under his arm. Ajali watches the deed with a nervous and spiteful expression. He is overwhelmed as usual by Johnson's eloquence, and also by his unexpectedness, but he resents his own feeling of confusion and weakness.

'Good evening,' Johnson says in his grandest manner. In spite of the bundle under his arm, he has great dignity. 'You call me liar, I say you, yas, I'm a liar—I don' tell you the truth—I don' tell you how much Mister Tring 'gree for me because you so little small ting like stink bug. How anyone tell stink bug about de glory of God—he only make so bad stink he make you sick for belly.'

Johnson's indignation is growing as he realizes it. He goes off saying to himself, 'You show um a diamond, he tink um broken bottle—you show um beautiful fine horse, he tink um rock rabbit— you give um bag of gold, he tink um snake's head with troat full of yaller poison—you bring um beautiful girl, he say she little dirty goat—he creep on his belly all over everyting like house lizard—he say all ting made of dirt.'

At the entrance to his own compound, he sees Sozy come dodging through the bush. Probably she has been lying in wait for him. He hears the thump of the pestles and the murmur of women's sing-song voices from the women's court and at once Ajali's insults disappear from his mind. He thinks of the surprise he is going to give Bamu. In his delighted anticipation, he even notices old Sozy, and with a lordly gesture spreads out the velvet cloth in front of her.

'Look at that, Sozy,' he says with the pride of an artist showing his masterpiece; 'the finest cloth in Fada.'

Sozy gazes in confusion at the cloth and from that to Johnson's face. At last she sees what is expected of her, claps her hands, wags her head, bends her knees and says, '*Da dadi*.'

'Nice—I should think it was—the Emir's first wife hasn't got a cloth like that. But, then, Bamu is more important than the Emir's wife. She is a government wife.'

Sozy, making a stronger effort at appreciation, bends almost double, clasps her hands wildly, wags her head like a toy mandarin and cackles, 'Oh—*da*—*dadi*.'

Johnson laughs and walks on with the old woman at his heels. She now has a solemn foolish and frightened expression. She is blinking and groaning to herself. She perceives that she hasn't used the right word about the cloth, but she cannot for the life of her think of a better one. She knows that she has failed Johnson and lost a great opportunity, and like other failures, she can't tear herself away from defeat. She is still hoping for another chance.

Johnson marches into the women's compound, where he finds Bamu and her half-sister Falla pounding millet in a large wooden mortar.

Falla is older than Bamu and has three children including the three-month baby on her back. She has been staying with Bamu for a month, because while she is suckling the child, she will not live with her husband. Falla and Bamu chatter all day, and whenever Johnson comes near them they both look at him with the same expression, as if he were a strange dog or an unusual and possibly dangerous beast. They look at him now with this expression; their eyes are as bright and hard as agates.

He puts the cloth behind him and cries to Bamu, 'I have good news for you, my dear wife—I have just seen the new judge and he has spoken to me most honourable words. He shook me by the hand many times and said that I was the finest man in Fada. He said to me, "Mr. Johnson, I hope you will give me your help in this government, because I know of your wisdom and of your great love for our noble King, the greatest King in the world." '

Bamu screws up her nose and says to Falla in a nervous voice. 'What does he say?'

Falla raises her pestle to begin work again and says, 'I didn't hear.'

'You did hear,' Johnson shouts. He dislikes Falla. 'I told Bamu that the judge had said honourable things to me and that she is the wife of a most distinguished man.'

Bamu screws up her face as if she has just sat on a thorn and says in a disgusted voice, 'What does he mean?'

'I don't know.'

'Look here, Bamu,' Johnson cries. He laughs and suddenly taking the cloth from behind his back, he stretches it before the two women: 'What do you think of that?'

Falla and Bamu both together drop their pestles and take the cloth. Bamu says indignantly, 'Dragging it in the dust.'

'Put it in the bokkis,' Falla says. 'Be careful.'

'I'll be careful.' Bamu goes away, carefully folding up the cloth. Falla, after consideration, trots after her, takes the cloth from her, and folds it again in the same folds. Her expression is full of sympathy while she handles the plush; Bamu looks on like an anxious mother while her new baby is being admired. They disappear murmuring warnings and advice to each other. After five minutes, they return with virtuous faces, as if from a sacrament, and take up their pestles.

Johnson, brightening at their reappearance, smiles, strikes an easy attitude and says, 'Well, what did you think of it?'

'You were spoiling it.'

'Aren't you glad I gave you a cloth?' Johnson cries.

'It's too dear,' Falla says.

'It's too good,' Bamu says. 'It's only fit for a chief's wife.'

'But you are a chief's wife, Bamu—bigger than any chief's wife—the wife of a government man. You're not one of the savage bush girls any more. You're as good as a white woman. That's why I give you a cloth fit for a government wife.'

'What's he say?' Bamu asks.

Falla aims her pestle at the mortar. 'I don't know—something about the chief.'

She strikes her pestle into the hollow wood and Bamu immediately joins in with rhythmic strokes. They continue their work, without haste or pause. Johnson throws up his hands, knocks his hat to the back of his head and slouches into the house. His walk is itself a dramatic expression of despair. He falls on to his box chair and stretches out his legs for Sozy to take off his shoes; he hears the sing-song begin again in rhythmic jerks: 'But Niji—had twins—of course—some demon—had crept up—in her belly—when she was asleep—on the farm—but she knew—the people would drive her—so she hid—one child for bush—behind yam store—she used to say—I fetch yam—she creeps out—suckles baby.'

Johnson gives a groan as Sozy kneads his feet. 'You damn women, always telling stories—I think you've got nothing else in your heads but all that nonsense about witches and devils and spells and corpse washers and twins.'

He hears from outside: 'So the husband—was sick—he began to die—he goes to juju man—juju man says—bad devil in your house—he comes to find devil—he finds the baby—is the devil—a very bad devil—they all run out—set fire to house—but Niji comes back—gives a scream—runs into house—she's all burnt up——'

Johnson rushes out in a fury and shouts, 'What nonsense you talk, you savage; there are no devil babies. A twin is not from the devil—how dare you tell my wife such a lot of lies.'

The two women stop and turn their absorbed faces towards him like sleepers reacting unconsciously to a passing noise.

'How dare you, Falla, you silly fool of a woman—do you want to frighten my wife so that she lets her baby slip.'

Bamu screws up her face and says in a resentful tone, 'What is he talking about now?'

'I don't know,' Falla says, gazing blankly.

'He's always talking like that,' Bamu says. 'What does he mean?'

'He's a stranger,' Falla says. 'He doesn't understand this country.'

'Then why does he talk like that?'

'He can't help it.'

'Oh, Gawd—oh, Gawd—what do you do with savages like that?' Johnson says in English. He staggers into the house and throws himself on the bed, where, to Sozy's terror, he lies and groans for half an hour as if he were dying.

However, in another hour he is in paradise; that is to say, entertaining the station; and not the least part of his pleasure is to see Bamu's disdainful air as she parades up and down in the new cloth, thrusting out her round stomach and answering all the compliments and salutations of the station boys with the same blank and aloof stare. She does not wear the cloth and carry herself so forwardly to be admired by such foreign animals, but for the sensation of her own pleasure. Johnson also serves his pleasure, but for him it is pleasure to admire and to create happiness.

The next day he rises, like any villager after a hunt ball, with a splitting headache. But he is still happy. His groans while Sozy pours cold water over his skull and then gently rubs his temples and neck are full of self-satisfaction. He feels that only a big headache is adequate to such a successful party.

'Allah damn you, you old skin; you're killing me.'

'*Ohey—ohey.*'

'Get out—go away. Here, enough.' He jumps up and escapes from her, staggering into the sun with his head in his hands.

'*Ohey—ohey.*' She, hastening in pursuit, strokes and pities the air.

'Enough I say, you old wooden fingers—I can't bear any more.' He puts his hat on his head and crawls drooping towards the office. But, catching sight of Tring briskly crossing the open ground, he at once becomes spry and brisk, forgets his headache, pulls down his coat, and swaggers up to the stoop like a sergeant-major.

'Good morning, Mister Tring—I pray God you sleep like a baby.'

'Good morning, Mr. Johnson—I think you're a little late.'

'Oh, sah, I tink office clock too fast.'

'The office clock appears to have stopped some weeks ago—there is an ants' nest in the works.'

'Oh, yes, sah, but he stop too fast. Mister Rudbeck say so.'

'We'll go by my watch now and the bugle. I expect you to be here at reveille.'

'Oh, yes, sah—I like to be here before the first blow—so I don' waste de King's time after de las' blow.'

'Very good, Mr. Johnson—now for the cash book copy—the monthly accounts ought to go in to-day.'

'I do him, sah.'

Johnson brings in the copy, which is beautifully written, especially the certificate at the front: 'I certify this to be a true copy of the cash book, etc., etc.' Only one line of numbers has been missed and this is soon discovered by Tring, who adds up the total and finds all the addition wrong. He puts in the amounts, and says only, 'A little slip, Mr. Johnson?'

'Oh, yes, sah. I knew there was a little slip.'

'Then why didn't you correct it?'

Johnson smiles affectionately at his adopted friend and says, 'I knew he was dar, sah, only I never find where.'

'Where's the cash book and the vouchers?'

110

Tring checks through all the vouchers and remarks that Mr. Suli has received a great many payments within very few days. Johnson laughs gaily as at an old joke and says, 'Oh, dat Mister Suli—his hand quite tired from making marks.'

'I suppose there is such a person?'

'Oh, yes, sah.' Johnson laughs. 'Very rich man.'

'Where's the native Treasurer, Ma-aji?'

The native Treasurer comes panting into the office with his clerk. He is an old man with a thin white beard; it is said that he can neither read nor write. While he is saluting the new A.D.O. with rheumatic bobs, the young clerk hands over the cash book. Tring checks it and complains that the figures are almost illegible and that some entries have been rubbed out. The old man, in consternation, begins to cry out that he has served the state for forty years, but Tring checks him and says kindly, 'Don't worry, old man, I'm not blaming you, but I think you had better learn the elements of your job. Come up again to-morrow and I'll show your clerk how to make figures. Who's this?'

Audu, the road treasurer, has come into the office, followed by Johnson, who can't resist this chance of showing his special knowledge. Audu, in a clean white gown and turban bought for the occasion, is grinning with all his teeth. He carries his cash book, rolled up in a piece of goat-skin, under his arm, and his pen-case in his right hand. He keeps on bowing to Tring and grinning all the time with an air of self-confidence. In fact, he is in a great fluster.

'Who are you?' Tring asks again.

'Road treasurer, *Zaki*.'

'The road treasurer, sah,' Johnson explains.

'Who is the road treasurer—I never heard of such an office.'

Audu keeps on smiling and bows still deeper.

Johnson explains that the road treasurer keeps the road money.

'Road money—what is road money?'

'For roads, sah—for road work.'

Tring holds out his hand for the book, opens it and sees rows of neat entries, payments for hoes, for innumerable small and large gangs, for rope and timber, for presents to chiefs. The name Suli does not appear anywhere.

Tring is astonished. He looks from the book to Audu and from Audu to Johnson. At last he throws himself back in his chair and says in a prim voice, 'I still don't understand, Mr. Johnson. What money is this? Where did it come from? Who authorized these payments? Are they from the government Treasury or the native Treasury?'

'Oh, sah, from both Treasury—it's the road money.'

'The road votes for last year came automatically to an end last month—the new votes arrived about a week ago. Am I to understand that this great mass of transaction, has occurred in a week? But no, I see the entries began in October last.'

'Oh, yes, sah—in de book.'

'Are they actual payments?'

'Oh, yes, every one. Audu here very good, honest man.' Audu begins to bob and smile again. The sweat appears on his forehead. He has no idea that anything has gone wrong, but he finds this important interview, on which depends his career, and that of his wife and family, a trying ordeal.

'Kindly let me see your Treasury note-book again, Mr. Johnson.'

Johnson brings the oblong book and Tring examines it. He remarks, 'Your last year's votes were exhausted in September. Or is this book also a fraud?'

'Oh, sah, all dem payments real. I keep book myself.'

'Where did this money in the so-called road Treasury come from?'

'De cash tank, sah.'

Tring turns red. He can hardly believe his ears. 'Do you mean it was taken from the cash tank and—and simply used, Mr. Johnson?'

'Oh, sah, we use 'um on the road—every penny go on road. Mister Rudbeck very particular—he pick Audu because he most honest boy he fin' anywhere.'

'And you falsified the cash book—the real Treasury cash book—between you?'

'Oh, no, sah—oh, no.' Johnson laughs with triumph. 'He all right, sah, de votes come out las' week—Mr. Rudbeck and me write all dem vouchers we make cash book all right with cash. He no false now—all dat cash in cash book really in de tank and Audu have forty-seven poun' five shilling sixpence and four aninis in the road box.'

Tring is now calm and as it were exhausted; like one who, being dragged through the most loathsome revelations of vice, can no longer be shocked by anything. 'So there is also a road cash tank,' he says.

'Oh, yes, sah, for de road surplus—old travelling cash box, sah.'

'And a road surplus.'

'Forty-seven pound five——'

112

'You understand Mr. Johnson that you have committed embezzlement and forgery.'

Johnson smiles and says, 'We write dem vouchers, sah, for Treasury,' as if to say that it can't be forgery to swindle a treasurer.

'Very well, Mr. Johnson—I think I begin to understand the situation. Tell this man to bring his illegal cash book here so that the stolen money may be restored to its proper place. We shall consider meanwhile whether to arrest him. As for you, Mr. Johnson, you are suspended from duty. I can't say offhand how far you may be held responsible for this extraordinary fraud on government, but I'm afraid that headquarters are not usually very lenient in such cases. You can go home and stay there till further notice. I would rather not have you about the office until I have looked into your papers.'

'But, sah, it's for the road—Mr. Rudbeck's road—de fines' road—I show you. And Mr. Rudbeck say to Audu and me, we pay every penny for de men, put it in de book.'

'An illegal cash book is an illegal cash book, Mr. Johnson, whatever it is used for. Kindly leave the office.'

Audu bows and smiles, now completely bewildered. The police orderly takes his arm and explains to him that he is under arrest. Johnson, horrified, runs all the way home, repeating to himself in astonishment, 'But he didn't understand—Mister Tring, I tell you—all de money spent for de road. Audu and me we no tief one little penny.'

Tring brings the surplus money to account in the cash book under the head of 'Surplus at taking over, described as road money.' He then sends an official report of the two cash books to the Resident, old Bulteel.

Bulteel is astonished and alarmed. Like all old officials anywhere in the world, he hates a fuss or a scandal more than fire. He says to himself in surprise, 'Funny thing for a sensible chap like Tring. Why didn't he send me a private chit if he wanted to do anything. But, of course, after all, he hasn't much experience.'

He drives down to Fada as fast as he can go, thanks Tring for his report, looks at Audu's cash book, checks it and says then with relief, 'Well, well, well, and you say the cash was all correct. So that's all right. And no harm done. Of course, I knew poor Ruddy hadn't helped himself—I need not say—but I was a little worried about the accounting. He's not a flier at the accounts—we've had rather a crop of queries about Fada, as a matter of fact.'

'Oh, of course, sir, I didn't want to make any trouble for Rudbeck.'

'Oh, no, no. Good heavens, no.'

Bulteel, who is a little fat bald man, with a pink head and small white moustache, the picture of shrewd good nature, throws up one fat little hand and shakes his head with earnest deprecation. 'Of course not, I quite understand that. No no, you were quite right to let me know—for Ruddy's own sake. I shall certainly warn him. But you needn't worry—it won't go any further. Trust me.' He throws himself back in his chair and smiles like a good papa. His little slits of eyes disappear altogether when he smiles.

'It was only that regulations had so definitely been ignored.'

'Quite, oh, quite—though, of course, you might say they are made to be broken. That is'—catching Tring's mild, curious gaze and expanding in fatherly good nature—'you must be careful of course. What I mean is that all these regulations meant to keep a check on every penny of expenditure are a bit of an anomaly. Anyone who wants to swindle the Treasury could make a fool of the rules any day—and as for the honest ones, they only find 'em in the way of real honest work—as here with poor Ruddy's road.'

Tring gazes with his mild receptive eye, like a pupil in the front desk, and Bulteel, much encouraged, sticks his forefingers in the band of his trousers, and closes his eyes in a thoughtful manner. 'After all, I suppose we're meant to be trusted—that's why they give us special conditions—and, really you know. Tring, we've got to be trusted or the whole thing would come to bits. I know we wouldn't have had even the Dorua road if we'd stuck strictly to the rules.'

'I'm sorry if I acted precipitately.'

'Not at all. Certainly not. You did perfectly right. And you can be sure that nothing more will come of it. There's nothing to meet the Treasury's eye, thank goodness.'

'Except the surplus. I brought that to account at once.'

Bulteel turns red and exclaims in amazement, 'Brought it to account.' He is going to explode when again he catches Tring's mild blue eye and suddenly he doubts his judgment of the boy. 'Is he so simple?' he thinks; 'I've always said he would get on and perhaps this is the very way he's going to get on. Certainly I'm no judge—I'll never be a governor.'

He therefore reflects a moment before saying mildly, 'Ah, yes, of course, that put's the fat in the fire.'

'Surely there was no other course.'

'Well, I suppose we could have arranged something.'

'I could hardly take over a division and pass bogus accounts.'

'No, no, no; though we know that funny things do happen to vouchers—once all mine were blown into the Niger by a tornado, but the Treasury wouldn't take that for an excuse. They demanded vouchers —and, of course, they had to get them.'

Tring listens to this with his polite, earnest expression and says, 'Do you mean that Treasury regulations are not to be taken seriously?'

'Well, after all——' Then, glancing again at the young man's sharp nose and pale blue eyes, Bulteel has another moment of doubt about him, the profoundest doubt. He thinks: 'Damn it, I'd better be careful. He may be one of the real go-getters. He may report me next.' He pauses therefore and says gravely: 'Certainly not disregarded. They are, however, a little inelastic sometimes, and I suppose Rudbeck's real idea was to get on with the motor road, which, I must say, no one else has managed to get on with.'

'Rudbeck meant well, but I scarcely like to take the responsibility of carrying on in the same style. Besides, I suppose one has a certain duty,' with a glance at the Resident.

'Oh, of course, of course, you did quite right. Well, well, well, poor Rudbeck. This is going to be a big dust-up.'

In fact, thanks to a private note from Bulteel to the Chief Commissioner, and because Bulteel's wife's first cousin is in the Secretariat, Tring's report, having stuck for two months in the provincial office, and another in the secretariat, reaches the Secretary at last only in the form of a précis in which the words 'embezzlement' and 'forgery' are translated into overspending votes and unorthodox accounting for expenditure. Rudbeck, on a new honeymoon in Devonshire, at a crisis when he has not spoken to Celia for three days and is prepared for murder and suicide, receives a strong reprimand and a warning; Tring is officially thanked for his close attention to duty. Audu and Johnson are sacked. It is only fair to say, as Tring says to Johnson, that he would not have been sacked if it had not been for his very bad reports.

'Both Mr. Blore and Mr. Rudbeck gave you very unfavourable reports and I'm not surprised, Mr. Johnson, that the department has no further use for your services.'

Finally the road work, since the entire road fund has been gobbled up by the Treasury as an unexplained surplus, comes to a sudden end; the gangs of axe-men are dispersed; the little foreman, Tasuki, is seized by the Emir, heavily flogged and thrown into gaol; and the Waziri is assured that if anything more is heard of motor roads to Fada, he too will be beaten.

The Waziri makes no protest. He hates roads as much as his master, but he knows his duty as Waziri, to suffer for anything which disturbs the Emir's temper.

Johnson makes no secret of his misfortune; in fact, he tells everyone on the road, including market women, passing traders or unemployed labourers, that he has been sacked.

He stops in front of each and shouts, 'Have you heard, friend—they've turned me out—me, the chief clerk of Fada and a friend of Mister Rudbeck? Did you ever hear anything like that? And all a mistake too. It's not Mister Tring's fault, you understand. He's been very nice and polite. It's the Treasurer, the Ma'aijin Gumna. I tell you, that man is sold to the devil. He is the deadly enemy of Mister Rudbeck, too. Of course, Mister Rudbeck knows his tricks—Rudbeck and me, we're a match for the Treasurer. But Mister Tring is too mild—too trusting—he has been deceived by that cunning rascal at Lagos. He believes all his lies, and so he's turned me out—me, Johnson, the chief clerk,' and so on; until by the time he reaches home, it has become a saga, and the women paying court to Bamu in their compound hear his voice on the other side of the mats explaining to old Sozy that he, the great Johnson, chief clerk of the province and the main north road, friend of Rudbeck, Tring, the Wazirin Fada and the King of England, has been utterly ruined by the plots of a wicked devil at Lagos who has removed Rudbeck out of the country, robbed him of forty-seven pounds five shillings and sixpence, and put a spell on Tring so that his ears are deaf to truth and his eyes are blind to justice.

'*Ohey, ohey,*' Sozy repeats.

'What do you think of that, Sozy?'

'*Ohey*, your poor feet.'

'Oh, God bless you, Sozy, you damned idiot, you never understand anything. Bamu, Bamu.'

He comes into the outer women's compound, shouting. Bamu within wraps her cloth more firmly round her, and continues to scrape yam. She is near her time.

'You hear that, Bamu?' Falla says in the special tone of a wife who speaks to another in the hearing of her husband. 'He's finished.'

'Yes, it seems so,' wiping her knife on her thumb.

'He'll go to prison now.'

'I suppose so.'

'I always expected it.'

'So did I.'

'You'd better get away quickly.'

'I was thinking so.'

'Before he wants to sell all your things.'

'Yes, he might.'

'Go then, quickly. Go and drag your box out at the back. I'll tell him you're sick.'

Bamu shakes her head.

'Why not, you silly.'

'I must ask my brother.'

'He will say, go.'

Bamu looks calm and indifferent. She repeats, 'I must ask him first.'

'I'll go and get him now.'

'Yes, but he'll come anyhow.'

Falla rushes off. When, an hour later Johnson is still relating his misfortunes to Bamu, the plots of the wicked Treasurer and the innocence of Tring, old Brimah arrives with Falla and begins to pack Bamu's tin box. Bamu assists. Johnson protests, screams, threatens; no one pays the least attention to him. He assures Bamu that he will soon be richer than ever; he will be a trader, he will make her the richest woman in Fada, and in the middle she turns to Falla and says, 'The big water-pot is mine too.'

'I love you, Bamu, and you love me. We've been happy—think how happy we have been—every day we sing, we play together. Then you put on your beautiful clothes and walk about the market, and everyone says, 'See Bamu, wife of Johnson. She is a happy girl because he would die for her. Why, Bamu,' Johnson cries, laughing. 'You think I'm broken. You think that now I'm not a government clerk any more I can't give you good things. But now I am going to be a trader, the richest in Fada. You shall have clothes like the Queen of England. You shall have silver bangles every day as big as ropes. You shall have kohl for your eyes as black and shiny as a new cash box. You shall have a thousand cigarettes every week—cigarettes from home with gold ends. You shall have red paint for your nails and scent in a barrel.'

Bamu, still folding up her clothes, says to Falla, 'He owes me six-pence for yams. What shall I do?'

'He must pay!'

'Yes, he must pay,' old Brimah says, 'and he owes me two pounds for the compensation money.'

Johnson shouts that he has paid already fourteen pounds. They dispute it and then claim that the original price was seventeen, that by losing such a good girl as Bamu, strong, wise, virtuous and affectionate, a perfect daughter and sister, they have lost the equivalent of twenty pounds.

At this moment the brother Aliu arrives with Waziri and young Saleh. Waziri has come in a hurry. He is breathless. But he manages to give Johnson a most polite curtsey and then shakes hands with him.

This politeness strikes all dumb.

'How are you, Mr. Johnson, in your health?'

'In good health, Waziri.'

'You fill me with joy. What is this affair? I hope you are not being troubled by this rubbish.'

'They want to take Bamu from me.'

Waziri throws up his hands and laughs. 'Ah, these bush men; what a lot. You have to take care.' He waves his hand at Brimah. 'Off with you.'

Old Brimah picks up his stick, gourd and bundle and calmly departs.

Falla bursts into cries of protest, but no one pays any attention to her. Waziri speaks a few words to Aliu, who then says to Bamu, 'You must stay with your husband, Bamu. He is a good man and it is your duty to take care of him.'

Bamu begins to unpack. Falla goes grumbling into the house. Johnson thanks Waziri with low bows and many handshakes. Saleh thoughtfully picks his face, and looks suspiciously at the fragments, as if at some treachery of nature.

Waziri and Saleh then depart. Falla rushes out and screams at the brother, 'What is that for—there's no sense?'

118

Aliu, picking up his stick and water gourd, shrugs, and answers with the sullen face of a private person worsted in conflict with official subtlety, 'It's Waziri.'

'Why do you listen to him?'

'He says the white man Mr. Rudbeck may come back.'

'How could he come back? He's done for.'

'God knows.' Another shrug. 'But that's what Waziri says. Oh, I suppose he's up to something. It's their job, those ones.'

He departs, much cast down.

Johnson is left in the highest spirits, thanks Bamu a thousand times for her loving goodness, and tells her that she is the most beautiful, the most intelligent, the most loyal and loving wife in Fada.

Bamu and Falla listen to this with the bored faces of attendants in lunatic asylums. They know perfectly well their own value and position. But Johnson, since he believes every word as soon as he invents it, grows more affectionate and more happy every moment.

He sends to Ajali for a bottle of gin and invites him to join in the celebration of his happy marriage. The gin is refused, but Ajali, out of curiosity, Benjamin, out of the fascination which Johnson always has for him, both come to the house. Benjamin, since his own sudden lapse at the Post Office, is still more correct and formal in dress. But he seems to grow more and more surprised at some thing or perhaps everything. He says to Johnson, 'It is very unjust for you to lose your job, but perhaps it is lucky. If you go for a labourer, they seem to enjoy life. They are so free from worrying about the bad condition of everything. Yes, and not about themselves too. The secret of enjoyment. Perhaps you think you waste your time if you go for a common labourer. I think so too. It would prevent all the enjoyment.'

'Yes, I waste my time—I waste everything. I go make money now.'

'How do you do so, Johnson?' Ajali asks with an easy condescension. He drops the 'mister' and his yellow face is full of that special joy which bored and self-centred people feel in the misfortunes of another; a mixture of self-satisfaction and pure nervous cruelty.

'I go trade in kola nuts.'

Ajali laughs. 'What, how you trade? You got no money. How much money you got to buy you nuts, Johnson?'

119

'I going to ask you, Mister Ajali, perhaps you join with me—we trade together. I go south and buy nuts.'

Ajali laughs heartily and says, 'What, I give all de money—you do all de trade?'

'I think that's a good idea,' Benjamin says; 'then you go about the country, see many people. Yes, that's what I would do if I lost my job. Yes, I would do so.'

Benjamin is quite animated. Goodness knows what ideas or rather feelings of adventure are stirring in his mind.

'I tell you, Johnson, what you do—you go for a small boy to Sergeant Gollup at the store.'

'But Mister Ajali, could I be small boy? How I live on four shilling a week? I got make some money.'

Ajali laughs. He is delighted by his suggestion. 'Yes, you come to store—I ask Sergeant Gollup. Perhaps he let you sweep de floor, wash his mammy's cloes. He pay six shilling a week.'

Johnson is at once full of new ideas. He sees himself clerk, the chief clerk and partner in the Fada store. He says, 'Thank you, Mister Ajali— dat's a good idea. I'll tell Sargy Gollup if he fit to pay me five poun' a month I fit to be his clerk.'

'Clerk?' Ajali cries. 'He no want another clerk. He wants a small boy.'

But when Johnson offers himself at the store next morning as a clerk, Gollup at once engages him, at two pounds a month. Trade in the store has been increasing fast, thanks to the new road, and Gollup sometimes finds himself compelled to serve at the counter. He considers this task beneath the dignity of a white man and is glad to set Johnson to it, at a cook's wage with a weekly deduction until Johnson's store debts are paid.

Johnson therefore moves home to a shack behind the store and sells everyday, cloth, knives, salt, cigarettes, tea, kerosene, sugar, clocks and beads to the Fada pagans; or buys hides by the weight.

His duties include sweeping the store, flattering Ajali and listening to Gollup's stories. Also he is obliged to bribe Gollup's woman, Matumbi, for otherwise, as Ajali warns him, she will accuse him to Gollup of trying to seduce her.

'De las' second clerk, she say he pinch her—Sargy come out with wooden hammer break his head, kick his ribs, break four teeth down his troat, trow him in de river, and every time he come up he shoot at him with a gun.'

Johnson opens his eyes. 'How much you give Matumbi?'

'If she ask a shilling, I give her sixpence—if she ask big tin of jam, I give her small tin sardine.'

'How often she ask you?'

'Tree-four times a week.'

'But how I do so, Ajali—for two poun's a month?'

Ajali makes a superior face and answers, 'I don't know, Johnson, how you do. I do like this.' He then goes to the petty cash drawer, fixed under the counter, opens it with a key, takes out a shilling and spins it in the air. 'I do so, Johnson.'

'You tief de petty cash?' Johnson cries, laughing and rounding his eyes.

'I tief de petty cash.'

'Aren't you 'fraid, Ajali—aren't you 'fraid for Sargy Gollup?'

'I no care for Sargy Gollup.'

'He no count dat money?'

'He count him every Sunday. But he pay all tings from dat box, beer, yams, cuku. He tink he remember how much he spend. When he find one shilling two shilling short, he tink he count wrong.'

Johnson is not surprised. He has seen political officers manage their accounts by the same method; paying their bills from the safe, balancing the cash book each week, and writing off the weekly debit from their personal allowance.

'But de key, Ajali?'

Ajali gives a superior smile, half-closing his eyes, and holds up a piece of flattened wire, bent at right angles, with a small loop soldered to the angle; a native-made key.

Johnson roars with laughter. 'Mister Ajali, I tink you too clever for dat Gollup.'

'I tink so, Johnson.' Ajali, in the admiration of Johnson, looks a foot taller. The effect is partly due to his half-closing his eyes and bending his head back so that he can look downwards at his assistant.

'I tink I get key like dat, Ajali.'

'You better be careful, Johnson. Suppose Sargy catch you, he kill you for sure.'

Johnson sees his mistake and returns to flattery. 'I never tink you dare to tief from de Sargy, Ajali.'

'I don' care for dat Gollup.'

But just then the Sergeant's voice is heard in the compound and instantly the two clerks dart to their places behind the counter.

Sergeant Gollup is a little man with a pale, lumpy face, a black moustache waxed at the points and round blue eyes. He is an old soldier. He parts his black hair down the middle, shaves carefully, and wears every day clean clothes, but not always in orthodox form. For instance, he will inspect his store and compounds in cotton drawers, a spotless singlet, a white linen coat, pale blue socks with green suspenders and white canvas shoes. He will go to bed in drawers and take an afternoon stroll in purple and green pyjamas, or he appears on the wharf in nothing but a pair of beautiful white trousers, carefully creased.

His store and compounds are kept as spotless as himself. Each path in the station is outlined with whitewashed stones and no stone is allowed out of place. But Gollup, like many old soldiers of the British Army, is not at all rigid in his ideas. He likes order, but it is his own order. He is a first-class trader, but he conducts trade by his own methods. For instance, when he gives presents in a village with which he seeks business, he does not give a big one to the chief, but many little ones to the people. He declares that he has doubled his turnover on a few bags of strong peppermint.

Gollup has built a fine store and a good trade. He struts about like a little king and when sometimes he looks round from his back stoop at the swept earth, the bright alleys, the new thatched roofs, all glittering in the sun, he purses up his lips in what is too dignified to be a grin of satisfaction. At such a moment the two points of his moustache rise as if presenting arms, and when he steps off on the left foot, he hollows his back like a guardee.

Gollup has an easy condescension to all the world, and just as, from the height of his military rank and native genius, he despises ordinary trader's and tailor's conventions, so also he refuses to condescend with the African sun. He scorns all topees, terais and sun hats and wears always, if he doesn't go bareheaded, a soft pearl-grey hat with a curled brim, which always looks new. 'Damn your old sun 'ats,' he says. 'Lot of stuff they talk. A real old coaster don't give a damn for the sun—and they're not the ones that fill the 'ospitals.'

Gollup, in fact, has had only three sunstrokes, and none of them has quite killed him. He is only inclined to lose his temper suddenly and violently, and to run a high temperature upon the least touch of fever.

He is precise and polite in all his dealings with clerks, labourers and servants; but impatient with slow ones. Stupidity causes him to lose his temper and then he is ready to use his fists or his feet, or any weapon to hand. Johnson, on his first day, is surprised to see the gentlemanly Ajali receive a tremendous kick in the backside for failing to understand that 'Over there on the right, you silly bawstard' really means 'On the left, four shelves from the bottom.'

He does not see any more kicks, because Gollup, having given this one with an unexpected power and dexterity which moves Ajali visibly into the air and causes him to utter a loud squeal, turns suddenly to Johnson and says, 'You didn't see anything, did you?'

'What, sah?'

'You didn't see anything 'appen just then—to Ajali's trousers? Because if you did, you better not. See. Unless you want something to 'appen to your trousers, only more so.'

'Oh, yes, sah. I see, sah.'

'No, you silly baboon—you didn't see. See?'

'No, I didn't see, Mister Gollup.'

'That's it. You don't see and you take bleeding good care not to see. neither. I know the law as well as you do, Mr. Monkeybrand.'

'Oh, yes, sah—I see, sah.'

Gollup turns upon him sharply and bawls, 'Oh, you do, do you? All right.' He swings up his fist.

'Oh, no, sah. I don't see.'

'Oh, you do see now—see—you see that you don't see. So that's all right.'

Gollup, pleased with the last joke, smiles, strokes his moustache and opening his mouth to show, unexpectedly, broken and blackened teeth utters a short laugh, 'Hawhaw.'

Johnson, seeing the joke, laughs heartily and both laugh together. Gollup then claps Johnson on the shoulder and says, 'I can see one thing—you got your 'ead screwed on—you and me's going to 'gree for each other. And all the better for you, see? I'm a good massa to the right uns. You stand by me and I'll stand by you.'

Nevertheless, half an hour later, when Johnson in the midst of some plan to make his fortune and buy Bamu a real diamond watch out of a store catalogue, buys a hide full of worm holes at the price of a sound one, Gollup sets up a scream, rushes at him and gives him a punch on the nose which jerks the boy's head backwards like a punching ball.

Johnson, his head swimming, his nose pouring blood, then sees the blue eyes glaring into his and hears Gollup say, 'I didn't touch you, did I?'

'No, sah.'

'I didn't go near you, did I?'

'No, sah.'

'I was in the next room, wasn't I, when it happened?'

'Yes, sah, in de nex' room.'

'What 'appened to you then?'

'I don't know, sah.'

'Yes, wot 'appened? Spit it out.'

'My face got a blow.'

'Wot?' raising his fist again.

'No, sah, I don't know.'

'A haccident—you see—that was a haccident. You got a haccident to your nose.'

'Yes, sah, an accident.'

'All right, you remember that, young fellermelad, or you'll get such a norrible haccident as you won't be no more good to your mammy than the backside of a billiard ball.'

But the same evening he presents Johnson with half a bottle of trade gin, slightly watered, and an old shirt. He likes Johnson, and Johnson likes Gollup because he perceives this liking. Of course, immediately after a punch or a kick he is murderous, but he forgets his injuries within half an hour in the ordinary course of his imagination, perpetually inventing something or other, and Gollup never reminds him of them. Gollup simply overlooks them. Five minutes after punching the boy in the face or mouth, he will come back in excellent humour and say, 'Johnson, old chap, get me a pot of that ginger—Matumbi 'as a fancy for something 'ot—'ot to the 'ot, as you might say.'

Johnson, still running with blood, will climb the shelves to get the pot and Gollup, taking it away, will say as thanks, 'Haw-haw, your mouf had a real misfortune, I see—regular bit of bad luck. I should put it in a bucket if I were you—or use the *bafu* if the bucket ain't big enough.'

'Trouble with me,' Gollup tells Johnson one afternoon. 'I'm too 'asty and I knows 'ow to do it—I used ter know Gipsy Joe w'en I was a kid and 'e taught me 'ow to do it. W'y, I b'lieve I could punch an 'ole in a boiler-plate if I was real annoyed. So w'en you see me coming next time, just take your frying pan out of the way. I don' want to kill you ole chap, 'cause I 'gree for you too much. You're a good kind for a, nigger, and I ought to know. I've known enough niggers by now, all sorts and both kinds, and I always say they aren't 'arf as black as they look if you treat 'em right. Naow, and some of the real hugly ones like yourself, the real wogs, isn't the worst, neither. That yellow Ajali, for instance—I wouldn't trust the bawstard farther than I could kick him. 'E's afraid of me, the cur. Can't look a man in the face. A chap may be a nigger—that's the way Gawd made 'em—same as 'e made wart-hogs and blue-faced baboons—'e can't 'elp being a nigger—but 'e can 'elp being a man. Wot I like about you, Wog, is you aren't afraid of me.'

'No, sah,' Johnson would exclaim proudly. 'I'm not afraid of anybody.'

'Nah, nah, don't blow off; that's the way you nigs always goes on—you got no sense. W'y, I wouldn't say that myself; it'd be stupid, because, look 'ere, Johnson, suppose you say you ain't afraid of any-body and someone comes and knocks your block off; w'y, you look a bloody fool. But, suppose you know a bit, like me, for instance, and knock 'is block off, then that's all there is to it. But look 'ere, w'y, suppose you didn't blow off, suppose you didn't say about being up to anybody and then you knock 'is block off; w'y, it's a bloomin' wonder. It's a surprise, see? That's the game, see?'

Gollup is a believer in routine. He is punctual to the minute; six o'clock in the store; seven, breakfast; eight, store; twelve, lunch; two to four, sleep; four to five, smart walk; six, drinks; seven, dinner, and between eight and nine, drinks again; ten, to bed with Matumbi on the mat beside him. On week-days, he is never more than half-drunk by bedtime and if he beats Matumbi, he uses only his feet or fists. On Sunday, with a special routine throughout, he is always roaring drunk at six, mad drunk and murderous in the evening, and dead drunk before midnight. On these days, he will sometimes thrash Matumbi with a stick, flog her or even batter her with a chair until she lies on the floor covered with blood, and the terrified boys expect to find her dead. In fact, she has suffered no more, in four years of Sundays, than a broken arm, a split ear, and a few deep scars. Matumbi, like Johnson, has a strong affection for Gollup. She is a huge, lumbering woman, dimpled all over in her soft fat. She is as soft and heavy as pease-pudding in a bag. Her face is so ugly that the labourers say, 'Some cow must have walked on it.' Her nose is as wide as her enormous mouth and its nostrils are turned outwards like two oven mouths. One of her eyes is almost closed. She has a sway back, great overhanging knees and long heels like a hen.

She is boundlessly greedy and lazy; she will not even scratch herself if she can get the small boy to do it. Her virtue is good humour. She will sit for hours apparently thinking of nothing, with a smile so good-natured that nobody can see it without feeling relief and comfort. Only Ajali hates Matumbi's smile, saying, 'Why she smile? She big fool to smile—I tink Sargy go beat her again nex' week. I tink she soon too old, he turn her out like rubbish. She don' smile den. I tink dem hyænas eat her like other old-woman rubbish.'

Ajali is obviously disgusted that Matumbi doesn't realize the insecurity of her comforts. He is like those others who, vaguely dis-satisfied or frightened within themselves, hate everyone else who seems happy or confident in the same circumstances. So poor people often hate other poor people much more than the rich; saying, 'It's a shame if So-and-So gets away with it—the way he goes on.' In fact, all people who think in terms of justice are apt to be spiteful and wretched. Even if they do not seem wretched, like Ajali, it is only because they do not know how much they have been wasted by boredom and loneliness and selfishness until they have become a new kind of creature, a sort of subhumanity which can smile and eat and live at a level of corruption and misery which would kill a real human being in a day or two.

Ajali hates Matumbi for her happiness, but he is always polite to her; she has a vindictive temper. It is not safe to refuse her anything she asks for. Like other lazy, greedy people, without much thought for themselves, she is reckless when crossed. She doesn't care what lies she screams in order to punish another for giving her the least trouble. Yet she is generous, she is the prey of all beggars; and she will even walk a short distance in order to intercede for a friend.

On Sunday mornings Matumbi has herself washed and oiled, and puts on her best cloth. A stranger seeing her smile on these mornings and smelling her scent would think that she was a bride preparing for her lover. In fact, she is always in the highest spirits on Sundays, because she knows that Gollup, as soon as he has finished his

126

afternoon sleep, will begin bawling from his little room behind the store, 'Where's that bitch, Matumbi? Hi, Johnson, where's that nigger Wog?'

Johnson jumps up smiling. He knows that 'wog' is a term of affection, and he is looking forward, like Matumbi, to the evening, which is always interesting and often exciting.

Gollup meanwhile comes out into the afternoon sun in a clean pair of cotton drawers and vest, the pearl-grey felt hat and slippers. There he stands for a few moments, slapping himself on the chest, bending his knees, shooting out his arms and admiring his own energy. Then he strolls round the huts in his first Sunday mood of humorous and truculent good nature. He will slap a labourer on the back with a noise like a pistol shot and laugh to see the man jump, saying, 'Hello, ole Haji' or 'Cheerio, young Ali' with such obvious good intention that the man will usually smile and bob. If he does not, Gollup will only be amused and call out, ' 'E's 'urt in 'is feelings; 'ow 'aughty we are to-day.'

He then takes Matumbi, Johnson and perhaps a headman or two into the bungalow and gives them all gin. After the first gin, he passes by degrees into the poetic and sentimental mood.

He takes Matumbi on his knee, where she perches smiling proudly and joyfully with her enormous arm round his neck. Her expression, with her smile and little screwed-up eyes, is exactly like that of a plain fat little girl delighting in a kind papa.

Gollup meanwhile talks to Johnson about his life, his home, even his wife and children. At first he is dignified. He describes his house in a London suburb, the beauty of the bathroom and the garden; the ornaments and even the carpets.

'I paid fourteen pound for the drawing-room carpet, but there, you don't even know wot a drawing-room is.'

'Oh, yas, Sargy, it's at home in England where you sit when you finish you chop.'

'Home. Haw, haw. Scuse me, Wog—always makes me laugh to ear a nig talk of England as 'ome w'en he never see so much as a real chimney pot.'

'Oh, sah, but I true Englishman for my heart.'

'You're quite right, Wog. And never mind wot they say. You got the guts even though you 'aven't the physique. 'Ere, drink up and forget your face. You can't see it, any'ow.'

127

But a little later, Gollup forgets some of his dignity. He describe how lucky he was to marry his wife Gladys, who was the daughter of a high-class tailor; what a beautiful and good girl she was, and how she forgave him when he got drunk on the honeymoon.

'Oh, yes,' Johnson cries. 'My wife, too, she mos' kind, loving wife in de whole worl'. When I lose my job, she say only, "I stay for you now make you happy." '

Johnson is carried away, not merely by friendship, but by something in the air, the exciting sympathetic spirit of the occasion which is like a real party, a drum party. This, of course, is what is delightful to Matumbi and Johnson in Gollup's Sundays and in Gollup himself. When he is drunk, he becomes of their own kind; he ceases to calculate and to reason; he wants to sing, to love, to talk and to tell stories; and above all, to make a certain kind of situation, romantic and exciting, in which he can live and feel more intensely. All drunk men at a certain stage of release have this desire, to create some extraordinary impression. They lose their timid fears of ridicule or criticism. They pour out their secret thoughts and innocently reveal themselves as philosophers, dreamers, saints and poets. Gollup is all four. In that exciting atmosphere of gin and poetic sympathy which belongs only to artists and drink parties, Gollup and Johnson often pursue their own creations simultaneously.

'Oh, when I tink of my dear good wife Bamu, how she say, I you wife, Mister Johnson, I fit to go with you always for richer or poorer——'

'The angel in the 'ouse—that's a real angel too. The light of the 'ousehold—making little 'eavens—and oo wants your bloody trumpets.'

'For sickness or healt', till deat' do us part.'

'You can't beat a woman's 'eart,' Gollup says.

Matumbi, feeling Gollup's enthusiasm, smiles affectionately and lays her enormous cheek on the top of his bristling head. He pays no attention whatever, but continues to develop his theme.

'And she's not one of the churchy ones, either—it's all 'er own—out of 'er nature.'

'No, my Bamu too—she laff at dem churches, she say, "Dis lil house my church, dis baby my boy to sing, here in my bress he drink dem god's wine." '

'Of course, it's their job. It's wot they was made for. But my Glad as made a proper good job of 'erself.'

'I tink all dem women have too good Christian hearts—dem born Christian.' Johnson gazes into the air, smiling broadly at his vision of the perfect woman.

'And my little Bobby, that's me eldest, height years old—you'd think he was a prince to look at 'im.'

'I tink he be a prince one day.'

'A prince—'e's better than any prince—and clever.' Gollup begins to tell a story about his son who has solved a problem in geometry that was too much for his own schoolmaster, 'oo's an Oxford professor.'

'Oh, sah, I tink he'll be a judge.'

'Judge be damned. Gladys and me, we always said we'd make an officer of Bobby—the Army, that's the job—the finest job in the world for a real man.'

'Oh, sah, I tink he be a general with a gold sword; I tink he be a duke all same prince stan' beside de king at pallement, marry dem princess.'

But Gollup, in a loud sing-song voice, is saying at the same time, 'Damn all the brass 'ats—Bobby'll stick to 'is regiment, or I'll know the reason w'y. That's a real life, that is, not a lot of bits and pieces. I'd sooner see 'im dead than doing that prance—sucking up to the millionaires and the noospapers. We get too much of that already. Yess. That's wot's the trouble with old England. You can't 'ave guts and money—they don't go in the same bag.'

Gollup has the usual hatred of the old soldier for the rich and their women, and in fact for all those who live easy and self-indulgent lives without risk or responsibility, that hatred which has made all countries with conscription inclined to violent revolution. Gollup regards the rich, in some mysterious way, as parasites on the soldiers and especially on his own officers, of whom he speaks, in comparison, with the deepest sympathy.

'Pore ole colonel on 'is 'arf pay, scraping along in some bloody 'ole on sixpence a week to screw out a education for 'is grandson so's to make a soldier of 'im too—offering 'is whole life to the country, and wot's the country done for 'im?'

'Poor Mister Rudbeck, make dem great road—greates' road in Africa, and den dat Treasurer, who got all dem millions of gold——'

'I tell you, Wog, 'e was the finest man in England, and is still. The finest and the greatest. The colonel of a first-class regiment—you don't see 'is picture in the snob rags. That's the sort the old Empire stands on—and I wouldn't change one of 'em for forty bleeding lords with oh de colon on their back 'air nor a 'undred millionaires. If God wills, Bobby'll be the colonel of the old regiment, and, mark my words, it's not a job God would give to any of your bloody Harchbishops. He picks 'is colonels careful—he knows wot depends on 'em. You look at our battle honours, from Talavera to the Somme—there isn't a country in the world where we 'aven't laid down our lives for the Empire, and that's for you, Wog, for freedom—the Empire of the free were the sun of justice never sets. Yess and will again wen they're wanted.'

'I tink some day we English people make freedom for all de worl'—make dem new motor roads, make dem good schools for all people—den all de people learn book, learn to 'gree for each other, make plenty chop.'

'Wot do we care if the school marms get in their dig wen there ain't no danger? Pore things, wot do they know about anything in the real world?'

'I tink all people be rich, dey be too happy together dey sing every day, make play——'

Half an hour later Gollup is in a melancholy mood. 'It's the hexile—you chaps don' know wot the Empire costs us——'

'Oh, sah, dem millions and millions of gold——'

'I ain't complaining—it's a duty laid down upon us by God—but the Pax Britannia takes a bit of keeping up—with 'arf the world full of savages and 'arf the other 'arf just getting in the way.'

Ten minutes later, he is astonished at his own sufferings. 'You don't know wot it is to leave your children—talk of hagony——'

'Oh, sah, I too sad for you.'

Gollup screws up his face like a child with some bitter medicine in his mouth and makes a peculiar noise at the back of his nose, like a sheep coughing. This is his form of a sob.

'Heugh—hew—worse than 'ell.'

'Oh, sah, I too—when I go away from my little baby—I feel my heart all burst—I say I fit to die soon. Only if I die, what happens to my poor Bamu and my little son?'

'It isn't a life, it's a bloody sacrifice. I ain't complaining. But you don' know wot it costs us, you nigs, to tidy up things for you—you ain't got the same feelings.'

'Oh, yes, sah—I feel it too—I too sad for you.'

'Wot the 'ell you grinning at, you?' This is spoken to Matumbi, who has caught Gollup's wandering eye. Matumbi, having smiled with Gollup's smiles, sympathized with his enthusiasm, is now shaking her head and grinning with his grief. At his sudden yell, she looks foolish and astonished.

Matumbi never seems to learn that Gollup's mood, on Sunday evenings, is likely to take a bad turn. She joyfully prepares herself, every Sunday, for a feast day, apparently without the least recollection that two out of four Sundays end in a beating for her.

'What?' she says, gazing at Gollup with a face like a blancmange just dissolving into its liquid form. 'What is it?'

Gollup thrusts out his jaw so that his moustaches rise up like bayonets and says slowly, 'You dirty——'

Matumbi, still more confused and alarmed, smiles with the foolish grin of innocence and at once receives a tremendous punch in the face which knocks her backwards on the floor.

She then begins to make a noise like three or four women and several men—bass, baritone, falsetto—abusing Gollup, asking for mercy, complaining and apologizing with yells, howls, moans and sudden piercing cries, while Gollup beats and kicks her.

Johnson meanwhile tries to prevent him from killing the woman, and to give her a chance of escape. In the course of six or seven fights he has taken out of Gollup's hands such weapons as bottles, jugs, clubs, chairs and received dozens of blows meant to smash Matumbi's skull or face. But the blows are accidental. Gollup, even in the most violent rage, never turns on Johnson. His only idea is to kill Matumbi.

The next day, of course, he is once more on good terms with the woman, who demands compensation and takes almost what she likes. Moreover, he bears not the least malice against Johnson for hearing his confessions and seeing him drunk. He meets him next morning with his usual greeting, 'How is it this morning, Johnson?'

'Very good, sah, tank you. I feel mos' well.'

'That's the style.' Gollup himself, in spite of greenish cheeks and sunken eyes, is brisk and lively. 'That's the lad—don't let it get you down. Keep it on the run.'

He has the air of one who has just defeated a dangerous enemy. In fact, Gollup always seems like an old soldier on campaign in enemy country; watchful, suspicious, enterprising, always on the alert, always in fighting trim; not too punctilious, scornful of convention; but, for all his good nature, ferocious and ready at any moment for any kind of violence.

Although Gollup has a corroboree every Sunday night, he doesn't allow drumming or drinking in his compounds. He objects to any lack of decorum on the sacred ground of the store. On the other hand, he approves of drinking. As he says, 'A chap needs a good drunk about once a week same as he needs exercise. That's wot's wrong with some of these teetotal mishes—they get fat on the brain.' He often gives the wharf labourers and store-men ten shillings to go and make a party in the town; on religious anniversaries, like the King's birthday, Easter, Empire Day, the Derby and Christmas, he often gives them a pound and strictly charges them to drink every penny of it. A pound's worth of Fada beer is equivalent to a hundred gallons of strong beer. Among forty men it is enough for a two day's party and a week's headache. It is not surprising that Gollup can choose his men and has the best gang on the river.

Johnson, before he knows Gollup's rule, gives his usual party in his compound on pay day. For this he receives a black eye and a split nose, and several of his important guests are kicked half-way home to Fada.

Johnson gives his next party in the town and invites the labourers as well as townspeople. He wishes to eclipse and make forgotten the shame of the first failure. He persuades even Waziri to come, by giving young Saleh a new looking-glass smuggled out from under Gollup's very nose in the seat of his trousers.

Johnson has drums, strings and two gramophones playing at once, gin for all the greater guests, the best impromptu singer and story-teller in Fada.

The party is a success. About one o'clock, when the first reserve of the guests has worn off and several have already thrown away their clothes, visitors begin to arrive, self-asked, with those shining eyes and broad anticipating smiles which show, in Africa, that the news of some extraordinary entertainment has spread through the town. These visitors, though perfectly sober, behave with far more abandon than any of the invited guests; they begin at once to shout, dance, sing and roar with laughter. They are like men born rich who from the beginning of their lives have a different standard of pleasure. At two, the party can be heard two miles away. Tring has sent an orderly to the Waziri protesting against the drums; but the Waziri, very drunk and without his turban, is tearfully pursuing Saleh through the compounds. Saleh, who now carries his left hand in henna, occasionally turns and hits the old man over his bald head with the wooden cylinder. In the outer compounds seven pagan labourers from the same tribe are performing a marriage dance with twelve women of all ages from twelve to sixty. All except the young girls are in a state of possession, blind, deaf and anæsthetic. Their screams and leaps make everyone laugh, while they themselves do not know probably even what they are doing.

Johnson walks through the crowd in his best white suit, new patent leathers, and a pearl-grey felt hat, exactly like Gollup's, on the side of his head. His face shines with sweat and his mouth is spread perpetually in an enormous grin. Every moment he shouts out some joke, some greeting, takes a step with the dancers, miming their leaps, throws a ball for the juggler or, all by himself, makes a little song and dance expressing some impulse of delight, pride or hospitable affection for mankind.

Ajali and Benjamin follow him everywhere. Ajali follows closely, thrusting his long chin over his shoulder, spluttering in his eye; Benjamin, wearing his stiff party collar and very long cuffs, has more dignity. He never moves with Johnson. When Johnson suddenly swaggers across the floor among the leaping, frenzied dancers in their erotic agony, to greet a new friend, Benjamin remains in his usual attitude of meditative distraction; his chin in the air, his eyelids half closed. But a moment later, as if upon some independent errand, he stalks thoughtfully in the same direction as Johnson, and takes up his stand within a yard or so. This movement of Benjamin is unconscious. He has no idea that he is the dependent spirit. On the contrary, he thinks of Johnson with gentle condescension.

'Very savage people,' he says to Johnson, looking at the dancers. 'But I think these people enjoy themselves greatly.'

Johnson suddenly crouches down like the dancers, wriggles and skips in that position; then jerks himself three feet into the air, bent backwards at almost a right-angle, with a scream even louder than the old ladies.

133

'How can you do so, Johnson? You seem so foolish in your English clothes.'

Johnson laughs and sings with the dancers, improvising:

'What you 'fraid of, little woman, hiding for bush.
I got no stick, no knife.'

Ajali thrusts his crab eyes and sloping yellow forehead almost into Johnson's chin. He roars with laughter and says, 'You give big party, Johnson.'

'Yes, I tink dis pretty good party.'

'How much you pay for dis party, Johnson?'

'Oh, I don't know—perhaps five poun'.'

'Five poun'?' Ajali roars with laughter and his eyes glitter with jealous rage. 'Have you got five poun'?'

'Oh, I gettum,' Johnson says, smiling, and he makes another crawl and leap. 'I got a little wife, round like de worl'.'

'You tink you tief fife poun' from Mister Gollup.'

'Oh, I gettum. She smooth like de water, she shine like de sky.'

'Mr. Gollup is an illegal man,' Benjamin says gravely. 'I advise you look out for him, Johnson.'

'How you nose feel, Johnson?' Ajali cries.

'She fat like de corn, she smell like de new grass.
She dance like de tree, she shake like de new leaves.'

Ajali turns round, laughing and drunk with his jealous excitement and shouts, 'Mister Gollup hits Johnson on the nose.'

'A very illegal man.' Benjamin sighs. 'But then he is not a gentleman.'

'She warm like de ground,' Johnson sings, crouching and touching the warm earth. 'She deep like de bush,' with a leap.

'You no frien' of Mister Gollup, Johnson,' says Ajali, thrusting his face up.

'How dee, little Bamu, I see you dar hiding.'

'Johnson say he frien' of Mister Gollup,' Ajali cries, turning to the crowd. 'Mister Gollup hits him on de nose, kicks him in de bottom every day.'

'How dee lil girl, I come catch you dar.'

'You no 'fraid of Mister Gollup, Johnson?'

Johnson cocks up his head, thrusts out his leg in a grand pose and says, 'I no 'fraid of him, Mister Ajali—I no 'fraid of nutting at all.'

Benjamin looks thoughtfully at his friend, 'But suppose he knock out your eye or break your stomach, Johnson, what good is that? He does not care at all. He has no education. I think you better be careful of a man like Mister Gollup—it is all simply stupid and senseless if a savage man like that can spoil your good health. For then you are done for.'

'Oh, no, Johnson no 'fraid no nutting,' Ajali cries. He turns round and shouts at the crowd, 'Johnson don't fear anyone in the world.'

'No, nutting.' Johnson wags his head to the music and bends his knees. 'Johnson got de big heart. He no 'fraid of nutting.'

Then, springing up and throwing out his arms:

> *'Johnson got a sojer heart, strong like a motor.*
> *He beat the war drums in his bress, poom, poom.'*

Crouching and weaving with his long arms like a boxer, he dances round the compound, shadow-boxing with imaginary enemies:

> *'What fool chile stand in de way of Johnson?*
> *What fool chile dis in Johnson's road?*
> *Out of the way, fool chile; when Johnson go walkum*
> *The whole worl' make path for him, all same for de lions of de forest*
> *De whole sea go dry for him all same dat King Moses from Egypt.*
> *De whole sky make light for him, all same de fire for Moses.*
> *De whole forest bow down for him, same for Mister Rudbeck's road*
> *Out of my way, fool chile, if you don' want to die.*
> *My eye burn you up all same sacrifice.*
> *My wind blow you down all same tornado.*
> *My feet walk you dead all same elephant.*
> *What, who dare say Mister Johnson 'fraid?*
> *Johnson say, what dat mean dat word 'fraid?*
> *What dat mean, 'fraid? Is it good to eat?*
> *Is it like a man's leg when I bite it off?*
> *Is it good to drink? Is it like a man's blood*
> *When I drink it up?*
> *What you mean, 'fraid. Show me some 'fraid.*
> *I don't know nutting about 'fraid. I tink he be ole savage word.'*

This song becomes even more celebrated than the song of Bamu. It is repeated with new variations at many beer parties. Since a Fada man, like most primitives, looks upon the making of free verse as part of ordinary conversation, and, like an Elizabethan or an Irishman, uses the most poetical expression even in casual talk by the road; since, therefore, songs in Fada are in continual production by every member of the public from two to eighty, they are not carefully recorded. A party which calls upon Johnson for the song of Bamu, or the song of the drum beat, does not expect the same words, but only an improvisation in the same theme. What's more, almost everyone who hears the song at once begins to improvise variations of his own and apply them to other circumstances. The drum beat, which is the idea most catching, becomes part of the popular imagination. Johnson, himself hearing the song about a warrior, does not know himself the author of the idea and joins in the chorus without sense of artistic jealousy.

> *'Big heart got a war drum in his chest. Poom, poom.*
> *To call his army for the war.'*

Johnson attends many parties at this time because he is not only a renowned singer, but he is also very rich. He has now perfected his method of trading. He buys hides for himself in the compound and then sells them to himself in the store, through his boy. For these hides he pays always top prices. Once or twice Gollup protests against the prices with a punch or a kick; but since Gollup himself is making 50 or 100 per cent., he is not a skin-flint. Also he grows more and more fond of Johnson. On Sunday night now, in his first sentimental mood, while he squeezes Matumbi, he will cry out, 'I 'gree for you, Johnson. You the best little nig I ever knew. It's not saying a lot, but I mean it. That's what I mean, I mean it. I like you because you're honest and because you know your place, and because you're a friendly little bawsted, too, and I like a chap who ain't afraid of me. 'Ere's to you. nig Wog; your face may be a bit of a mistake and you ain't got much to talk about in the short ribs, your nose is no good to me, a chap might as well scratch his knuckles with indiarubber. but you got some guts. I'll give you that. You ain't afraid of me, are you?'

'No, sah, I'm not afraid of you.'

'And you never was, neither—came up smiling first time.'

'No, sah, I never fear you, sah—I got a big heart.'

'Yah, I'll say so—I still remember the first kiss on the smeller I give you—just got you coming up—it was as nice a bit of timing as ever I engineered—damn near broke your bloody neck.'

'Yes, sah, he good strong blow. But I didn't care—I just laugh at you knocking me.'

'Struth, and so you do too.' Gazing at Johnson with his blue eyes, 'I say, you're too good for a nig, Johnson—ah, it's a pity—you ought to bin born one of the 'igher races, wot got the hintelligence too. You got the nature, but you ain't got the hintelligence.'

'I no 'fraid of nutting in de worl',' Johnson says.

'Struth, I don't believe you are; no, struth, I 'gree for you, Johnson. I'd raise you if the company could stand it.'

The next night Gollup has an engagement. He has gone out with Tring to find a lion. For some time, Tring, who knows that Gollup has shot several lions in Fada, has been asking him to organize a lion hunt. Tring is very anxious to shoot a lion on his first visit to the bush, because, as he says, 'You never know when you'll get another chance.' It is as though this very junior officer does not expect to return to a bush station. Meanwhile, he wants to squeeze from the bush all that it is capable of yielding to an ambitious young man, including a lion.

Gollup does not like political officers, whom he regards as the natural enemy of all soldiers and rational government, but he has not been able to refuse Tring's polite but firm invitation. He leaves at five o'clock with his old Service rifle, his valise, a load of food and a native hunter, for a village where some lion has lately eaten a woman. His last words to Johnson are, 'Gawd knows wen I'll be back from this party—young Mister Tringaling as got to 'ave 'is cat-skin if it costs me 'arf a week's walky and six week's lumbago. These mammy boys are very obstinate on being 'eroes. All I say is, if I don't come back to-morrow, don't forget to put out the cat's milk—I mean give Matumbi 'er bottle of stuff—and don't 'ave no nonsense with 'er neither—if she comes sneaking in the store, give 'er a bust on the conk. And none of your own games, either—see, young nig? Oh, I know you. All gammon and grins till you think you can get away with it. Well, you can't, see? If you get dipping your blubber in my *barassa* (spirits), I'll knock it through your back 'air, see; and none of your matey parties on my

137

pre-myses, see, or I'll take your tripes out and tie em round your silly neck—see, young nig? You know me and I know you. We've played 'appy families very 'appy, so let's go on in the same 'appy way or by gee I'll alter your domestic arrangements so you 'ave to feed yourself with a bicycle pump and go to by-byes in a 'orse-sling.'

Johnson smiles and cries, 'Oh, Sargy, I take care of everyting too well.' In fact, he takes up a broom at once and begins to sweep the floor. Even after the sergeant is out of sight on the station road, Johnson is still full of zeal and responsibility. He checks the money in the till. He also opens the cash drawer with his private key, checks the balance there and, finding it three shillings short, takes out only three more, for current expenses.

He sends then to invite Benjamin for a quiet evening in his own compound. Afterwards it strikes him that he has not given a party for a long time; four days at least. He invites two policemen, five or six young townsmen, a single drummer and Matumbi. An hour later, by general agreement, he sends for two more drummers, more beer, and more women. Matumbi summons a few of her own kind; a dozen or so barrack girls, who begin to scream like horses or curse like carriers even half a mile from the party.

At half-past eleven, when there are perhaps fifty people in the store compound, making noise enough, since they are mostly from the station and the barracks, for two hundred, a tornado breaks. There is a clap of thunder that shakes the face of the ground, lightning like the explosion of the hot sky; rain like a burst dam. The dancers and singers take cover in the store itself, and Johnson, who sees that the party needs sympathetic encouragement, brings out gin. The party revives, the noise increases. It is impossible to say, at any moment, whether the store is shaken by thunder or the dance; whether the crescendo which makes one feel that the top of one's head is about to split off is rain on the tin roof or kettle drums under the counter; whether the demoniac appearance of the naked dancers, grinning, shrieking, scowling, or with faces which seem entirely dislocated, senseless and unhuman, like twisted bags of lard, or burst bladders, is due to sheet lightning reflected from the river through the front windows, or the success of the party. Johnson feels that it is a success; a triumph. He stands, in his best white suit and pale grey hat, in the middle of the floor under the hurricane lamp, with a serious expression; streaming with sweat as if dissolving in his own warmth of feeling, and opening his mouth now and then to give a yell or whoop, of the same quality and almost the same force and duration as an air-raid syren.

He has just completed one of those long ululations of victory and his face is regaining its look of calm content when the back door from the compounds, behind the counter flap, is burst open, and Gollup, in soaking bush kit, comes whirling in. He is as silent as a bomb. He ducks under the counter flap, takes a leap of six foot into the room and knocks the first man in his way, a huge bargeman, into the drums. He then sees Johnson under the lamp and makes for him like a charging bush bull. There is no time even for Johnson's expression to change before Gollup's fist strikes him in the nose and knocks him heel overhead.

Johnson, as it were instantaneously, is seen resting on the back of his neck with his long, thin legs waving horizontally over his face. The bystanders, spotted with blood from that one blow, are wiping their cheeks as they fling themselves backwards.

Johnson, bewildered and half-stunned, gathers himself up again, slowly rises to his feet, and instantly receives another punch in the nose which causes him to turn another back somersault. This angers him very much, but when he reaches all fours, he stays there, with blood pouring on the floor, and cries, 'I no 'fraid for you, Sargy Gollup.'

'Get up, you bleeding bawstard, get up and let me 'it you a real one.'

'I no 'fraid for you, Sargy Gollup; you no fit to hit me; you go way now.'

'By gee, I'm no fit to 'it you, ain't I. Get up, you filleted 'ore drop and you'll see who's fit.'

Johnson suddenly springs up and leaps at Gollup, with whirling arms and kicking feet. Gollup, amazed, gives a furious punch in the air which misses by several inches. Johnson's knee strikes him in the stomach, his flying fist takes him on the angle of the jaw, and he falls down as flat as a sack. His blue eyes gaze at the ceiling, still with the same amazement, and his right fist clasps and unclasps several times as if feebly rehearsing a series of knockouts. The points of his moustache rise slowly and stiffly like the antennæ of a dying insect. They stick at their highest elevation and the hand slowly relaxes and lies open.

Johnson, who has fallen forward in the violence of his effort, is on hands and knees, peering at his master's upturned nose with horror and incredulity. There is breathless silence.

139

Then screams and yells of terror break out, and every man and woman in the room except the stone-struck Johnson rushes for the door. The store rocks, wood is heard to split, a crushed woman shrieks and rustling steps diminish in all directions. The place is empty. In five minutes the compounds and the nearest ward of the town are empty, and Waziri is galloping up to Tring's house.

Tring, very annoyed by the failure of his lion hunt, and by the noise from the store, appears in pale blue silk pyjamas, frogged with pink. 'What on earth is it, Waziri?'

'Clerk Johnson has killed the merchant Gollup.'

Tring at once blows his whistle, calls the sergeant, pulls on slacks, coat and boots, and comes to the store. It is still lit up. Voices are heard within. Tring, revolver in hand, pushes open the door and sees Gollup sitting upright on the floor and Johnson squatting in front of him. Gollup has one hand on his jaw, the other raised in a prophetic gesture. Both look at Tring with surprise. Gollup then gets up, dusts his knees and says, 'Hexcuse me, Mr. Tring.'

'You aren't murdered then? Did Johnson attack you? Do you want to charge him?'

'No, Mr. Tring. Certainly not. A slight haccident—that's all.'

'So you don't want our assistance?'

'No, sir.' Gollup refuses this intervention with cool dignity.

Tring withdraws. Gollup turns to Johnson and says, 'I don't 'old with washing the company linen in public, and it wouldn't be fair to you, neither, Johnson. I know it was a haccident—you couldn't 'ave done it if you 'ad meant it. But you understand that I can't 'ave that sort of thing 'appen without taking notice. I got to keep discipline 'ere, or where should we be. It was a fracass, whatever you say, and in public too. So I'm afraid I'll 'ave to give you a month in loo. Sorry as I am, Johnson, real sorry, I couldn't 'ave anyone around my store after a breach of discipline even by haccident. I 'gree for you, Johnson, but I got to think of my responsibilities 'ere—got to keep things running. 'Ow much is it? Three pound six and heightpence, less five bob for fines.'

Gollup goes to his safe, pays off Johnson, takes a receipt and tells him to be out of his house before six o'clock in the morning.

'But I'm sorry, old Wog, real sorry—the best nig I've 'ad, and you never was afraid of me.'

'No,' Johnson says mournfully. 'I never was 'fraid of you, Mister Gollup.'

They part with a handshake, and Johnson, taking his lantern and going away, repeats to himself, 'I wasn't 'fraid of him.' He enters Bamu's hut and finds her already sound asleep. He wakes her up and she stares at him with wonder.

Johnson stretches himself up to his full height in the lantern light and says, 'You see dat, Bamu? I knock Mister Gollup down so that he was like dead. And the judge come with the police.'

Bamu shuts her eyes again. Old Sozy creeps to her beloved's feet and pats them.

'You hear, Sozy? I kill that white man.'

'Oh, *da dadi*.'

'Come along, Bamu, my dear. We must pack up.'

Bamu says in a sleepy voice, 'Where are we going?'

'We're going south where all the trade is—we're going to be rich, my dear. You shall have that motor car like a big Lagos lady.'

Bamu says nothing. She gets up and begins to pack her tin box. Sozy grows alarmed and stares at her. She murmurs once or twice, '*Da dadi*.'

'Come on, Sozy—get the kitchen things together.'

Sozy is at once relieved. She knows that she is still needed. She gathers together pots, gourds full of flour and peppers, salt and sugar, the bottle of ground-nut oil, the kerosene, two chickens and bundle of dry sticks.

At dawn there is no trace of Johnson or his family. It is only known that he has taken the southern road.

Tring is not due for leave till December. He finishes his overhaul of the Fada office in August and is just writing a special report on 'The Organization of a Bush Office' when some of the English newspapers, during the holiday season, demand prison reform. In the next three weeks Tring rebuilds the native prison in Fada with separate hut cells for the convicts, photographs them, with some carefully washed prisoners, and sends in a special report on 'Native Prison Organization,' by J. S. Tring. It is afterwards quoted by the Governor in his annual report, and it is discussed at home, where prison reform is still in the newspapers and the air.

Nobody, not even Bulteel, calls Tring an eyewasher, because he is in fact a highly competent officer. He does a good job as well as it can be done. His prison is a model. But he is certainly one of those people who, by a natural and probably unconscious art, can always catch the right eye at the right time. When he applies for early leave, in October, on urgent private affairs, he gets it at once and goes home by the next boat to take a short course on criminology, and to give lantern lectures on 'A New Life for the African Delinquent.'

Tring leaves behind him the certainty, even in native minds, that he will never return to such a bushy place as Fada. He has even bagged his lion. Blore has been invalided. There is no one available for Fada except Rudbeck, who, coming back from leave in November, is therefore sent back to his old division, under a strict injunction from Bulteel to keep his accounts in order.

'Yes. Can't take any chances,' Rudbeck says.

'No, as a family man—did I hear by the way—the M.O. here said something about——' Bulteel looks like a benevolent family doctor.

'Well, it's a bit previous—they're letting her come out.'

Rudbeck has got over his first squeamish delicacy as a married man. He talks of Celia's pregnancy with careless frankness. 'About seven months to go, anyhow—but she seems to be sure about it.'

'My dear boy, I'm very glad.'

'Yes, it's not a bad idea. Same old kuka tree—I thought you were going to root it up.'

Rudbeck is looking out of the window. His voice expresses keen pleasure in recognizing the decayed kuka tree in front of Dorua Residency.

'Yes, it's still there. Glad to be back?'

'I am rather.' Rudbeck looks mildly surprised.

'Well, well, I'm glad to see you. You saw what they said about your road—H. E. gave it a special mention.'

'Yes, but that poodle-faker Tring has cobbled all the funds.'

'Very unfortunate.' Bulteel screws up his thick little lips, then suddenly bursts out, 'It's had the most surprising effect on provincial revenue—most surprising.' His voice is full of wonder and self-satisfaction. Bulteel has read half a dozen reports from Rudbeck urging the road on the grounds that it will improve trade and he has minuted them all 'Mr. Rudbeck's views deserve serious consideration when finances allow of further road expansion. A large increase of local trade might well be expected.'

142

But he is astonished to see that even thirty miles of road, without through connections, has produced a large increase in trade. He is like all those other old officials, who, having written a thousand reports, are as astonished to see one of them take real effect; as if the paper on their desk—say, a warrant for arrest—should cry out and bleed beneath their pen-points.

'Really quite surprising,' he continues, raising his eyebrows. 'Even our market here has almost doubled. It made a very good showing in the annual report.' He utters a chuckle, which makes him turn red, and looks at Rudbeck. 'We even got a pat on the back—first for years. Oh, yes, my stock is looking up.' Then he shakes his head again. 'A real pity we can't go on with it.'

'Trade was there all the time,' Rudbeck says, walking over to the other window and making his bush boots thump on the echoing floor. He is restless, like a man tired of holiday and eager to use his energies. 'Any fool could have seen that.' Then he colours slightly and frowns. He feels that he has said something wrong, but he does not quite know what it is. Bulteel smiles and his eyes disappear again. He is not offended because he knows that Rudbeck's meaning was not 'You were a fool not to see it before,' but 'I do not claim any credit for seeing it first.'

'If we could put it through we'd transform this province.'

'Ah!' Bulteel says. 'That would be very nice—very nice for everybody.' He laughs. 'I should be quite the golden-headed boy.'

'They'll make you a gumna, sir.'

'As long as I've something for the report, I find I get along nicely in poor old Dorua—after all, the clock golf is second to none.'

He chuckles until he is crimson, and Rudbeck grins and frowns at the same time. Suddenly Bulteel becomes serious and remarks, 'All the same, it's a pity.' Obviously he feels that the development of transport would be more interesting than clock golf. 'But where's the money coming from?'

They look at each other. Then Bulteel says, 'You mustn't take any more risks.'

There is a pause. Bulteel remarks with sudden liveliness, 'And how are things at home?'

'The usual bloody mess.'

'Oh, yes, of course, yes—it's bad.' He shakes his head and begins to look serious. 'Extraordinary these slumps—nobody seems to have any idea what to do.'

'Looks as if the whole show is going phut.'

'Yes, civilization's in a bad way.'

Both sit reflective.

'Getting on a bit too fast,' Bulteel says, shaking his head and pursing his lips.

'Or not fast enough.'

'Yes, there's that too.'

Just then Bulteel smiles, out of pure good spirits at seeing Rudbeck again and discussing with him the success of the road and the annual report.

Rudbeck says in a gloomy voice, 'Only thing is quite certain—there'll be hell to pay sooner or later.' He looks up, catches Bulteel's smile and looks interrogative.

'Of course, there are a few votes lying about here,' Bulteel says.

Rudbeck loses his gloom in the same instant. The necessary ritual sacrifice, to the time-spirit, has been performed. 'Well, if I could get hold of a hundred—even fifty to start with——'

'I dare say we have more than that in the province—but you mustn't take any more risks with the Treasury, Ruddy. I'd never forgive myself.'

'That's all right, sir. I'll be careful. I'll put Suli on the job as an accumulator.'

'Suli? Who is Suli?'

'Suli, to making twelve *dogarai* uniforms, cloth and materials.'

'Oh yes—yes.' Bulteel raises his eyebrows and then suddenly bursts out laughing. 'Oh, well, well, well. Suli is a very valuable member of the administration.'

'Don't know how this country would work without him.'

'Well, there's not much red tape about him, of course.'

'Nothing much about him at all—the invisible Pooh Bah.'

'Yes, yes—ha-ha. The only thing is, Ruddy, you've got to look out for yourself—as a married man, you can't afford——'

'I'll be careful, sir.' Rudbeck is slightly impatient. 'How much do you think I can count on?'

'Remember that no administration can overlook a breach of financial regulations.'

'All right, sir, it's my funeral. Do you really think you could raise a hundred?'

'I don't see why not—if we get at the Dorua native administration too. The Emir won't mind. I've just got him a rise. There is some money

144

in Works Recurrent, as a matter of fact, and a grant for the new native court. Then the station gardener has just passed out. Why shouldn't we use his pay for one of your road foremen—two, in fact?'

'Two Sulis.'

'Two what? Oh, yes, yes. But in fact his name was Joseph. We'd have to stick to the name or there might be a question. Don't want to lose my gardener.'

'Joseph will make a nice change on a voucher. But what about your vegetables, sir?'

'Oh, I'll put some of the native administration prisoners on to that and the police sergeant can look after 'em—we could give him a dash now and then out of stationery.'

'Thank you, sir—I could do with more regular staff.'

'Of course, a purely temporary arrangement.'

'Oh, of course.'

'We'll have to kill Joseph before I go on leave.'

'I dare say Suli would take his job on.'

'Who? Oh—ah. Well, yes, but you must be careful, Rudbeck. It doesn't pay, I warn you. Stick to the rules, as near as you can. That's the way to get on in the service, my boy, and you know you want to get on. As a family man.'

A week later countrymen, visiting Fada town, ask, 'What's happened here?' and hear the answer, 'Judge Snake has gone and Judge Pigsneck is back.'

'I noticed the market was crowded.'

'Yes, and the Emir has given the prison chief ten lashes.'

'What for?'

'What for? Why, he was Snake's great friend. He had a terrible swelled head. If you want anything done now, you'd better go to Audu or Tasuki.'

'What, the road man?'

'Yes, the road man. Pigsneck took him out of prison the first day.'

Native states in Nigeria are accustomed to sudden changes of power and tempo. Each new district officer is likely to have his own tastes and his own policy. The important thing for the native ministers is to know beforehand what his tastes are and to cater for them. Does he like ceremony? Then he must be met with camel drums and royal salutes. Does he like wandering about on the farms and talking crops? Then he must be provided at once with a few reliable farmers primed to tell him the right things. Does he hate sinecures? A council must be held to decide which of the Emir's old pensioners is to be sacrificed.

Tring has proved an unpleasant surprise. He has been described by Waziri's agents, as a hamfish or *mallam* judge—that is, an office keeper; one who loves to sit at table and write. This is the most harmless and least feared of all judges. He never finds out anything. He writes all morning, plays some game in the late afternoon, drinks with other white men in the evening and talks about the English news. This is the judge who believes everything in the official reports, because he writes the same kind of reports himself. He is the dream of all native administrations, of all Emirs and Waziris; every kind of corrupt swindler and petty tyrant.

But Tring has turned out to be a busybody, who, in his first week, made surprise visits both to the native Treasury and gaol and at once sacked half a dozen officials. He had nearly been the death of Waziri, for the Emir, after his first meeting with him, returned home in such a palsy of rage that he ordered Waziri to receive a hundred lashes with the big execution whip. He had remitted the sentence only upon the recollection that Waziri, being the sole intelligent official in the place, was indispensable to the outwitting of Tring.

Tring has taken the N.A. by surprise, so that there is relief when the new clerk, Mr. Montagu, gives the news that Rudbeck is coming back. Rudbeck's tastes are known. All the bridge-builders, the road foremen, drummers, unemployed labourers, hurry at once to Fada town; the drink shops lay in supplies of beer; and the lowest class of town whores the soldier's women and barrack bawds, buy new clothes. In one day the prisoners in the gaol lose half their rations, stolen by Tring's new gaol chief, and their separate cells, which are a nuisance to the guards.

The season is bad. Prices are low because in Europe and America, the office men, buyers and sellers of paper, have first bought too much and then tried to sell it again, all at once. Children are starving in Fada, bush villages and the slums of London and New York for exactly the same reasons. There are therefore hundreds seeking work on Rudbeck's gangs. But though he does not take them all, he takes more than ever

146

before. It is understood that a new road is to be made. Some say, but nobody believes, that he has talked of making a road to join Fada direct with Kano and Sokoto.

What is certain is that there are now half a dozen road camps instead of one, that six bridges are being built at the same time and that Rudbeck is hardly ever seen in the office. The mails are taken to him in the bush; telegrams are sent by bicycle or runner; the poor clerk, Montagu, wears out so much shoe leather in walking to and fro between Fada and the touring office that he throws dignity away and goes barefoot. Such upstarts as Audu march about like kings and wield power over hundreds.

Audu is reporting to Rudbeck one morning in the bush office, which is a mat hung upon four crooked posts, when the messenger Adamu, who, even in the bush, is a stickler for routine, is heard abusing some member of the queue which waits for employment.

'Thief and rascal!' Adamu shouts. 'How can you dare to show your face here.'

The rascal is a lanky youth dressed in a filthy pair of drawers and the brim of a soft felt hat. He is accompanied by a young woman, also in rags, with a baby on her back. The moment Rudbeck turns his head, this petitioner takes off his hat brim and calls out, 'How do do sah? God bless you, Mister Rudbeck.'

'Be silent, scum!' Adamu shrieks.

'By God,' says Rudbeck. 'It's Wog—I mean Johnson.' He goes down the line and shakes hands with Johnson. 'What the devil have you been doing to yourself, Johnson—lion-taming?'

'Oh, no, sah.' Johnson laughs. 'I been in business.'

'I didn't know you were a tailor.'

'Tailor, sah. No, sah. I been in business.'

'What kind of business?'

'All kind, sah. I do any kind of business. But when I hear you back here, sah, on road, I tink I come and see you.'

'Well, Johnson, I haven't got any jobs except labourers jobs, at sixpence and ninepence a day.'

'I like dat very much, sah.'

'Dammit, you can't work at ninepence a day.'

'Oh, yes, sah. Sometimes I work for nutting a day.

Just then Celia Rudbeck comes out of her grass hut, carrying a sketch book and a folding chair. She is changed, not in looks, but in manner. Once she had the air of someone who has never been anywhere before; now she seems like a traveller so experienced that she is at home everywhere. She sees Johnson, hesitates, then comes up to him with a smile and says, 'It's Mister Johnson—how nice.'

She shakes hands with him, looking at him with that maternal affection which everyone feels towards a devoted servant, and says, 'We're very old friends.'

'Oh, yes, mam,' Johnson says. He suddenly begins to cry. Tears roll down his cheeks. 'I tink you my frien'. God bless you, Missus Rudbeck.'

Celia looks at him in surprise and then, noticing his rags, says, 'Poor Mr. Johnson. You lost your job, didn't you?'

'Yes, Missus. I get too bad report.'

'Who gave you a bad report?'

Johnson catches Rudbeck's eye and says, 'Everybody, mam. I no good clerk.'

Rudbeck smiles and gives him a slap on the shoulder. 'You were wasted in the office, Johnson—this is the place for real work.'

Johnson is made secretary to a native court at two pounds a month and is put in charge of a gang. When his gang do twice the work of any other, Rudbeck goes to him and finds him strolling about in a new straw hat, followed by a small boy with a stool, and three drummers beating with all their might. Every moment Johnson opens his mouth and utters a fluctuating cry, which is followed by a roar of chorus from the working gang.

'You seem to get a lot of work out of your gang, Johnson.'

'Dey good men—very good gang. Dey wanna make road.' Johnson has no idea why his gang does more work than the others.

Rudbeck promotes him headman of all gangs, except the bridgemen under Tasuki. Johnson at once engages twenty more drummers, not apparently to improve the rate of work, but simply to please himself. As he says to Rudbeck, 'I like to hear dose drum when we work. De men like to sing too much.'

He also buys himself a new canopy chair, a white helmet and a pair of patent leather shoes. He wears the shoes on Sunday; on the other days he goes barefoot, followed by a small boy, carrying the hat and the chair. He is never seen to sit in the chair. Whenever he visits a gang, it is set up and the hat laid on the canopy, like a royal crown above the chair of state. Johnson himself, having thus displayed the marks of his rank, goes among the gang, to swap jokes with the drummers or improvise a chorus. Sometimes he takes a hoe or a matchet, but though he makes with them the most tremendous gestures, he does not actually strike the ground or the scrub. He merely illustrates and expresses the act of digging and chopping, so that the actual workers both laugh at him and make a kind of poetry of their own hard work. They laugh while they sing with him:

> '*Bow down, you king of cotton trees;*
> *Put your green heads in the dust;*
> *Salute the road men of Rudbeck,*'

and yet at the same time they wield their weapons like warriors, utter war-cries and scream insults at the big trees standing in their way.

When Johnson describes the wealth and glory that the road will bring to Fada, the tough old labourers shout at him, 'That's a good trick and sixpence a day for me,' but when he sings,

> '*Here come the motors, foot, foot, whang,*
> *Full of beer and salt,*'

they join in with the cry

> '*Out of our way, this is the king road.*
> *Where he flies, the great trees fall*
> *The sun and moon are walking on our road.*'

Everywhere on the road the gangs shout jokes after Johnson, call him 'slave-driver,' 'the tricky one,' 'little-songs,' 'the thief-clerk' and so on. They perfectly understand why they are working harder for him than any of the old headmen, and yet they continue to work harder, to sing and to cry with sincere appreciation of their own efforts, 'Allah, what a road!'

One day Bulteel comes with Rudbeck to inspect the first fifty miles. He congratulates Rudbeck, who gives a nod towards Johnson, in attendance as aide-de-camp.

149

'Here's the chap who does it.'

Johnson laughs at the joke and shakes his head.

'He's the man with the ideas,' Rudbeck says. Then, staring at Johnson under his long lock which droops over his right eye, he says in a tone of gratified surprise, 'In fact, if it wasn't for him and Tasuki there wouldn't be a road even up this far.'

Bulteel chuckles and says politely, 'Yes, yes, I've heard of your excellent work, Mr.—ah—Johnson.' He doesn't believe that anyone does excellent work. But Rudbeck is still surprised by his own remark. He gazes at Johnson thoughtfully as if trying to get a new conception of him. Then he gives a snort of laughter, which means that the accepted idea will have to do for the present, and says, 'He keeps us all merry and bright.'

'Oh—yes—yes—I must borrow you, Johnson, for some of my jobs at Dorua. By the way, Ruddy, about this town-planning circular. I suppose it's chiefly meant to save somebody's face, but we'll have to write something.' They walk away in conference about important matters. Johnson hastens back to the camp to give warning to Celia that the Resident has arrived.

'Thanks, Wog—that's very thoughtful of you. How did you guess I wanted to know. You'd make an ideal husband.'

'I am a husband,' Johnson cries, delighted.

'Why, of course you are. How many wives have you?'

'Only one, mam—you know her. You say she very nice, beautiful girl.'

'Of course I met her,' Celia says. She is a little absent-minded and does not always notice what is said to her or even what is happening in her neighbourhood. She is now quite careless of África; never goes to see it; and sometimes complains of its dust, heat and night noises. She does not rush about all day as if she had bought a week-end ticket to Fada and is under obligation to her conscience to get every pennyworth of sights out of it; she occupies herself very much as if she were a housewife anywhere in Europe, discussing meals, contriving supplies, feeling the breasts of chickens, inspecting pots, looking at the small boy's tongue, sewing a patch on Rudbeck's trousers, knitting and darning, reading novels, smoking cigarettes; or simply lying in a chair and gazing at her husband with the absent-minded expression of one who looks through a window in the dusk and cannot quite make out the landscape.

150

She is getting a little fatter and plainer. That is to say, the smooth pretty face which seemed to have come out of a beauty parlour is giving place to a new face, with prominent bones in cheek and jaw, broad, rather flat lips, square jaw, which causes Rudbeck to say sometimes, when he notices it, 'I say, are you all right, dear?'

'Absolutely full of fit, as Wog says.'

'No, I mean, you haven't anything on your mind, have you?'

'Good God, no! I believe the thing's dead.'

But to Johnson it seems so beautiful that he cannot help smiling when he sees it or remembers it.

Celia is not disconcerted by Johnson's admiration. She doesn't pay more particular attention to Johnson than to the rest of her surroundings. She carries on conversations with Johnson and even with Rudbeck and does not hear a single one of their answers.

This does not annoy Johnson, who perfectly understands that to Celia he is like part of her household, but it irritates Rudbeck when he finds himself obliged to say something twice.

'I'm afraid the road job is a bore,' he says.

'Oh, no, darling. I'm awfully interested.'

'Oh, I don't mind. Why should you be? It is a bore to anyone else. I'm sorry.'

Celia says nothing and obviously she considers the matter too trivial for a quarrel. She has the absent-minded air of a busy person with important responsibilities who is pestered by a child. This, no doubt, is what she feels. But though she is slightly bored by Rudbeck's work, she is still interested in his character, which apparently surprises her very much.

One day at the bathing pool below the camp she sees that a row of new mats has been built along the road above. As she swims lazily about she keeps looking at these mats.

It is just after six and chilly. Johnson, on the bank, having finished his own swim, is shivering with the small boy in attendance. Rudbeck is floating on his back in the middle of the pool, kicking up a huge fountain of water with his hairy legs. He is full of impatient energy. The birds, too, in the tall trees of the river bank are flying here and there in a hurry and screaming simply to use their voices and wings.

Treasurer Audu is now seen approaching, in a white turban, a white gown, with his book under his arm. He is grinning as usual with a frank delight in himself and his job. He has been so happy in the last months that obviously he has a quite different idea of the world and its possibilities. He stands grinning shyly on the bank until Rudbeck comes out and gives his orders for the day.

Rudbeck is mauve and pink with cold. He scrubs his legs and hisses like a groom.

'Zzzzzz, what about number three bridge? What's the hell stopping it—who's the headman—is he p-perished of the—of the pox or is he only asking for the boot?—zzz—the swamp road—what about it—I don't know—ask Mr. Johnson—zzz.' Rudbeck's body, now streaked purple, blue green, pink and salmon, coated with thick hair on breast, belly and legs, gives Audu acute uneasiness. He keeps on turning his face away from it, with a nervous smile, as if from some diseased object, unsuspectingly exposed by an innocent.

Celia languidly swims ashore, and stands in her red trunks skimming her flanks and gazing at the mat wall. Johnson and the small boy hasten to throw a bath towel and a bathing gown over her. She says to Rudbeck, 'Why the wall, Harry?'

Rudbeck is in his shirt. He pulls on a pair of soldier's shorts and draws the tape at the waist. 'Peeping Toms.'

'But it's a public road.'

'Much too public. Don't go away, Audu. I want to see the state of the accounts. I'm coming to the office now.' He strides up the bank, as if Celia's affair had been dismissed. But she is still at his shoulder.

'Do you really mind?'

'Well, dammit, don't you?'

'No, not really, I feel quite dressed, you know.'

They climb the bank with Johnson, laden with mats and towels, dodging at their heels like a faithful hound. But they don't notice him any more than a faithful hound.

'Would you mind at Bournemouth or Brighton?' Celia asks in an amused tone.

Rudbeck says nothing. He thinks he has made a fool of himself, but he can't be sure. He wishes he were sure, and he feels a vague resentment, as if somebody ought to have told him what to think.

'You're not jealous, are you?'

'Good God, no—of a lotta apes like that.'

'But if they were really monkeys?'

152

'Damn it all, Celia, why not let it go at that? Or must you analyse everything I do?'

Celia, in a pensive but sad voice, says that she never dreamed of such a thing. He answers, in a polite manner, but with an irritable tone, that that's all right then, and both remain a little depressed for twenty minutes. Rudbeck and Celia have not had a violent quarrel for ten months, but they have their little differences almost twice a day, and then they are much depressed. For the rest of the time, they are avoiding the differences by a careful selection of words and tones, adjusted to the other's comprehension and taste. Thus it seems to them that their life together, apart from the routine satisfaction of various appetites, has become a series of mild depressions and mild deceits. They have no idea that they are in process of constructing a relationship so complete and delightful that, in another year or two, each will be indispensable to the other, that in twenty years, their friends will say of them, 'What a lucky couple—so exactly suited to each other.'

About February, it appears that the road cannot be finished before the rains. Money is running short and the new villages, deep in the northern bush of Fada, send no labour. Rudbeck has been disappointed in the villages all along the road. They take no interest in the work and send few recruits to the labour gangs. Recruiting speeches by the headmen, including Johnson himself, have brought in only a dozen here and there, chiefly from larger and richer villages already provided with markets. It seems that the poorer, more cut-off people do not want roads and have not enough energy or imagination to break out from their poverty.

Now that the road is cutting through this primitive country, where scattered villages, lost in the bush, are not visited by a stranger in a year, the volunteer labour comes to an end. Only the professional gangs are at work, at ninepence a day. It is even difficult to obtain food for them. Rudbeck decides to spend what is left of his fund, scraped together from Dorua votes as well as his own, on the bridges. The road itself will have to be finished next dry season, after the year's farm work is done.

Tasuki and Audu are much depressed by this suggestion, so much so that Rudbeck, even in his own disappointment, is amused. He says to Tasuki, 'you ought to be pleased—your job will last another year.'

Tasuki shakes his head and looks surprised. He has not thought of his own future.

Even the labourers are disappointed. They have been singing for two months:

> *'Here come the motors, foot, foot, whang.'*

The rate of work begins to fall off. A road to be finished next year is too dim and vague for the imagination. No one can see this year's sun and moon walking upon it.

Johnson, feeling the depression and disliking it, goes about saying to the labourers, 'Soon finish now—we finish this year,' to which they answer with surly glances and sometimes a clod of earth, hard as a brick. Johnson is surprised and angry and shouts, 'It's your fault, you rubbish, if you don't finish.'

To Rudbeck he says, 'I tink we finish dis year.'

'But we've already decided not to—it can't be done.'

The next day Johnson says again, cheerfully, 'I tink we finish dis year,' and Rudbeck says angrily, 'For God's sake, don't talk ballocks, Johnson—we haven't got the cash nor the men.'

'Oh, sah. I tink dem village men come—we soon finish.'

'They won't come even for pay—a lot of drunken sods.'

'Perhaps they come for beer, sah—we make a good play—den we finish dis year.'

'My dear yamhead, beer costs money—beer strong enough to interest these bloody pagans costs threepence a calabash.'

'Yes, sah, but we got plenty money for *zungo*.'

'What d'you mean?'

'Why, sah, we got more money dis month—more traders come.'

The *zungos* have in fact been paying fifteen pounds a month, clear profit, into the two Treasuries, and the Treasury department has already sent queries to know why the receipts during one month have fallen off.

'What d'you mean?'

'Perhaps if we take more money, Treasurer no say nutting if money same as las' month.'

'I see, you want me to steal the *zungo* money to make pagans drunk.'

Rudbeck scowls and then laughs. 'You're not exactly a credit to your mission, Johnson.'

'But, sah, we take de road money.'

'But, damn it all, don't you see the difference between taking government money for government work and stealing *zungo* dues to make a lot of bare-arse pagans tight?'

'Oh, yes, sah.'

'I should bloody well hope so.'

'But, sah, I tink we finish dem road.'

'Oh, run along, Johnson, for God's sake.'

'And if dem village people came?'

'Damn it, if—if—but they don't.'

The next day Johnson and Audu appear in a village not far from road-head and make their usual recruiting speeches.

The village assembly listens in silence. The harvest for the year is over, it is holiday time; the days grow hotter. The women are brewing the new year's beer. Every week there is a hunt; the grass is set on fire to drive the deer, the men lie in wait for them and afterwards there is a feast of meat. There are songs and dances, drumming all night. The whole village gets drunk. It is the happy time, the good time of the year when, after months of hard work, a man can live, day and night, in friendship and the joy of his heart. He hunts and his father, uncles, and brothers admire his prowess or sympathize with his misfortunes. At night he squats singing, their voices in his ear, their thighs touching his; he dances with the young men and the young girls spring and wheel before him. He knows them all, he has played with them from their babyhood, they know each other like brothers and sisters; they are like parts of one being and now every part is mad with the same frenzy, laughing at the same joke; feeling the same ache in their bodies. Their bodies are playing the same tricks, and while they jerk and leap, they burst out laughing at their strange appearance, their lewd inventions and their serious greedy faces. They fall into each other's arms with the same hungry rage and creep away into the dark bush among the rest; butting their heads angrily at the scrub which stands in their way, weeping with indignation at the tie-tie which scratches their backs and swearing at each other when they bump in the dark.

In the morning no one gets up till the sun is high and warm. Everyone has sore eyes, sore feet, sore heads and many are bruised and cut all over. One has a torn ear, he does not know how he hurt himself

Another has a bite in his cheek, but he does not know what woman has bitten him or why. He lolls in the shade with a group of his friends, all sulky and languid. Some have strings tied round their heads to ease their headaches. The girls wander about in groups, with their arms about each other's waists; they too groan, feel their heads, show their cuts and bruises. But they are not so languid. They laugh among themselves and some of them, telling a story of the night, sketch a dancing step. They have not drunk so much as the men and they are not so exhausted by love-making.

When the village is brought together to hear Audu-the-road-money and Johnson-the-clerk, the young make the front rows, leaning against each other in the shade of each hut. The children tumble between the legs of their mothers and sisters or crawl among the groups. The elders with the chiefs sit in the middle, the women and girls squat behind, pressed closely together; the old disappear, hiding in the bush or the huts.

Audu speaks first of the importance of the great road which will make them all rich. It will bring every day traders to the village wanting shelter from the men and food from the women. Along this road motors will come to take them and their produce to market. But to make the road all must work, not much but a little.

The young men languid with their sore heads, lean against each other, draw pictures in the dust and think of nothing. Their brains are asleep. Their bodies enjoy the pains, bruises and languor, which are part of their holiday, of peace, of do-nothing. They know that soon there will be more hunting, meat, beer, songs, dances and love. The first rains, the beginning of work, are at least two months away, so far that they can't be imagined. The girls and women know that the speech is none of their business. They will do what they are told. They fix their sleepy eyes on the speaker and allow their usual train of feelings to continue; I'm rather thirsty—my leg is itching—Ojo hurt me last night—I don't like him—yes, I like him—who is that squeezing me—Edi—why does she do that—I suppose she wants me to like her better than Zinna—but Zinna is my friend—is that a pain—no, it's nice. I know I shall laugh in a minute if Edi goes on—who is this man talking now in trousers— he talks in a funny way—he's a foreigner—I don't like him—he has a bad eye. I wonder what's he made like—they say foreigners are dangerous to girls—I would like to see him—from a hidden place—if he comes near me, I shall scream.

Johnson wears nothing but dirty slacks and a dirty white coat without buttons which falls open when he waves his arms. He is flourishing a matchet. He is speaking about the road work. It is like a game. He shows how a great tree stands in the way. He chants the road-song:

'He says to us of the road, go away, you ants, be quiet, you monkey,
I am Rimi the king of the trees, I stand here a hundred years,
The sky is all my palace, that little small sun my fire,
That little moon hangs in the roof, for my lamp,
The thunder comes to war, he tries to fright me with his trumpet,
My war horse is the strong earth, he prances through the sky,
He tramples over the thunder and pushes him down with his big chest,
He cannot throw me off, I sit upright.
I hold my head high up, I say nothing.
All the trees in the forest bow down to me and whisper
Agaisheka, King Rimi, god prolong you,
Go away, you little men,
Or my horse will trample you down.'

Johnson declaims this in a lordly voice, holding up his arms like branches. Then suddenly he chops the air.

'Get out of my way, King Rimi, the road is coming,
It does not stop for kings, it is little judge Rudbeck's road,
Get out of my way, King Rimi, here are the road men
To chop you down at the feet, kerplunk,
To chop you to little pieces.
Bow to the road men, King Rimi,
Salute the road men with your whole length
Put your hands on the ground
Put your face in the dust.'

The village young men continue to draw in the dust and enjoy their lazy headaches; a young girl in the front row, finding that both her arms are fixed in the clamped mass of women flesh, scratches her nose on the next one's beads; the village chief raises his eyebrows and half shuts his eyes. He is impatient to know what Audu and Johnson are going to ask.

He is an intelligent chief. He has a good farm. He is rich. He dislikes

157

change. He hates motors and especially their drivers. He has heard that when motors come to a village the people begin to grow restless; to go on journeys, and to be impudent to their chiefs. Like the Emir, he objects especially to the northern road because it will bring in strangers to Fada.

Johnson finishes his speech with a dramatic picture of the motors coming down the road and bringing the rich traders ready to pay silver for yams. Then he asks for the men to fetch their hoes and matchets and come to the road play.

No one moves and the young men continue to draw in the dust.

When Johnson repeats his appeal, some turn their heads away like young children to whom nurse is beckoning. The girl with the itching nose tries to scratch it on her own shoulder, but gives up the attempt and gazes once more at Johnson with dreamy eyes like a cat in the morning. Audu and Johnson then summon the chief to a private conversation and tell him that there is a prize of five pounds for the village which wins the road play.

'What play?' the chief asks.

'Clearing the bush—the village which clears most bush for each man in one week will get the prize.'

'Who gets the prize?'

'It is paid to the chief.'

'Five pounds.'

'Yes, to the chief, and there will be presents to all villages which cut bush, according to their work.'

'To the village.'

'The money will be paid to the chiefs for the village. Do you think your village will come to the game?'

'It is possible.'

'When?'

'Next week, perhaps.'

'The sooner they start, of course, the more work they will do. It will be good for them if they think of starting to-day. Do you think that perhaps they will think of starting to-day?'

'It is, of course, possible.'

'If they start the road play now, there will be beer for them to-night.'

'Beer for those that work.'

'Much strong beer. That is part of the play.'

The chief smiles. 'You call it play. We call it work.'

'It is a village play—the men get beer, the chief gets a prize.'

'Five pounds for the best village.'

'That's it. Will you ask your people now? Don't forget the beer.'

'I may possibly mention it to them.'

Half an hour later sixty or seventy young men are lounging towards the road with matchets and hoes. Their eyes are blank, their faces sulky. They have heard of the beer, but they do not believe in it. They do not even want it. As for the road game, it is something new and therefore to be hated. Suddenly they hear the drum and fife, a loud song wavering like a water organ, the whack of axes, the clop of matchets, and the sudden crackle of falling trees.

They come upon the road head in high forest near the Fada river. A big tree has just been cut and rolled away; great mounds of chips are burning and sending out long sausages of blue smoke which blow along the narrow clearing. Under the cliff of foliage at the blind end of the road, twenty axe and matchet men are chopping and singing; behind them forty hoe-men, stooped double, are walking backwards, swinging their enormous two-handled hoes in time to the band to chop the roots and break the ground.

These hoe-men, pouring with sweat, have the glazed eyes and mad expressions of men performing automatic movements in a trance.

The languid villagers gaze at the scene with wonder and disgust. They are divided into two gangs; for matchets and hoes. The matchet men are led into the dark green cave at the road end and set to cut scrub round the big trees. They are received at once with yells of greeting and chaff.

'They have caught you, have they?'

'You seem to be enjoying yourselves.'

'Did you think it was a hunt?'

'We're not working here—it's a game.'

The sulky villagers scowl and look about them.

'Go on, convicts.'

'Tired already?'

'They're a weak lot—everyone knows that.'

Chaff and abuse fly round them. Two or three languidly begin to chop. There is nothing else to do. Meanwhile the new hoe-men stand sulking behind the ranks until one of the workers calls out, 'Hi, this is the way—in case you don't know.'

'No, they don't know—they're too foolish.'

159

'If you ask them to hoe, they'll cut their own feet.'

One of the visitors starts, frowns and makes a swing with his hoe. He almost chops his feet. There is a shout of laughter.

When Rudbeck comes through in half an hour with the survey gang, from the blazed line which marks the road direction in front, he finds the new matchet men chopping with all their might; each of them with skilful side-shots, uppercuts and draw cuts is showing off, if only to himself, his skill and strength with the matchet. The new hoe-men cannot be distinguished from the old. They too swing like automatic farmers; their backs pour sweat; their great six-pound hoes cut through root and vine, and every time the blade bites between their feet they all grunt together, 'How-oouch.'

The pipers and drummers stroll after them as they swing back step by step, and Johnson, marking the time with a matchet, leads the song:

'*Oh, you king tree, hundred feet high (grunt).*'

At night, tired, blistered, the new recruits are still among the noisiest in the camp. It is the bush pagans who have never been outside the village before who are most eager to show off their feats of acrobatic dancing and to drink the most beer. They have already, in five hours, forgotten their dread and contempt of the stranger and their resolve to keep themselves to themselves. In one afternoon they have taken the first essential step out of the world of the tribe into the world of men. The yells and drumming from the camps surprise even Rudbeck after two months of bush fighting. He apologizes to Celia, kept awake. 'These villagers have probably brought their own beer. It is the time when all the pagans get drunk three times a week.'

Celia answers thoughtfully, 'I thought I felt something just now.'

'Felt something?'

'Something move inside.'

'It's much too soon yet, isn't it?'

'Yes, must have been a wamble. Give me a cigarette, will you, dear? I must say Wog's party is unusually vocal to-night.'

'Don't set your net on fire.'

Every day now the villagers come in, some to clear only a few yards, some to work for days, according to their fancy. There is no compulsion upon them to stay, only to begin. A chief in Africa can usually persuade his young men, or some of them, to go to a task, but he can rarely keep them there. But many of the Fada road gangs, from villages which have never seen a motor and think of a road as a foot track, camp out beside their work night after night, talk about their road and come to believe that they are engaged in some important and glorious enterprise.

In two or three weeks after the local villages come in, the first pioneers cut through to the main north road. The last three bridges are begun. Rudbeck rides or walks along the whole length, marking the ditch on the upper side of the track.

Now, simply because the road is certain to be finished soon, work becomes a kind of festivity, something between a spree and a battle. The drummers beat all day till their fingers bleed, the workers strike at the bush with savage fury and yell their songs like curses, or burst into shouts of laughter; all the songs, jokes take a more brutal note and edge; a wilder exuberance; the headmen themselves are swinging axes; Rudbeck is seen stripped to the waist, so black with sun and dirt that he is not much lighter than Tasuki; Johnson, in a torn pair of trousers and a carrier's straw hat, is chopping, swearing or singing, improvising and exhorting from before dawn till long after dark. He is always dirty, streaked with layers of sweat and dirt in which the new sweat trickles crookedly like water on a varnished boat, leaving bright, black trails. His cheeks are hollow with tiredness and his eyes are inflamed with wood smoke. But his voice still conveys the most energetic feeling and his legs, body, and arms change every moment from one expressive posture to another, in sympathy with the voice. He is like a witch-doctor possessed by the spirit. Johnson, in fact, has no notion that he is tired. He doesn't feel anything except music, noise, the movement of the work, the approbation and nearness of Rudbeck and Rudbeck's triumph, which is his own. He lives in this glory, which is expressed in every yell, in every obscene joke, kick, jump or swing of the matchet. He does not need to think, 'Rudbeck's road, the great, the glorious, the wonder of the world, is about to be finished and I have helped to finish it.' He knows it in every muscle. It is there all the time, part of the music, the shouts, the shining sweaty backs and their rhythmic muscles, the yelling songs, the triumphant, intoxicating drums, the blue smoke of the fires, the trees toppling and crashing like cliffs, the suddenly exposed sky. It is like the mat under him when

he wakes at night, the firm ground by day. He sings like a defiance
to the forest:

> '*Bow down old lords of the world,*
> *Put your green heads in the dust.*
> *Salute the roadmen, children of the sky;*
> *Come, sun and moon, walk now in the dark wood,*
> *Walk in Rudbeck's road with your long shining feet.*'

Rudbeck is fond of saying, 'When we open this road.' Tasuki,
Johnson and Audu say to each other, 'Ah, when the road is open' in
the tone of prophets who look forward to the opening of paradise, to
the sound of angels' trumpets.

Foot travellers, of course, and petty traders are passing through
every day. Hausas especially, who travel into every new crack of the
bush like water out of a reservoir, have been using the first survey path
and fording the streams since a year ago. This trickle has gradually
increased into a stream. In the last four months, salt caravans, herds
of cattle going south to the great markets of Oyo and Yoruba land,
family parties carrying kola nuts to the north and native women taking
loads of shea butter to the Fada store, have passed continuously
through the gangs, who are so accustomed to them that they have
ceased to abuse them, and treat them only with good-natured contempt.

For some reason, all the road gangs, even the raw pagans after they
have done an hour's work on the road, despise traders like an inferior
species; creatures who do not make roads, but only use them, beings
without appreciation of road work; without imagination. Traders, in
fact, bringing wealth to Fada, receive no welcome anywhere; the
villages curse and plunder them.

They are exceedingly glad of the *zungos*, provided at three places on
the road as well as in Fada itself, and the dues received increase rapidly
to twenty and twenty-five pounds a month.

But the road is not open.

One day, however, a party of hoe-men are working about ten o'clock
near their own village. They have fifty yards of ditch to finish and they

work like fury. Every now and then one of them straightening his back for a moment, and flicking the sweat from his neck, looks up and down and repeats the formula, 'Allah, what a road.' Then all stand and answer with some current phrase, 'It is a road,' or, 'A road, friends, yes, a road,' in a high-pitched tone of wonder.

The road, at this place, is merely a long narrow strip of hard mud, littered with half-burnt chips, which passes out of sight in both directions into the high, primeval bush, familiar to them all. On every side the enormous columns of the trees stand dusty and motionless as stone, under the dark roof of foliage. The narrow crack in that roof, which lets in a strip of light sky above the brown strip of road, is like a single knife cut, already closing. Branches reach across overhead, at a little distance the edges seem to join.

The little group of hoe-men, their naked bodies glistening with sweat, who stand under these enormous vaults in the hot gloom, are at home. They smile at the road, because they have made it and sung of it, but they have no idea of its beginning or end. They are still like men brought up on a forgotten island far from ship routes, to whom the rest of the world is as much a mystery, a blank inhabited by monsters, as to their ancestors of the old Stone Age. They do not even imagine it. Suddenly, in the immense silence of the morning, familiar as the forest twilight, which seems like the very substance of it, they hear a strange noise, between drumming and gunfire. It increases quickly. Two of the pagans dart among the trees and disappear into the silence. The rest stiffen. They do not seem to move, but each muscle is tense; their eyes open widely and stare with fixed and blank apprehension.

A lorry comes pounding out of the shadows, and at once they know what it must be. Two or three voices together cry, 'Motor!'

All grin with astonishment and delight. They lift their hoes and rush forward, shouting greetings. The lorry driver, a tall Yoruba in blue dungarees, with a stub of cigarette stuck to his lips, pays no attention to them. He clanks and rattles past and disappears from sight. He doesn't even know he is the first man to drive over the Fada road. The gang burst into excited talk. One of them dances, another gives a whoop. Rudbeck is seen cantering towards them on his brown pony. He pulls up and asks, 'Did you see a motor?'

'Yes, master, a motor—a big motor.' They surround him laughing, shouting, waving their arms. 'It was a motor—from the north—he went through, poot, poot.'

Rudbeck says, 'I suppose that means that the last bridge is finished. Have you seen Tasuki?'

'No, we haven't seen Tasuki, but it was a motor—a big motor.'

Rudbeck, with a puzzled, disconcerted expression rides away to find Tasuki. He has not realized perhaps that the road would open itself.

But next day the villagers, except a few ditchers, are going home. Tasuki has discharged the last bridge gang. The chip fires are still smouldering in the clearing, but there is no sound of drum or axe. In the bush camp, Johnson, Tasuki and Audu are counting tools and paying off the headmen. Rudbeck is answering arrears of mail and listening to cases. He is surprised to find how much his court work has increased in the last three months, not only with cases due to the new road, such as disputed bargains, complaints of extortion, adulteration, fraud, highway robbery; but purely local ones, such as theft, assault, quarrels between villages, disputes between chiefs and their people, disputed claims to all kinds of rights; and even wife-beating, kidnapping and divorce. There is a crime wave in Fada and every time the Waziri reports to Rudbeck, he mentions it and says with the appearance of innocence, 'It is a most strange thing, but all the thieves and black-guards in the country have come to Fada, especially from the north. The Fada people, too, have never been so insolent. They are getting spoilt.'

'You can't say it's the motors—there's only been one.'

'Oh, no, Zaki, it's nothing to do with your road. For that we are all grateful—we thank God for it. No, but for the last six months a lot of new people have been coming to Fada. I don't know why; small traders and rascals of that kind, from the north. They always make trouble. They stir up the people against us even in the villages. I fear there will be big trouble—we need more police already.'

Rudbeck authorizes four more police on the Emir's roll and warns the Waziri against the prejudice that roads and motors bring trouble to a state.

'When the motors begin to use this road, you will see the advantage of it. Fada market will be twice as big and all your people will get good cash prices for their produce. Motor roads are very good things, Waziri. The Governor himself has given the order for them. Native officials and even Emirs who try to prevent them by spreading false reports that they do harm will displease the Governor very much. In that case, of course, it is possible that their pay will not go up; it may even come down.'

Waziri bows to the ground and cries out, 'Master, lord, but the Emir admires motor roads above everything—and so do I. We pray for them and for you. We pray that you make still more roads and bring many more motors to Fada.'

'All right, Waziri. I salute the Emir. Good-bye.'

'God be with you, lord, provider of roads, benefactor of Fada.'

Waziri goes home in a fright and the next day, not only he, but the Treasurer, the Master of the Horse and the Chief Justice all come ten miles down the road, to the first bush camp, in order to congratulate Rudbeck on the road and to assure him that it is a blessing to them all.

Rudbeck is most gracious and promises them a golden age for Fada. But when they have gone he is left with a sensation of confusion and disappointment. He feels that something is wrong, but he can't make out what it is. He suspects that he has been misled and even that he has misled others; but how, when or where he cannot discover. He shouts, in sudden anger, at a headman who is dragging a bundle of axe-helves across the camp, 'Don't kick up all that dust—isn't there enough as it is?'

He is disgusted with the camp. The place where he has enjoyed some of the happiest hours of his life, of which he has loved even the fire glow half a mile away, has become a squalid rubbish heap. Everywhere there are heaps of filth, broken tools, cracked calabashes, rotten mats, tottering huts, half-burnt embers, rusty tins. All the trees about are splintered, singed by fires, their branches are broken and their leaves shrivelled. Over all there is a stink, never noticed before, of rottenness and badly sealed latrines.

The Fada road is finished, the great idea is realized, and suddenly Rudbeck feels as if life holds nothing more for him. There is, of course, plenty of work waiting for him; the new assessment, a new census, a questionnaire about the infantile death rate, another town-planning circular, as well as arrears of office and court work. But he thinks of them merely as routine jobs, figures to be gathered, columns to be filled.

165

'More eyewash about sanitation,' he says to Celia, throwing a blue circular on the breakfast table.

'Poor darling.' Celia already has a maternal kindness for her husband; and the maternal absent-mindedness.

'As if you can plan towns without cash—and there won't be any cash to spare in Fada until we have some real trade.'

'Yes, darling, more motor roads.'

Rudbeck looks still more gloomy. 'We can't do any more. I've tapped all the local trade with this north-south route. Now we can only wait for the other divisions to do something—and the central government.'

'Couldn't you do just one more little road?'

Rudbeck glances at her and says, 'Keep the children amused.'

Celia does not answer. She is counting her knitting stitches. Probably she has not heard Rudbeck. He continues to stare at her for a moment and then gives a snort of laughter. She looks at him affectionately and says, 'Three more lorries went through this morning and one of them was loaded.'

'You're interested in roads, what?'

'Oh, dear, is that another hole in your shirt?'

'No, it's only a bit of dirt.' He disappears into the store hut and can be heard snorting again there. It is his only protest against the maternal distraction.

It is time to go back to Fada. After breakfast Celia begins to pack. She is neither depressed nor pleased. Her air is still that of the accomplished and cheerful traveller who carries her home with her, and sets up her household, complete with family and knitting bag, even in trains and tram shelters. She packs with careful art and when each uniform trunk has been dusted, papered and carefully filled with exactly folded clothes, her glance of appreciation, before she closes the lid, merges at once into the look of pleased expectancy with which she opens the next one and says to Jamesu, 'We ought to get the rest of the bush kit in here if we don't waste any corners.'

Rudbeck hates packing even more than he dislikes putting figures into forms. He wanders about the camp, pipe in mouth and wonders vaguely why he feels so wretched, bored and disgusted. It is exactly as if he has just returned after three months' debauch to ordinary life and finds it more stupid and pointless than before.

Even the road gives him no pleasure. He looks sulkily and doubtfully

166

at the great raw cut extending through the forest as far as the eye can reach, until on the horizon it becomes a mere nick in the dark sky-line, like the back sight of a rifle. A grand job. Far bigger and grander than he had ever thought possible. But what was it doing to Fada? Where were all the good results? Could it be that dirty old savages like the Emir and Waziri were right in their detestation of motor roads; that roads upset things, brought confusion, revolution. And wasn't there confusion enough? Wasn't everybody complaining that the world was getting into such confusion that civilization itself would disappear.

Ideas like these, or rather feelings which cannot take form as ideas for lack of clear definition, are as common to Rudbeck as everyone else who reads the newspapers and can't distinguish between their sense and their nonsense. Over a thousand lunch tables and camp fires he has discussed them with his friends, and tossed about these words, 'confusion,' 'chaos,' 'breakdown of civilization,' without offering or reaching any kind of conclusion. He knows only that certain conclusions are not popular with his seniors. He has said to Bulteel, 'But, sir, if native civilization does break down, there'll be a proper mess one day.'

Bulteel takes off his hat, lifts it in the air in a line with the sun, and then at once puts it on again. They are taking their evening walk along the river road at Dorua.

'Ah! That's a big question.' Bulteel hates talking shop out of office hours.

'We're obviously breaking up the old native tribal organization or it's breaking by itself. The people are bored with it.'

'Yes, yes, and I'm not surprised,' Bulteel says.

Rudbeck is greatly surprised. 'Don't you believe in the native civilization?'

'Well, how would you like it yourself?' Bulteel smiles at him sideways with a kind of twinkle.

'Then you think it will go to pieces?'

'Yes, I think so, if it hasn't gone already.'

'But what's going to happen then? Are we going to give them any new civilization, or simply let them slide downhill?'

'No idea,' Bulteel says cheerfully. He takes off his hat again and replaces it at once because he finds it a nuisance to hold at arm's length above his bald head.

'I suppose one mustn't talk about a plan,' Rudbeck says.

'Oh, no, no, no. They'll take you for a Bolshy.'

167

'Well, sir, an idea. I suppose some people do have an idea of what life ought to be like—the Catholics did and the missionaries do, or ought to—and I suppose old Arnold did.'

'Oh, Arnold, the Rugby man—yesss.'

'I don't mean their ideas would do now, but only that a general idea might be possible—something to work to.'

'Well, what idea?'

'That's the question.'

'Yes, that's the question.'

There is a short pause and then Rudbeck, seeing that Bulteel is not going to make any suggestions, says, 'But it's a question you mustn't put up to the Secretariat.'

'Oh, no, no—no. Not at all.' Bulteel pauses. He dislikes this kind of conversation, which, as he says, gets you nowhere. But after a moment his affection for Rudbeck overcomes his disinclination to spoil the evening's walk and he says gravely, 'But don't think it's the Secretariat's fault—people think they've been held up by the Secretariat when it's really Service conditions.'

Rudbeck perfectly understands this phrase. He accepts it as a reasonable explanation of the fact that obstacles stand in the way of every constructive plan. He understands that people in themselves, full of goodwill and good sense, can form, in an organization, simply an obstructive mass blocking all creative energy; not from any conspiracy or jealousy, but simply from the nature of rules and routine, of official life. He accepts this cheerfully and says to Bulteel, 'Ours not to reason why.'

'Exactly; the higher the fewer or words to that effect. It doesn't do you any good or anyone else,' and, stopping at the station garden, he says in the same good-natured, laughing tone, too cheerful to be called cynical, 'What do you think of my zinnias? I hope you don't despise zinnias. They have one great merit as flowers—they always come up.'

Rudbeck has at once dropped the problem from his mind. He has not thought about it again for perhaps a year. He is too busy.

But now his road work finished, he notices it again, and for a moment, it seems so large and urgent that he wonders how he ever forgot it.

The road itself seems to speak to him. 'I'm smashing up the old Fada—I shall change everything and everybody in it. I am abolishing the old ways, the old ideas, the old law; I am bringing wealth and opportunity for good as well as vice, new powers to men and therefore new conflicts. I am the revolution. I am giving you plenty of trouble already, you governors, and I am going to give you plenty more. I destroy and I make new. What are you going to do about it? I am your idea. You made me, so I suppose you know.'

Rudbeck, staring at the road, feels rather than understands this question and he feels again a sense of confusion and frustration. It seems to him, not to his reason, but his feelings, that he has been used and driven like a blind instrument. This gives him a very disagreeable sensation. He stands for several minutes smoking and gazing, with a kind of disgusted surprise, and then gives a snort so loud that a passing headman bobs a curtsey and says in a mildly apologetic tone, '*Zaki.*'

The headmen, with their usual nonchalant and world-worn air, are collecting their stores for return to Fada. They are not depressed. They have forgotten already their enthusiasm for the great Fada road. It is already a part of Fada to them, like the ground and the air, Johnson, too, shouting to Tasuki across the dusty waste, is in excellent spirits.

'Tasuki, hi-monkey-beard.'

'*Naam*, clerk.'

'What about the pot you borrowed from Waziri?'

'He took it back.'

'I mean the other one—the one that didn't leak.'

'It got broken when number three gang had that fight.'

'What, another shilling pot broken?'

'Allah, clerk, it wasn't my fault.'

Rudbeck turns away towards the office hut. It has been surrounded three deep, for at least two hours, by applicants and petitioners. He gives a sigh, taps his pipe with his thumb, and slowly makes his way towards a boring duty; rolling in his walk, swinging his arms, stooping his broad thick shoulders as if his burden of confusion and blind treadmill effort has turned into a physical weight on his back.

Rudbeck finds the office even hotter and more foul than the camp outside. Old Adamu, spotless and austere, is waiting by the rickety table which was a shaving table at six and breakfast table at seven. Rudbeck sits down heavily on a chop box and says in a tone of martyred resignation, 'All right, Adamu. Native courts first.'

A native scribe comes in, bows with a shy and anxious air, sits down and begins to sing out a list of cases.

'Alhaji, male, forty years of age, north ward, Fada, arrested for repeated refusal to rebuild his house wall which dangerously overhangs the road. Also for insulting my lord the Alkalin Fada when reprimanded. Fine of two pounds.'

'Does he appeal?'

'Yes, lord. He's here waiting.'

'On what grounds does he appeal?'

'He says he was away trading and his sons neglected the wall.'

'I'll see him afterwards. Carry on.' A deep sigh.

'Marimi, married woman, twenty-two, claims divorce. Grounds, her husband beat her. Husband declares she has spent all the tax money on new cloths in the markets. Divorce granted. They are Mussulmans.'

'Any appeal?'

'Yes, lord. There is a dispute about the bride's price to be returned.'

'I'll hear that one with the Chief Justice.'

'In Fada—or shall the Alkali come here?'

'I suppose it must be in Fada.' Another sigh. 'Next, please!'

'Amadu of Bauchi, trader, arrested for an assault on the police, also for violent language against the Wazirin Fada.'

Rudbeck sighs again. Outside he can hear Johnson shouting in Hausa, 'But, Tasuki, we'll want all the calabashes.'

Tasuki's voice chatters from the distance, like a monkey from a high tree, 'Allah, there isn't a good one left.'

'Then who took them all?'

'Allah, how should I know? These bastards of labourers would steal the smell off a goat.'

'They couldn't do that for you, monkey-beard.'

Johnson and Tasuki both laugh and Tasuki chatters, 'Shut up, your mother was a what's his name. All the same, old chap, there's going to be trouble about that bag of bolts.'

Rudbeck gives another deep sigh. The *mallam* is in the middle of another case. '. . . declared that he had already paid his *zungo* fees; he hit him over the head with a shoe. Fined ten shillings.'

'Does he appeal?' Another sigh.

'Yes, lord. He claims that he paid both fees.'

'Both fees—in two *zungos*?'

'No, lord. Both fees in Fadá *zungo*.'

170

'Oh, he had cattle?'

'No, I mean the lodging fee and the road fee.'

'What the devil is the road fee?' Rudbeck is at once suspicious.

'The fee for the road, lord, instead of ferry fees.'

There is now general alarm. The *mallam*, a young polite boy new from a central school, falters and stammers. He can see that something is wrong; but he doesn't know on what scale. The other court clerks, older and more experienced, understand at once that there has been extortion. They all glance sidelong at each other as if to say, 'Here's a nice mess.'

'What is a road fee?' Rudbeck demands.

'Lord, he said he paid—a road fee.'

'Where is he?'

At once a huge Yoruba, who has been attending closely to this exchange, bursts in and shouts, 'I paid a penny for the sheep and a penny for a wife and a goat, that's a halfpenny each, and then I paid a penny for the road. Then he asked me for the whole lot all over again.'

'Who took the penny for the road?'

'The road boy, of course,' bawls the Yoruba.

'Who the hell is the road boy?'

'He takes the money for the road.'

'You wait here, all of you.'

Rudbeck goes to Celia and tells her with gloomy ferocity, 'They're on the rob again—in the *zungo* this time. I must go myself.'

He gets out the car, drives into Fada as fast as it will go and makes straight for the *zungo*. He finds the road boy actually on his rounds, collecting a penny from each trader for the use of the new road.

He arrests the boy, who says that clerk Johnson appointed him road boy. This is confirmed by the *zungo* policeman. It appears that about a month before clerk Johnson sent this boy to collect the money, which has amounted to an average of ten shillings a day. The money has been paid, after 10 per cent. deduction for the collector and 10 for Waziri, direct to Johnson.

Rudbeck drives back in a rage, and arrives dirty, thirsty, shaken by the road and still more angry. He shouts for Johnson, who can't be found; then for Audu, who has also disappeared. Celia, astonished to see her husband in such a rage that he won't even take tea, asks what is wrong.

171

'Only another swindle—Johnson and Waziri this time.'

'Not Wog?'

'Why not? They all do it—you can't trust any of 'em anywhere any time.'

Audu is found by the orderly. He comes in trembling, cash book in hand, and falls down on his nose. 'Oh, lord, I didn't take any of it—I gave it to Johnson.'

'What did you give Johnson?'

'The *zungo* money.'

'*Zungo* money—but that's in the cash book, isn't it?'

'I mean, what we didn't put in the cash box.'

'Oh, you didn't put it all in the cash book—but what the devil have you got to do with the *zungo* money?'

'The *zungo* policeman gave it to Johnson and Ma-aji.'

'And they took a slice of it.'

'Lord, they paid in more every week.'

'But not all.'

'Lord, it was only three pounds they took last week.'

'I see, expenses weren't so heavy last week. I suppose Mr. Johnson didn't buy so much gin.'

'Lord, but it wasn't liquor—it was the store bill. Mr. Ajali said he must pay for the new chair. So Mr. Johnson said to me, "I will borrow a little this week—only borrow." '

Audu's eyes, though still fixed on Rudbeck's face, take on a glazed expression. He is inventing. Rudbeck says shortly, 'The *zungo* money went for the store bill, but what about the road pennies?'

'That was another matter, of course. The boy was foolish and thought he would play a game. So——'

'Give me your cash book. Orderly—keep an eye on Audu. He may be for jug.'

Rudbeck, in magisterial gloom, strides up and down. Celia begins to fear that he is going to be a nuisance both to himself and her. She is a little anxious about him and about her own peace of mind. She says in a caressing tone, 'Never mind, darling. They all do it.'

'But I trusted the blighter.'

'But I'm sure poor Wog didn't mean to do any harm.'

'What did he mean then? He's put up the whole swindle. This poor devil Audu didn't know what he was doing and that old fool Ma-aji was never more than quarter-witted. It's your friend Johnson that's worked it all.' He goes to the door and yells to the orderly, 'Have you got him yet?'

'No, *zaki*.'

'Then get him quick.' And he says to Celia, 'He thought he could make a fool of me.' As he says this, he grows still more furious. A sense of frustration that has been boiling inside him for two days blows up in hot rage. 'He thinks he can pull the wool over my eyes. He did too.'

'But, darling, do you think Johnson really——'

'Blore told me he was a crook and, by God, he was right. Look at this game going on for weeks—right under my nose.'

Celia is feeling worn-out and she knows that this is bad for her. The doctor has strictly commanded her to have an easy mind, to worry about nothing, to sleep well, and she carefully obeys him. As a modern young woman she has great faith in the expert and, moreover, she likes to make a good job of things, from her marriage to a baby. She therefore gives up the defence of Johnson and hastens to make Rudbeck happy. 'It certainly looks queer.'

'But there's no doubt about it—don't you realize—the thing's proved? I've just——'

'Oh, yes, of course, darling—I do realize—I only meant that's it so odd in Wog——'

'Odd? It's just what Blore told me to expect——'

'Yes, I'm afraid poor Wog was always a bit of a bad egg—the only thing was, he looked so honest——'

'Of course he did—he's been at it for years.'

Johnson is found that night in his hut. He has slipped back to Bamu and is just going to bed when the boy Jamesu hears their voices and comes peeping. Rudbeck charges out with a lantern and shouts, 'Johnson.'

'Yes, sah.' Johnson, in a pair of bright pink pyjama legs, comes into the lantern light. He smiles innocently and says, 'How you do, sah. Good night to you.'

'Have you been stealing *zungo* money?'

'Oh, no, sah. How I do such thing?'

'Didn't Ma-aji give you three pounds?'

'Oh, sah, I forget—perhaps I borrow two-tree shilling from Ma-aji—perhaps he take it from *zungo* money.'

'Why did you say you didn't steal the *zungo* money?'

'I never steal anything, sah—I borrow small small.'

'Anything else?'

'How you mean, sah?'

'Did you borrow anything else from anywhere? Did you take any other money out of the *zungo*?'

'Oh, no, sah. How I ever do such ting?' Johnson opens his eyes wide in innocence. 'I never tink of such bad ting.'

'What boy is this who has been taking road money in the *zungos*?'

'Oh, yes, sah. I remember um.' Johnson laughs. 'Dat small boy from my house—he go make a lil collection—to buy beer for labourers.'

'A collection—he threatened to turn anyone out who didn't pay—he took four pounds last week.'

'Oh, sah, dat beer cost plenty—he got to be very strong beer for village people.'

'Do you realize you've committed embezzlement and *sojan gwona* too?'

A *sojan gwona*—that is, a soldier of the farm—is a man who collects money on pretence of being a government official. He is an offender heavily punished in Nigeria.

'But, sah, I put him all for book.' Johnson dives into the hut and comes out with a small notebook which he offers to Rudbeck. It is a penny notebook with a black cover, curled back at the edges; a contemptible object. No one could respect such a cash book.

'Look, sah. My beer cash book. I put everything in it—money for *zungo*—and money for beer and money for chiefs. All like Treasury cash book.'

'Audu says you had three pounds from the Treasurer; you say a few shillings.'

'Oh, sah, I forget—perhaps it be a pound—but I no take one lil penny for myself. I put all for cash book just like de road cash book.'

'How did you pay your last store bill?'

'Oh, sah, out from my pay.'

'And the new canopy chair.'

'Oh, sah.' Johnson laughs. 'Perhaps I borrow small small from Ma-aji to pay dem chair.'

'Why do you tell such lies, Johnson. I can't believe a word you say.'

'For Gawd's sake, sah, I never never tell you lie. Oh, sah, you my father and mother, you my good frien', I never tell you one small small lie.'

174

'But you're doing nothing else. Look here, Johnson, you've been robbing the Treasury for weeks and you know I ought to run you in. But you've done useful work here and I don't want to jug you. So clear out quick.'

'Oh, sah, perhaps Ma-aji len' me twenty shilling—look um book, sah—in my cash book.'

Rudbeck suddenly loses his temper and shouts, 'Get out, I tell you—can't you understand this is a let off?'

He marches away. Johnson runs after him, crying in dismay. 'Perhaps I take two pound—I don' remember.' The orderly catches him and sternly orders him to pack up and go. Tasuki and half a dozen headmen surround him and urge him to hurry. They explain that Rudbeck is very angry.

Johnson is now angry as well as confused. He shouts loud enough for Rudbeck to hear that there was no harm in borrowing two pounds three shillings, or perhaps four shillings, from the Treasurer. He explains that all that money was spent in beer for the labourers.

'Except those new silver bangles for Bamu,' the orderly says.

Johnson has forgotten the bangles. He can never remember how he spends or what has happened to his takings in the last month; not only the *zungo* money and the road pennies, but bridge money collected at all bridges not immediately under Rudbeck's inspection at the moment. The new bangles, his new suits, pyjamas and bed, the canopy chair, the new patent-leather shoes, and various presents to his friends, have no doubt been paid for, either from his salary or the money that continually pours through his hands, but he doesn't know how. There is much more not paid for yet. He has never troubled himself about money; he has much more interesting things to think about. But he knows very well that he has given all his devotion to Rudbeck and that what he may have spent on some trifling necessities for himself is nothing to what he has paid out for Rudbeck's road.

'I got it all in my book,' he shouts towards the far side of the camp, where Rudbeck's compound is hidden under the dark wall of trees. Nothing can be seen of it except the door hole brightly lit by a hurricane lamp hanging from the flat straw roof within. Half the lamp appears below the door lintel, containing the flame, and two legs in pale, washed-out khaki trousers, Rudbeck's evening kit, project from the right side into the middle of the mud floor. He is probably reading his weekly *Times*, only a fortnight old. Celia is entirely out of sight.

Probably she has gone to bed. Legs and lamp flame are perfectly still; even the shadow of the lamp's guard-frame thrown across the uneven dust heaps of the camp almost to Johnson's feet does not waver. It looks like a mark on the ground.

'In de beer cash book,' Johnson shouts towards the lamp and the legs. 'I keep my accounts all good as Treasury cash book—dey balance every week. Mister Rudbeck no fit to say I tief—I put all dem money for cash book.'

'Come on, hurry up,' the orderly says. 'Or do you want jug?'

'I go now.' Johnson's voice is full of anger and despair. He is speaking to the legs. 'But I never no tief—I put him all for my cash book—de beer cash book. Why Mister Rudbeck no look um? Why he no look at my cash book?'

'Hurry up—hurry up.'

'I go now,' Johnson shouts. 'I go now and don't you say nutting to Mister Rudbeck becas I no fit to stop any more. He call me tief. I no fit to stop along of Mister Rudbeck. Never no more. I go now, orderly.' Johnson stops and stares at the legs. But they are still motionless. The flame is as still as if it has been painted in the bright miniature of a domestic interior. 'I go now, orderly,' Johnson bawls, using his utmost lung power. 'But don' you say nutting 'bout dat to Mister Rudbeck. Don' you tell him I never fit to come back.'

The orderly gives him a push. 'Now then, clerk, you don't want big trouble.'

Johnson goes into the hut and looks at Bamu, who is packing her tin trunk. He says to her, 'That's right, Bamu, pack quickly. Mister Rudbeck has insulted me. I am not going to stay with him—no, not for a minute.'

Then he goes out again and shouts that all the money is entered in his cash book, opens the little notebook to show how neatly it is ruled and holds it up towards the legs. 'It all same as Treasury cash book—but don' you tell Mister Rudbeck. I no 'gree for Mister Rudbeck no more.'

He goes on like this for an hour. Sometimes he urges Bamu to pack quickly; advice to which Bamu, who has been packing since Audu's first disclosure, pays no attention whatever. She believes in slow and careful packing. She does not intend, for instance, to spoil her plush cloth by squeezing it into tight folds. But Johnson does not notice Bamu's indifference. He is full of despair, anger and self-pity. He is now convinced of his innocence. He is sure that he has been honest and careful to an extraordinary degree. When he holds up the cash book for the fourth or fifth time towards the motionless legs and commands the orderly, in a voice audible half a mile away, not to tell Mister Rudbeck that Johnson has entered all the money in the beer cash book, he believes himself a most injured man. He grows more innocent, more injured, more tearful, and more haughty every moment.

At last, after ten o'clock, Bamu comes out from the hut and ties the kitchen load to the canopy chair. The orderly helps her to put this on Sozy's head; and then to put her own tin trunk upon her own head. The baby, sound asleep, is already swaying on her back. She says to Johnson, 'We're ready, clerk.'

Johnson, still dressed in his pink pyjamas, is standing with folded arms gazing at the lighted hut. The legs have disappeared, but the lamp is still burning.

The orderly pushes him. 'Go on now.' Johnson gives backwards, and the orderly, having discovered this method of moving him on, continues to push. Johnson retreats slowly and jerkily backwards down the road. The two women follow.

Johnson throws all his power into a final yell. 'I go now, but don't you tell Mister Rudbeck. He no fit to stop me now. I no say good-bye to Mister Rudbeck. I don' bless him at all.'

He then turns round, takes stick and lantern from Bamu and places himself behind the women to light their path through the immense canyon of the new road. Every now and then he repeats, 'I don' bless you, Mister Rudbeck. I don' say good-bye and I don' bless you now. My heart is not kind to you now.'

Johnson spends that night in a village and doesn't reach Fada till the next afternoon. His fall is then known to the whole country. He has been Rudbeck's chief minister for three months and prime ministers are more noticed than kings. When he passes through Fada town, the market women, old headmen, old dependents and flatterers, quickly avoid his path. A fallen chief in Nigeria is still dangerous to know; his trouble is more contagious than leprosy and much more fatal.

177

But Johnson swaggers through the streets, smiling into curious eyes and laughing at timid frowning looks like one still full of greatness and conscious of power.

Bamu, following behind with the heavy box on her head and the baby dozing on her back, has her usual expression of self-possession. She is neither humble nor swaggering. She is simply a wife doing her job and neither expecting or challenging notice. Old Sozy, carrying the chair, several calabashes and two chickens, gasps and reels five paces behind Bamu. She is probably aware of nothing but the need of keeping up with her party and not losing her last place in the world.

Johnson has, of course, no money. He sells his new watch for a shilling and goes to the *zungo*.

It is now about four o'clock when the town inn comes to life again after its sleepy day. The traders who have been in the market all morning and the newcomers from the road who are too late for that day's market are pouring through the narrow arch of the guard tower to find places for the night. The town falls into the deep, hot tranquillity of the African afternoon, but the great quadrangle of the *zungo* is in turmoil. It is like a huge stew pan boiling on the still red heat of the town square. The flood of new arrivals swirls round the outer edge. This stream is continuous, because all African travellers have an objection to the first empty hut that they see. They dislike the empty cubicles, though they are, of course, exactly similar, and always find that they want one which has been chosen, at the same moment, by somebody else. Then they argue for an hour, call the guard, are driven off at last by bored neighbours, and frantically begin their search again.

In the middle of this whirlpool, there is a mass of bobbing heads and loads; goats, sheep, cattle, donkeys, on some of which an old rich trader, or veiled woman, still sit calmly awaiting their servants. There are even two camels who throw up their chins high above the seething crowd with looks of disgust. The noise of several hundred voices, in twenty different languages, over the shuffle and scrape of feet, is like a tremendous bubbling and spitting of steam. From all rises, like steam, a huge column of fine dust, glittering forty feet high in the afternoon sun.

Johnson, who made this *zungo*, takes no interest in the scene and feels no glory in his own creation. He only notices that it is crowded and therefore stops at the first cubicle, near the gate.

This is the most unpopular of all, because it is under the nose of the guard. Also anyone who passes in or out of the courtyard can stare into it or dip his head into it over the low front wall. It is always the last occupied.

A Hausa family is considering it. That is to say, the woman of the house, her nose extended over the wall, is sniffing at it, two small children are chasing each other round it, and the man, having placed one end of his six-foot load on the front wall, the other on his stick, has just withdrawn his head. He is pouring with sweat, as if his whole body is melting grease. His lungs are opening and shutting like the gills of a fish just caught. His eyes are glazed with exhaustion. His load probably weighs a hundred and twenty pounds, and he has carried it twenty miles.

'Do you want it?' Johnson says.

He stares at Johnson with wonder. He can't understand him Probably his brain is out of action.

'Do you want this room?'

The woman draws back her neck, looks at the guard who stands, spear in hand, just behind Johnson and makes a face. Like all women, she does not care to be near authority. She bawls at Johnson, 'No, it stinks!' Then she gives the man a prod. 'Come on, it stinks—it's unlucky too.'

'Wha.' He gazes at her.

She stoops and seizes her own household load, a huge bale of gourds and calabashes, enclosed in a net. 'Load me.'

He stoops; both heave up the load and place it on her head. 'Come on.'

'Wha.'

'It's unlucky I tell you—it's a bad place.' She makes a vigorous gesture as if to lift another load. He scowls angrily. He is beginning to comprehend her. But even while making ready for a protest, he obeys the hand, bends his knees, puts himself under the load and throws up his chin to balance the weight. He gives a deep groan, seizes his stick and lifts the load off stick and wall. Then at last he understands what is happening and exclaims angrily, 'What? This is all right.'

But the woman is already staring down her nose into the next cubicle. The Hausa slowly and carefully turns, in case the swinging load may break his neck, says to himself, 'But, damn it all—Allah—Allah,' and walks slowly after her. The two children scamper out and dart round his legs.

'Here we are,' Johnson says. 'The best cubicle of the lot—what luck. On a Sunday, too, which is the big day's market after the police are paid. You see, my love, that I'm the lucky man.'

Bamu slightly raises her eyelids at the cubicle and walks past. Johnson gives a cry, 'But here we are.' Bamu has already examined and rejected the next one. So, after a complete circuit, they return half an hour later to the first and find two bush pagans examining the inside with delighted grins. Both Johnson and Bamu immediately shout at them, 'Go away—what are you doing in our house?'

The pagans, abashed, creep out with fearful looks and dart away; Johnson triumphantly unloads Bamu, opens the canopy chair, unrolls two mats on the floor, hangs up the muslin nets, and puts on his shoes.

Sozy picks up her dry sticks and disappears to find firewood and water. In half an hour the fire is made and three different pots are simmering in holes among the ashes.

It is past five; the evening sun throws its bright blue shadow across the whole courtyard to the foot of the eastern rooms. All the rooms have been taken and many have two famillies. Only a few belated wanderers are still going round the edge seeking a lodging. The yard itself is a huge bivouac. Scores of family parties sit round their fires among the tethered cattle, which stretch out their necks towards the smoke and stare at the flames with round, alarmed eyes. The smoke makes a hundred little french blue columns in the still air, which seem to support a canopy of bright blue and gold above the *zungo* roofs in the sloping sun rays.

All these hundreds of people are chattering together with the peculiar lively note of sociability and evening happiness. Any voice that can be distinguished is full of gaiety, and now and then someone gives the loud sudden laugh of anticipation; there are everywhere calls of greeting.

The few who are moving about; three or four young boys, a servant carrying a bucket, an old woman with a stick, make their way through the confusion with purposeful ease as if in streets and lanes. In fact, what seems like confusion is seen to be exactly ordered as a beehive. Each family or caravan is a unit grouped about its own fires and pots. The haltered animals are secured somewhere at the edge of the circle; and the space between the groups however narrow is as clearly apparent to the passer-by as a street. So he can walk confidently, without disturbing anyone, through what looks like a solid mass of bodies.

Nothing is more charming than the voices of peoples at rest in camp after a long day's work or long march. They make together the very sound and note of friendship and self-forgetfulness. They are full of contentment and no one hears them without feeling reassurance and a new peace. It is as if he has forgotten during the hard work or anxieties of the day that underneath all the conflict and perplexity in life itself there is an immense common happiness and peace, shared by all creatures in their simplest feelings.

Johnson, sensitive to every breath of feeling, is himself keenly happy. He sits beside the fire with his new white hat on the extreme back of his head. Sometimes he stirs a pot and sometimes looks round him, sometimes at Bamu, who is squatted down on a bundle of sticks, suckling the baby.

Only Sozy is restless and keeps rummaging in the calabashes and muttering. She feels that she has forgotten something necessary to the supper, but she can't think what it is. Sozy has forgotten how to be happy. She is always on the defensive.

Johnson, like the rest, is gossiping, talking for pleasure and saying the same thing many times with the same broad smile, sure of appreciation. 'Yes, it's lucky—I'm a lucky chap—this is a good thing for me. Bamu. I stayed too long on the road. Allah, what is the good of roads, A road headman, who is he? Nobody. Of course, Mister Rudbeck depended on me and I couldn't go away from him. I promised him to finish the work and I finished it. But I tell you, my dear, it's lucky it is finished. It is a lucky thing, too, that Mister Rudbeck and I had that little argument, because it just gave me the excuse to go away from him. Yes, my sweetheart'—throwing another stick on Sozy's fire—'what I was afraid of was that Mister Rudbeck would keep me for headman and you know I am too kind. That is my fault. I am a very good-hearted man. I get fond of people just like a woman and then they make use of me. Yes, I have been robbed and misused by people, my treasure, and that's why you have had these bad times. But now I'm going to change all that. I'm going into trade and I'm going to be a rich man. Perhaps, my dearest, you think that it is just talk, but I'm not a man who talks. When I say things, I do them. Look at those keys I got—everybody knows of that bold daring act. It was a wonderful deed. And I shall trade like that too. I'll start to-morrow. What's more, I start with a great advantage. I'm a pretty big man in the country and the Waziri's best friend.'

181

Johnson watches Bamu for a moment and smiles. 'Don't think I've forgotten about the gramophone either or the motor car. Why, my darling, my gift from God, I've just been waiting to get away from that road until I could make you a real big woman for this country. For what a good wife you've been. How good you were to me when I had to resign my appointment at Sargy Gollup's; a good faithful wife, you never said a word to me. May God bless you now and bring down the milk as sweet as yourself.'

Bamu says to Sozy, 'More salt for that one.' Sozy gets up, runs here and there, looks into three different gourds.

'That one,' Bamu says, and throws in a handful of grey desert salt.

Johnson stirs the salt in the broth, and smiles at her, admiring her. She is certainly a pretty girl and deserves her name as a belle, but Johnson takes a delight in her proportionate with his natural power of feeling. He gazes with wondering eyes and a broad smile at her brown, polished shoulders, her nose shining like oiled bronze, her soft, curly lips, the beautiful shell curl of her nostrils, the round, small forehead, smooth as a bowl, the eyes set within their firm, thick lids as if by a skilful and decisive carver.

'Yes, you good beautiful wife, Bamu—I love you too much—I love you stronger than the tree grows—I love you more than the sun fills the air.'

'More water, Sozy.'

Sozy rushes at the sticks. Bamu, crooking her arm under the baby's belly, gets up and reaches for the water, which she dribbles carefully into the broth. The breast falls out of the baby's mouth. His legs hang down in the air, curling over each other. He draws his bald skull into his fat neck like a tortoise and gives a sharp disgusted squall, like a punctured balloon. Bamu sits down again and puts him again to her breast. Johnson stirs the cool water into the stew and hums a carrier's song, half humming, half singing:

'*Now I see far off the smoke of a village.*
Like a woman it bends towards me and beckons me,
Saying, Here is rest, here is food and drink.
Headman, blow your pipe now for we are near.
Oh, labourers, your thighs falter like a horse's wither.
Your necks are breaking with the load pain.
Oh, blind ones, running with cast down eyes.

182

You cannot breathe any more, there is blood in your nose.
Listen, I hear far-off women's voices.
Headman, blow your pipe now for us coming.
We come, come fast, the labourers, we run because we are so tired,
We run in case we shall fall down before we come.
Blow, blow, headman, make the pipe sound.
Tell them we come, we come, the labourers,
Oh, women of the house, we thank you beforehand.
We salute you now, we repent to you, we the labourers.
We rely upon you, oh, kind women of all the world.
Our mother, our sister, our daughter, our wife.
Blow, blow, our headman——'

Bamu flips her nipple out of the baby's mouth and jerks him under her arm into the cloth. The baby howls; Bamu gets up and goes towards the *zungo* gate. Her brother Aliu has just come in. Bamu gives him a bob curtsey; he holds up the palm of his hand and mutters some pagan salutation.

Johnson rushes up to them. 'Hi! What do you want?'

'Nothing, clerk.'

He turns to Bamu, 'You're not going with him?'

'What?'

'You're not going away?'

Bamu makes no answer. The brother says to her, 'I heard something had happened.'

'Yes, we came here.'

There is a short pause. The baby doubles itself up in the cloth and utters terrific screams of rage. Bamu reflectively gazes past Aliu at the porter's spear; Aliu looks over her shoulder towards the setting sun.

'What happened?' Aliu asks.

'I don't know.'

Another pause. The baby suddenly stops screaming and relaxes with its nose buttoned on the edge of the cloth.

'White man's work.'

'Yes, some foreign work.'

Bamu raises her eyebrows slightly and shifts her gaze to old Sozy, who is blowing up the fire. Aliu glances sideways at the huts and frowns. The baby is already asleep.

'Time for supper,' Johnson says gaily. He walks round them like a dog excluded from a reunion on the street corner. If he had a tail he would be wagging it, now and then, at half-cock. He says again 'You hungry, my sweetheart? Aliu, you would like supper?'

Neither speaks or looks. He goes back to old Sozy, builds up the fire, stirs the pots, and hums the tune of 'I see the smoke of a village far away.' But he is depressed and thoughtful. Suddenly he remembers that it is Sunday. He pauses a moment, makes a grimace, draws himself up and walks thoughtfully out of the *zungo*. In ten minutes he is standing behind the store compound. From within he can hear the screams of Matumbi and Gollup's calm, unangry shouts of abuse. Gollup has reached the moral stage. Johnson slides barefooted like a shadow between the mats, past the boy's huts and into the back door of the store. Gollup's bedroom door stands open. Johnson looks through the crack of the door and waits till Gollup, having got Matumbi down, stoops to punch her face at leisure. He then glides past the opening into the store. He still has his key to the cash drawer under the counter. He opens it, puts in his hand and finds a heap of small silver. He fills his pocket, shuts and locks the drawer and slides again down the passage. He sees Gollup in the act of jumping on Matumbi with both feet, and as he slips down the steps, hears him say in a grave unthreatening voice, 'I'm going to make a real job of it to-day, you bitch.'

Johnson flies back to the *zungo*. Bamu is cooking the supper; her brother is dandling the baby in the canopy chair. They are a family group.

Johnson rushes up to Bamu and pours a shower of shillings and sixpences over her. He calls out to the neighbours supping round their fires, 'Come, it's a party.'

In half an hour there are drummers, dancers and beer. Johnson is jigging and singing:

'I got a lil girl, she roun' like de worl'.'

The moon rides above the walls of the *zungo*, throwing a ray like limelight on the dancers and on the group by the door. Bamu looks thoughtfully at the moon, and then at the baby dozing in her brother's lap.

Bamu picks up the baby, puts it in her cloth, and ties tightly. The brother gets up and gives his gown a twitch. Johnson makes a jump towards them and shouts, 'Where are you going?'

The brother holds out his spear and says, 'She's coming home.'

'But she can't go home. She's my wife.'

'She has the right,' Aliu says.

'How long will you go?'

'For as long as she likes,' Aliu says.

'Bamu, you don't want to go?'

'Yes, I'm going now.'

'But, Bamu, I'm just about to make you rich.'

'I don't want to be rich. I want to go home.'

'But, Bamu, don't you 'gree for me?'

'No, I don't.'

'Haven't I done work for you?'

'Yes.'

'What then do you want?'

'You're mad.'

'She means you're mad,' Aliu explains.

Johnson suddenly rushes to the gate and shouts, 'Don't let them out. He's stealing my wife.'

The *dogari* on duty, a stupid, truculent-looking fellow, gazes at him and says, 'Who is it?'

'It's clerk Johnson, and if you let these people out, I'll tell Waziri.'

'Oh, oh, Waziri. And this is your wife, you say.'

Bamu just then tries to walk past and this action causes at once an idea in the guard. He is ready to stop people from doing things. He drops the spear across the gate and says, 'Here, woman, wait a bit.'

'That's it, keep her till I come.' Johnson runs to Waziri's house at top speed.

Johnson is refused admittance at Waziri's front porch. A sleepy old man says that it is too late for visitors. But he goes in at the back through a hole in the mat wall, known to him on many private visits, and makes directly for the old man's compound.

The hut is brightly lighted. A young southern boy, old copper colour, with round, plump limbs, is in the act of putting on a blue gown. He stops with both hands in the gown sleeves and looks at Johnson with childish interest and arrogance.

'What do you want, stranger?'

'I want Saleh.'

'Who is Saleh?'

'The Waziri's friend.'

'I never heard of him.'

'Oh, yes, Saleh with the long neck?'

'Oh, you mean that Saleh.' The child makes a little grimace between laughter and disgust. 'But he isn't Waziri's friend—he treated Waziri very badly. He was most ungrateful.'

'But where is he? I must see him.'

'I tell you he's not here. They drove him out, the nasty boy, and serve him right.'

'Oh!' Johnson suddenly understands. His gaze of wonder becomes an anxious and polite enquiry, 'But perhaps you know where Waziri is?'

The boy shakes his head. 'Not just now.' Then with a coquettish air, 'But I rather expect I may know in a little while.'

'Oh, he's a friend of yours?'

'I'm a friend of his.' With a lofty glance. 'He likes me very much.'

Johnson pulls out a two-shilling piece and holds it out. The boy laughs, takes it, and runs to a tin box in the corner. He hides the coin under a tumbled heap of clothes, ropes, mats, in the box, and then says to Johnson, 'You can wait if you like.'

Johnson waits a quarter of an hour, gloomily biting his fingers and twiddling his toes, while the small boy chatters about the extraordinary affection and respect with which Waziri regards him. 'He tells me everything.'

At last Waziri's asthmatic breathing and shuffling feet are heard on the hard earth outside. Johnson runs out of the door and salutes him.

'Waziri—forgive—excuse me—it's Johnson.'

'Wha-at.' The old man starts backwards in panic and snatches up his gown as if it may hide a snake.

'It's your friend Johnson, Waziri. You know my wife Bamu, whom you gave me.'

'Oh-h.' Waziri drops his gown and looks calmly at Johnson. In the moonlight, his face seems like sun-dried clay. Its creases are sharp as cracks. 'How do you come here?'

'I had to come, Waziri; it's urgent. My wife Bamu suddenly declares that she is going back to her family.'

'But, tell me, they say that Judge Rudbeck has turned you out.'

'It is false—I left my work on the road, that's all.'

'You left Judge Rudbeck?'

'The road was finished, you understand. But excuse me, Waziri, the matter of my wife, it is very urgent—she's packing up to go.'

'I don't care what she does. What are you thinking of, you rubbish, coming here with such nonsense in the middle of the night? How dare you?' Waziri suddenly loses his temper. He screams at the top of his voice. 'Thieves!'

Half a dozen house slaves or servants, who have probably been listening to the conversation, start up with sticks and spears.

'Catch him!' Waziri shrieks. 'How dare he come here into my private compound? Beat him, knock his eyes out—smash his face in—tear his guts out.'

Johnson is thrown on the ground. He kicks and fights like a maniac. He hears a voice say, 'Shall we take him to prison, lord?'

'No, no,' Waziri shrieks. 'Beat him only—throw him out—go on, you fools, don't kill him—only cripple him.'

Johnson, tearing, spitting, yelling, is dragged away by the feet, beaten with sticks, kicked and trampled into insensibility. In the morning he wakes up half-naked, covered with blood and bruises, in the town ditch, buried deep in rubbish. He crawls out, and since his visit of ceremony is over, takes off his patent shoes and hangs them round his neck by the laces. They are, to his great relief, undamaged. He limps back then to the *zungo*, where he finds his cubicle completely bare. Bamu and her family have taken even the water-pot; even Sozy. While Johnson is gazing with surprise at the bare floor, the guard comes up and says, 'You're back, are you?'

'Yes, clever one. Why did you let them out?'

'They said this morning that Waziri's men had beaten you to death.'

'They tried.' Johnson laughs. 'But you see that they didn't succeed. No.' His spirits begin to rise. 'I was a bit too much for them.'

'You owe me a penny halfpenny.'

'What about my property? Are you the guard or not?'

The guard is alarmed. He says, 'But I didn't know——'

'Suppose I go to the judge now, Judge Rudbeck.'

'But Waziri has already laid a complaint against you.

'When?'

'This morning—he says you broke into his house at night—he says you tried to corrupt the boy—he wants to put you in prison.'

'Oh, does he,' Johnson cries. 'He'd better look out—that old villain. I know too much—I could tell stories about him too. Let him be careful, that's all.' Johnson walks angrily up and down. 'I'm not afraid of anybody—I wasn't afraid of Sargy Gollup, and I'm not afraid of a savage like Waziri. I'll beat him—as I beat his men last night. I don't care anything for any of them—or you either.' Johnson makes a violent gesture which causes the guard to grab at his sword. Johnson laughs at this and looks round for an audience. He shouts out, 'See here, friends—your brave soldier is afflicted—he is sick for belly.'

A crowd of beggars, idle labourers and half-grown boys, carriers, unemployed while their masters or parents are sitting in the market, gathers at once and listens with enjoyment to a word battle between the offended constable and Johnson. The former threatens a complaint to the Emir, prison, stocks, a flogging; Johnson answers with chaff.

'King of guards, emperor of the *zungo*, lord of the dung-heap and flea-pit, I repent at your feet. You are my father and mother and I am an ass.'

The guard retires at last, cross-eyed with rage, into his private cubicle; Johnson, followed by the crowd of his admirers, walks through the *zungo* relating to everyone the events of the night, the treachery of Waziri, his victory over the Waziri's assassins and his triumph over the guard.

He imitates in turn the little boy, Waziri wheezing and shuffling through the moonlight to his tryst, the Waziri's terror at Johnson's voice, the rush of men to rescue him and their panic when they realize that it is Johnson with whom they have to deal. Finally, their utter defeat and humiliation.

'They tore your clothes a bit,' somebody remarks.

'Did they?' Johnson looks down at his tattered rags. 'So they did, the blackguards. That shows you what a fight it was. Just look at my trousers.'

'And your eye.'

'And my eye. My friends, it was a big fight. They roared like lions and I really believed at first that some lions must have attacked me. I said, they can't be men—they're too fierce—they even smell like lions.'

Johnson sniffs the air, opens his eyes wide, and spreads out his hands like claws. At once the audience, not only the half-grown boys, but the old labourers, marked with the bald patch, worn by ten thousand miles of head carrying, the old traders attracted from their packing by the crowd, open their eyes too, wrinkle their nostrils slightly in the sketch of a sniff, and crook their fingers. Johnson holds them. An hour later he is still describing his victory, which has become an epic. In six months, a year, perhaps five or ten years, carriers and traders as far away as Tripoli, Khartoum, Mecca, Lagos will tell the story of clerk Johnson and the Wazirin Fada.

Meanwhile he has his choice of chairs, fires and meals at the *zungo*. He is among the most welcome and honoured guests in all Africa, men of imagination, the story-tellers, the poets.

At night when Ajali and Benjamin come to seek him in the *zungo*, he is presiding over the biggest drum party that they have ever seen. It is not like a party of the townspeople, with its regular routine and well-known dances; it is a witches' night for all nations. There are twenty different dances; a gang of mountain pagans come to clean the parade ground are jigging in one corner; a group of Hausas are acting a kind of mime in another; single and lonely persons are inventing their own steps and shouting their own accompaniment; in the gate corner an old one-eyed Pathan, who carries for papers a chit from a political officer in Kashmir, and a transport order signed by a district commissioner in the Eastern Sudan, is clapping his hands for two thick-set Yoruba girls, dancing an American fox-trot together. Behind, in the middle of the yard, among small fires with little flames not much bigger than candles, a few quiet family parties are still supping and murmuring together. Beside the red embers, half a dozen carriers, arrived late with heavy packages, and unable to find lodgings, lie heaped together like corpses, one's head on another's thigh; a third on his face, a fourth, flat on his back with both knees in the air and one finger across the bridge of his nose, his head twisted sideways against his load. A sheep, trailing its halter, is nibbling the load; beyond them a cow stands with lowered head and glittering red eyes as if about to charge the dancers; then suddenly takes fright and dashes away kicking and converting with a tail stiffly bent like a pump handle.

Johnson, still in rags, but wearing a battered white helmet, presented by some trader, is walking among all the groups, laughing, encouraging them, dancing with each and then imitating and embroidering the steps;

189

or suddenly, upon the impulse, throwing up his hands and whirling in a dance of his own; acting some scene of his exploits; breaking into high-pitched song.

> *'Clerk Johnson no 'fraid of nobody, nutting at all.*
> *Clerk Johnson got strong heart, go all by himself.*
> *Clerk Johnson got a heart like a motor car, prompety, foot, foot.*
> *He go by himself, no one fit to stop him.*
> *He full of fire, he full of hot, he full of strong.*
> *He no want nobody, no judge, no Waziri.*
> *He make all dem strong judge for himself.*
> *He no want no frien'.*
> *He make all dem frien' for his own heart.*
> *He no 'fraid of no nobody, no nutting at all.*
> *He got a heart like a lion, go round inside his bress, krong, krong.*
> *He fight 'em like a horse stand up ten foot high.'*

Johnson rises on his toes, boxes the air like a stallion, tramples the ground, and gives his tail a jerk behind.

'Good evening.' Ajali thrusts his face towards him. 'How you do now?'

'I do very well, Mister Ajali—have you got some strong beer?'

'I hear Waziri go beat you.'

'You hear wrong, Ajali—I beat dat Waziri, I make him wish he be dead.'

Benjamin gazes at Johnson with intense curiosity and says, 'What, you leave your job with Mister Rudbeck?'

'I leave him.'

'Now what do you do?'

'I, Mister Benjamin, I go walkum all everywhere in de worl'—I go make my fortune.'

'I think that would be a good plan. Yes, I think so.' Benjamin still gazes at Johnson. 'Where are you going?'

'I go where I like, Mister Benjamin. Perhaps I go with dis gentleman—very rich man.'

He waves towards the group which stands always round him, admiring him, or waiting for his next joke, his next song; and says in Hausa, 'I am one of you now—I come with you.'

An troldader in a large dirty turban wags his head slowly and gives a loud cackling laugh. Then once more he fixes his little blackbird's eyes on Johnson, waiting for amusement. He is a famous man on the road—one of the richest. Down on the southern border he keeps a royal state in his huge household, with cars, many wives and servants. He is a little man with a singularly small, thin face, crinkled like a prune.

'I shall go with Alhaji there, that old rascal, and steal some of his wives.'

The old man gives another cackle and says in a high voice, 'Trading—that's not for everybody—it's a life.'

'Yes, a good life.'

'It is perhaps a real life,' Benjamin says thoughtfully in English. 'What do you say, Johnson, if I lose my job, perhaps I come too?'

'Look at you, Alhaji, you old rascal, with a new girl every month and young ones too. Are you made of silver to be so hard on them?'

The crowd shouts with laughter, the old man cackles and wags his head till his turban falls over his eys. He pipes, 'It's as God wills—and there's luck in it too—much luck.'

'Oh, but I'm the lucky man. Clerk Johnson is the luckiest man in the world.'

'Where's your girl, den?' Ajali cries, grinning. 'Where's dat Missus Johnson?'

'Missus Johnson?' Johnson is surprised. He has forgotten about Bamu.

'Bamu,' Ajali prompts him. 'I hear she leave you now you got no money.'

'Oh, dat poor, savage girl—I let her go home for while till I get new house.'

'Where you make your new house, Johnson?'

'I tink perhaps I take the Emir's house, pull him down, make something fit for gentleman and his family.'

Benjamin stares and shakes his head as if he dislikes this levity. He murmurs, 'No, it is better that you go away from this place. There is nothing here—not even civilized houses.'

Ajali bursts out laughing and says, 'How you make new house—perhaps you make him out of you trousers?'

Johnson looks at his rags, smiles and says, 'I make him out of money, all de posts of dollars, all de roof sticks of shillings, and all de thatch of coppers. I make my bed of gold with silver legs and I make my net of little, fine silver threads all lace together.'

'I nearly lose my job once,' Benjamin says. 'If I lose my job, I think I shall come with you, Johnson. Yes, I think that would be very wise for me.'

'Come then, Mister Benjamin—we are going to be rich soon. We go home to England, we see de King and Pallament.'

He begins to sing 'England is my home, de King of England is my King,' and dances with the peculiar, loose, boneless step which expresses his patriotic sentiment.

The old trader laughs, claps and even moves his feet. The rest hum the tune. Benjamin goes on talking about losing his job and taking the road. He explains at great length that he has stolen the stamps from the post office and that Mr. Rudbeck ought to have sacked him. He gets excited, in a grave way, drinks beer, and the people laugh to see him still talking to Johnson, explaining, arguing.

Only Johnson is not surprised by this peculiar conduct in Benjamin. He keeps on saying, 'Yes, Mister Benjamin, you come with me; we go walkum everywhere.'

'Yes, it is necessary for me,' Benjamin says. 'I am too lonely here. Yes, that is it—it is the loneliness. There are not enough civilized. Of course, I am drunk now, but I know that I speak very good sense.'

A little later in the evening Benjamin is found without his tie, dancing among the pagans. The pagans and Ajali are laughing, but he is still serious and his dignity makes their laughter cheap. For though he dances, he has lost not dignity, but only his stiffness, something foreign and pompous. His new dignity is graceful, strong and afraid of nothing, like all great art. It accords for some reason with the dancer's melancholy face. He has ceased to be grave and become as proud and mournful as a Greco saint. His forehead wrinkles, his lower lids seem to drop outwards, his long cheeks are hollow.

'Look at the drunk clerk,' the crowd cry.

Benjamin does not notice them. He sings or sighs through his nose, 'He go by himself, no one fit to stop him.'

Johnson comes in with the refrain:

> 'He's got a heart like a motor car, prompety, foot, foot.
> Full of fire, full of hot, full of strong.'

At nine o'clock, one of the beer-sellers, an old woman from the town, comes to demand her money. Johnson assures her that she will be paid, but she begins to shout.

'Now then, ma, you know I got plenty money,' Johnson tells her.

Ajali gives a shout of malicious laughter. 'Where you catch dat money, Johnson—in you trouser pocket.'

Johnson holds up a key hanging from the purse string round his neck. 'Plenty, Mister Ajali—a whole box full.'

Ajali's crab eyes stick out. 'What's dat key?'

Johnson throws up the key and catches it. 'How much money in my store to-day?'

'You store, Johnson?'

'Did you work hard to-day, Mister Ajali—at my store.'

'But what you do now, Johnson. What's dat key?'

'De key to get my money from my store,' Johnson says. 'What's de time, Mister Benjamin—moon no rise yet. No, I tink perhaps I go get some money for you and me.'

'For me, Mister Johnson. But where are you getting this money?' Benjamin gazes in mild surprise at his friend.

'He go rob de cash drawer for Sargy Gollup,' Ajali cries, effervescing with delight and excitement. His lips bibble. 'He go dis minute.'

'But you cannot do so, Johnson.' Benjamin raises his brows. 'To steal money like that—that's not the same as taking Mister Rudbeck's keys—it's a bad kind of robbery.'

'He my money,' Johnson laughs at him. 'He my store, Mister Benjamin—because I got de key to him.'

'But, Johnson, if all people did so—there would be robbery on every hand—there would be nothing but bad trouble everywhere. There would be no civilization possible.'

'Did you sell plenty cloth to-day, Mister Ajali? Did you buy me some good hides? Did you make plenty money for me? I go see now. Perhaps if plenty money no live, I give you de sack.'

Johnson, smiling and tossing the key, strolls away. In half an hour he returns still smiling and goes towards Ajali and Benjamin who are drinking beer with the old cattle-trader.

Ajali is still effervescing, jumping up and down on his seat, but Benjamin looks grave and sad. His sadness is once more judicious and resigned. He looks more like a missionary than a saint. He is still without a tie, but he has buttoned the collar of his shirt.

Johnson comes before them and spreads out his arms. In each hand he holds a bottle of gin. The two clerks gaze. Ajali gives a scream of excitement.

'Sargy's gin—oh, my Gawd—Sargy's own gin. Where you get dat gin, you Johnson?'

'I get him from my store. I keep first-class store. Drink up, Mister Ajali. Drink up, Mister Benjamin. I got plenty gin in my store. Gin from home. English gin. What else you want? Kola nuts, cigarettes.' Johnson takes a two-shilling piece out his pocket and tosses it to a passing labourer. 'Bring cigarettes.' Another, and throws it to a small boy, 'Find kola-nut merchant and bring nuts.' Another to a woman, 'Give it to the drummers and tell them to make the king's tune.'

He is surrounded now by a crowd, laughing, holding out their hands. No one is astonished except Ajali, Benjamin and the rich old trader, Alhaji. The poor are not surprised by anything that money may do; they do not wonder to see a fountain of silver rise from a pauper's hand. He has been lucky; money has favoured him.

Ajali and Benjamin jump up. Their eyes follow the curve of the flying money. Ajali cries as if in pain, 'But he find out—he count money.'

'On Sunday he count money.'

'Yes, on Sunday. In six day he know somebody tief money.'

Johnson laughs at Ajali's terrified and astonished face. 'Six day—dat long time. You make me plenty more money in six day.'

Ajali stares at him not comprehending. 'And how you do so, Johnson. How Sargy no see you? He no drunk to-day, and the gin live under his bed.'

Johnson laughs, delighting in Ajali's wonder. 'I go to store—I look—I wait behind door'—drawing himself up to tiptoe—'till I see Sargy light cigarette—it shine for his eyes.' He screws up his eyes. 'I go down.' Johnson suddenly sinks down on his haunches. 'I go past quick, quick.' He moves along the ground on his heels with a waddling gait, like the second figure of a hornpipe; but with surprising rapidity and silence. 'I go for store, take my money. But I bump my head against de shelf—all de tins fall down, plank, plunkety. Sargy shout, "Whossat comes for store?" I go down'—crouching down with his hands over his head—'by de counter. Sargy lookum store—because he so dark—I go out—see his room empty—se dem gin under bed—so I tink—Ajali and Benjamin like some gin.'

194

'What, you take dem gin from under his bed when he go for store.'

'I do so, Mister Ajali.'

'What, for Gawd's sake happen to you if he come back den, you fool chile.'

'I knock him down again.'

Benjamin, who has been following Johnson about with growing amazement, now exclaims, 'But Johnson, that is a bad way to go on. It is impossible.'

'Dey put you for prison,' Ajali cries, 'for sure now.'

'Dey no put Johnson for prison.' Johnson, at the word 'prison.' looks angry and frightened. He shouts as if at unseen enemies. 'No prison—take away dat prison. I no fit to go in dar.'

Ajali pokes out his long, crocodile chin. 'How you stop dem, you fool chile?'

Johnson whisks out his cook's knife and makes it flash in the firelight. 'Dey no catch me.' Ajali jumps back a yard. Benjamin growing more agitated, begins a long expostulation. He assures Johnson of his friendship and admiration, but points out that crimes of robbery and violence are dangerous to civilization and that therefore they are wrong and wicked. Moreover, they would be very likely to cause remorse. 'I fear you will be sorry, Johnson. It is always dangerous for a Christian to do serious crimes.'

Johnson smiling in his face, but not listening to him, flourishes his knife and cries, 'Take away dem ole prison—dey not fit keep clerk Johnson for no prison.'

'How so, Johnson. What, you think you king of dis Fada country?'

'I king of dis Fada country.'

'Den dey put you in prison at Kaduna.'

'I king of dem Kaduna. I king of all dem country. I say to all dem policemen, open up dem prison, for clerk Johnson come out.'

'Oh, Johnson, dat fool talk now.'

'How it be fool talk, Ajali? Dey my prison. I catch dem key.' He holds up the knife in front of Ajali's eyes. 'Me king of all dem prison in de worl'.'

He laughs at them, puts the knife back in his belt, and walks among the crowd, tosses a shilling, a sixpence, and calls out, 'We are happy now—we are happy, friends.' The crowd shouts back, 'We are happy,' and hold out their hands to catch the sixpences and threepennies which fly up between the yellow light of the camp fire and the white light of the new-risen moon, sparkling gold and silver, and curl away into the tossing waves of black.

Ajali and Benjamin follow closely. Benjamin, looking at the money with a mournful shake of the head as if to say, 'This is wrong and bad.' Ajali, amazed, excited, sweating with the thrill of Johnson's deeds, and grinning with condescension for Johnson. But the grin is fixed and uncertain. It is contradicted by the raised eyebrows, the popping eyes. He is astonished by Johnson's triumph. It seems to him that Johnson defies the very laws of being; and still goes unpunished. It is most unjust. He keeps on turning to Benjamin and shouting, 'Dey catch him dis time for sure.'

Benjamin shakes his head mournfully. 'He is very clever, but I am afraid it will not be good for him to look back in his old age and say, "What have I done with my life." '

'Johnson clever—he perfect fool chile. Dey catch him dis time for sure.'

The next day, when Ajali goes to the store, he is very thoughtful. When Gollup comes to the shop he says to him, 'Funny ting, sah—dis cash drawer got a scratch round keyhole.'

'I suppose you've scratched it, you poop.' Then the sergeant looks at the drawer, which has been marked for years and says, 'It is scratched too. Now, oo's been at it?'

'I tink we no put money for de drawer, sah; he not safe.'

'You think perhaps we leave the money in the till and you tief 'em. Not in these trousers, Mister Poldedoodle.'

He opens the drawer, counts the money, strikes a balance with various accounts and comes to the conclusion that the cash may be short by a pound or two. The sergeant is not good at accounts; he hates arithmetic and often does not strike the balance of his petty cash for a month. He cannot now be sure if one or two pounds are missing, or if perhaps the present he gave Matumbi, on Sunday morning, was two or three pounds instead of one. But he is taking no risks. He puts a note in the drawer showing the total, and makes Ajali balance it each evening.

On Wednesday morning, the drawer shows a deficit of fifteen shillings. Also Matumbi swears that somebody has passed through the back passage at three or four in the morning. She has heard the floor creak. Gollup thinks, 'Some labourer has been copying keys.' He lies in wait with a double-barrelled gun under the store counter. Nothing happens before two. He falls asleep then and wakes up at six with a yell, aiming the gun at a suit of clothes hanging from a shelf. The drawer has not been touched.

On Friday night he has just sat down under the counter, about eleven o'clock, while the labourers are still talking in their huts, when the store door, left ajar, swings slowly back. Nobody is seen; Gollup's hair rises. Then he hears the click of a small lock and the chink of money. He springs across to the door, points the gun at the drawer and shouts, 'I've got you! Hands up!'

At once something long and dark, with a bright flash before it, seems to uncoil from the floor, straight at his breast. He fires and feels a thump on his bare chest. Then his legs give way and he says in a surprised voice, ' 'Ere, 'ere. Wot you playing at?' He's dead.

The murder is reported at the station within ten minutes. Matumbi brings the cook's knife from Gollup's house. Ajali, trembling and sweating, says that Johnson had such a knife. Johnson is missing from the *zungo*. But it appears that he has been scattering money there for a week past.

Rudbeck turns out the police, not with any expectation that they will catch anybody, but simply as a necessary official act, like putting on a uniform for the King's birthday salute. He knows that if the murderer is caught, it will be by the native administration. He therefore sends a message to the Emir, saying that a white man has been murdered and that the murderer must be found. Also he would like to speak to Mr. Johnson. The Emir sends for the Waziri and tells him to provide a murderer, either Johnson or another, within twelve hours or take the consequences, which will be severe, since the murdered man is white. The Waziri sends out his mounted messengers, who gallop along the bush tracks. Before dawn every village head in Fada, every ferryman, is prepared to arrest any stranger at sight. No wanted man in Fada has ever escaped from the Waziri, for no one in Fada can sleep in the bush. There are too many leopards. So that fugitives from justice have the choice of being caught in the first village or being eaten alive. Nevertheless, four days pass; Gollup is already buried; but no murderer, no Johnson is found anywhere. On the fifth day, just after dawn, at Jirige, Bamu and old Sozy go down to the river, to fetch water. Bamu carries the pot, Sozy dodges round her, trying to feel useful. Both women at this hour are chilled and silent. Bamu steps into the shallows, puts down the pot, and presses its lip beneath the surface to let the water pour in. She says to Sozy, 'Get some leaves, Sozy.'

Sozy runs up and down, then comes to hold the pot. Bamu patiently surrenders the pot and goes to fetch a twig of leaves.

Her father's old dugout lies, bottom up, just within the edge of the scrub. While Bamu breaks off a twig, she sees this dugout move. Before she can scream, it lifts, a thin face plastered with dirt peeps out from, beneath it and Johnson's voice says, 'Bamu.'

'It's you, is it?'

'Yes, it's Johnson.'

'What are you doing there?'

'I'm hiding here—but it's a bad place.'

'Yes, it's bad.'

'Can you hide me in your house a little while?'

'I don't know—is that the best thing?'

'I'm hungry, Bamu. I've had nothing to eat since the day before yesterday.'

'You're hungry, are you? What would you like?'

Bamu knows that it's her duty to feed a husband. 'Shall I bring some food here?'

'Take me to your house first. Is anyone about?'

'I don't know.'

Johnson creeps out. He is almost naked. His trousers are two leg-holes in a rag of cloth and his coat has lost its back. It is two sleeves held together by a collar. But the patent-leather shoes still dangle from his neck.

Sozy, staggering up with the full pot, sees him, and nearly lets it fall. She thinks that he is resurrected from the dead. She gazes with a deeply wrinkled forehead, murmurs to herself, uncertainly, '*Da dadi.*' But she doesn't believe him yet.

Bamu rescues the pot, throws in the spray of leaves to keep it from spilling and says to Sozy, 'Load me.'

She says then to Johnson, with the pot on her head, 'Very well, husband, come to the house. Luckily I have some meat—good meat.' She turns up the slope. Johnson glides, in his peculiar crouching gait, round by the scrub behind the compound, and so through the back mats into Bamu's hut.

He sits there trembling and dejected with his face towards the door. Sozy peeps in, and then runs away again. She can't make out exactly what has happened, and this throws her into terrible agitation. She has come to know that every strange event is a danger to the old.

Bamu quickly blows up a fire, mixes yam flour, warm water, some salt, pepper, a few shreds of meat powder. She puts it in a clean calabash and brings it to Johnson.

'Is that right for you?'

'Yes, it's magnificent. It is the best I ever had. How good you are, Bamu. You have saved my life.'

'More salt perhaps?'

'No, thank you, my dear one. It is perfect.'

Bamu goes to her brother and says, 'What shall I do? That clerk is here—I mean my husband.' The brother says, 'Which way does he look?'

'Towards the door.'

'Then make him turn round.'

'But what will you do?'

'That's not a woman's business. It is a man's business.'

Bamu goes back to Johnson and says, 'But why do you sit like that on the floor? Use my chair.' She pulls her chair round, back to the door, Johnson, surprised by this affectionate thought, sits down. At once the brother enters the door with a club and hits him a tremendous blow on the head. Johnson falls like a tree. Bamu and the brother tie him up with a straw rope and send for the police. Johnson wakes up in time to see four native policemen enter with ropes, chains, spears and swords. They chain his ankles and wrists, tie his wrist to his neck, and drive him along with frequent prods and thumps.

Sozy runs distracted to and fro between Johnson and the village. She can't make out what has happened to her family, or which half requires her. But suddenly Bamu is heard shouting, 'Wood, Sozy.'

Johnson says, 'Go and get the wood for your mistress, Sozy.'

Sozy's face clears. Her problem is solved. She rushes back towards the compound, muttering to herself, '*Da dadi.*' But at once she begins to look anxious. She is asking herself, 'What is this difficult duty? Shall I be equal to it?'

Johnson is much depressed. He can hardly walk. His neck sags. But when at last he approaches the town and the main road, he sees the other travellers running to get out of his way. Then he perceives that he is a remarkable man; only the most desperate criminals have an escort of four. He sits down and says, 'Wait.'

The native *dogarai*, always rough with prisoners, threaten him with their spear butts. 'Get up.'

He shouts at them, 'But I must put on my shoes.'

'Get up, son of a dog.'

Johnson shouts furiously, 'I am not the son of a dog, but an English gentleman. If you were not rubbish, you would not propose to take a gentleman barefoot through your disgusting town.'

The *dogarai* give way. One of them, such is the power of Johnson's character, even stoops to tie his laces, which he cannot manage, one-handed, for himself.

Johnson jumps up, revived. He straightens his back, swaggers his shoulders and, passing through the market place, he even waves his free hand at the staring awed crowd. He enjoys his last triumph.

He is thrown into the old common dungeon of the gaol, now brought again into use after Tring's departure. It is a long, twilit chamber of thick mud, with window holes six inches square. Here thirty prisoners, chained in pairs, are squatted on the floor, or lie against each other with their rags pulled over their heads, in a stupor of boredom.

Few look at Johnson; none shows any interest or curiosity. He sits down in a corner and admires his shoes, turning his feet sideways to catch the light on the varnish, rubs his chafed ankles. A couple comes shuffling towards him, a tough little pagan with bandy legs, a lanky youth with swollen joints and hollow stomach.

The youth takes his hand and cries, 'Mr. Johnson.'

'Saleh, how strange to meet you. So we are both prisoners.'

'But I have suffered terribly. I cannot describe it, Johnson.'

'I heard of your trouble.'

'No, no, you can't understand what it is like.' Saleh gives the chain a jerk and makes an imperious gesture; the pagan smiles and bends his legs; Saleh is able to sit down. The pagan then crouches beside him.

'I came here to ask you. Speak to Rudbeck. Speak to the Governor. You must save me.'

'My poor boy, I can see you've had a bad time.'

'No, you can't see anything—you can't believe how bad it is,' Saleh says, weeping. 'A terrible injustice—I haven't done anything. Waziri says I am a thief—but it is all a lie. It is all that nasty Yoruba boy that he has bought from the Bororro.'

'They said he was adopted.'

'Yes, adopted. What's the difference? And, do you know, they set on me and took everything I had, my new gown and my rings and my box and my money and they beat me and sent me here. Oh, how could God allow such a thing. You couldn't believe it. You don't know what can happen in this world, Johnson.'

The boy goes on weeping and bewailing his fate. The little pagan sits patiently. He does not utter a word. Sometimes he stretches himself, sometimes he examines his own stomach, sometimes he looks at Johnson for a long time with his bright, mountain eyes, smiling like a deaf mute at the play, or again he glances enquiringly at Saleh as if to ask, 'What is he, after all, my companion? What sort of boy is he?'

'Oh, I shall die,' Saleh cries. 'I can't bear it.'

'But if it is only for six months.'

'You will save me, Johnson? You will speak to Rudbeck?'

'But I am a prisoner, too.'

'Yes, but I know you are going to Rudbeck to-day.'

'To-day.' Johnson is cast down. 'That's quick—too quick.'

'Yes, to-day, and you will tell him, won't you, about my sufferings—how they have abused me—how that nasty Yoruba boy has robbed me?'

'I'll do what I can.'

'Oh, but you must. It is necessary. And, Johnson, look at my feet, they are ruined with the rough ground. Give me your shoes.'

'But, Saleh, I need my shoes.'

'Need them—what good are they to you. In two days they will hang you. Oh, Johnson, do not be so cruel. I am only a boy. I am so unhappy. I can't bear this life. I cannot walk over the rough ground, and when I stumble, they beat me. You will give me your shoes now.'

Johnson is taken aback. He begins to reason with Saleh. 'But, Saleh, they are special shoes—the best English shoes.'

'Oh, how selfish you are. You are a brute.'

Johnson is moved. 'But, Saleh——'

'Yes, a heart of stone. You see me suffer here and care nothing.'

'But, Saleh, it is not so bad for you if you cheer up. Keep up your heart.'

'Oh, how cruel you are, Johnson. You don't understand what suffering is. You don't know how cruel people are. They say they love you, and they are nice to you, but suddenly they don't care at all. And then they betray you and beat you for nothing. You're as bad as the rest. You see me here dying of cold and misery without a friend.'

Tears come to Johnson's eyes from pure sympathy. 'But, Saleh, I am your friend. I am truly sorry for you. Here is my coat, then—it will serve for a pillow.' He takes off his coat.

'I see you're going to put me off with rags and lies, like all the rest. You are cruel to me—and how selfish. What good will those shoes be when they hang you to-morrow. For it will be to-morrow, I promise you.'

'Well, damn it all, Saleh, here you are, then.' Johnson pulls off the shoes. Saleh seizes them and gives them to the pagan, who, smiling, rolls them up with the coat and puts them under his arm. Though he acts as Saleh's slave, his expression is full of the pleased curiosity of one who studies and enjoys new experience. Saleh then jerks the chain and says sharply, 'Get up, pagan.' The pagan rises quickly, taking care not to jerk his professor's leg-irons, and the couple jingle rapidly back to their own corner, where their loot is carefully rolled up in a mat.

Johnson sits looking at his bare feet for a long time, with an air of surprise. Then he says to his nearest neighbour with a voice inviting gossip, 'That boy, Saleh—fancy him being here.'

The neighbours, sitting on their heels against the wall, with their long thin arms hanging out over their knees, move only their eyes. They are a pair of cow Fulani, thin, dry and taciturn as only Fulani can be.

'A most surprising thing,' Johnson says in wonder. 'That boy was a most influential person—the Waziri's best friend—he had great power, and now, poor chap, well, you saw him. It makes you think, friends.'

The cow Fulani do not even move their eyes.

'It makes you think that a chap has to look out for himself—yes, you've got to be careful.'

A *dogari* opens the door and shouts an order. The prisoners, who have been resting after the first spell of work, form up two by two and file out into the sun, to the task of cleaning the market and emptying latrine buckets.

Two constables enter. They have come to take Johnson to the station guardroom. They know him well and greet him with that nonchalance which all police show to known criminals, the professional *sans gene* which means 'We understand each other—it's all in the game.'

Johnson is happy in the guardroom. He is not chained and the police do not look upon him with dismay and horror. They behave as usual, lounging with their buttons undone, chewing nuts and spitting through the door into the sun, throwing out those disconnected remarks which are only heard among soldiers, police, and among large families in privacy. One, for instance, a veteran of two wars, with a long row of ribbons, lying against the wall, spits and says, 'That Moma.'

The sergeant of the guard utters a short laugh and replies, 'Well, Dog-nose, what did you expect?'

A third man, polishing his buttons, thoughtfully scratches his back with the button-stick and says, 'But, oh, my, what a girl.'

All laugh, and the old soldier Dog-nose, drawing up one leg to examine his big toe-nail, mutters, 'Give me a shilling, any day.'

'Yes, you,' the sentry says through the door.

At this everybody laughs except Dog-nose, who turns up his blood-shot eyes beneath his little wrinkled forehead and growls in a disgusted voice, 'Funny, isn't it?'

Johnson, already part of the company, laughs with the laughers and looks grave with the offended old soldier. Then he asks, 'Is that Moma's girl then?'

'That's it.' The smart young sergeant looks at him. 'You know her?'

'No, sah.'

Button-stick, still polishing, says in a meditative voice, 'Well, you see, clerk, Moma comes in and gives her a clout in the gutbag.' He is also old and wrinkled. His voice is a deep bass.

'Thing that bothers me is, what did happen to the beer?'

The sentry, a brisk little man with protruding teeth, widely gapped, again stoops his head and says through the door, 'Ask Corporal Lousy.'

'Shut up, Fish-teeth. You know he's a friend of mine.'

'Did the corporal drink Moma's beer?' Johnson cries.

'That's about it, clerk.'

203

'What does he know about it?'

'Leave him alone, Pepper—he's going to be stretched, anyhow.'

'I beg your pardon,' Johnson says. 'I didn't mean to hurt your feelings.'

The old soldier Dog-nose growls angrily, 'Never mind his feelings, clerk. He's only a blasted pagan rooky, anyhow, with the usual crush on the corporal.'

The young pagan called Pepper mutters to himself and falls into deep sulks. There is a long silence. The old soldier then yawns like a dye-pit, showing a magenta mouth stained with kola nut, and exclaims in a deep voice, 'God bless us all.'

'What I say is'—Button-stick stops in mid-speech to breathe on each button in turn—'that to stop a chap sixpence for dusty legs is a dirty shame.'

'*On* a windy morning,' Dog-nose growls.

'*And* a bachelor.'

The brisk sentry pokes in his head and cries, 'Well, Soapy, if you're afraid that a wife would eat you right up——' and laughs at his own joke. The little pagan suddenly forgets his sulks and gives a shriek of laughter, looking round to see how his admired friend is appreciated.

Soapy, the button-stick, holds up his buttons in the slanting light from the door to admire his work and says mildly, 'I've oiled my own legs for fifteen years and never been stopped before.'

'Pig's-neck all over,' Dog-nose growls.

'All over.'

'Goes off to the bush for a week and comes back and jumps on your legs.'

'It's to show how smart he is,' Teeth suggests.

'I told you he was particular about legs,' the smart young sergeant says in a severe tone. 'And quite right, too.'

Dog-nose rolls his eyes at the sergeant and makes a peculiar humming noise. Soapy breaks into a song, hummed at the back of his throat:

> '*Farewell, my village, farewell, my mother dear.*
> *For I'm off to the white man's war.*'

Two other voices at once take up the song, humming and singing softly:

> '*Farewell, my sister, do not weep.*'

The little room of yellow mud is full of the evening sunlight which pours through the door. A cool evening breeze comes with it, but the walls are as hot as a stove from the afternoon sun. The men are enjoying both heat and breeze, in the disinterested manner of long-term soldiers and policemen who do not count time or take much regard for the passing moment.

The sentry is heard chanting in the sunlight outside with peculiar grace notes of his own:

> *'Fare-hoo-well, my lit-hit-til house, my si-his-ter dear.*
> *They've to-hook me for the white man's war.'*

And he adds the imitation of a bugle, 'Too-hoo-tle.'

All the voices rise together in the chorus and Johnson sings with them, 'Fare-hoo-well, my li-hit-til house.'

The indolent cadence, the languid attitudes of the singers in the stifling heat, even the heavy smell of flesh, button polish, saddle soap, rifle oil and hot earth, make Johnson feel indifferent to his own fate. Anxiety passes out of him as if into the song and the voices of the old soldiers, taking it up and carrying it away into the air. He relaxes into their mood of the everlasting camp, of pilgrimage.

> *'Farewell, my mother, it's because I was strong and big,*
> *Because I was your favourite son,*
> *They took me for the white man's war, too-hoo-tle.'*

As the voices die away, Soapy, the button-stick, is heard remarking. 'It isn't as though Pig's-neck comes on parade every day. No, friends.

> *'Too-hootle.'*

A long silence follows and then suddenly Dog-nose brays, in a raucous nasal voice:

> *'Far away that land of corn,*
> *I see you no more.'*

This is another of the soldier's songs, all full of good-byes and memories. Yet they sing as usual in an indifferent tone without sentiment. When Dog-nose draws out the note on 'far away' into a sentimental wail, he manages to make it sound like a cynical joke.

> *'Fa-ar awa-ay that la-and of co-rn.*
> *Bright bending in the wind.'*

Johnson and Soapy sing together in chorus:

'*I see you no more.*'

The singers all stop except the pagan, who begins with enthusiasm a new line and then, finding himself alone, stops abruptly. There is another long silence in which nobody moves a finger. Johnson says then in a sympathetic voice, 'Yes, it is bad for you old soldiers leaving your homes.'

Nobody moves. It is as though Johnson has spoken in an unknown tongue. After a long time, Dog-nose slowly turns his bloodshot eyes towards him and stares at him. Then he spits and ejaculates, 'Pig's-neck. Ah-h.'

'Never looks at your blanket or your ammunition.'

'Nothing but legs, belts and carbines with Pig's-neck.'

'Judge Rudbeck is a friend of mine,' Johnson says.

Fish-teeth sings out gaily beyond the door, 'Was, you mean. Too-hootle.'

'Do you think perhaps he'll let you off?' Soapy enquires.

'He's my friend.'

'Doesn't make any difference,' says Dog-nose. 'Not if you've killed a man.'

'He's been good to me.'

'*Far away that land of corn.*'

'It's the law. If it says you've got to be hanged, why he'll have to hang you, see.'

'*Bright bending in the wind, toohootil.*'

'Don't you get down about it, clerk. It doesn't hurt.'

'*For they too-hook me for the whi-hite man's war-hor.*'

'See, friends, a louse on Pepper's neck. He knows where he's a home.'

The sentry challenges some unseen passer-by, 'Who go dar? Pass friend and all's well.' He turns again towards the guard-room, 'It doesn't hurt. I saw it done at Rairai—they hung a chap down a well. No trees up there, you know—the chap didn't even give a squeak.'

'Mister Rudbeck say I good friend to him—he say he 'gree for me too much.'

'Yes, that's Pig's-neck,' Soapy declares.

'Pig's-neck all over. Legs, belts, and a little splash of old friend to wash it all down.'

'Don't you believe it, clerk,' Dog-nose says. 'Don't you let 'em make a fool of you. You're for it all right. Here, have a chew,' holding out a piece of green tobacco.

Johnson is trembling, but he laughs and says, 'I don't trouble for hanging.'

'That's it clerk. You're the plucky one. Don't you be bamboozled.'

Johnson is indignant with himself for trembling. He says, 'I don't care for anything,' and he begins to brag. He tells the story about his fight with Gollup. In the middle of this triumph, a messenger appears and calls out to the sergeant, 'Bring dem prisoner Johnson.'

Two constables hastily put on their belts, and march Johnson over to the office. On the office stoop there is a large gathering of witnesses, Ajali, Benjamin, Aliu. Johnson is brought into the office, where he finds Rudbeck seated at his table in full uniform. He open his mouth to greet him, but, seeing Rudbeck's judicial pose and gloomy air, he thinks that perhaps it would be unwise. He therefore stands silent, effacing himself as much as possible behind the constables while the court arranges itself. Intrusive witnesses are sent back to the stoop and Mr. Montagu, the new clerk, brings a Bible and a Koran.

Rudbeck is, in fact, feeling gloomy and aloof. It seems to him pure bad luck that he should have to try Johnson. But he has been in a disgusted temper for some weeks; since the comments on the provincial report, passed to him from Bulteel's office.

The comment underlined for his notice, and for reply to the Secretariat, is this: 'Mr. A. D. O. Rudbeck should be asked to explain why serious offences against property and the person have nearly doubled in Fada since he took over the division from the late Mr. D. O. Blore. His suggestion in the report that a certain number of bad characters have found their way to Fada with the improved communications is beside the point. Analysis of the figures shows that nine-tenths of the crime is among Fada natives and the remoter villages.'

A private note from Bulteel is attached: 'What's wrong in Fada. Are you sure that there isn't some dirty work going on. You know how things get started. I could let you have a few more quid on miscellaneous

207

services if you want to make some private enquiries. Shall I lend you the chap who ferreted out the Emir's little game here when we had those palavers on the southern border—he's first-class on a trail and fairly trustworthy, because he knows that I could jug him for several little things. Whatever you do, don't let things slide. Tell them something soon and show you're awake to the very serious nature of the figures, or something like that. They like people to be awake to figures. As dear old Robey might say, "They stop and they look and they listen." But whatever you do, don't let it pass. Tell them something. You can't afford another bad mark.'

Rudbeck has refused this kind offer in a formal letter, which is the first symptom of his new reaction to the conditions of the Service. He writes that a satisfactory explanation will be provided in due course.

He doesn't, however, send any explanation. There is something a little spiteful and malicious about his formal and correct feeling, his refusal to be put out.

To Celia about a fortnight later he says, 'I suppose I'd better cook up some eyewash for the brass-hats.'

Celia, now growing round in her fifth month, but still firmly resisting the doctor's attempts to send her home, looks at him dreamily and says, 'Yes, dear, I should.'

'It's all they want—eyewash.'

Celia brings him into focus and remembers that she has been a little disturbed about his odd speeches and behaviour for some time. She says, 'Poor Harry, it's awfully bad luck.'

'What is?'

'Poor Wog.'

'Oh, well'—gloomily—'Blore warned me that he would come to a bad end.'

'But it's horrible for you.'

'Just one of those things that happen—got to get used to it.'

Celia looks at him again doubtfully, but then forgets her mild curiosity and says, 'You might remind me to write to Mother about that nurse.'

Rudbeck, annoyed by Celia's preoccupation, says, 'Write to Mother about that nurse?'

Celia is not even annoyed. She says, 'Not now, darling. I meant when I am writing. What was the other urgent thing? Oh, yes, the wool.'

Rudbeck grins at her and walks off. He is perfectly aware of his attitude and its cause. He perceives that there are different ways in which a man, crossed or offended by his seniors, can get up against Service conditions. He can write rudely or sarcastically, or in a tone of martyrdom, or he can turn himself into a robot who submits gracefully and carries out instructions to the letter in order to make a fool of them. It is in this latter mood that Rudbeck has composed all his recent official correspondence.

Bulteel, who, fifty miles away, has diagnosed the young man's trouble, common enough among juniors at their first serious check, has filed these long, elaborately empty letters without comment. He hopes that Rudbeck will soon get tired of malice and settle down, like the others, to do his job, as a job, fill in his forms, draw pay, play golf and bridge, bring up his family and instruct his own juniors in their turn, 'No long views—the age for long views ended twenty years ago—and above all, not too much zeal.'

But Rudbeck, at the moment of the trial, is still in his most gloomy and disgusted mood. His formal air, while he sits, upright like Blore, in his official chair, is a protest against a world of Trings, Blores and Bulteels.

He reads the charge in the cold, official tone, and then gives, as usual in a district officer's court, a short description of the law; what is wilful murder, what manslaughter, what merely a homicide. Then he explains to Johnson that the charge amounts to murder and asks him to plead.

'Oh, sah, I guilty—I kill poor Sargy Gollup.'

'Not guilty.' Rudbeck says in his mechanical tone. He writes it down. 'We'll call it not guilty.'

'I guilty, sah. I tink I save you trouble.'

Rudbeck calls the witnesses in turn. Ajali testifies to finding Gollup's dead body, also that he saw Johnson with the false key and heard him boast that he would steal the money.

Matumbi, her eyes swollen with weeping, is full of spite against the man who has spoilt her comfort. She swears that she saw Johnson stab Gollup.

Rudbeck, acting counsel for the defence, questions Matumbi and makes her contradict herself. She confesses that she has been telling lies and adds a good many more to explain the fact. She is sent away.

Other witnesses prove that the knife found in Gollup's chest was Johnson's; that he had shown it to many people in the town and boasted that if he were caught thieving, he would never be taken alive.

209

Rudbeck asks Johnson after each testimony, if he has any questions to ask the witness; finally, if he would not like to call any witnesses for his defence.

Johnson smiles and shakes his head. He is not troubling now. He feels cheerful and often smiles either at Rudbeck or simply to himself. The soothing procedure of the court, the calmness of the judge, the quiet voices, all reassure his nerves. Like most natives in a court, even on the most serious charge, he cannot, in spite of any warning, feel the extent of his danger.

Rudbeck reads over the evidence to him and says, 'It comes to this. They say you meant to rob the store, that you took a knife in case anyone caught you in the store, that sergeant Gollup caught you and then you stabbed him.'

'Oh, sah——'

'Wait a minute. You needn't say anything, and if you are only going to agree with the evidence, I advise you not to. But I want you to understand what it amounts to—that you were prepared to kill the sergeant before you started for the store. If that's true, you'd better say nothing. But if you feel that you didn't intend to kill the sergeant, then you'd better make a statement.'

Johnson answers with the same polite and reasonable air, like one who does not wish to make difficulties, 'No, sah—no statement—I don' want to give you all dat trouble, sah. I jus' done it, that's all. I 'gree for dem Sargy too much—I never 'fraid of him—but when he come to catch me, I 'fraid he take me for prison.'

'Wait, you must take the oath. Now, you say that you liked the sergeant?'

'Yaas, sah, we very good frien'.'

'Did you mean to kill him, then?'

'Oh, no, sah, I 'gree for him too much. I didn't want to hurt Sargy one lil bit.'

'Then how do you explain the evidence we have just heard, that you stabbed him.'

'I frightened, sah. I thought he catch me—I jess made one jump push him away.'

'Do you mean that the knife struck him by accident?'

'No, sah, I jess didn't tink what I doing with dat fool knife.'

'You understand, if you plead that the killing was an accident, that's one thing—but if you say that you lost your head, that's another. A thief who kills to get himself out of a corner is still guilty of murder in the first degree.'

'Oh, yes, sah. I kill um—I understan',' Johnson says with a cheerful air. He is greatly enjoying the chat with Rudbeck. Gratitude makes him eager to please, in his turn. He is ready to say anything that seems likely to be satisfactory.

'But your statement just now was that the killing was an accident? Do you want that to stand or not?'

'Oh, yes, sah—what you like.'

'But it's what you like. Was it an accident or wasn't it?'

'Oh, sah, I jess forget what I do with dat damfool knife—I too surprised. And so I kill poor Sargy.'

Rudbeck sighs and then with a gloomy and resigned air, writes a note.

'Now, Johnson, listen to this and tell me if this is what you mean. Prisoner elected to make statement and was duly sworn. He states, I had no intention of doing any harm to Sergeant Gollup. He had treated me well and I liked him. But he took me by surprise in the store, and I lost my head and jumped at him. I have no recollection of stabbing him with the knife, I simply did not know what I was doing.'

'Oh, yes, yes, sah,' Johnson cries. He has never dreamt of this interpretation, but now it seems to him true. Tears run down his cheeks. The marvellous Rudbeck has detected the truth that he did not know himself. But he is not so much moved by Rudbeck's outstanding wisdom, which was to be expected, but his kindness. He thinks that he means to save him. He has heard of the plea of irresponsibility and knows that murderers have escaped the gallows on the grounds of not being responsible for their actions. He cries and laughs at the same time, 'Oh, sah, it's true—it's true—I didn't mean it—I didn't know anything how it happened—you write it better dan I could tink—you save me now. You are my father and my mother in de whole worl', God bless you, sah.'

'Very well, Johnson. We'll let that stand.'

Rudbeck reads over his minutes and then writes that the court finds the charge proved. Sentence, death. Underneath this he writes the usual report for the Governor, who must confirm or remit the sentence: 'Mr. A. D. O. Rudbeck begs to recommend a reprieve on the grounds of the prisoner's youth and nervous instability. His statement can be accepted as true. He did not premeditate the murder, but carried a weapon for defence and lost his head when he found himself in a corner.'

Rudbeck does not read out the finding, the sentence or the report. He says only in his official resigned voice, 'Very well, that's over. Sergeant, take the prisoner back to the guard-room.'

'But, sah, what dey do to me? You tink perhaps dey don't hang me?'

'We'll have to wait till the minutes come back from headquarters. Take him along now, sergeant.'

Because Rudbeck is in full uniform and the trial has been a murder case, he calls the sergeant, 'Sergeant,' and not 'Sargy.'

Rudbeck sends off the minutes the next day. But the legal authorities see no reason to advise the Governor-General that Johnson should be reprieved. The papers are returned with a note in red ink against one question: 'Verges on a leading question; better put in the form, "Do you know the prisoner," not, "You know the prisoner, Johnson," ' and a confirmation of the sentence.

The envelope contains a sheriff's warrant to hang Johnson and duplicate forms for the coroner's inquest after the hanging. Rudbeck is both sheriff and coroner. There is also a piece of thin, bluish paper, mimeographed in smudged blue ink with a list of drops, so many feet of rope for a seven-stone prisoner; so many for eight-stone, nine-stone. The heavier the prisoner, the less drop.

Rudbeck looks at this with surprise and disgust. He has never before had to do with a hanging. For a moment the disgust is overwhelming. But at once he covers it up with his new armour of the ranker-robot, and says in the very tone of the private grousing against the sergeant, 'God damn it all! That's all very well but how the devil am I to weigh the chap. Suppose they think I keep a bloody railway station in the office box.'

He throws the paper into a basket and for two days does nothing. He is, as it were, in the condition of dumb mutiny known to every sergeant and officer.

Young soldiers in this state wear a special face on parade, at once injured and truculent, and they often combine a smart turn-out with a dirty rifle, or at kit inspection they lay out a complete and spotless kit carefully arranged in the wrong order.

Rudbeck carries out his usual office routine with great exactness and even exaggerated precision. Every morning, when he pays his usual visit to the fort, he first inspects the guard, and then steps into the guard-room.

'Good morning, Johnson. Any complaints?'

'Oh, no, sah, dey too good to me here—I tank you, sah. You too good to me, coming every day.'

'That's the regulations,' Rudbeck says in a gloomy voice, as of refusing to take any credit. 'Chop all right?'

'Oh, yes, sah, he too good. I live here just like my home.'

'Well, let me know if there's anything you want,' and he goes off with the same expression, at once dutiful and defiant. But he takes no steps to execute the warrant.

On the fourth day a wire comes asking for an immediate acknowledgement of the warrant, and the date of the execution. Rudbeck says to himself, 'Oh, very well,' in the tone of one who says, 'You've asked for it.'

He goes over to the fort. Since it is late afternoon, he can hear a loud chatter of voices from the barracks. Somebody in the fort is beating a drum tune on a kerosene tin. As he approaches the gate, three or four voices in the guard-room porch sing a line together. Then they stop and Johnson's voice is heard solo, improvising. There is a loud laugh. The sentry catches sight of Rudbeck and gives a challenge. After shouting the words, 'Halt! Who go dar?' his lips are seen to move again, though nothing reaches Rudbeck. In fact, he is giving a warning to the sergeant. As he presents arms, Johnson's song and laughter are suddenly cut off and the sergeant can be seen stooping under the tin porch with his hand already at the salute.

Rudbeck puts his head into the hot, frowsty guard-room and sees Johnson sitting against the wall, arm in arm with two constables. All three jump up. Rudbeck says, 'What do you weigh, Johnson?'

'Weigh, sah, I don' know.'

'And we don't happen to have a weighing machine, do we? Sargy, get that palm rib over there—the big roof stick.'

The sergeant fetches a palm rib from the cluster leaning against the fort wall, ready to hand for building new barrack huts.

'Sling it up to the porch by the middle.'

They hang up the rib, tie an office chair to one end on four ropes; and a chop box on the other. Rudbeck throws a few chunks of earth into the chop box to balance the chair. He asks Johnson to sit in the chair and hold tight.

'Open the cash tank, Sargy.'

'The cash tank, sah.'

'That's it, Sargy,' with the same air of 'They've asked for it.' 'The cash tank.'

The sergeant moves his chair and bed, which always lie on the cash tank; and uncovers a slab of galvanized iron level with the earth. He unlocks two padlocks and raises the slab to show a great heap of money bags, in all cloths and colours, sealed, some with Blore's eagle, some with Rudbeck's stork.

'Put 'em in the box, Sargy.'

The sergeant puts bags of silver into the box until the chair rises and the box is on the floor.

Johnson, who has watched this proceeding with interest, asks now, 'How much I weigh, sah?'

'How much is that, Sargy?'

'Four bags, two shillings, sah, one bag shilling, one bag sixpence,' the sergeant says.

'Five hundred and fifty pounds in silver—at twenty-five pounds a hundred. That's five fives are twenty-five and five twos are a hundred and twenty-five, plus twelve and a half are one hundred and thirty-seven and a half. Say eight. Go and get some jam, Sargy, plenty jam.'

'Jam, sah?'

'Yes, dammit—go and ask cuku, and take care you don't let Mrs. Rudbeck see you coming away with it.'

The sergeant departs. Rudbeck calls after him, 'And one tin flour.'

Johnson asks, 'Why you weigh me, sah?'

'Regulations, Johnson.'

'I eat pretty good, sah—I tink I get fat.'

The sergeant returns with one tin of flour, and seven of jam, which Rudbeck hands to Johnson one by one; when he is holding the tin of flour and three tins of jam piled crookedly in his lap, the balance slowly tips and sinks. Rudbeck reckons in his offended tone, 'That's what did I say minus four of flour and three one-pound jam—seven.'

'One hundred and thirty-one, sah,' Johnson says.

'Is it, yes. Damn the tins. All right, Johnson. Thank you, Sergeant.'

Johnson goes back to the guard-room; the money is put into the tank; the tins return to the store-room, and Rudbeck to tea. Three minutes later a message comes from the guard-room—the prisoner wants to see the judge.

Rudbeck has given orders that any prisoner can send for him at any time. Dutifully he goes to the guard-room. He finds Johnson squatting in a dark corner.

'Excuse me, sah—I beg you pardon for troubling you—you go hang me, sah.'

'Who said anything about that?' Rudbeck's disgust breaks into anger.

Johnson is quick to soothe him. 'Nobody tell me, sah—I guess by myself. Only I tink you do it youself, sah. I don' tink you let Sargy do it.'

'But the sergeant——'

'Oh, sah, you my good frien'—my father and my mother—I pray you do it—I tink perhaps you shoot me.'

The very idea startles Rudbeck so much that he does not contemplate it at all. He says at once, 'But that wouldn't be possible, Johnson. I'm sorry, but you know the regulations.'

'Yes, sah, but I 'gree for you too much; you do so good ting for me. You do dis for me, I no mind it one lil bit. I tink you shoot me quick by yourself. Like old judge live for Guri.'

'What judge? What do you mean?'

'Dem old big judge live for Guri. He shoot dem prisoner when he sleep. He say he gentleman—he no fit hang people—he on'y fit shoot dem.'

'I'm sorry, Johnson, but I have to obey the law. I shall have to sign a paper that I've carried it out exactly.'

Johnson steps back and says in a polite voice as if apologizing, 'Pardon, sah. You too good for me, I no fit bring you all dis trouble. I no good for nutting.'

'I'm awfully sorry, Johnson, but really——'

Rudbeck goes away still more depressed and resentful against the mysterious enemies that close him in, regulations, conditions of the Service, and luck, whatever they are. It's more bad luck that Johnson should ask for something impossible.

The execution is fixed for Wednesday morning at eight o'clock—that is to say, when Celia will be taking her walk in the station garden. This news is not given to Johnson, but he knows it the night before from the police who chat to each other so, 'Beer to-morrow, Sargy.'

'You shut up.'

'Well, it's a quid at least for Sargy.'

'Old Sargy Bluebag got two at Rairai.'

Young Pepper comes in, takes off his belt, gives a long 'O-o-f' of relief and says, 'Has the rope come?'

'Shut up, pagan—shut your crack.'

'Oh, well, if you're going to be nasty.' The little recruit falls into sulks.

'Don't you mind him, clerk. You see, he was asking about the—the rope for the well.'

'Oh, no, tank you. I don't mind him.'

'We like you, clerk—you're a nice chap.'

'I like you policemen; you are kind people. God bless you all.'

'That's all right, clerk.' This from a tall Nupe, bland and lazy. 'We're sorry you're for it. Wednesday morning—why, we don't think of it.'

'Shut up, Stink-fish.'

'Well dammit, what did I say, I was telling the chap we agreed for him.'

'Yes, all of you are most thoughtful and attentive. I shall tell my friend Mister Rudbeck how good you are to me.'

'Oh, as for that, Pig's-neck can hang himself if he likes—instead of you. We wouldn't mind.'

Johnson from his dark corner thanks them again. His legs are trembling, but he does not feel unhappy, only strange. He looks round him with surprise at the walls and the evening sun coming in at the window holes. He stares at them as if he had never seen them before. He creeps to the door and looks out at the bare, hard earth of the fort, the low ramparts almost washed away in thirty years of peace, the broad gap below the guard-room through which can be seen a corner of the barracks, some children playing with toy spears, and beyond, at the other side of the station, the office building and the dark-green bush.

Johnson doesn't sleep. He sits by the fire chatting with the men on duty or in the doorway exchanging stories with the sentry. At earliest dawn he goes to sit in the porch, to see the sun rise.

Just before six, the sergeant, who is asleep on the cash tank, gets up, washes his mouth, rolls up his mat and puts his deck-chair in its place. He is a little yellow man, lately promoted and still full of anxiety. He turns quickly and darts at the little American clock lying on its back in a hole in the wall. He calls out, 'Six.'

The sentry takes up an old rusty matchet and strikes with the back of it upon a short length of railway line, hung under the porch by a bolt-hole. He strikes six times, counting, '*Daia—biu—oku—fudu——*'

The sergeant puts on his jacket, sits down in his chair, and then gets up again to brush the seat. The Nupe, Stink-fish, comes lounging out of the guard-room and sits down in the sun beside Johnson. He says, 'God bless the warm.'

'God bless it.' The sergeant begins to yawn and then clicks his mouth shut impatiently, as if to restore discipline. Two other constables come out, wearing their blankets over their shoulders, and squat down in the low rays of the sun. One, a fierce little Shua Arab, very black, the other Soapy, the button-stick. The Arab blinks at the sun as if half-inclined to take it down a peg, then smiles and yawns at the same time. 'Ow—yow.' His yawn is like a bark.

Button-stick gazes dreamily at the pale sky, and says in a meditative voice, 'I've got that pain again—in my belly.'

No one replies to him. Little Pepper, the recruit, steps briskly forth and cries, 'Salute, day.' He walks restlessly up and down in the porch, rubbing himself, shivering. 'What a cold night. It's to-day, isn't it?'

'Yes, to-day,' Johnson says, laughing

Rudbeck's orderly is seen coming through the fort gate with a bottle of whisky in his hand, which he presents to Johnson.

'What's this?'

'Judge's cook give it to me and said take it to the prisoner.'

'Oh, yes,' Johnson says. His legs begin to tremble again. 'Mister Rudbeck is my frien'. He give me plenty present.'

The row of sleepy policemen squatting on each side of him in the doorway, blinking languidly in the new sun, turn their heads and eyes and gaze wondering at the bottle.

'It's whisky,' Johnson says, 'from England, from home. The best whisky in the world.'

The sergeant in his chair takes the bottle and holds it up to the light draws in his breath excitedly. 'Beautiful—beautiful—like gold.'

'That costs money,' the Nupe says.

'But why does he give you whisky, clerk?'

'You know,' the little pagan says, rubbing his arms. 'Cause of you know what at eight irons.'

'Shut up, pagan,' from the Arab.

'Well, I didn't say anything.'

'Yes, that's it,' Johnson says, laughing. 'It's because he's going to hang me to-day. Oh! Mister Rudbeck is my friend—he's the best man in the world.'

Johnson is a little light-headed after a sleepless night, but this makes him lively. The trembling in his legs makes him restless and disinclined to sit still. He sways about from the waist, laughing, and says, 'At eight o'clock—that's two hours—that's a long time.'

The police look at him gravely and the Nupe says, 'That's it, clerk.'

'Have some whisky, clerk.'

'No, thank you. It's for you, my friends.'

The police wake up at once and lean forward from the wall. They urge him to drink the whisky. But Johnson shakes his head, hands and body. 'No, no. I want to give it to you—you are my friends.'

'But it will cheer you up, clerk.'

'No, I'm cheerful. I don't need that whisky. No, I don't care for anything. Here, Sargy, drink for me.'

The sergeant takes a drink and all the men cry, 'Now, then, Sargy.'

The bottle goes along the row. The Arab, next Johnson, claps him on the back and cries, 'I had no idea you had any guts, clerk.'

The bottle goes round again in silence. Then the Arab begins to hum and sings in falsetto like a cracked fife, 'In the morning when the sun is new.'

Soapy, scratching his back on the wall and gazing upwards with a romantic expression, throws in the accompaniment by humming in the back of his throat, 'Ooom—oom—aah.' He adds at once, 'Yes, a bad pain.'

Little Pepper, walking up and down, suddenly gives a jump into the air, cuts a caper, and turns round in the opposite direction. The Nupe murmurs, 'Go on, Pepper. Show us how the baby-eaters do it.'

The Arab yawns again and then asks briskly, 'How much will you get, Sargy—two pounds?'

'Mister Rudbeck is very generous—he is my friend,' Johnson says.

'So are we.'

'Yes, all of you are my friends.' His body is trembling as well as his legs. He sways from the waist and dances his feet up and down in time with Pepper; then joins in with Button-stick: 'Oom—oom—aah.'

The Nupe takes Johnson by the arm and sways with him; both sing with Button-stick: 'In the morning when the sun comes up, I say to the trees, all you my beautiful sisters.'

Button-stick takes Johnson's other arm and sways with him; he is still providing an oboe accompaniment sometimes through his nose, sometimes in his throat.

'All you, my beautiful sisters,' the voices chant. The sergeant claps his hands in time to the swaying bodies and sings in a high, sweet tenor, full of sentiment,

> *'I hear you calling me with your soft voices.*
> *I see your breasts shake when you laugh together.'*

'Oom—oom—aah,' Button-stick intones.

Suddenly the song stops, cut off as if at a signal; but there has been no signal and no one is surprised by the sudden end except Johnson, who remains trembling, laughing, his mouth open for the next verse.

'Ay-ee,' Button-stick yawns. He says thoughtfully, 'Friends, I've got that pain in my belly again, only worse.' But no one pays the least attention to him.

'Eight irons, that's a funny time for a h'm.'

'All right, clerk.'

'Yes, friends, I don't care for hanging.'

'You're the brave one.'

'It's surprising how brave he is,' the Arab declares, looking at Johnson and sticking out his lower jaw.

'H'm! Well, some clerks are not so bad.'

'I don't care for anything. Mister Rudbeck is my friend.'

'All friends here, clerk. We admire you. You might almost be a soldier.'

'We'll be sorry to say good-bye.'

'So will I, friends. Have some more whisky? I don't mind hanging, but I don't want to say good-bye.'

'Oom—oom—aah,' Button-stick sings:

> '*I said good-bye to my little house.*
> *Good-bye, my little house, my little dog.*'

Stink-fish, Johnson and Button-stick sway together, to the rhythm of Button-stick's oboe and the sergeant's soft hand-clapping. Then Pepper and Stink-fish join in:

> '*Good-bye, my little father, my little mother.*
> *I'm going for the white man's war.*'

Johnson is trembling in every muscle, and as he sways, singing, the trembling seems to make his body light as if every part were detached from the bones. He is merely a trembling nerve or string which vibrates to Button-stick's oboe, the sergeant's hands, the soft mournful song and the swaying bodies of his friends.

'Oom—oom—aah,' they croon together.

> '*Good-bye, my little river, my little village.*'

'Good-bye,' Johnson sings, gazing at the sun, which is now throwing a strong ray against his face and sending the shadow of the sergeant's chair clear into the guard-room behind.

'Good-bye, my sun,' Johnson sings in English.

'Oom—oom—aah.'

> '*Go give me fire when I no got no wood.*
> *Go give me light when I no got no kerosene,*
> *Go walk with me when I poor man got no frien'.*
> *Put you han' in my bress all same brother.*
> *Warm my heart now in the cold morning.*
> *Never ask for nutting for youself.*'

'Ooom—oom—aah.'

Johnson is laughing and trembling, so that he does not know whether he is drunk with fear or happiness.

'Good-bye,' the men sing in English; the sergeant and the Arab strike an octave higher. 'Gooo-bye.'

'Good-bye, my wind.' Johnson takes up the rhythm:

> '*You so beautiful as de diamind.*
> *Fan me when I hot, blow away all dem fly.*

Clean all dem bad stink out of my house.
Dry all my cloes when I get too wet.
Never say give me, never ask for nutting.'

'Ooom—oom—aah,' and Pepper throws in an impromptu flourish
through his flat nose, something like a bassoon.

> *'Good-bye, my rivers, wash me with you soft hand.*
> *Play with me all morning, tickle my belly,*
> *Rub my feet, make me laugh when I poorly.*
> *Laugh to me with your bright shining lips.*
> *Never ask for nutting for youself.'*

'Oom—oom—ooah. Trumpety.'

'Good-bye, my worl', good-bye, my father worl'.
Carry me on you head, give me chop.
When this fool chile hear you breathe in the dark he no more 'fraid.
I smell you like de honey beer in de dark night.
I see you bress shine in de moon,
I feel you big muscle hold me up so I no fit to fall.
Good-bye, my father, you do all ting for me, never ask for nutting for
>   *youself.'*

'Oom—oom—aah. Terompty.'

> *'Good-bye, my mother sky, stretch your arms all round.*
> *Watch me all time with your eye, never sleep.*
> *Put down you bress when I thirsty; never say give me.'*

'Oom—oom—trompetty pom.'

> *Good-bye, my night, my lil wife-night,*
> *Hold me in you arms ten tousand time.'*

Just then the sentry from the gate calls out, 'He's coming, Sargy.'

The sergeant hastily puts on his cap and tightens his belt. The men
jump up and straighten their jackets, grab their carbines. 'Guard, turn
out!' the sergeant cries in his shrill anxious voice.

They rush to the gate and fall in; the sergeant shouts, 'Guard, thup—
slope, pup—present, hup.'

The guard present arms with a rattle of carbines. Rudbeck, without
a hat, is seen approaching the gate. Since he is hatless, he does not

return the guard's salute. But he is neatly dressed in a clean uniform; and his hair is brushed.

The sergeant trots beside him, as he makes towards the guard-room, and salutes.

'All correct, sah. One prisoner live.'

'Yes, you got things ready?'

'Oh, yes, sah. All ready, sah. Put up posts for old rest house, like you say, sah. Nobody see—fix rope for roof, sah—dig dem grave for bush.'

'Thanks, sergeant.'

Johnson, standing in the guard-room door, says, laughing and visibly trembling, 'Good morning, Mister Rudbeck. God bless you—I like to see you.'

'I'm sorry about this, Johnson.'

'Oh, yes, all dis make plenty trouble for you, sah.'

'Headquarters say they won't do anything.'

'Oh, no, sah, you do you best.'

'You're very good about it—you've plenty of pluck, Johnson—I was wondering—you wouldn't like to send any message?'

'I tink dat good idea, sah.'

Rudbeck waves him into the empty guard-room, turns round the sergeant's chair just within the door and takes out a pocket book.

Johnson squats down and dictates a letter to Bulteel, thanking him for all his kindness. He ends, 'I bless you and Judge Rudbeck for my happy life in de worl'.'

Rudbeck looks doubtfully at the boy, but he sees that he is perfectly serious. He is too nervous and excited to play the hypocrite. His face and body run with sweat, his knees tremble violently, and his expression changes every moment. He smiles suddenly, then looks grave and licks his lips, raises his eyebrows as if in dreamy recollection, and then smiles again as if at some memory.

'Any more, Johnson?'

'Oh, yes, sah. I tink I write to my wife Bamu.'

He dictates a long letter to Bamu, thanking her for being such a good wife to him and admonishing her to bring up their son as a good Christian gentleman 'all same Judge Rudbeck.'

Rudbeck sits silent for a moment and gives a faint snort. Then he says, 'Any more letters, Johnson?'

'No, sah. I don' tink of any more.'

222

There is another short silence. Then Johnson asks, 'Is it time, now sah?'

'Never mind the time.'

'I tink perhaps I like to wait small, small. I jess remember someting.'

'Another message?'

'Oh, no, sah. Jess someting I forget—I forget all about dat time I was in Guta with Mister Jones.'

'Has that anything to do with your trouble here?'

'Oh, no, sah—I jess remember he very good time. I nearly forget him.'

Johnson speaks as if he has nearly committed a fault. In fact, he feels that he has only just escaped a piece of ingratitude towards the good time at Guta.

'And Mister Ajali's birthday—bless my soul—I was nearly forgetting dat time—it nearly loss altogether.'

Rudbeck sits silent and gloomy. Then he says, 'Look here, Johnson—you remember that advance you asked for?'

'Oh, yes, sah.'

'I suppose it wouldn't have made any difference to your little difficulties—getting a few bob in advance.'

Johnson sees his drift. 'Oh, no, sah.' He laughs. 'Oh, I owe too much money—I trow away all money you give me.'

'I see.' But he remains gloomy and depressed. 'That report of mine—I don't know if I was quite fair to you.'

'Oh, yes, sah.' Johnson shakes his head while he quickly seeks a means of restoring Rudbeck's opinion of himself, and also, of course, his own idea of Rudbeck. 'Oh, no, sah—I much more bad den ever you tink—I do plenty of tings behin' you back—I steal plenty times out of de cash drawer—I sell you paper to Waziri—I too bad—I damn bad low trash, good for damn nutting tall.'

'And when I sacked you from the road——'

'Oh, sah, I never mean to stay at dem road. I tink I get more money for trade.'

'Oh, you had another job in your mind?'

'Yes, sah. I tink dis work for road don' finish—I tink I go make plenty more money, go tief Sergeant Gollup's money.'

'What, you meant to go thieving even then, did you?'

Johnson has no recollection of what he meant to do, but his imagination has never failed him in a pinch, whether to glorify a story, his own deeds or a friend's opinion of himself. 'Oh, yes, sah,' he cried. 'I always say so—I always say, I go tief Sergeant Gollup's money—if he stop me—den I go kill him. Oh, Mister Rudbeck, you report quite true—I very bad man.'

'So you don't think this trouble of yours is partly my fault, perhaps.'

'You fault, sah? Why, if you didn't be so good frien' to dis Johnson, he tief all every place in Fada, he murder plenty people, all kinds, he most wicked, bad-hearted kind of man you ever see. If I tell you how I tink every night, I go tief, I go murder, you tink I too bad.'

Rudbeck sits hunched in his chair. He is still dissatisfied, not with Johnson's explanation, for he knows that Johnson is actually a thief and a murderer, but with everything. He feels more and more disgusted and oppressed, like a man who finds himself walking down a narrow, dark channel in unknown country, which goes on getting darker and narrower; while he cannot decide whether he is on the right road or not.

Johnson, seeing his gloom and depression, exerts himself. 'Don' you mind, sah, about dis hanging. I don' care for it one lil bit. Why'—he laughs with an air of surprise and discovery—'I no fit know nutting about it—he too quick. Ony I like you do him youself, sah. If you no fit to shoot me. I don' 'gree for dem sergeant do it, too much. He no my frien'. But you my frien'. You my father and my mother. I tink you hang me youself.'

They look at each other, Johnson smiling, full of confidence and enterprise; Rudbeck, perplexed and disgusted. He shakes his head as if to say, 'That, at least, is out of the question.'

A loud clang of iron makes them both jump. The sergeant has sounded the first stroke of eight on the railway iron. They sit silent till the last. Then Johnson says in an uncertain voice, 'Is that the time now? I tink perhaps you give me time make small small prayer.'

'As much time as you like.'

'I tink he proper ting, make prayer now.'

Johnson goes down on his knees beside Rudbeck's chair, joins his palms in front of his nose, and shuts his eyes. He does not pray. He thinks of forms of words which he might have used, still more expressive of his own indifference to Fate and his devotion to Rudbeck. He peeps through his fingers at Rudbeck who sits in the chair with his elbow on his knee and his chin in his hand, looking more gloomy and oppressed than ever; and thinks of further consolation and encouragement which he might offer him. One or two phrases occur to him and he examines

224

them critically. He is in the state of feeling often noticed in people before a dangerous operation. Apprehension at a certain point of intensity, like a boiling kettle, becomes still, but all the quickened powers of the soul pursue their favourite task, with exaltation.

Johnson feels extraordinary lightness and cheerfulness. His mind is full of active invention. He wants to do or say something remarkable, to express his affection for everything and everybody, to perform some extraordinary feat of sympathy and love, which, like a statesman's last words, will have a definite effect on the world.

But at the same time, physically, he is glued to the floor. His body and legs are not heroic. They are so languid with fear that they seem to be dead already. Their exhausted nerves seem to say, 'Do what you like to us, but don't ask us to do anything.'

He hears Rudbeck's chair creak, and, peeping, sees him get up slowly. He says to himself, 'I no 'fraid of nutting—Johnson no 'fraid of nutting in de worl'.' But he sinks down a little lower. His body is almost fainting.

But Rudbeck does not say, 'It is time now.' He goes stealthily out of the hut. A moment later, Johnson, peeping, sees him returning across the bright sunlight with the sentry's carbine in his hand. He stops in the porch to glance into the breech.

Johnson knows then that he won't have to get up again from his knees. He feels the relief like a reprieve, unexpected, and he thanks Rudbeck for it. He triumphs in the greatness, the goodness, and the daring inventiveness of Rudbeck. All the force of his spirit is concentrated in gratitude and triumphant devotion; he is calling all the world to admit that there is no god like his god. He bursts out aloud 'Oh Lawd, I tank you for my frien' Mister Rudbeck—de bigges' heart in de worl'.'

Rudbeck leans through the door, aims the carbine at the back of the boy's head and blows his brains out. Then he turns and hands it back to the sentry. 'Don't forget to pull it through.'

He is surprised at himself, but he doesn't feel any violent reaction. He is not overwhelmed with horror. On the contrary, he feels a peculiar relief and escape, like a man who, after a severe bilious attack, has just been sick.

He is mildly surprised to notice the sentry's nervous gesture as he takes the carbine and almost lets it fall; and to hear the sergeant's voice crack as he shouts some incomprehensible order.

The anxious young sergeant has lost his head. Although he has already once turned out the guard, he turns it out again. It is perhaps an instinctive reaction of terror and respect. The men, surprised and alarmed, rush together and present arms. Their movements are ragged, but they stand at the present with backs so hollow that they seem to be dislocated. You can see right down their hairless nostrils; but their eyes are not looking to the front; they are all fixed on Rudbeck. The little sergeant, at the salute, is staring at Rudbeck. His teeth are bared, his eyes are like bull's eyes with a ring of white all round. Beyond the sergeant the whole population of the barracks and station, the constables, the barrack women, the little market women, are standing in a crowd, pressed together like one animal, and quite still. Not a rag moves. But all their eyes are fixed on Rudbeck with the same expression of greedy interest.

As Rudbeck walks towards them, they press away in a panic, a woman screams, the sergeant shouts curses from behind.

Rudbeck pays no attention to them. He goes towards the office with his usual rolling gait. He is insisting with the whole force of his obstinate nature that he has done nothing unusual, that he has taken the obvious, reasonable course.

The clerk Montagu comes, neatly dressed, perfectly correct, an excellent clerk who never makes a mistake. He too shows bare teeth; his lips curl back as if in fear. He mutters something inaudible and, with a quick nervous bow, puts two papers in front of Rudbeck.

Rudbeck is now slightly irritated. He looks at the clerk with a polite but enquiring expression, as if to say, 'What's wrong with you?' Mr. Montagu makes another nervous bow, and suddenly darts out of the office.

Rudbeck looks at the papers. They are the forms of a coroner's inquest, No. 5 in duplicate—one for himself, as sheriff, one for headquarters.

'Protectorate of Nigeria.

'In the court of the coroner of Fada district an inquisition taken at Fada on   day   of   19   before   coroner on the body of   then and there lying dead; who having to enquire when how and by what means the said deceased came to death, finds that the death of the said   was caused at Fada on the   day of   19   by

Rudbeck hesitates, seeking a legal form, and then writes, 'By hanging, duly executed according to the law, and signs 'J. H. Rudbeck.' He fills in Johnson's name, and calls, 'Messenger.'

Adamu comes in and makes his morning bow. Adamu shows no agitation. For him, an old-fashioned Moslem, men are always responsible before God, and there is nothing surprising in the fact that Rudbeck, as a ruler, should discharge that responsibility according to his own unique conscience.

'Good morning, Adamu,' in an absent-minded voice.

'*Zaki*.'

Rudbeck holds out the forms. '*Akow*—for mail—and tell him to date it.'

'*Zaki*.' Adamu sweeps out.

Rudbeck sits still without doing or thinking anything. Like a convalescent, he feels not only escape, but weakness and apathy. Nine strikes from the fort. Breakfast time. He notices that he is tired and hungry, and glances through the window hole, under the eaves of the stoop, to see if Celia is coming back from her walk. She is twenty yards away, obviously very hot in spite of her sunshade. She marches heavily forward at a good pace with the resolute air of a young soldier on a training route.

Rudbeck goes out to intercept her. She glances at him, and asks unexpectedly, 'Haven't they decided yet what they're going to do about poor Wog?'

Rudbeck's forehead wrinkles. He looks, as usual when he reflects on any serious matter, perplexed and troubled.

Suddenly and unexpectedly to himself, he tells her the story. She looks at him for a moment with the same face as the clerk's, astonished and horrified as if at a murderer. Her lips move as if she is going to cry.

But Rudbeck, growing ever more free in the inspiration which seems already his own idea, answers obstinately, 'I couldn't let anyone else do it, could I?'

ALSO BY JOYCE CARY

"Second Trilogy": *Prisoner of Grace. Except the Lord. Not Honour More.*
"Even better than Cary's 'First Trilogy,' this is one of the great political
novels of this century."—*San Francisco Examiner.* "...the richest, most
fascinating saga in modern English literature."—James Stern, *The New
York Times.* NDPaperbook606, NDP607, & NDP608

A House of Children. "...my favorite Cary novel. The organization—the
progress of children toward maturity by means of sudden epiphanies—is
remarkable. The characters, based on Cary's cousins and aunts and the
author himself, are charming. The language is intoxication. No one writes
more wisely about childhood than Joyce Cary. He remembers what most of
us have forgotten."—Edwin Christian. NDP631

PUBLISHED BY NEW DIRECTIONS